DOOMSDAY!

Vol. 7 of the
Three Worlds Saga

Carol A. Strickland

Other books by Carol A. Strickland

Touch of Danger – vol. 1 of the Three Worlds Saga

Lost in the Stars – vol. 2 of the Three Worlds Saga

Stalemate – vol. 3 of the Three Worlds Saga

Worlds Apart – vol. 4 of the Three Worlds Saga

Mind Shift – vol. 5 of the Three Worlds Saga

Secrets of the Worlds – vol. 6 of the Three Worlds Saga

Doomsday! – vol. 7 of the Three Worlds Saga

Applesauce and Moonbeams – wacky soft sci fi

Nothing Personal – ditto but wackier

Burgundy and Lies – sweet historical romance

Star-Spangled Panties – the full nonfiction tea on Wonder Woman!

Carol A. Strickland, publisher
www.CarolAStrickland.com

Publisher's Note: This is a work of fiction. Names, characters, places, and incidents are a product of the author's imagination. Locales and public names are sometimes used for atmospheric purposes. Any resemblance to actual people, living or dead, or to businesses, companies, events, institutions, or locales is completely coincidental.

Book Layout © 2017 BookDesignTemplates.com
Cover figure produced by AI and Rebecca Finkel, https://www.fpgd.com.
Doomsday! / Carol A. Strickland. -- 1st ed.
ISBN 978-1-941318-70-6 ebook
ISBN 978-1-941318-71-3 paperback
Some publishers require other ISBNs and you'll find them on those sites.

A hearty round of applause for my two editors, Rosa Bosett-Roberts and Jill Marshall!

Also thanks through the years to the now-defunct Heart of Carolina Romance Writers group. Let's not forget the Rhine Research Center, Radleigh Valentine, Sue Burton, so many at Hay House, and all those best-of YouTube psychics for keeping me educated on spiritual/psi matters and techniques.

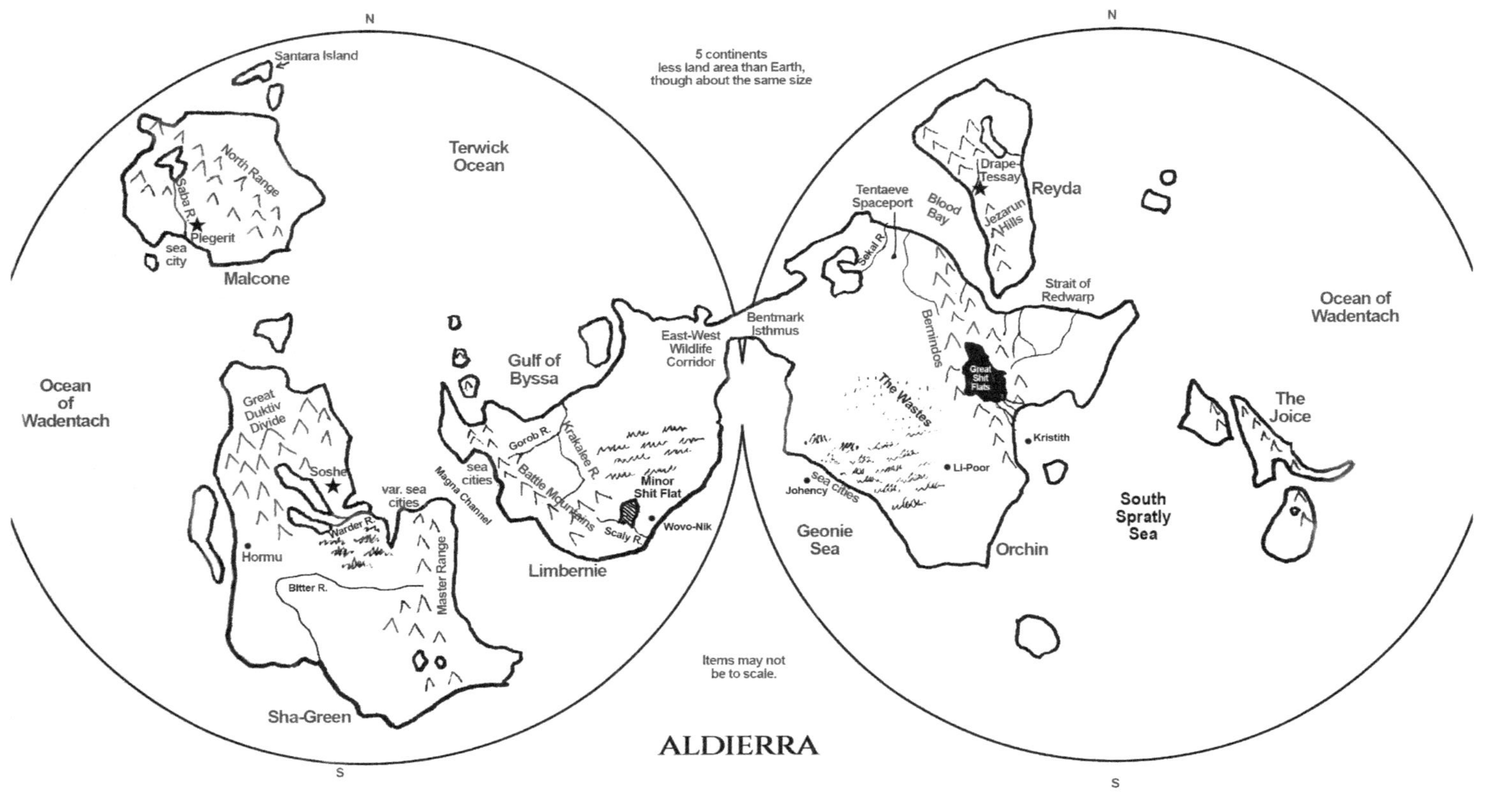

N
Santara Island
Terwick Ocean
5 continents
less land area than Earth,
though about the same size
N
North Range
Saba R.
Plegerit
sea city
Malcone
Drape-Tessay
Reyda
Tentaeve Spaceport
Blood Bay
Jezarun Hills
Sekai R.
Strait of Redwarp
Ocean of Wadentach
Ocean of Wadentach
Great Duktiv Divide
Sosha
Gulf of Byssa
East-West Wildlife Corridor
Bentmark Isthmus
Bernindos
The Wastes
Great Shit Flats
Gorob R.
Krakalee R.
sea cities
var. sea cities
Magna Channel
Battle Mountains
Minor Shit Flat
Kristith
Warder R.
Hormu
Scaly R.
Wovo-Nik
Li-Poor
Johency sea cities
South Spratly Sea
The Joice
Bitter R.
Master Range
Limbernie
Geonie Sea
Orchin
Items may not be to scale.
Sha-Green
ALDIERRA
S
S

The Aldierran Ultimatum

I *am Aldierra. I am your mother, your nurturer, the source of your life. I have loved you for eons but you have tried to destroy me. No more! I will not take this abuse any longer!*

I am an advanced being and I need to evolve. I can do this with you or without you. Make your choice. Stand by me; support me and love me, and I will continue to support you, too. You will receive my bounty in abundance. And in turn you will evolve, become more loving toward each other. Happiness will come within your grasp.

But continue to forsake me, to destroy me and the life that lives upon me without remorse, and I shall have to destroy you. Lovingly so, for you are my children. But I say I will not take this abuse any longer!

DECIDE! You have three seasons to make your choice and act. Your deadline is the equinox.

Please, my children, do not forsake me. I have enjoyed your presence until these last few centuries. I wished to be your home as you matured. But sometimes you have to cull the herd, thin the seedlings so that others may survive. I will do this if you force me to.

DECIDE. By the equinox after next!

Inform my Chosen and I will know.

1

"I am taking back my power," Lord Generalissimo Patriarch Lupoff of Aldierra declared, his chin defiantly set.

Jae Starhart, aka Neutrino and the Minister for the Three Worlds, had done him the respect to show up at the Patriarch's offices instead of via video. Like many here, white-haired Lupoff's skin held deep, orangy-bronze tones. On a world too full of underfed humans, he was chubby. His tailored uniform was red and studded with medals, which Jae had always thought odd because the Majority Army wore green for the most part. Perhaps Lupoff wanted to stand out from the crowd. Being as he usually sat, standing out would be a problem.

There was a small crowd of army officers in here to reinforce the Patriarch's positions.

Before Jae could say anything, Lupoff added, "Taking it back as of now. This has gone on too long."

"Excellency," Jae said in level tones. He bowed respectfully and gave the Patriarch the *"pelzire"* sign: the fingers of both hands touching in front of his chest to make a triangle. "I recognize your soul as being connected to mine; we are one," was the simplest meaning for it. "We have not completed our mission. We have not taken Aldierra through Deadline. There's still a half-year to go."

"You've taken it far enough. Everything has been disrupted. My aides tell me things are now beyond repair."

Mama had always told him, "Patience, Jae-Jae. Take a moment to truly listen to what the other is saying. What comes out of their mouth may not actually be what they mean. Or they may blurt the truth and not realize it."

Patience, Jae reminded himself. "We have had to tear down and clear out some of the most offending parts of your world, Excellency. Now we are re-building as we can. These areas are much better than before, and provide a foundation for a healthier world. Perhaps you need to wait a while to see more clearly the direction things are going. We were given the directive to better this world, its people, its flora and its fauna."

"Not by me," Lupoff growled.

"By a power even higher than you," Jae said. "By your world herself. She has existed for billions of years, and will be here for billions more. She is dis-pleased at what her humans have done to her and her other inhabitants."

"I don't believe it." Lupoff snorted. "Don't believe it!"

"Yet you heard her message clearly, as did every other Aldierran-born hu-man."

"It was a trick! That so-called Speaker is a telepath–"

"A telepath who couldn't even begin to communicate with twenty billion people instantaneously." Jae set his facial expression at, oh, he chose Expression Number Two: patient and listening. "When you heard it, you knew for a fact it was the voice of Aldierra. Everyone did. I and my spouses all heard it; we had no doubts."

Lupoff swayed and shifted in his wide chair, leaning heavily on his arms to help him do so. Left and right. Left and right. Behind him, an aide (dressed in green) eyed him nervously.

"You know duty," Jae urged. "Years ago you set yourself in charge of Aldierra's ruling council, over the entire population. Since the Ultimatum you have given us carte blanche to do what we can. You have a duty to see to your people's welfare. Their welfare depends on the welfare of their world as well."

The Patriarch licked his lips even as his eyes practically sparked flames. Those were the same eyes that Jae often imagined had marked the visages of the men who had ordered his own world destroyed. "My duties are primarily toward the Majority Army and its sovereignty over the people of Aldierra. You are dismantling it," Lupoff growled. "No. No! You cannot do this. You are prohibited from diminishing any part of my army!"

For that Jae brought up a mid-air screen and made a show of studying it. *Patience, patience.* Even if he did want to shake Lupoff until he understood. And maybe his teeth fell out. "We were discussing this just before I came here," he said. He reversed the screen so the Patriarch could see it. "Just this morning the Protector reported that he'd finished disbanding the Yellow Army."

Jae gave the Patriarch an approving smile. "I like how your world names your armies, after colors. It's so cheerful. Plus it provides instant visual identification of the various ones. Most worlds name them after political movements or nations, planetary governments, what have you. But the Yellow Army is no more."

"I'm talking Majority Army! He's shredding it!"

The Greens had absorbed the Red Army and renamed themselves the Majority, no color involved. "You heard us declare that war is now forbidden. My husband Londo – the Protector – has been doing what he can to help the armies disarm. Like the Yellow Army. They are of no danger to anyone anymore. Your Majority Army needs not defend itself from them. The last of the Yellows have been volunteered to help in our efforts to detoxify the world."

The Patriarch set both hands firmly on the arms of his chair to rise a few inches. His aide stepped forward in case he needed help. "I mean my Majority Green Army! What is he doing to it? What are you all doing? It must remain as I built it!"

He sank back into his chair to hear the response.

Jae blew out a shallow breath. "We are listening carefully to the advice Field Marshal Bracken gives us. He's been generous in his aid and military knowledge, as well as how it pertains to the culture of Aldierra. We are grateful for his wisdom." Jae bowed his head, giving a small smile of quiet satisfaction. Lina had called it his "Buddha smile." He'd have to look that up.

"As for the Majority Army, since you no longer need it so much for war, we are re-engineering it for peace. Not completely, but for the most part. Your soldiers make fine constructors and wonderful hand labor for those projects that need it. Which are very, very many. Your engineers are building the things your people need most. Their help in building a better world is invaluable." Though

it would be nice if more of them arrived sober and skilled at what they'd supposedly been trained to do.

"But how are we supposed to return to status quo after all of this is over?
How does my Majority Army – and frankly, my position as Patriarch – get
reestablished after Doomsday?"

"Deadline," Jae corrected automatically.

"How am I supposed to re… re…"

"Re-conquer?" Jae couldn't stop an eyebrow from twitching.

"Re-organize everything after you three have torn everything apart? You're
teaching people who shouldn't be taught, and what you're teaching them are
things they have no business knowing."

"We are indeed focused on making Aldierra's population literate."

"Even the women!"

"Yes, even the women."

"The idea! And homosexuals – you've legalized what they do!"

"Now, Your Excellency, I'm sure that at the very least, when you were
young, you–"

"I never. I never!"

Jae shrugged. "A lack of enthusiasm on your part should not preclude others
being able to explore their own curiosity and proclivities."

The Patriarch sat back to glare at Jae. His mind was shouting at him so Jae
was able hear without peeking: such language!

Such darkness of purpose.

Jae switched to Expression #3, then #1, before returning to #2 just to appear
to be listening raptly rather than daydreaming. Lupoff didn't need to guess what
he was *really* thinking. Over the years Jae had developed a catalog of facial expressions to show the world. He wanted to keep his own opinions private.

"You will formally hand power back to me this evening. Tomorrow morning
at the very latest," Lupoff declared. "Yes, tomorrow morning. You'll need time
to prepare. You will hand over any and all files that detail what has happened to
any and all armies and their personnel. And their weaponry. We will arrange a
telecast at…" He turned to his aide, who showed him a padd with schedules on
it.

"I'm afraid we can't do that, Your Excellency." Jae pitched his voice so it wasn't condescending. Well, not too much. Patient but powerful, which required Expression #3. "We have projects we cannot and don't wish to stop. We have operations we are trying our utmost to expand. Again: Deadline is six months away."

Jae leaned forward to make his point. His voice was deadly. "Aldierra will not die under my – under *our* watch. Her people will live no matter what we have to do to assure that."

"I won't–"

"You will," Jae said. "I have taken a holy oath that Aldierra will not suffer the fate the people of my home planet saw. Never again. Never again!"

Again, he gave the pelzire and with that he silently signaled distant Lina to port him home. He had other duties for today.

CHAPTER

2

The jail cell was unusual in so many ways. Not only was it located in a top-security penitentiary in the remote Atacama Desert of Chile, but a top-security penitentiary for paras and even mega-paras like Yusuf.

The cell walls were fifteen feet thick. The interior width was about twenty feet across and twenty in length, including the private bathroom, which wasn't that private of course. Squat robots delivered meals and water, then took away wastes, as there was no plumbing. Inside were many amenities of home: a comfortable bed, desk (with restricted Internet access), a disappointingly limited supply of streaming video, a few small pieces of gym equipment, microwave and mini-fridge, books…

Cyrus Alexander, aka Alexander the Greater, né Yusuf Joshi, sat at his computer monitor, his mind blank as it so often was in these days of isolation. He could talk to other selected prisoners, so perhaps it wasn't perfect isolation, but it was–

He whirled at movement.

Two tall men stood before his short couch, their lean bodies encased in colorful armor. Transparent faceplates let him see their features. One looked… familiar. From TV or somewhere.

Yusuf unleashed a sharp blast of glacial cold at them.

The air in the cell glistened with ice crystals that began drifting to the floor. Thick frost glazed the men's armor, but didn't freeze it solid. In fact the men shifted on their feet, in a way they shouldn't have been able to do.

The other one was definitely more than a cop. A soldier, from his stance. The first, slightly taller: same stance but… easier. Commanding in a non-military fashion. Regal.

"Mind if we visit for a while?" that man asked in the language of Yusuf's childhood. His face protector and then helmet slid away, revealing medium-brown features. They were perfectly placed, the very physical concept that men's expensive cologne ads wanted to present. His eyes were piercing blue and a subtle gold design tattoo had been set on his forehead, above his nose.. A mop of blond hair with bangs topped it off. Were those pointed ears peeking out?

He motioned to the cell's couch, and his companion took a seat.

Both looked around before bringing their gazes back to him. Yusuf lifted the cold. Why waste energy on something that wasn't working? But he couldn't allow them just to walk in, or however they had arrived.

"What are you doing here?" he demanded. "This isn't legal. I want my lawyer present, right now! I want the warden! I want–"

A bejeweled staff appeared next to the blond man. Lightly he struck it on the floor.

Yusuf couldn't speak. He couldn't form a question. His attention was solely on the man and what he would say next. The other man might not even have existed, so focused was Yusuf's concentration.

The man said, "I am Jaeson Starhart, and this is Erik Gallad. Also known as Neutrino and Sunstorm, from the Affiliated Systems Megaforce Legion. Though we don't come representing that group."

"It sounds pretty good, though," the other put in. Unlike whatever multilingual technique the blond was using, a small marble floating next to this man's face translated his words, obscuring his true syllables.

Yusuf took a moment to digest all this information, as well as his privacy – and mind – being interrupted. Despite him loosing his powers and these two teleporting in, no alarms had gone off. Yet.

"Megaforce," he repeated to buy time to collect his thoughts.

"It's a large interstellar organization, next galactic sector over," the seated one – Sunstorm – said through his translator. "We're–"

Yusuf pointed at the standing one. The important one. "You're one of the Three Worlds," he accused. "Am I under arrest Out There? You can't– You don't have–"

Neutrino made a calming motion with his hands. Yusuf noticed his staff had disappeared. To where? "Give us a chance to explain. We've cleared this visit with the prison and the local planetary justice system. We are here to offer you, ah…"

"A choice," Sunstorm suggested.

"Yes. A chance to walk a new path, to re-define yourself," Neutrino said, even while nodding at Sunstorm. "There is a world out there, Aldierra, who needs your help."

"I've heard of Aldierra," Yusuf said slowly.

"It's experiencing an ecological crisis as well as a sociological one. Now, I don't know why you and your cold-producing powers haven't been helping out here on Earth, but–"

"I get paid for using my powers. Paid well."

Neutrino's mouth set in a tight line of disapproval. Then he said, "And look where it's gotten you. You are imprisoned for life, aren't you? You've been here for three years. Your life progress is stymied. They don't know what to do with you. They're afraid. Even if your crimes didn't warrant long imprisonment, which they do, they wouldn't release you for fear of what you'd do when you got out."

The seated man held out his hands, index fingers extended, and began to… play. A pen blew off Yusuf's desk and, without touching, bounced back and forth between those fingers on a breeze. A breeze that had never risen before in this unit. The man, Sunstorm, didn't seem to pay much attention to the process.

Yusuf refused to be distracted. "They are inferior."

"They seem to have gotten the best of their superior."

They were offering him a deal. Yusuf met the gaze of the standing man, this Neutrino who'd been on the news. Earth rarely received any news from Out There in the universe other than to acknowledge that other civilizations existed on other planets, but feeds had been arriving as to what was happening on Aldierra. One of the Three Worlds was Valiant, a premier Terran megahero.

Another was his new wife, Leena or Lina or something like that, a newcomer to the mega scene. This was the third of the group. He'd also married Valiant. They were a threesome in all ways.

Valiant had been the mega who'd captured Yusuf.

And this Aldierra world was in dire straits.

"I get paid for what I do," Yusuf reiterated. How much would these desperate people pay?

Neutrino shrugged. "All our employees do as well."

"I don't," Sunstorm put in.

"You are a volunteer," Neutrino countered. "But when you do major work for us, we'll be paying you."

"Oh. Okay. I'll probably donate it somewhere."

"What you do with it is your business."

"I'll donate it to Three Worlds."

Neutrino smiled before returning his attention to Yusuf. "We propose a deal. We teleport you to Aldierra, and you use your cold-producing powers to reduce the temperatures at the planet's poles – in a precise and controlled manner that we will lay out for you."

He gave another shrug. "Now, Valiant could do this with his parabreath. I could do it with my powers. But the poles are very large regions, and we have our hands full in other places, doing other things."

This Neutrino paused a moment before continuing. "People will die if Deadline comes and there is little change. Twenty billion. Do you understand? People dying. Children dying."

"What do I care about children dying?"

"You were almost one of them," Sunstorm said. "You were, what do they call it here? Illegitimate. What a concept. In a primitive society that dealt with transgressors harshly. Your father never gave you more than his name. Your mother managed to hide herself and you until they discovered her. By then your powers had begun to manifest. They decided to keep you."

"Like an animal," Yusuf spat.

"Like an animal," Neutrino said. "Which is how many of the girls and boys who don't live up to Aldierra's standards are treated."

Neutrino took a step closer. "They need a hero they can relate to. Someone who can show them how to find strength in themselves and live up to it. But first you need to find your own inner strength, Mr. Joshi. Set a goal you can be proud of, one that illuminates the truth you carry inside you. The amazing possibilities.

"We have almost unbelievable psychiatric help available. We can get you past the blocks your past has raised. Blocks even more limiting than this cell." He raised his arms to take in the scant square footage.

The inescapable square footage.

"We need you to help save Aldierra not only physically, by helping to lessen the global temperature, but by embodying an inspiring story as you have the potential to realize, so that the downtrodden of the world can follow. Not to aggrandize yourself, but by being yourself. Being who you can be."

Neutrino's hands formed fists, and his beautiful face set into determined lines. "Aldierra's people will not die so long as I have breath in me to help them."

Sunstorm pointed to the desktop computer. Yusuf's gaze riveted upon it in surprise. It held an informational page about Aldierra, the world many lightyears away that had lately popped up on so many Earth newscasts. Earth didn't even have intra-solar system capabilities yet, except for a tiny handful of space agencies and para-powered individuals.

Neutrino gestured to Yusuf's wall. Instead of blank whiteness, there was now a giant screen.

"Like this," Neutrino said, and gestured in a peculiar, broad way.

The screen lit up, revealing… another world. A horrible-looking place. A sky laden with purpleish, leaden clouds. Yusuf could smell the sourness. The rot. The landscape held high, high buildings. Flying cars flitted between them, but many people – men, it all seemed – walked on the ground like a vast but slow-moving ant army. Some were pedestrians; some had set up destitute scrap camps along the roadways.

Neutrino gestured again, in a slightly different way. The screen changed to a desert setting. Three mud huts were set on a hilly venue, with sparse bushes here and there. The air smelled dry, but only slightly sour compared to the city. Boys sat on the ground looking as if they'd given up their last sparks of energy. Men squatted with them, their heads bowed. All were so emaciated.

Then some kind of flying vehicle came into the picture. Everyone perked up except one or two. The vehicle landed and what could only be soldiers emerged, for they were dressed in drab uniforms with bright vests. The vests held the symbol of what Yusuf recognized as the one for Three Worlds – a large starburst containing a circle that framed a triangle.

They and some robotic vehicles carried boxes to the huts. The men rushed forward as they could.

"Women and children first!" the guards shouted at the running men.

Yusuf saw that the speech had been translated, for it didn't match the mouth movements.

Soldiers went into the huts and soon were helping withered women outside.

The people were dressed in tatters. In addition to being practically skeletons, these women showed dark bruises and abrasions. Not one had all her teeth.

And the babies. The toddlers.

Yusuf didn't want to look, but he did.

Along with these, the soldiers helped elders. Men who had been injured or who showed body deformities.

The boxes were opened. Tables set up. Food produced. Much of it seemed semi-liquid and thus more easily eaten.

Soldiers waving things out of *Star Trek* moved through the crowd. They motioned to the others. Some of the people were separated from the rest, to be surrounded by soldiers obviously offering some type of medical aid.

The people were being fed.

The men who hadn't been included in the first wave were now allowed to sit for a meal. They fell on it like animals. They poured water into themselves with celebration.

More boxes were unloaded. Many more. A protective shelter was set up, and the boxes were set into that.

The soldiers helped the women, younger children, and the injured into their vehicle. The man leading the unit explained that they were being taken away for further medical help. He left the area with a small communications unit they could use to check on their relatives.

Should they be interested in doing so.

The man also told them that they now had enough supplies to last a month, and that another shipment would arrive a few days before then.

Neutrino made another peculiar movement. A menu in Yusuf's native language came up at the side of the screen.

"I prefer English," Yusuf said. To hell with his father and his people.

The translation changed to that.

Neutrino directed the screen to a picturesque fly-by of a river where hundreds of men toiled at clearing junk and trash. This was the Three Worlds at work.

"I remember people like that desert scene," Yusuf said slowly.

Neutrino and Sunstorm waited.

"I was one of them. Denied food. Denied medical care. Skin and bones, while others feasted."

Neutrino nodded.

Sunstorm said, "We're working for the day when none of that happens again."

They gave him long minutes to consider, then Neutrino said, "If you decide to try this, the process will take at least three weeks to go through your Earth legal system." He made a gesture, and Yusuf's computer screen changed.

"Here are the provisions of your contract with us."

Yusuf didn't look. "And if I break it?"

"Then you have me. And Valiant. And the Speaker for the Three Worlds, all of whom will track you down and return you here."

Valiant. Yusuf certainly knew him. He and Maximus were supposedly the most powerful beings at this end of the galaxy. Valiant – he'd walked through the worst Yusuf could throw at him. Yusuf liked to think there'd been effort on Valiant's face to do so, but that was likely wishful thinking on his part. "The… Speaker?"

"My and Valiant's wife. You saw what she did to that Ruby Guard."

"Without powers," Sunstorm put in. "Ah yes. Impressive and more than a little frightening."

Yusuf had seen the stories. The rogue Ruby Guard had attacked Olympia, the legendary megaparahero, leaving her barely alive, her body in shreds. She was now off somewhere not Earth, literally being reconstructed back to health. The

Ruby Guard had been defeated despite possessing one of the most powerful weapons known in the galaxy – certainly on Earth – by the Speaker, Lina or Leena Starhart, who had had her powers stripped from her at the time by some kind of extraterrestrial device.

Neutrino gave him the moments to ponder. "But it would be best if you entered this agreement on your own free will, with the expectations that this is your chance to change your life. To leave the negativity behind you and choose to walk toward what you want to be. What you truly are."

Yusuf glanced at the screen. It listed what he'd be expected to do. What kind of quarters he'd be given. His salary. His benefits. He'd be expected to regularly work with mental therapists, beginning immediately.

It was that last that made him pause longer than he normally would. Lately he'd become aware of a weight interfering with his mind. Maybe it was the "emotional baggage" that so many people talked about. Whatever it was, it sapped him, his enthusiasm, his purpose, even his sense of accomplishment. He'd actually been considering requesting a psychologist here, one from outside the prison, someone he might trust. Who might be able to deal with problems no one else had ever had to wrestle with. "I, ah…"

"We will give you three days to consider," Neutrino told him. "After that, well, there are other temperature wizards Out There we can enlist. In fact, we may sign on one or two just to help you."

"I could do this work," Yusuf said slowly. "Two poles, you say?"

"Aldierra is of similar size to Earth," Neutrino said. "Less land surface ratio to that of ocean, though, which makes this trickier to adjust temperature. We will leave you a device to learn the language quickly."

"And I have to finish this in… how many months? Far beyond your Doomsday."

"Please don't call it Doomsday. The people are terrified enough. It is our 'Deadline.'"

"Doomsday, Deadline… It isn't possible. This would take years. Decades, probably."

"The planet only has to see positive movement to correct her problems before Deadline," Neutrino explained.

"If I'm on Aldierra when the Deadline hits—"

"The planet has vowed that no non-Aldierrans will be culled," Neutrino assured him. The world of Aldierra was reported to be sentient. "After Deadline, live native human population or dead one, there will still be much work to be done."

"Much work," Sunstorm echoed.

Neutrino pointed. A tiny module sat on Yusuf's desk. "Contact us if you're interested."

And then both men disappeared.

CHAPTER

3

As soon as they materialized in the Landmark Fifty's Three Worlds conference room, Erik caught Jae as he began to collapse. Lina Starhart rushed forward.

"I've got him," Erik assured her. He helped Jae into the waiting floating chair.

"Are you all right?" Lina asked breathlessly as she brushed Jae's hair back to inspect his face. Her loving concern washed over him, and he returned it with reassurance. Satisfied, she relaxed her hold on the black cat she held in one arm. "And you?" She checked Erik's as well when he retracted his Legion armor.

"We're fine now. Erik was solid backup," Jae told her. His own armor retracted into his normal blue and white Neutrino uniform. "Don't bother with me. Though I did have a bad moment or two there. Couldn't let him see."

"I'd never have suspected," Erik told both of them. "Jae pretty much preached the shit out of him. 'This will be a way you can re-imagine yourself,' and all that."

"Well, it's true enough."

After Lina set down the cat Jae eased back in the chair to raise his face so that Lina could more easily give him an unhurried welcome-home kiss. The relief in her green eyes was evident even to a non-telepath. Then she bestowed upon him one of her special smiles, and Jae's insides shivered with wonder and lust. And relief to be home.

She was short, his bride, only six feet tall in Terran terms. Limited Terran terms, that was, utilizing an outdated measurement system that they'd be changing in the next few years. She had pale skin and amazingly luxuriant, curly dark hair that held red highlights in bright sun. Maybe that had been when he'd first fallen in love with her: out on that beach with the wind lifting her hair so it surrounded her in a fiery halo. She'd been an elemental goddess. He'd had to catch his breath.

Jae had never particularly had a preference for one type of female shapes – he was a lover of both genders and could appreciate almost any healthy body that came his way – but Lon loved what he called "brickhouses," amply-endowed women with an underlying athletic build. Lon had chosen Lina before Jae had met her. Jae was learning how special such women could be, how exciting to explore. Add that to a sharp and humorous mind, and he'd known he was hooked.

Another floating chair appeared next to Jae. Erik regarded it and then clambered on. "Don't mind if I do," he told Lina. His skin was a medium-light brown, his head topped with a thick fuzz of blazingly red hair. "Thanks. Just don't tell Gorgeon."

Dr. Riz Gorgeon, head of Legion Med, had been treating Erik after his injuries during the Mind Control Tour right before the Worlds had begun working on Aldierra. Jae was newly released from being seriously injured last week in dealing with the rogue escaped Ruby Guard and his powerful weapon.

"I'm not looking at you," Jae assured his teammate in the medical chair. "Last I heard, officially you were here for a few days' R&R. I'll just remind you that you're due to report in for reduced team duty in two days."

"I'll be ready. Just taking it easy until then. Building up my strength." Erik flexed an arm that had once been drilled with small holes by laser fire. He grinned at Lina. She breathed a sigh of relief.

They filled her in on their meeting with Yusuf Joshi and Lina sent off the usual numerous emails to staff for them to prepare for his arrival.

"We can probably get his release moved up to a week, week and a half," Jae said.

Lina scribbled notes. "You still want to house him at a pole?"

"Security will be easier, and he'll probably be comfortable there. With our planetary transporters we can reach him quickly if needed."

"Hm. Santara Island? It has a few villages. Is that a good thing or a bad thing, Joshi-wise?"

Jae made a checkmark motion with his index finger toward his wife. "Let's try it. We'll keep a close eye on him."

Lina walked beside the two gliding men to enter the larger of their living rooms, lined with charts and timelines. "Your guy on the Krakalee says that with just fifty more men he can get twice the work done." She gave a dubious look to Jae, which he returned.

"That's probably Montue. He's quite impressed by himself." Jae paused the forward momentum of his chair. "Still… I wonder how he'd do if we sent him seventy-five. He might hit that mark."

"Seventy-five," Lina confirmed. She brought up some screens of her own. "Londo's dismantling the last of the Yellow Army on Orchin. There might be seventy-five in today's bunch."

Jae nodded. "Then that'll be the number we send Montue."

"Ah… A suggestion?"

Jae gave his wife a wide smile. "What can I do for you, beloved?"

She smiled back as if letting the endearment sink in. Then she said, "People should realize how vital the icky parts of this mission are. Cleaning portalets."

Erik snorted even as he fished in his chair for some liquid refreshment.

Lina continued, "The squads on portalet duty in Malcone have been doing that for some time now."

Jae floated up to the spare work desk in the room, away from the main entertaining/conference. "So we should transfer them to Limbernie and have them wading through the polluted waters there."

"The Krakalee is more delightfully fragrant than is a portalet. They'll appreciate it." She beat on her chest with two fists and shook her head back and forth so that her dark braid danced behind her. "'Ah! Outdoors! Fresh air!' Well, relatively speaking." Aldierra's air was not the greatest thing to have to breathe unfiltered. Yet.

Jae nodded assent.

Lina pointed at her screen and whoever might be on the other end. "Make it so," she intoned, and then snickered. "The army leftovers will scrub portalets until we can find some other unsuspecting recruits to replace them."

"And so on, and so on," Jae said. He glanced to his side as a floating screen appeared.

Jae's assistant, Leefe Tanshield, was center screen. "The Patriarch wants to see you again, this time privately. As soon as possible."

Jae and Lina exchanged glances.

Erik let out a laugh. "He's still afraid of meeting with Valiant. He thinks you're the weak target."

"Not me?" Lina asked.

That warranted another quick laugh. "He has no idea what you're about. A woman, and yet the Speaker for the Worlds and the key to all this Aldierra Doomsday stuff." Erik raised both splayed hands in shock. "Impossible!"

"Please don't call it 'Doomsday,'" Jae said automatically as his mind spun in a different direction. "Likely he just disregards her as he would any woman. Any way to get more info on deflecting his commands, Leefe? I want to know protocol we can bend if needed. It's not like we haven't seen it coming. What's he after now? What angle is he going to take?"

"He was being obtuse. I think he was getting a kick out of that."

Jae nodded. "Give him our regrets, but we're trying to get caught up after all our medical trauma." He heaved a sigh. "Lost a lot of time lying about in hospital. I will get back to him. Soon. Tell him we wish no disrespect."

"Yessir."

"On the other hand," Lina said, "all this was a good test of our support system. I think everyone did splendid jobs. Well, with a few exceptions here and there. We know where the weak spots are now and can correct them."

"Before the next time this happens," Erik said darkly.

"Next time?" Lina asked sharply.

"You three are workaholics," Erik declared. "Don't know how to rest now and then. You'll have to learn that, otherwise you'll collapse from the strain. You'll have to release the reins on things more before this is all over."

"Release the reins?" Jae asked.

"I've had time to see how you run your Legion team," Erik said. He had indeed recently been promoted to Jae's Alpha team. "Speaking off the record, sir…" He raised an eyebrow at his Team Leader.

Jae closed his eyes a moment, then nodded his permission. "You do realize that Wiley has the three of us recording 24/7?" All three Starharts wore earrings packed with micro electronics.

"Off the *Legion* record," Erik insisted. "You micromanage. I don't think you trust us – sometimes – to achieve our mission goals by ourselves."

Lina cocked her head at Jae, taking in information new to her.

"I give you plenty of leeway," Jae declared.

Erik shrugged. "When it suits you. You're awfully hard to read, Jae. Sometimes we don't know if we're supposed to follow the rules by the letter or break out of them – like you do every so often. Like during the Sarastor Invasion. *That* was as far against the rules as you could get."

"We were backed into a corner," Jae said. "No other recourse but to throw our enemies off-balance. Wiley got AffSys defenses up and running. Lina was our wild card with coordination. I merely provided… diversion."

"I hate to think what might have happened if they'd figured out that you were just crazy and they shouldn't expect a logical military move."

Jae nodded. "I will watch myself for this micromanaging thing you're claiming."

"We should trust our staff," Lina told him.

Still onscreen, Leefe nodded.

"To a point. Most of them are newer than new."

Lina leaned in closer to Jae. "And in the meantime? The Patriarch? He's going to cause trouble. My guides tell me he's already doing that. Who can we get to investigate this?"

"You should remind him a few more times that he officially handed over power to Three Worlds," Erik said. "He must have been overwhelmed to have done that."

"Having a planet make a worldwide ultimatum can do that to you," Lina said.

Jae chuckled. "Even so, letting us have full run of how we carry out this mission? He should have thought a few more seconds before he gave away his power like that."

– – –

ORCHIN. ALDIERRA'S LARGEST CONTINENT. People had died there to-day, been badly injured too. That last-gasp war by the Yellows had been a tiny but potent version of Armageddon all the same.

Could Lon have saved anyone else? Whom did he miss as he plowed his way through the maelstrom? Had even one innocent died or been hurt because he hadn't been faster or more observant?

Londo Rand Starhart groaned and raised up from the otherwise empty bed. Adam had told him that when he couldn't sleep he should get up, do something else for a while, and then go back when his mind, or at least a part of it, had been diverted.

So Londo eased himself around the cats who had been nestled around him, blinking sleepily as they used minimal energy to reposition themselves on the mattress. The hiss from the far corner could only be Molly. Both Bran-Bran and Katie stretched, their butts raised in the air before they extended their front legs to complete a feline Sun Salute.

They followed him to the living room. There he settled in the reinforced chair designed for his strength. He motioned for a screen.

Hal had sent him an email with attachments. There was a video introduction.

"I thought that you'd like to see these, son," Hal – Papa – told him. "I have lots more, but these will get you started. I know you don't have much personal time out there." The message was cc'd to Grady Jackson.

Grady had been Papa's therapist for ages. Surely for most of that time he must have known Hal's Secret – that Hal was Lon's biological father. The two heroes had arranged for him to oversee them and their sessions concerning their rocky reunification. Lon's therapist, Adam, would be kept apprised and might step in on occasion if they thought he was needed.

They were over the worst of it: the accusations and blazing anger. Deep hurts still lingered, but they would work on those. Above all else, they loved each other.

The attachments opened to reveal photographs and videos of Londo, Hal and Lon's mother when Lon was a baby, growing into a toddler.

Lon had never seen pictures of himself under age seven before. His identity had been a mystery.

It was curious; Lon's skin was several shades darker back then than it was now. After a puzzling two minutes Lon shrugged to himself. He'd been through a lot of alien experimentation. Now he recalled that he'd noted his lighter self, back during those terrible years, and thought he was sick because he'd gone pale. The Lectori, his kidnappers, used this belief to assure him that they were actually taking care of him. He hadn't been captured; he was in "medical quarantine" for safety reasons.

The very thought of the Lectori made him ill. *D'accord,* their experiments had affected his melanin. That was just a cosmetic thing. Lon double-checked the images he'd been given. It hadn't affected his eyes or his hair. They were the same as before.

The only important different thing about him was his gold tattoo, about the size of the center of a toonie, emblazoned on the back of his right fist. His starburst logo enclosed Lina's circle, which enclosed Jae's triangle. They all had the tattoos, though on different parts of their bodies. They sealed them to the Three Worlds and this mission.

He settled to studying the photos. Maman. She had been so beautiful. The videos showed her doting on both Londo and Hal. There'd been a special formal "family" photo that Hal arranged, with baby Lon tucked into Maman's arms. Hal had wanted to marry Maman. She'd refused.

Lina had also refused Lon, several times.

"Maman must have been just as smart as Lina," Lon concluded to Katie, who lay along the arm of his chair, looking at the screen with him. Bran-Bran was curled asleep in his lap. "That's a pretty high bar. You have to admit it's *fou raide* to marry a Rand. We both have armies of enemies after us."

Guilt twanged in Lon's gut. Well. Lina had powers, primarily the power of escape. He'd make sure she retained them and was never imprisoned again. Plus Jae would keep an eye on her when Lon wasn't there to protect her. He'd protect Jae as well, when needed.

"*Eh bien*, like it or not, you're a Starhart now," he reminded Katie as she closed her eyes.

Lon had been a pretty cute kid, he decided. A little precocious. Maybe a little spoiled. He laughed at some of the situations the videos portrayed. Apparently Hal's billowing white cape had been a source of great interest to the toddler, because little Lon pulled on it at every opportunity. Hal came across a lot sillier in the scenes as well. He was showing off for Maman.

It was too bad that Mama Ruth and Papa Mike weren't in any of these. They hadn't met Londo until he'd escaped the Lectori and Hal had taken him in. They'd found out Hal was his real father at the same moment Lon had, just a few weeks ago.

Lon snorted as a therapeutically approved way of letting out some pent-up emotion. Hm. He congratulated himself on doing that. It showed creativity and got the job done fairly well. To test the hypothesis, he snorted again. Twice.

After three more videos he decided he was sleepy, then headed back to bed.

CHAPTER

4

Jae's gaze traveled the length of the workers' camp. What had this morning been neat rows of pitched tents, ready for the men who worked cleaning the area's waterways, was now piles of ripped material, dismembered cots, bashed-in portalets… and no electronics. Anywhere.

Four of his Aldierra Corps men stood before him, two drunks slung between them.

"You were supposed to be on guard," Jae growled at them.

He didn't need his sensors to know that not only were these two inebriated, but wildly so. "Call medical," he instructed a Corpsmember. Then he turned back to the drunks.

He could feel not only the familiar, fermented sweetness of alcohol in their systems, but something else. "Tell them it's an emergency," he urged his man, who was already sending out a call.

Body systems were beginning to shut down. The drunks swooned.

Silently Jae spoke to their systems. That chemical he recognized, knew how to negate. Dangerous to do so without knowing what else was operating, and there certainly was something else that shouldn't be there, there. He tried to go through compounds one by one, talking to the devas and substances themselves, getting them to *change*.

The one man's eyes seemed to droop less. "Uhh," he managed to say before his eyes closed again.

"Wake up," Jae demanded. The man's companion seemed worse off. "Where are those medics?"

"Right here." It was Lina's voice. She'd teleported a medic in with her. It was a woman, and she whipped off her equipment bag while opening it in one smooth motion.

Jae watched her as she scanned the men. "What is it?" he asked.

She began reading a list of substances.

"There's poison present," he told her. "I can feel it. What is it?"

"Execlin," she decided as she reached into her bag.

"Execlin," Jae murmured. Ah, yes, he recalled the stuff. He'd run into it once. It had felt like… Lazy, with a dark purpose underneath. "I've got it. I'll handle that. You take everything else."

Together they worked on the men, the medic countering the substances they'd imbibed, and Jae actually changing them while they pulsed through the men's systems.

He took no notice of dozens of men entering the area around him. He knew that back at HQ, Jae's Chief of Staff, Walker Sentristone, was coordinating as well as Lina and her staff with supplies. But Jae's focus was deep inside the bodies of these incompetents. He tried to hold back his anger. Anger solved nothing and it certainly impeded his power.

Someone laid the men out on blankets. Slowly they were coming around. Sobering up. The medic looked up at Jae expectantly. When he lowered his outreached arms and nodded, she attended to finishing her aid.

"Out of danger," she reported. "Very little intoxicants now as well."

"Good," Jae said. He scowled at the wakened men. Traitors. "Who gave you the drugs?" He didn't care about the why. They were incompetent traitors, that's why. "Who?"

"Ah, ah…" The men looked at each other.

"You can't get into much worse trouble than you already are," Jae told them. "Look around you."

They did: chaos. Sabotage.

"I didn't do it."

"I didn't either!"

"You deserted your posts. You allowed this to happen."

"B-But…"

"You do this often? Get high while on duty? After you've been certified sober and ready to work for the day?"

"But nothing ever happens, Minister! Every day it's the same. It's boring."

"Which is why we keep you on rotation." Jae tried to keep his features and voice even. "Who slipped you the drugs? The drinks?"

"It was, it was… that guy. He comes around every once in a while."

"Guy?"

"He likes to talk with me," the one confessed. "He's always been nice before. He's got a family just like mine, one he wants to stay away from. He said he runs a bootleggery now, drugs and booze. It's good stuff."

"This time it was poison stuff. You were about to die."

If nothing else, that sobered them up. "No. No!"

The medic paused in her duties. "Yes," she assured them. "If it weren't for Neu– the Minister here, you would be dead. I couldn't have neutralized the poisons in time."

The men gaped first at her, then at Jae.

"So this was a 'guy,'" Jae urged. "Give me a description. Tell me what direction he came from. If he seemed well educated, what kind of regional accent he had…"

As they talked, Jae searched for a picture in their minds of the man. It had been just the one.

Apparently that was all the Patriarch had needed to scuttle this operation.

Others had been on the guard rotation. Others would know of this man, and might be able to add to the description. Jae made notes of ways to keep track of what his guards were up to when they were left alone.

Lina's schedule had her return to quarters to sleep, but one of her aides remained in her office an on monitors to direct supplies. "We've got new tents that should arrive in three hours, Minister," the man reported from his station. He chuckled. "New portalets. We specialize in those. These damaged ones will be repaired when possible; recycled if not. Meals haven't been affected; they're still en route, though we'll need new tables, dining tents and chairs. The Protector's office is lining up new electronics."

A flitter appeared in the sky, which soon deposited Walker, who traipsed around the camp with two aides furiously taking notes. When he returned, he reported to Jae.

"There's poison in the water, a fish kill to begin with."

"I'll handle what I can," Jae replied. "Warn the Corps; they should be wearing overall protection until we get past this. Priority HAZMAT protocols in place until given the green light. Call the Protector's office, see what equipment we have already for water purification. Let's catch this before it can spread too far downstream."

"Surveillance footage shows it was set on a loop. We don't have video evidence of the perps."

Jae nodded. "We'll adjust the systems to report looping. I doubt if these two are smart enough to be able to do that." His nose wrinkled in distaste at the thought of those who would be. Too many. "Continue the questioning here. I want to catch every last person responsible."

Though the person behind it all was Lupoff. Lupoff and the cohorts who wanted to feed off his power.

Lupoff had to be dealt with.

– – –

IT WAS A BEAUTIFUL NEW DAY, more or less, though here it was already past noon. Lina's schedule took her around the world and was set up to gradually advance in time zones so she could attend better to diverse regions on a regular basis. Two and a half weeks ago she'd been beginning her day at dawn.

The bubble overlying the new Starhart estate was tinted like polarized sunglasses: a protective security forcefield. As it arced above the two *oveng* trees its optical polarity changed, a combination of color and opacity. Lina knew that in that area it would let rain through, but she wasn't sure precisely what else it did. It was to protect the trees, but also partially expose them to the environs in preparation for the day when they could withstand the world's true, healed elements.

Once they got through Deadline, Lina was determined to learn all – okay, *most* – of this newfangled Out Here tech that was so different from Earth's. Until then, she could ask lots of questions as needed and fake things when there was no time to ask.

Because of Aldierra's perpetual smog, the estate forcefield dimmed the area into almost shadow. The trees weren't dimmed. She'd have to see if they could adjust the effect to get some more light everywhere. She didn't want her staff affected by such bleakness. Things were bleak enough as they were.

Though it did seem as if today's overcast wasn't quite as oppressive as it had been. Her imagination? She should check the reports.

"Does it look lighter to you, baby?" she asked Obi, her cuddle-loving but shy calico. His only answer was a contented purr as she carried him down the gravel path. She planted an arc of tiny kisses across his fuzzy forehead.

A sharp rock edge delineated this side of the estate. On a ledge below, two of Lina's personal guards kept watch over the landscape.

More guards were stationed around the compound, as they were whenever the Speaker was home. Squads were stationed in locales around the world and used a flitter fleet to more easily accompany her. In emergencies, they utilized planetary transporters that Lon and Jae had set up. They followed her schedule, arriving an hour or two before her appearances.

They were a great bunch, even when pushing aggressive people out of her way. Lina had talked with them all and confirmed to herself that they were not only expert but loyal to Three Worlds and its mission. It was kind of embarrassing that Lina seldom noticed them at work. They tended to blend in. They were just always… *there*.

Thank goodness. The old days – a couple weeks ago? – were over. Most people no longer bowed or groveled to the all-holy Speaker. Now she was just a person. A female person, to the consternation of many. A possibly vulnerable person.

The ancient Romans had had a famous saying about fame being fleeting, but she couldn't recall it. Besides, it was in Latin. They talked funny back then, something about a non-lady named Gloria. Whatever. *Veni, vidi,* Visa. I came; I saw; I shopped. Now *that* was useful.

These days Lina tried to keep her psychic antenna up. "Aldierra is dangerous," Lon's voice rang in her mind.

The rocks formed a safety barrier for moderate cliffs. They led down to the west to a significant wildlife migration route, a massive valley sculpted over the eons within mountain foothills that had been newly cleared of urban sprawl and planted. Some flora had already attained good size.

Chloroplast… that is, the ex-Legionnaire Nesh Inagar, was remarkable. Her power could accelerate plant growth. Of course she had an entire world to attend to, but you could see the spots she had chosen here. Between them volunteers and armies had carefully prepared the ground to plant seedlings in the multitude of types that Aldierra's ecosystems people reported were native to this area. In a decade-plus this would be a breathtaking view.

But against the higher ground behind Lina, stood the Monstrosity.

She frowned at it, then gave Obi an apologetic kiss in case he thought that had been directed at him. "I shouldn't call it that, not even to myself," she confided.

She'd first seen it from a video of a location on a different continent than this, where it looked antiquity-old and intriguingly different, if a bit large. In person it was too huge, too moldily-garish with its onion domes, too rundown if not rotting in spots, to call it anything else. Lon assured her that once it was rebuilt it would be a glorious palace for them to live in.

She didn't particularly long to live in a palace, but Londo had a bit of claustrophobia after being locked in a tiny room for most of his childhood as a kidnapping victim, so she wasn't going to argue. This was not a hill to die on. Besides, living in the posh hotel in Plegerit for almost three months as she constructed the staffing for Three Worlds had made her realize just how much office, visitor, cat, and employee space they needed. Just for starters. When they expanded after Deadline to handling three planets, the organization would only get larger.

Jae just laughed quietly whenever he might glance at the Monstrosity, but he didn't object. He was more concerned here with finishing the walkways and landscape around the score of tents that had been erected this past week, as well as the area that would become recreational, just for the family to enjoy. He already had his future garden space staked with boundary markers.

The Boys had been patient at Lina's insistence on keeping the existing low trees so the cats could climb them. Plus Lon promised a pool.

Imagine, a home with a pool! Well, Starhaven might have a pool as well. Starhaven was Lon's – *their* – mountain-sheltered mansion on Earth in Wyoming. Currently under construction, it was planned as their primary residence.

Lina bent down to adjust the markers for the future pool to make it just a liiiitle bit bigger. Obi took the opportunity to jump from her arms and run back to the trees and other cats.

Those poor trees would be the most pampered on the planet, for the Starharts' seven cats liked them a lot. Already they were back there whenever they could, climbing and swatting at each other from low, neighboring tree limbs. All except ancient Fafhrd, who clambered up shallow steps to a bench that overlooked the view.

Lon had purchased the condemned property here as well as moved in the Monstrosity with the help of some para friends and his father, Maximus. Hal, that was. That quiet bench had immediately become Faf's favorite spot. Jae had rigged the bench so the seat warmed when Fafhrd was on it. If you liked looking on miles of acreage where only green sprouts, young trees, and orange erosion control groundcover stuff had been set, the view was smoggily fabulous.

Lina did. She often sat with Faf in her arms and visualized a lush, peaceful future for this world whose people and places were becoming more dear to her. She only managed a few precious minutes there a day, away from the chaos that was her new life as Speaker for the Three Worlds.

Lina's earring buzzed softly as she strolled. "Yes, Tidda," she responded to her primary executive assistant. Tidda's schedule was a near-mirror to her own, poor thing. "Give me a few minutes to breathe and get ready for the day."

Tidda reminded her of the first three hours of appointments on her schedule. They had until Deadline to get every Aldierran, all twenty-plus billion of them, involved in improving all aspects of their world. That was a hair over six months left now. Or was it less? Lina frowned. She'd find out when she made her daily report this evening. She'd lost track of time when she was in a coma in Duke Hospital last week, but Puter was programmed to include the countdown in her report. It and Tidda and the rest of her assistants were the only way Lina could keep track of time anymore.

What it boiled down to was: Everything had to be done now. Now, now, now, and have things ready for Jae and Londo for the next round of whatever they were doing.

"The group from the Netting Institute are queued up on video," Tidda reported.

"Ten minutes. Please make sure my guards have things ready for the visit to Sha-Green. I'll need last week's reports about landscaping equipment availability there, plus Wiley's staff's suggestions for cleaning the lower continent's ground water. I think I saw some report from an AffSys world where they tried it a few centuries ago. Daisy, some name like that. It wasn't thorough, but it was a start."

"Probably Daidie," Tidda replied. She was from the AffSys and knew its local celestial cartography. "I'll find it for your data file."

"Thanks. I'm going to forget this, but please add a note to our Tuesday meeting, the personal one. We need to reorganize Starhaven's plans."

"Oh?"

Starhaven was where their new Earth home was. "I've been thinking. I know both Lon and Jae think security is our most important priority, but we'll be needing some kind of house staff. Aldierra has proven that. The kitchen will have to be enlarged or something to accommodate. They'll need a break room. Bathrooms. Maybe beds? Maybe in the guards' quarters that Jae was talking about? And Lon has been waffling on how exactly we're going to ship visitors and guards and such in every day. He needs to commit to a plan. Anyway, make a note, please."

"Done."

"Yes, you'll get to visit when it's done."

Tidda couldn't stop the small squee at that.

Lina was in charge of coordination, supply and transportation, and it seemed to her that she also had the most contact with ordinary Aldierrans. Jae and Lon were the ones who actually got out and did things. They all researched as much as they could. This world, situation, and people were all new to them.

At least their big secret was out. She no longer had to worry obsessively about letting the news of their three-way marriage slip. Now she could smile at Jae in public without people thinking dark thoughts her way. She could hold Lon's hand without hesitating to make sure he was Lon and not Jae. She could relax a little.

"Royce Hristin says he needs to talk with you asap."

Lina closed her eyes. "I'll get him as soon as I come in. Tell the Netting folks I'll be late by, oh, another ten minutes."

"I'll remind you."

Tidda maintained a tight rein on Lina. That's what she'd wanted in an assistant: someone to keep her on track. So many things to do.

God, she needed a stim.

It was still too soon to ask for one, not since she'd experienced some nasty repercussions during the Mind Control defensive tour three months ago. To get everything done while helping save the sector, she'd gone a little crazy by taking massive stimulants. This wasn't a great thing to try, not when she was also going more than a little crazy merely because of her new Perilous Life with Megaparas Where Megavillains were Trying to Kill Her.

PTSD was a bitch.

"Nileen Brody–"

"I'll talk with her after my first two appointments. Not before."

And now she was coming off another megavillain-created crisis, darn them all, this one from just a few days ago. Thank goodness she was under the care of Legion Medical. Boy, did they know about PTSD. She now had a therapist who patiently listened to her a time or three a day and doled out great insight. Her other doctors were allowing her a limited number of caffeine drinks per diem (two, as long as they were low-dose), but hadn't okayed hard stims yet.

Tidda: "How about the videos for the latest Plegerit neighborhood? And that Spring thing you wanted to do in Orchin."

Lina considered a moment. "Give Plegerit a B ranking on my to-do list. B+ for the Spring thing. We've got to get that continent ready to go. We need more volunteers, and they'll need training. Have Ardi or Forlus signal the Blue Army to stand by to add to the ranks. Lon was saying they were just sitting around on their hands after that big to-do last month. Contact our eco-experts to tell us what specialties we'll be most needing. We can fill in from there."

"Right. Don't know why that reminds me, but Kanti said Dari Signet wanted to speak with you. You know Dari Signet?" There was awe in Tidda's voice. "I guess you would. Rich people."

"I met her before I got rich," Lina replied. "Some people were trying to kidnap her and her son, and I happened to stumble upon the scene. Wonder what she wants? Is she okay waiting a couple days? I really want to get Orchin straightened out. And Limbernie and Sha-Green. But I don't want to insult her."

"I'll contact her."

"Speaking of money–"

"Jae has told me not to bother you with money matters. He phrased it as kind of an order."

Lina *hmf*ed to herself. "I get the impression that Jae doesn't really understand the concept of money. Not in large amounts."

"And here he is, married to the richest woman for sectors around. Richer than I bet Dari Signet could imagine."

"If only–"

"Do not worry about the money. Tell you what; I'll get whichever accounting complex was the last one to attempt the job before they panicked and ran away, to tell me if we're still good."

"Thanks, Tidda. You're a gem. Don't tell Jae I asked."

"Do not tell me not to tell one of your husbands. They've both given me instructions about that."

Lina rolled her eyes. No one was around to see, other than her ever-present spirit guides. "I've given their aides instructions, too, for me."

"So you're all even. Are you coming into work today?"

"Almost there; I'm not porting in. I need to ground myself."

"Right."

Lina should find an independent stim supplier who wouldn't rat her out. It didn't take a genius to realize she'd be needing them before all this was over.

She strolled down the rough walkway toward her new office. That office was no longer on the top floor of the Landmark Fifty, formerly one of the snazziest hotels in Plegerit. Now the Starhart-owned Landmark was going all-office, all Three Worlds, with the exception of a floor of luxury rooms designed for visiting VIPs, and of course the ground-floor restaurant whose chefs were determined to reestablish fine Aldierran dining.

The Starharts were helping the former owners reno the even larger building next door as a hotel, to tie directly into the Landmark and its new reputation. Good for them. Three Worlds was why they'd needed to move out. The Fifty-One, or whatever it would be called, could handle the numerous elite people from all around the AffSys who were arriving every day, curious about what was going on on Aldierra.

Coming around a corner, she spotted her temporary office. It was a white tent, though it was so very much larger than the one on that TV show they'd kinda-sorta modelled everything after. So many other tents nuzzled it like kittens around a mama cat. Parallel to its side but beyond a protective zone for construction, lay the Monstrosity, so could one call it all a Compound?

It was more a village. Tent after tent of different sizes clustered, some connected departmentally, and others separate for whatever reason was needed. One of them was a large garage with flitters and larger vehicles that guards and staff could utilize. Another was a good-sized casual dining café to service the staff.

This village operated 24/7, which wasn't quite 24/7 since this was a different world from Earth with different rotation and revolution rates, but that was the gist. They had a world to save.

Yet most of the ever-expanding Three Worlds offices were still over at the Landmark Fifty. *Ca-ching. How much* was all this costing?

Tidda interrupted Lina's thoughts with word of a handful of upcoming tasks that would need extra equipment and volunteers.

As Lina listened, she frowned at a new sign outside that big café tent: "TBD Bistro."

"Tell me," Lina asked her assistant. "'TBD Bistro'…That name's probably going to stick, isn't it? There's a sign here and everything."

Tidda chuckled. "Too probably."

"Let's have a contest. Open to staff only: name that bistro."

"Winner gets…?"

This time it was Lina who laughed. "My first impulse is to say a week's worth of non-Aldierran meals."

"The food here *is* pretty grim."

"We're working on that." Lina's pressed her lips together and puffed her cheeks as she pondered. "Okay, a week's worth of meals from any world they want, or any cuisine. That won't insult the cook staff, and they don't even need to know what the winner wanted."

"Sounds good. It's certainly motivating. This contest runs a week?"

"Yes. Put on Lon and Jae's schedule that we choose the winner one week from today. Pick a time."

"Got it. You still coming in to work this week?"

"No one likes a nag, Tidda. I can't ground when you're whining in my ear. Almost there."

Aides were different from assistants like Tidda, working on a higher level. Lina had four of them, with another two kept as backup which seemed wise as they too were already going full steam every day, and three more because Kanti Cloutier, Lina's Chief of Staff, said they needed them.

Kanti was one smart cookie. Lina was so glad she'd hired her. Of course it had taken Lina's guides literally to throw them together. Kanti had her own large tent linked to her office, and her deputies – Lon's title for them, though Lina wasn't sure of the difference between a deputy and an aide – shared one of the larger secondary ones next to it. All of their offices had sound-barriered walls. People contacting the Speaker's section had a tendency to shout.

Grouped with the major tents for Speaker, Protector, and Minister departments was Starhart home quarters. It had its own small kitchen, various parlors for company and just for family, and two bedrooms for Lon, Jae and her. They'd discovered that with their crazy schedules, it was often disturbing for one to climb into a bed that already contained one or two sleeping spouses. Even with giant mattresses that masked movement, the disturbance could be jarring. The fact they were all telepaths didn't help the matter.

They needed their sleep.

Darn it. Lina missed that other thing they did. As newlyweds, they should be able to do that often. Real often. Too often it seemed to her that she was living with strangers.

Sexy hot-guy strangers whose mere glance could melt every bone in her body at inopportune moments.

But their schedules were crammed.

She slowed before the door to her offices to observe the lines of movers lugging furniture into the various tents. Trusted staff oversaw the efforts, with AI monitors set to catch any shady dealings. Lina had made sure the designers knew the difference between office furniture, family living furniture, and fancy-wancy furniture. None of that latter stuff, please. Once the Monstrosity got finished there'd likely be a few fancy rooms, but for now she didn't want to worry about what pieces the cats would be tearing apart or Londo would be accidentally stubbing his powerful toe on, wreaking havoc. Mama Ruth, Lon's grandmother, had warned her that both Londo and his father went through a lot of furniture quickly. Best not leave the good stuff sitting around.

Ready, Lina. Jae's telepathic call came in from Sarastor, where he'd been arranging with AffSys researchers about how best to normalize ocean currents on Aldierra. One of those was bringing instruments to do on-site research.

Oh right. Two to beam in. Lina tapped her earring three times, the signal for Absolutely No Interruptions for Five Minutes – the maximum time she could take for interstellar teleporting and biofiltering – as she took a breath, preparing to port them in.

CHAPTER

5

"Don't bother her," Lina called out to whoever it was in her reception room this afternoon. There were sociologists and researchers waiting to be invited in. From the corner of her eye she could see someone bending over Fafhrd as she lay on a favored pillow.

"I think she's dead." The voice revealed that it was Hal, her new father-in-law, aka the legendary Maximus.

"She's not dead," Jae's corrected from the screen that hovered in front of her. "She's just a million years old. She needs her sleep."

Hal plus Londo entered the Speaker conference room without Tidda announcing them. For this family occasion Lina could forgive the lapse of protocol, but Tidda was timid; this was not the first time she'd done this. Lina would have to help her grow a better backbone if she wanted to retain her position as chief executive assistant.

Even so, Lina could understand. Just think: Maximus. Yikes.

He was a hair taller than Lon, quite a few shades darker of skin tone – it was so dark that Terran news organizations had difficulty getting his image to pop well when he stood next to people in the upper half of skin lightness. His amazing muscles gave him half again the width of Lon. His lightning emblem was familiar beyond the local galactic sectors, and his short white cape had inspired Jae to wear one for himself, though longer.

Hal's secret that he was Lon's biological father had only been revealed a few weeks ago. When that had happened, Jae had removed the cape from his uniform. Now that Hal and Lon were trying to regain their relationship, Jae's cape was still absent.

Lina approved of the no-cape look. Without it, she could admire his butt more.

And Lon was looking good as well, finally relaxed next to his father after the falling-out. Black pants and boots, black vest, black-striped gray shirt; light brown skin and black hair, overlaying a physique many compared to that of a Greek god. His trademark frown was almost missing, and his brown eyes looked around to take stock of what was what. He was ever looking for trouble, her wonderful husband, but here he was safe. She could feel the otherwise terrible tension in his shoulders was eased, at least by half, since the two men had been through intensive therapy. Jae had told her that Lina's arrival Out Here a few months ago had eased Lon's tension by at least half as well. How must he have been before they met?

At least he'd had Jae to lean upon, though at that time he couldn't even touch him. Lina had taught them both how to touch without harm.

At one end of the room Wicker Greenweave, their chief of PR, was communicating with various publicity outlets about the Southern Aldierran hemisphere and how its new growing season needed to be handled for the public. Lina had gotten permission to broadcast some Terran specials about the formation of Earth's first national parks. That Ken Burns series was a gold mine, and AI had just finished translating it to Farrani. Mace Lafayette, their Terran Chief of LGBTQ+ Operations, had double-checked it for accuracy and word flow.

"Now I need to plant a tree," he'd told Lina when he checked in.

There were sub-articles in Wicker's proposed information release about Central Park in New York City and Brazil's Ibirapuera Park. Maybe they needed to televise a historical biography of that guy who'd designed Central Park. He'd also worked at Biltmore, which was pretty impressive, and some river walks and such. Might inspire some designers here. Lina made a note, adding that countries more unfamiliar to her would also have had big-name nature designers.

More research was needed. More time.

But everything was now, now, now.

A screen popped up next to Jae's. It was Mace, reporting on his normal operating programs. Jae told him, "Give me an hour," and signed off even as he physically entered the room and the screen holding his image vanished.

Nesh joined them. She motioned to Lon, who gave her a "wait" gesture. Taking a seat, she opened a video conversation with her own planetary flora staff, Lon's, and who knew who else.

Conversation in the room created a continuous not-so-low rumble.

Lon was covered with dirt, his normal state these days as he deconstructed most of the planet's cities. "She's faking," he accused of the "dead" cat. "I saw her just yesterday running like she was the Bolt. *J'te jure,* for a few minutes I didn't know where the new cat had come from."

That reassured Lina. Running Fafhrd meant that she was happy. "That reminds me," she told the group. "Dr. Mart says he's not returning to Sarastor."

Lon cocked his head at her expectantly. Dr. Mart was undergoing Terran veterinary training while he was technically on medical leave from Legion Med.

"He says the staff at the vet school took him out for Indian last night and he's not leaving until someone assures him he can order Masala dosa in the AffSys."

Hal chuckled, and Jae scratched his chest as he was trying to understand.

"I've never had Masala dosa," Lina said. "I wouldn't know if it had magical hypnotic qualities or not." She eyed the family group facing her. "I said, 'I've never had Masala dosa.'"

Londo quickly said, "We will get you a plate of it. And for Jae too."

"I know a place in Bangalore…" Hal volunteered. "Yeah. Very good Masala dosa."

"We will go there," Lon declared.

"Well okay then. Mart says to give them two, maybe three more weeks and the vet school will throw a graduation party for him, if he decides to go home. The staff wants to use him as an excuse to hit some new restaurants before they're done."

"We will get everyone in Legion Medical Indian food," Lon promised. "We'll hire a band. With dancers. *Attache ta tuque!* Is this graduation what that sliding 'cat spa day' is on the calendar?"

"Yes. The vet school will begin with complete grooming for the entire herd – god help them with that – then move on to any checkups the cats might still need. They're fairly up to date on their annual exams. Molly's is coming up before that. Graduation night three doctors will accompany Mart to Sarastor and then do checkups using AffSys equipment to double check and calibrate. Five different AffSys med schools are going to be watching it. Why don't most people in the AffSys have pets?"

"I can't believe you got Legion Med to okay this," Hal told his son. He was here to begin training in case he was needed to take over from Londo for some reason. "They're really okay with the idea?"

Lon gave a long gallic shrug. "It's on the outskirts of what the Legion provides for family medicine. Gorgeon okayed it. Stoan hasn't said a word."

"If he ignores it, it doesn't exist," Jae put in about the Legion commander, to which Lon nodded.

But their attention was brought back as Lina said, "Ah, here it is. Info starting to come through now." She brought up some screens for them to look at. "Sabotage," she told them. The screens showed one, two, even a third location where the rebuilding of cities was taking place. A split screen showed large industrial vehicles crashing into walls.

Lon's eyes narrowed as he studied the screen. "It's cosmetic damage but it's still too much," he growled. "Bet the driver or drivers wound up in a medical facility. I'll–"

"Three local psychic groups came up with warnings for the Scaly River in Limbernie," Lina told them. "Acidic taste, gasping, lack of air…"

"Someone's poisoning more rivers," Jae surmised.

"Maybe not yet," Lina said. "Back on Earth, Elena got the eight of Wands out of it when she ran cards. That means it's fast approaching but it might still be in the planning stages."

"Anyone ask who was behind it?"

"Something red."

Lon's frown reappeared. "That's helpful. Red Army? Santa Claus?"

"Elena and Cartrell kept coming up with the Emperor card. So did nine of our new Aldierran tarot groups."

"Emperor?" Hal blurted. "Yanist-Glory?" From the neighboring star empire. The man who'd kidnapped and tortured Lon when he'd been a child.

Lon's mouth drew into a flat line. "*Pantoute*. Lupoff. His red uniform."

Lina nodded as she tried to form a picture in her mind. "Could be. I see a lot of black swirling around that big red blotch. It has smaller colors, rather distinct, that dot it as if it were bits of other armies. Isn't that how the Red Army in particular works? Incorporated into other armies? We haven't really been here long enough to make solid imagery connections."

Jae slapped his hand on the desk before he straightened in disgust. "I'll get moving on it now."

— — —

"IT'S AN AMATEURISH JOB."

Wiley's image stood next to him, life-size against the equipment screens that lined Legion Lab #4 on. Sarastor. They faded around the edges of the viewscreen.

Jae examined his own equipment to compare the readings in the lab some 340 parsecs away. This snowy landscape showed stained tracks of boots, maybe a half-dozen men, that led to the refrozen melt from a landed flitter.

"They made it past planning stages."

The wide but shallow Scaly River had begun to emerge from its winter freeze in time to be sabotaged. It might have been worse: the river might have been cleaned before whoever it was did this.

Jae tasted the river with his mind and compared it to what his screen's chemical analysis showed.

"Give me some time here," he told Wiley, and his teal-skinned Legion colleague absently nodded.

Jae took off, using his Legion Array of ring, wrist, and ankle bands to fly over the river. The chemicals had left a faint reddish stain, moving downstream – but not far. They'd caught this in good time.

Jae searched for that vibe, that energy that responded to him: devas who controlled matter and energy on an elemental level, working with the energies of the world. "Change this," he commanded them. "Sodium bicarbonate will mesh with the river's natural properties. Feel the balance it imparts. Reach for that. Change it."

The devas approved and sorted through the stuff of Creation to shift atomic and molecular structures to Jae's wishes.

"Some iron over here. A little calcium. We're balancing the environment. Bringing it up to health." The devas within the poison were willing to change, looking forward to making something different.

Jae kept tweaking even as he referred to historical records of how this river's water had tested hundreds of years ago, before pollution overtook the world. It wouldn't be a perfect river, but what river was? He could fine-tune things as Spring arrived.

But for now the situation had been neutralized. A few poisoned fish and amphibians floated downriver, but even they now had their systems purified. They'd feed the rest of the food chain without harm.

Lina stood beside Wiley's screen when Jae returned. "All set," he reported.

"Wiley's got three possibilities of where the poison was manufactured," Lina told him. "He said—"

"I said you should set up a net of monitors along Aldierra's rivers," Wiley interrupted.

Lina held out her hands, revealing a dozen tiny cameras.

"We'll need more than this," Jae said as he examined one. Not quite standard Legion issue.

"You'll have them in two hours," Wiley said.

"Lina has a sleep period."

"I can stay up," she volunteered.

"You'll sleep," Jae told her. "They can wait until tomorrow. I'll have the networking in place by then, with people assigned to watch for the next event."

Lina nodded, and Wiley signed off.

— — —

OSTI DE TABARNAK DE SACRAMENT! Londo startled when he heard the call for help and took off. That women's shelter had just opened four days ago. There were three others in its area, none of them publicized. Like the others, this one was a nondescript gray building complex, only six stories high and encompassing a small city block. Its central courtyard had smog-filtering camouflage screens so that higher neighboring buildings couldn't see clearly into it.

From offices in military public relations and services centers, women seeking safety were discreetly funneled far from their Houses to these shelters.

Or at least they'd thought so.

Londo hurtled through the sky, aiming at the small facility. It had been less than a minute since the emergency call had come in. A swarm of shouting men rushed past a corpse directly in front of the shuttered main House gates. A disguised loophole through which defensive weaponry could be aimed from the inside still glowed dull red from being super-heated for a moment.

The mob was almost upon those gates. Energy beams flashed in beats of light from their ranks against the walls of the place. The building's armor was strong as military issue, but even that wouldn't hold up to a long-term barrage.

Londo landed with a directed thud that toppled the leading members of the mob from their feet.

"Go back!" Londo commanded in his naturally amplified voice. He assumed his Commanding Leader stance, the one that reinforced his position as one of the two mightiest beings this side of Galactic Center. They recognized who he was and what he personified, and paused their march. "You know you are not welcome here!"

"Give us our women!" One of the men yelled, and within moments the entire mob repeated the demand.

"You will not touch them!" Lon replied. How had they discovered this place? He'd have to relocate the shelter, reconfigure it to look different. Reconfigure the others as well, or perhaps design normal buildings that had the same types of facades as these shelters. Misdirection. Find where the leak was that had disclosed the location.

Likely from the military. He could sense Jae in his mind, wondering if this was Patriarch Lupoff's work, but Jae didn't want to interrupt Londo.

Lon heard the women inside scrambling to find a way to safety through their panic.

"These women are safe here," Londo told the mob even as he knew the women would hear as well. "I will see to their safety. None will be harmed. None will return where they do not want to go!"

"They are ours, not yours!"

"The Protector wants them all for himself!"

"The Protector" was Londo. Valiant.

"Give us our –" and the words used for "women" were foul indeed.

Ah. Lina was talking to the shelter inhabitants now, informing them that they'd be moved to a new, very secret place. They shouldn't fear, but should pack quickly.

"You're living in the shadow of the Deadline." Lon tried to reason with the mob. "Why are you provoking your world by doing this? These women want to live their own lives."

"They are our property, not yours!"

"They are not mine either. They belong to themselves. They are free beings."

Again, a string of foul synonyms for "women." And some worse words directed at him.

"Get back! Go home!" Londo insisted.

Three beams of weapons light caught him in the chest, in the face. Instead of blowing him apart, he remained standing. Unaffected.

"Go home now," Lon warned them. "I will not hold mercy for what happens here. I assure you that punishment will be dealt to anyone who doesn't leave. Now. And never returns."

The answer to that was more pulsed blasts from the hand weapons the men in the mob carried. They hardly rifled Lon's hair. A handful of men decided to retreat, but they were by far the minority.

"Final warning," he told the swarm.

The air between him and the mob lit up with blaster fire, spitting in targeted attack until they became a wide, steady barrage.

Londo extended his left arm. A shimmering Shield appeared on it, widening to Londo's mental command. He brought it closer to his body, where it could catch all the fire–

And reflect it back onto the mob.

Screams. The smell of burning flesh. Shouts of pure terror.

Stoically Lon held the Shield in place. He might have commanded it to absorb the energy, but an example needed to be set for the entire planet to witness. Twenty billion people needed to be saved.

Sometimes killing was warranted.

When it had to happen, the trick was to make sure it was quick and as painless as possible, with no innocents harmed. Any wounded would have to be attended to quickly.

Army troops were arriving at the back of the mob but left safe space from all the energy rebounds. They set up force shields for protection. He could hear Jae's voice on their communications telling them to let the ones who'd already walked away, go.

But the ones who'd remained…

Londo deflected the few remaining blasts on the Shield. He held out his right hand and caught some more on his palm, but they didn't reflect nearly as well as the Shield let them. The pavement in front of the shelter melted in a stench and sizzled with the refracted energy beams.

Lon advanced on what remained of the mob. Even now men shot at him. A few puffs of his parabreath knocked them down, their clothing aflame.

Then he let the Shield disappear. He extended both arms to his sides and crashed his hands together. The atmosphere thundered as the air displaced so violently.

What men remained on their feet now fell down before the shock wave.

He motioned for the unsteady army troops to come forward and surround the writhing mob.

"What do we do with them?" the soldier nearest, a senior lieutenant, asked.

"Medical aid for those who are still alive," Lon said. "Imprisonment upon medical release. Mark them for castration. Separate the younger ones, say, sixteen, seventeen years old or younger, from the rest. We will do reversible castration on them. And then…"

The lieutenant's gaze on him was hard but respectful. "Then?"

"I will take them to the Shit Flats," Lon replied with a snarl. "They can help this world whether they want to or not." He'd constructed a large penitentiary there where inmates spent most of their incarceration in full, protective bodysuits to insulate them from the unbelievable stink. They worked to rehabilitate that vast basin to health.

There a small court would confirm or deny his own pronouncement.

Then he turned around to consider the building and the best way to transfer the people and their possessions inside. Lina shouldn't tire herself out trying to port it all. He was tempted to fly the building intact somewhere, but there might be a good replacement purpose for the place right here, and it would be more difficult to determine where the women had gone. There were lots of homeless on this world. This was already set up as a home for perhaps a thousand families. There wasn't much time before Deadline.

But re-purposing was no true answer if someone was just going to leak the position of the next shelter.

I'll track it down, Jae assured him, but he had a good idea where the core of the problem lay.

CHAPTER

6

He hadn't realized he'd been so happy, but it had been all he'd known in his young life.

Jae Rallene was ten years old. He wandered the flourishing forests of Feith with his family: his father, two mothers, and sometimes his sister and her husband, or perhaps a grandparent or three.

They lived in a spacious tent with thick rugs on the ground and pillowed beds that made him feel weightless when he was tucked in at night, a favorite toy by his side. The family sang and danced as they worked. Daddy was the most adept at spotting disease, which he taught Jae meant "dis-ease," in the flora they encountered. He taught Jae how to sink his mind into matter and right physical problems by speaking to the devas of substance as well as the auras of the trees, and urging them to change, to cast off any clinging negative energies. He also made the best breakfasts ever.

Jae's Mama was more the animal expert. She taught him how to approach wildlife so they wouldn't be spooked, and to treat their illnesses. She was the best dancer of his parents and showed Jae how to throw himself full-heartedly into movement.

Mummy was more domestic in her approach to life. She taught Jae formal subjects as well as esoteric ones. She told him the history of his world and people, and how the universe was structured in ways that couldn't be seen unless you knew the secrets of how to look.

Every moment of every day Jae could feel his parents' presence in the back of his mind. It was an ever-fluctuating but always loving link to them. It was like breathing; it was *there*.

After a while, though they searched and searched, they couldn't find any disease or illness in the landscape. They sent out messages to other travelers, and the answer came back: all of Feith is well.

That's when they moved to the City.

Feith didn't have many; its population was small, though its people lived long. How long, Jae didn't know. Time was a slippery concept to his ten-year-old self. The city was called Chiline, and it consisted of low, hand-made buildings decorated by their inhabitants so each was unique. It was fascinating to see what marvelous frou-frous were hidden in the details.

But Jae hardly had anyone to play with. Oh, the adults were happy to take time and romp with him, but he was the only child his age. In fact, his sister Jarra was the only other Feithi near in age to him, but she was thirty years older than he, and newly married into a dual arrangement, which seemed odd to him. But she and his new brother-in-law were so happy. Jae was happy for them.

Eventually the adults' attention was diverted by some kind of big matter they had to discuss. Around the world, in the few cities there were, the word went out that people should gather.

Jae attended one of these meetings in a large, white amphitheater whose not-quite-stone seats allowed him to bounce about. After a while he got tired of bouncing. The adults were talking, talking, talking, and it was boring. He asked if he could leave and explore a bit.

Explore is what he did. In the next month he explored all over the city and the forests that surrounded it. He kept up his studies, but had much time to be curious.

One day a small spaceship descended into the city. Jae laughed because it was so silly. It was a big container! Surely people didn't actually use that to travel in space? He'd never seen a Feithi ship, but he knew his people were extensive travelers in the cosmos, especially to the surrounding planetary confederation, which was called the AffSys. They got around somehow, all by themselves, and Mummy assured him that someday he would know how they did it and travel himself.

But now there was this antique spaceship. Some AffSys man had come to speak before the assembly. He left his ship's door open. Well, just a little. There were other men standing around the ship, but Jae used what Daddy and Mama had taught him and slipped by them, unnoticed.

The control room was filled with bright, colorful electronics and picture screens like the kind Jae recalled from his history lessons. Electronics were used by civilizations who didn't know how to utilize their personal energies. There were certainly enough crew standing around to have controlled needed operations on their own.

What other old stuff was here? Jae wandered the ship and peeked into corner after corner. The metal structure was machined and sterile looking. Someone somewhere seemed to have been depressed, for colors were dark and lighting, dim. The only brightness came from the electronics, scattered within easy reach of the humans who traveled on the ship. Sometimes Jae would recognize the purpose of something and congratulate himself quietly for being smart, unwilling to let others know he was here.

He felt his parents reach out to find him and he mentally assured them he was okay. **Just looking around,** he told them.

But the novelty wore off. He found a bed and lay down.

When he woke it was to vibration. The ship was taking off! From a viewscreen he saw Feith quickly become a globe beneath him.

He called out to his parents. **Help!**

It's all right, beloved, Mummy told him. **It's okay to be afraid. I love you.**

I love you too, my little one, Mama said. **Remember that Source always protects you, though you may not understand how.**

I am so proud of you, my wonderful son, Daddy told him. **Hold fast to who you are. We are with you always.**

And then there was…

A Scream.

Millions of them, screaming as one. It took only an instant.

It seared Jae's brain like the brightest of laser lights, blinding him for minutes.

In panic he ran out of the room, feeling his way down the corridor as his vision returned, into that control room, shouting his terror. He had to catch himself on one wall, for the ship was suddenly pitching this way and that.

"A boy!" someone shouted in the AffSys language.

And on the screen behind her Jae saw the globe of Feith glowing with terrible heat. He could feel it from here, though not physically. His world was being incinerated.

Every last thing on it – he could feel it wither away.

Dead.

Every person.

Mama, Daddy, Mummy.

His sister and brother-in-law. Grandparents who had laughed with him through the years. Friends.

Through the utter confusion the wild movements of the ship came to him only as a background amplification of the terror. Smoke began to pour from the electronics. Flame. Air pressure oscillated, making his ears pop.

"See to the boy!" someone shouted, and suddenly there were arms pulling him this way and that. Someone shoved him into a small cabin.

The door remained open as the adults on the ship ran, shouting. Great shrieks of metal tearing made him grit his teeth. He clamped his hands over his ears.

More shouting. Screaming.

Something hit the door to the cabin. It closed with a hiss. Something happened; it took a moment to figure what it was: movement. Weightlessness.

There was a tiny window and outside it he could see that ship. It was disgorging tiny ships, maybe things like what he was in.

And then that ship quite soundlessly blew up.

– – –

HE SAT IN A DAZE FOR HOW LONG? Eventually he rummaged through the cabin. There was a tiny bit of food to eat. A water dispenser that held how much?

No one came to get him. All there were, were stars and Feith's sun and the husk that had once been Feith to look at outside.

The air was beginning not to support him. He found some things he couldn't identify and changed them into good air. That lasted for a while.

After how many days? he'd converted everything he could to good air. He wasn't sure what exactly was in good air, which frustrated him because there was still pressure in here. He needed to change whatever it was to something breathable. He'd been able to give the general idea to the elements he changed, but now he needed to be more specific to replenish it.

He just didn't... *know*.

Over and over he sent his mind out, hoping Daddy or Mama or Mummy would answer. Maybe his sister Jarra...

Nothing came back. No presence.

All was emptiness.

He was absolutely alone.

And he was getting dizzy. Not sure if he was seeing anything real or not. Hoping that he'd die so he could be with his parents again. They would be all right. Mummy had told him what happened after an incarnate life was over. Now he wanted his life to be over as well.

Instead at some point the wall hit him on his side. Some bit of his mind woke a little. He had floated to the wall – fast – and the collision was abrupt.

He didn't really care.

But outside the window he dimly made out... something. A human form. Angels? Other spirit beings? No, it didn't shine like angels did.

It was a man. Difficult to describe him, as there was just the tiny spark that was Feith's sun out there, but Jae could see that the man wore a white cape. He looked into the window, and the light from within illuminated his face. His gaze spotted Jae.

– – –

LINA FOUND JAE AT THE OUTLOOK, the bench overlooking the valley behind the Monstrosity. He had Fafhrd on his shoulder and was petting her, though he seemed a million miles away.

"Am I interrupting?" she asked.

He blinked, then turned to her. He patted the bench. "Just getting some fresh air." He sniffed. "Such as it is."

The semi-permeable forcefield over the trees allowed a trace of the outside polluted air through. Lina almost always wore the filtering necklace she'd been given. Jae's Legion equipment performed the same function for him. "Whatever you say," she said as she took a seat beside him. "Another dream?"

"More like a memory than a dream. I've been flashing back a lot, especially since Arient."

Both Jae and she had been injured there two weeks ago, enough so they'd been in comas for a few days. Jae had been in his two days longer than Lina. Not that they were competing with each other. Lina snuggled up to his side. She gave Fafhrd's chin a loving scratch, then turned her attention to petting Jae. He had a most satisfying head of blond hair, like a thick pelt.

"And yes, I've talked with Saichan," Jae said. His therapist.

"Deadline is getting closer," Lina said. "You spoke with Lupoff. A few tarot groups keep drawing the Devil or Emperor cards when they look ahead. Has he started the pushback everyone said he'd make?"

"Mm-hm." Jae nodded. He patted his knee and gray-furred Ember jumped to take her usual place, followed by Molly with all her long hair, much of it following her in a golden cloud to eventually fall upon what seemed mostly dark fabrics. Usually Londo's uniforms. Then Jae reached for the drink that sat on the table next to himself, took a sip, and set it down before returning his attention to the cats.

Lina shared the duty. "Does Saichan have any instructions for Londo and me?"

Jae shook his head. "It's just… stress. And the basic situation."

"Lord help Lupoff then," Lina said, and Jae allowed himself to smile. "So he's going to be trouble?"

"Oh yes. But he doesn't yet realize we've got Bracken fully on our side."

Field Marshal Bracken was still head of the Majority Army.

"What do your guides tell you?"

Lina paused in her thoughts, centering herself before trying to lift herself into a higher vibration.

****Jae needs your support,**** her spirit guides said helpfully. ****But trust his decisions in this. He's been in these kinds of situations before. He's trained in what to do, plus he utilizes his imagination to good effect.****

"They say to trust you, I guess."

"Good advice." Jae chuckled.

****Troubling times ahead. Trust yourself. Trust the universe. Ask for help. It is not a sign of weakness. We are always here for you.****

Lina gave a nod to them. She squeezed Jae's arm. "Just tell me if I need to do anything or say anything or look twice at someone to help out. Oh, your mag-net-mobile arrived. Lon's bringing it in now."

Even as she spoke Lina could look up and see a dot far off the sky that was her other husband. Above that dot was a dark cube that dwarfed it. As he got closer the cube revealed itself to be as large as a convenience store.

For the truly bulky items they required from off-planet, Londo would have Lina port him there, then lift them into space and use his puter to help him aim it in a mighty heave that would convey it through hyperspace. Days later, following the puter's directions, he could fly from Aldierra into hyperspace to retrieve the shipment. If he weren't there to do so, it would continue across whatever hyperspace was, not easily retrieved again. Hyperspace required one to know the exact theoretical position of what they were trying to connect with. Miss by an inch – and you'd missed entirely.

He hadn't missed. Easily he flew the equipment to the side, beyond what their outcrop would let them view, and two minutes later he alone flew to join them. He took an adjoining metal seat. Molly hissed at him but he ignored her.

"Ready to clean up the last bits in your two rivers," Lon announced to Jae as he stretched his back. "I'm not sure how it can be programmed to differentiate between scrap metal and rocks, but I do know it won't pick up anything that's organic."

"No sweat. I'll see to it."

Jae was techno-savvy, Lina knew. He'd spent most of his adolescence in Wiley's labs at Legion HQ. "We have video crews covering the befores and af-ters," she said.

Lon's stretching must be contagious. Jae rotated his shoulders and the cats on him set their claws into his clothes more firmly. He smiled at them; smiled at his spouses. "In case I forget to mention, I love that we're linked as we are. The constant… knowing." That made both reflect contented expressions to him. "It reminds me of what I used to have."

Lina rubbed Jae's arm. "We're family now."

"Always," Lon added.

"That doesn't mean that I'm not scared that we're also business partners," Lina told them. "We hardly have any personal time. Eventually we're going to have to re-sort priorities."

Lon grimaced agreement. "After Deadline. Remember when we thought all we'd have to do on Aldierra was come here now and then to lend a hand, if they needed one?"

"Did we really say that?" Lina asked. Fafhrd climbed off Jae and onto her shoulder, so Lina nuzzled her. The cat began to blow contented drool bubbles as Lina massaged her ears.

Lon picked Molly hair off his pants.

"We did. Oh, to be so innocent again. I've insisted that we get some personal time on the schedules now," Lon told them.

"But that keeps getting cancelled for emergencies," Lina countered. "We're up to our eyeballs and beyond in this mess we call Aldierra. Riots and men running screaming through the streets for no reason and people beating up on others just because they can and not even bothering to use a toilet when they need to relieve themselves."

Guess who was in charge of portalets? Lina would be happy if she never needed to bother with one again. Instead she directed entire companies around the globe to distribute them, clean them, and chase people down when they decided to just go in broad daylight on a crowded street.

Aldierra. What were they going to do with it?

"At least everyone's excited about the food contest," Lon said as he brought up their combined schedules in front of them. "You sure you're up for this, Jae? I'd be happy to take your place."

Jae gave a belly laugh. "That's the only thing I've been looking forward to," he said. "Lon, you can eat anything and never blink an eye. I've seen you eat solidified acid."

"It wasn't my favorite. Rust is worse. I like regular food." He gave a rude scoff. "My tastes are every bit as good as yours."

"Right. You can eat the leftovers in this, if there are any. We'll have a live audience."

"Don't you go eating everything, Lon," Lina warned him. He did seem to be hungry a lot. Then again, he performed a lot of heavy work, like bashing sky-scrapers with one fist while carrying warehouses in the other hand. "I'll collect some winning recipes and we'll have the kitchen here prepare them the next day. Would you like that, Faffy? Would oo?"

Fafhrd blew another bubble.

"My men will be happy to have anything better than their army rations," Lon declared. He made a face at Jae. "At least your armies get some local food."

"Hey, we're giving your guys local food too," Lina tried to work herself up to give her protest a little oomph, but Faf was trying to sleep. It was important that they talk about these relatively unimportant points as well as the big jobs. She checked the schedule.

"The magnet-mobile goes here, to the Saba River, right?" she asked Jae.

"Magnet-mobile?" Jae chuckled. "Right. Yes. We'll need to start it at the top of the river, though, Lon. I made sure it could handle mountain terrain. It also adjusts for waterways of narrow width."

"Like streams. *Vadontoé; c'est cool.* I'll reposition it," Lon assured him. "Just tell me where you want it."

"I've got trucks ready to collect whatever it picks up at forty different points along the main river," Lina said. "We haven't been sure how you'll be handling the tributaries…"

CHAPTER

7

It was supposed to be a fun, morale-boosting event: the finals in the planet-wide cooking contest for best *scanner* recipe. Scanners were a pocket sandwich, like the AffSys' *spielette* or some Terran pasties. A savory filling wrapped in a dough.

And people were pounding others about it.

There had been fifteen actual sizable, related riots in the two weeks leading up to this. All three Starharts had broadcast to the world that they were supposed to have fun competing. Utilize their creativity. Celebrate their heritage. Rediscover the joy of cooking that historical media insisted the world had once possessed. Some Houses might even (unthinkable!) collaborate with others on their entries. This was food, not atomic weaponry. Not everything had to have life or death consequences.

People should chill.

Jae strolled through the expansive army kitchen. Metal utility tables had been laid out with white tablecloths for the televised event. Occasional colorful decor such as flowers or shiny rocks dotted the area between presentation platters.

But the finished piles of scanners were missing. One table had overturned. Fried dough, boiled dough, baked dough lay in bits and pieces all over tabletops and on the floor. Fillings were smeared into the tunics and aprons of the men who were here to present them. Some of them still threw scanners at each other, grinding them into their opponents when they could. Decorative rocks and bric-a-brac had sometimes been put to other uses, and blood mixed with spatters of savory fillings. Various colorful ingredients added a certain piquantness to the mayhem, as did the purpling bruises upon the orange-skinned Aldierran brawlers.

The presentation dishes held only a few remnants of the food entries. Luckily, most of the fighting had begun after preliminary judging had been completed. The finalists and their entries had been rushed out of the kitchen and taken… somewhere.

Jae hoped someone knew what had happened to them – and that they were safe. He had skipped lunch to make sure he had room for this.

The director of the show rushed up to him, his lips flapping as he tried to find the right words. "Catastrophe!" He pulled his green hair in horror. "We cannot air this!"

"We can and we will," Jae replied. "First–" He materialized his Staff and then thumped it on the floor.

All action, all noise in the room ceased.

The attention-focusing Staff had been an Investiture present from the Worlds themselves, like Lon's Shield and Lina's Flute. "You will halt your fight," Jae informed the room. "Anyone still fighting within the next minute will be hauled away. I don't know where to. You probably don't want to know anyway."

He matched gazes with the anger, fright and disgust in the eyes of the room's chefs as he let his Staff disappear. Then he shook his head. He let out a theatrical sigh. "You fight about this. This. Can you be more petty? It's just food."

"It's the honor of my House!" one man dared to exclaim.

"It is food. Period. We're trying to get some enthusiasm going. We're trying to find something to feed our people and enjoy the process. How does this–" Jae indicated the kitchen and the remains of what looked like an attempted massacre – "show honor to anyone or anything? Look. Look at yourselves!"

A few dared to mutter. Jae stared them down.

Finally he straightened his stance, took a deep breath, and asked loudly, "Does anyone know where the top entries are?"

Eventually wary judges emerged from a set of double doors. They ascertained Jae was there and that the fighting had stopped.

After bustling about, the finalist entries were arranged on a long, clean table and Jae had a short conversation with the director.

So when the televised occasion began, only the tempting entries filled viewers' screens. In their homes they could smell the delicious aromas of the food.

The announcer gravely announced the contest and that these were the top contestants from all over the world. Then the cameras showed the watching crowd of cooks and chefs: bruised, some bleeding, their clothing torn. Food scattered hither and yon amid stilled chaos.

"Here are the honors of the Houses," Jae told the camera as it took in piles of doughy conflagration.

A voice from those Houses: "The contest was unfair! Some Houses advanced when they had no right to!"

Jae didn't bother to look back. "We will investigate. We will watch future contests like this closer. We merely assumed that the great Houses of Aldierra could hold an honest, innocent contest with some kind of integrity. We didn't think we had to set a low bar."

He sighed. "But let's look at these finalists. Where have those judges gone to? Have them wait in another room for a few moments."

The plates had been labelled only with numbers written on placards. Letting the cameras watch him, he relabeled the numbers with a pen someone produced. A tattered and stained tablecloth lay on the floor. Jae picked it up, motioned to some of the bruised men, and they held it between the table and the cameras as Jae reorganized the plates. Again in front of the cameras he shuffled the cards, then assigned them one by one to the newly-placed entrees.

"I have a record of what the order was before," he told the audience.

The judges entered from another room.

"Come forward, come forward. If anyone tries to harm you or yours, now or in the future, they will be dealt with. Harshly."

They studied the offerings one by one as the emcee asked what kind of things they were looking for in a good scanner.

Crispness of crust. It shouldn't get soggy. The filling had to have an exciting element, or at least traditional flavors, maybe with a twist. There were sauces to sample as well.

Jae followed the judges at the end of the line and listened closely to how they were rating the entries. He tasted the vegetarian ones. After the judges had been seen noting their rankings, he went back for another bite from two of the entries. "Really good," he declared, and for another said, "This reminds me of a Sarastoran tuddly. It's a favorite breakfast for many there." The scores were then averaged.

The bloody crowd stood breathless as the final rankings were revealed. The names of the Houses responsible for each splayed across the screen. Third place… Second place… "Grand winner!" the announcer shouted in triumph, and one of the bloody groups jumped about, grabbing each other in joy.

Someone back there made a lunge and Jae pointed at them. They stopped in mid-step, then retreated.

"Better," Jae said.

The judges presented the winning House chefs with a large golden spoon trophy. Originally someone had suggested a glorified chef's knife, but thankfully that idea had been nixed.

"Now, although we have a Grand Champion, I think all these recipes, finalists and semi-finalists alike, will be incorporated into the daily menus of the companies and staff members working for Three Worlds. They deserve some good food.

"We'll be publishing the recipes so everyone can try them. Some of you might think you can do better. All right, we might have a rematch in the future.

"But our next contest will be for a breakfast. Something we can make for the many, many people who are out there in the field, working to make your world a better one. We need something that is inexpensive, can be made in large quantities, maybe doesn't need extensive storage – it won't go bad too soon – and is delicious and hearty to start one's day.

"You all have three weeks to go through your local levels of competition on this. I want to see the finalists here in four weeks – and acting civilized, having been through a fair and unbiased process. Pelzire."

He bowed to the audience over the hand sign.

Jae grabbed another scanner before the director called a cut.

– – –

"STIM?" WILEY ASKED LINA. As usual, his short, purple hair stood on end from him constantly running his fingers through it as he thought about the zillions of things he thought about.

Those thoughts were a reason why his eyes usually operated differently from each other. He had what, seven? Was it eight or nine now?, sensory inputs available to him, most of them digital. Only when he was truly concentrating on something did his eyes work together, indicating that all five brilliant minds were coordinating.

She'd gone to Legion HQ in person to ask the teal-skinned man. Was it too soon to do so? At the moment his eyes weren't coordinated; good. He wasn't paying full attention. "We've got a crisis going on."

Wiley's mouth turned down. His left eye focused on Lina. "It's Aldierra. There's always going to be a crisis. Are you even out of your caffeine limitations yet?" Before he could respond, he said, "You are. This is a serious step above that. No."

"Crises in fifteen different locations today. We're hiring more people all the time, but they need to be trained before they can truly help. Please, Wiley. I need one now. I'm already beat for the day and there's at least six more hours of work needed."

Wiley checked in with Gorgeon. "Absolutely not," she told him. "Besides, I am the one to provide stims. Me or one of my staff."

"Please, Wiley," Lina begged once the screen had cleared. "Just this once. To last six hours. That's not long."

He actually seemed to be considering.

"This Aldierran crisis is going to be a once-in-a-lifetime event," Lina urged. "Twenty billion people. I only need six hours."

A groan seemed to emanate not from Wiley's mouth, but from his entire chest. "Just this once," he muttered in surrender.

"Oh, thank you! You're an angel!"

— — —

JAE COULD NOT REMEMBER ever having to make so many media appearances. The Legion scheduled them regularly, which as a full-time member and Alpha Team Leader had been once a week. Now as Minister of Aldierra it seemed cameras surrounded him several hours a day, as they were now.

As Minister he was assigned to guide the world to a better future. He'd chosen to specialize in the world's water systems, whether fresh water, ocean water, or ground. Today he had told the mostly volunteer army he had cleaning the local waterway, Orchin's Sekal River, to stand down for an hour – and look up at the sky.

Locals from Tentaeve joined the gathered crowd, their faces unsure as they glanced up now and then, trying not to look insane. They muttered to their neighbors, looked down at their feet, and then cast a furtive peek upward.

Up until this morning the sky had held its normal solid overcast. Now distinct layers of dark clouds drifted past each other. A light-colored cloud layer filled in gaps.

"I am not using my power to do this," Jae told the cameras. He used Expression #5: Confident, with a pleasant smile. "This is the result of a lot of hard work performed by thousands, even tens of thousands of people."

The crowd murmured expectantly.

Jae fretted to himself. Wiley had better be right about this. His brilliant friend and mentor had sworn on all five of his minds that it would happen today. This afternoon. Here.

Wan light played upon the center city's towering buildings as the sky's cloud systems shifted along a front coming through. Shadow followed darker shadow followed lighter one.

The crowd's noise level increased as a noticeably lighter spot appeared in the sky. They urged the clouds that were moving quickest to move even faster. There were several places almost as light, forming the front's leading edge. Occasional, hopeful exclamations erupted as tantalizing veils of whitish cloud wafted by before the crowd silenced again, disappointed.

Jae fought his tension. Almost triggered the tranquilizers stored underneath the skin of his left arm. He fought to keep himself from flying up to speed things along. That would be cheating. Don't deprive the people the chance to celebrate seeing...

A sliver of bright violet sky.

The crowd shrieked even as clouds covered it again.

Then they stood steadfast, waiting until another patch cleared. And another, farther along the front. Another.

Finally an entire small section of sky shone free and clear, the color that history told them it was supposed to be.

Jae hadn't heard Londo approach, but he heard the breath of relief he heaved. Jae turned to him with a hard hug.

"Great job," he told his husband. The job of ensuring planetary clean air had been given to Lon. "This is just the start."

Londo nodded. "And it will encourage others to help."

Lina, of course, was sending out messages. "All of Aldierra is getting the feed," she reported. "I'm going to add pictures of the Saba River to this now that so much of it is clean. I want to see people dancing in the streets."

"They already are," Jae said and pointed to the celebrations breaking out.

It was one small section of sky, already getting a little smaller as cloud layers shifted...

Only the rest of a big world left to go. Less than six months to do it all.

CHAPTER

8

They'd found nine more attempts of river poisoning.

Two large fires had broken out in the Battle Mountains' forests on Limbernie. A chemical refuse fire was raging just north of Soshe.

Arson.

I'm supposed to be setting up infrastructure for new sections of Hormu, Lon complained in Jae's mind. **Instead I'm putting out fires that shouldn't have started in the first place.**

Nesh stopped some bulldozers trying to get to her new meadows in the Bentmark, Jae replied sourly.

A screen popped up next to his elbow, the picture on it showing that more had tried the same near Londo's forests. It was Field Marshal Bracken.

"We've interrogated the river vandals," he reported. "They were all members of the Green Army. It took some effort to get information out of them, and we didn't get much. 'Just following orders,' they said. They're the type who don't question things. Most thought the chemicals were healthy ones and that they were actually helping."

Londo's growl came through the screen, the same as it did in Jae's head.

"Lupoff's an egomaniac," Jae told them.

"He is. He has his own program, his own goals, and he must be stopped," Bracken declared. "We can't allow this."

Jae could feel that Lon had his own ideas about the quickest way to stop Lupoff. Lon could be violent if someone threatened what was under his protection.

"I will do that," Jae said.

Bracken's face was dark. "I can do it quickly," he said. "No need to involve either of you. He will suffer an unfortunate accident."

Lon's face gave away his train of thought. He wrinkled his nose, then grimaced. Then his mouth slid to one side as he raised both eyebrows. "Maybe not yet. I'm open to other suggestions. What were you thinking of, Jae?"

Bracken interrupted, suggesting going through Patriarch Lupoff's support staff. Not the uppermost echelon; those were leeches who would grab any chance to replace Lupoff if weakness were shown.

"Let me feel out some of them," Jae said. "As for Lupoff, I'm meeting with him tomorrow. There's got to be a way to at least stymie him until we can make him understand that he can't do this."

"Don't approach from a position of weakness. We aren't groveling to him," Lon told him.

"And yet we need him to stop this immediately." Jae scratched his chest absently. "There must be a way to get through. Even he can see that all this will kill his world."

Bracken brushed that idea off with his hand. "That doesn't bother him. All he worries about is himself."

"And it *is* worry," Jae mused. "Fear. He's afraid of the possibility of him appearing weak, so he will lose standing. Position…"

Lon cocked his head at him.

"Let me handle this," Jae assured the two of them.

— — —

THE GROUND THEY MET ON was not neutral. It was instead the inner sanctum of the Majority Army, deep within the ultra-armored Command Fortress located within one of the peaks of the Battle Mountains on Limbernie.

The Council kept the room dark so that the all the displays glared brightly upon the retinas of Jae and his retinue – or it would have had Montue not warned them to wear protective contacts.

Montue was recent army, still half in its ranks but known to hold a high position in Jae's Three Worlds section. Walker Sentristone was former army and comfortable in its ways, even as he occupied the chair of Jae's Chief of Staff. Gebbage and Bluespring were heads of their Minister Operations branches. Gebbage was ex-army; Bluespring came from eco-research institutions. As with any Aldierran male of lower mid-class or higher, he'd endured two years of compulsory enlistment in his youth.

Across the table from them were part of the Great Council of Military Governors. Patriarch Lupoff sat at one end. Jae sat at the opposite.

"Where is Bracken?" Lupoff demanded as he glared at them all. He might be stout and stiff, but he vibrated with his own kind of dark energy.

"The field marshal is coordinating with Orchin police networks to contain those riots that have been threatening Tentaeve Spaceport," Jae replied. "Aldierra needs its food shipments or entire territories will starve."

"Police? Civilian police?" Lupoff settled back into his chair smugly. Jae could almost hear him gloating to himself that even the Three Worlds couldn't tear Bracken's loyalties from Lupoff. He wasn't here because he didn't want to work against his Patriarch.

Little did Lupoff know.

"We have encountered sabotage of major projects," Jae began. "We feel the actions point back to this council, or some entity associated with it."

Lupoff pretended astonishment. He was actually a fairly good actor, Jae thought. "I assure you that cannot be true. We are well aware of the Doomsday pronouncement. We wouldn't do anything to impede progress with that." He turned to Flimmettre, a general of the Orange Army. "What have you heard?"

"We would have quashed it as soon as we had word of it," Flimmettre declared. "There has been nothing coming through our intelligence… unless it's something the Gold Army is doing. They've gone rogue, you know." He finished with a sniff, daring Jae to contradict him.

Jae had monitored the questioning of the Gold Army personnel who had run like berserkers through Orchin a few weeks before. They were frustrated, backed up farther than they could stand. Food shipments were not getting through in their area for some reason. Lon had made sure extra shipments went there first now. Someone was egging them on, willfully causing the disasters that provoked conflicts.

Jae was fairly sure he was looking at those instigators.

Though hopefully some were not, or were unwilling participants. As his own people and Lupoff's talked, Jae studied what he could. Lina had advised him to ask angels to help point out possible allies.

He thought three of the men here had small glows above their heads, yellowish or white in the darkness. Tipton. Siekesh. Dule. Fotter Dule was a major in the Greens. Tipton was an aide to Siekesh, and Rei-Gone Siekesh, well, he had something to do with the uppermost echelons of the intelligence community.

That was one more than Jae had come to this meeting thinking he could convince. He studied them, watched their body language. The Mega-Legion trained its personnel well in sussing out such, filtered by planetary cultures. How they used language also helped his research. A few of them belittled the opposition with personal insults. More referred to the general population as inferiors. No one in the room of course, dissed the Three Worlds or their mission here.

"We're nearing the halfway point," Jae reminded the room. "We do not want anyone on this world harmed. Neither do you. The Majority Army is a huge organization, planetary in its extent. What ways can you see it working directly to the mission? Building instead of destroying?"

Lupoff protested, "Aldierra still has several ongoing wars, despite your commands to stop fighting."

Jae nodded. "Of course the Greens should see to stopping those. You are best equipped for that. Your men are trained. But these are minor wars…"

The discussion went on with little advancement. Lupoff resisted every suggestion as to the reassigning of units and companies. He positively sputtered at the idea of them joining forces with the Orange and Blue armies.

Jae shrugged. "The Blues are mostly cleaning latrines these days anyway," he said, and the entire room chuckled. "They're too busy to do anything of real value."

Lupoff wanted Lon to stop destroying their weapons. He'd been taking the worst into Aldierra's sun, where they'd disintegrate with no harm to anyone.

"You need guns, small weaponry," Jae said. This they discussed. At length. Plus Lupoff's men brought up vehicles they needed in top condition, vehicles that other armies had that should be handed over to the Greens.

"We can do that," Jae promised.

He left files for the Greens to utilize to repurpose a quarter of their army, with schedules they should attend to. Jae doubted that much would come of that. But he thought he'd spotted another man who might be amenable to some… subterfuge.

It was a good start. And he'd thought of one more person who needed to be brought into the plan after he'd run a few queries.

– – –

WEEKS AGO JAE HAD had his staff research Patriarch Lupoff in depth. Now he asked obscure search engines and library sources to do the same. Then his computer combined them all, leaving nothing out, and presented it as a thorough file to him.

He settled in the Starhart lounge with a couple fingers of *heilov*, the sharp Aldierran liquor he favored, then poured a dollop more. He needed it to think clearly, to dull the outside matters that kept popping into his head.

Lupoff was sixty-eight years old, the former commander-in-chief of the Red Army and now Supreme Commander over the Green Army, the Majority Army. He still wore a red uniform, though technically the Red Army no longer existed.

He'd been born toward the middle of a pack of sons. There were three older than he. His extensive natal nuclear family had no daughters. They must have been killed at birth or before so as not to sully the family honor.

For generations the men in Lupoff's family had been renowned for their viciousness as well as military standing. They were Reds to the core. As Lupoff had grown up, his brothers, as brothers will do, sometimes bullied him. When they chose the wrong day to do so, young Lupoff would give them a lesson by beating up their mothers. The family might kill their daughters, but they held their mothers in some kind of esteem. They'd been war prizes or otherwise symbols of the boys' fathers' importance that they were able to bring such women into their group.

Lupoff was not above attacking his own mother in order to rile his father. He did that several times, as she had been quite the prize. Lupoff's father had utilized her to marry up into the stratosphere of society.

Lupoff's father often angered him so Lupoff killed his mother when he was fifteen. He claimed it was her fault; she'd provoked him. The fatality was likely a sloppy mistake on his part. He wasn't charged with a crime, though the threat of that might have been what had sent him to join the Red Army immediately afterward.

Over the years his brothers tried to protect their wives from him, but he managed to rape at least two. One of his nephews might be a bio son.

Even so, those brothers teamed up with him as he advanced in the Red Army. Lupoff's promising father had been stymied in achieving full military power, and the brothers took it upon themselves to punish those who had stood in his way. In this manner they themselves rose in the system.

Lupoff learned to create his own internal network of spies and moles, most reporting back to him and not the bro squad. There were deals to be made, bribes to be paid, careers to enhance. Lupoff did most of it from the shadows.

In one operation, one of Lupoff's brothers privately cautioned him to be careful. The operation failed, and the brother's body was found soon after. No assassin was ever named.

Red soldiers learned that helping the Lupoffs would be helping themselves, or at least make their lives more secure.

When Lupoff gained control of the entire army he set his sights on the larger Green. For years he'd worked shadowy and even blatant alliances there. After all, both forces were after the same thing: keep the civilian population off balance. Draw military spending to support themselves. Gain power from the system.

Jae brought up a wall of diagrams showing how they'd done it: taking over the Greens without dismantling that army. The Greens absorbed them without much complaint after Lupoff's publicity campaign to make it seem as if it had been their idea, their strength that had cowed a lesser rival.

They were the Majority Army and had historically been the one given more patriotic space in history books and public opinion. But Lupoff and some few others among his brothers and the Reds never gave up their red uniforms to re-mind the Greens of who truly was in charge.

From then it was never a matter of vanquishing other armies. They thrust and parried, but war was too lucrative a business to stop. They put on a good show of piety and patriotism.

Lupoff amassed a harem of six women (two now dead) and ten legally rec-ognized sons. Most of the latter were approaching middle age. Some were Greens; some were Reds. It all depended on ability. He had had one daughter who had survived to adolescence. Curious.

Only two of the AI units reporting the stories to Jae included Lupoff's con-sistent use of lies and misdirection in herding his people. The human reporters would not have dreamed of containing that in their reports, for Lupoff was a violent man. Most of the time he hid the worst of his acts, and often it seemed he assigned others to commit them for him. On occasion it was him killing either swiftly or through lengthy torture, never anything in between.

Jae could see the paths and patterns that his plans took. Lupoff took time and effort to achieve his goals, worming his way bit by bit, often approaching from behind. He seemed to possess zero ethical barriers. Zero empathy.

But the potentials of Aldierra seemed to have waned. It must have become boring. It had been conquered. Lupoff had set his sites on distant Sarastor, the rich but weakly defended capital of the Affiliated Systems. He had then-Admiral Bracken commanding his new space fleet, and Lupoff's or maybe Bracken's op-eratives had managed to trick the majority of the protective Mega-Legion off planet to rescue a hyperspace mega-cruiser. The legendary Aiko, Lon's ex-girl-friend, had been killed in the sabotage, as had almost a score of passengers and crew. But no more than that; the Legion had seen to things.

They'd just left Sarastor defenseless.

It had been only Jae and Wiley left in HQ, plus a prisoner, Lon's new bride, Lina. Together the three had commandeered planetary defenses and fooled the invasion fleet long enough for Bracken to surrender.

Bracken. He would have to be brought in on this, Jae mused. Lon was con-vinced that the man was now fully on their side. If so, he'd be the best to offer counsel as to the paths Jae needed to take in this.

Jae put through a private call.

CHAPTER

9

There was a high wind over the ocean today. So far from polluting land to obscure much of the view, Jae could see scheduled rain approaching in the distance.

The crew were members of his Aldierra Corps, men drawn from both army and civilian sources. They wore fluorescent orange jumpsuits with built-in flotation devices and non-slip boots as they bent to their work.

Aldierra had manpower to spare, so two large groups of men bent to hauling in nets full of debris. As soon as they left the water, the nets were manhandled over to machinery that sorted live animals from the rest and deposited them back into the ocean. Men stood by to double-check the results and correct the machine's choices into memory so it would do better.

The debris also got sorted, this time by a different small army of men and machines. The vessel was a large one, but after being on patrol for so long, was getting near full.

Major Fotter Dule seemed an average enough Aldierran: average height, average build. Maybe a little darker orange skin than median. The thing that stood out about him to Jae's eyes was that he acted more… crisply… than others. His salutes snapped. His walk was precise. His medals shone in mint condition. Here was an officer who worked closely with the Patriarch and the Great Council of Military Governors. His exacting manner had helped him to his current position.

And also, from what Jae had been able to discover, the man was excellent at his job.

The crash of waves against the ship, the shouts of the crew as they worked, and even cries from some curious seabirds (whose numbers seemed already to be rising) covered up their conversation. Jae made sure his Legion sound equipment didn't completely mask their voices. Someone might be listening, and he didn't want it to be obvious that they weren't talking about things they were supposed to be talking about. Sometimes surrounding noise made an even better audio mask than did electronics.

Jae gave a leisurely wave at the crew as if he were discussing them and their work. Dule listened raptly.

"I have an operative who is getting up to speed on your office and its duties," Jae told Dule pleasantly. In response, Dule nodded with an expectant expression. Good actor.

"I want to bring her in–"

"Her? A woman?"

"She is female. Not human. She'll be disguised as a human Aldierran man."

Dule's expression slipped to reveal a momentary frown.

"She's an Alpha-ranked Legionnaire," Jae explained. "Like me. She's an expert in disguise. We've decided she'll use the name Nobrin Muvvik in this role. She'll have another disguise and name she uses while at our headquarters so she won't be linked between the two locations. I'd like her to take the role of your aide, so she can make reports and devise strategy from a different viewpoint than you. If it comes to it, she can protect you. Alpha Legionnaires are rigorously trained in defense of all kinds."

"Does she… know technology?" Dule asked hesitantly.

Jae chuckled and pointed out a section of the workline as if that's what they were talking about. "She's quite proficient at AffSys technology, which for the most part is a small step above what Aldierra has come up with." Jae shrugged. "Some of your tech is beyond that of the AffSys, but she's also learning that. I have faith she'll be able to learn things much quicker than you think. You don't have to worry about that. If she has a problem in some area, she'll ask you and I hope you'll point her to the proper learning materials."

"And military culture?"

"Bracken is briefing her on that. You'll find her more than satisfactory." Bracken was briefing Mimik on a lot of things, now that he had been informed of Jae's secret plans.

"Bracken." Dule heaved a sigh, then must have remembered himself and looked around the deck and its activity with curiosity. "A woman."

"You'll be pleasantly surprised at what she can accomplish. She's the Protector's second in command on Sarastor."

Dule nodded. "And what I get out of this, out of this mutiny… of this treason…"

"Who is the traitor here?" Jae asked quietly. "Lupoff is acting to doom the entire population in order to increase his own power. What power will he have if he, like everyone else, is dead? You will be working to save your world."

"This will not involve assassination?"

"Not from your aide. Hopefully not from anyone. We just want to remove Lupoff and his immediate supporters from the scene. We want Aldierrans to act for themselves, and not follow some leader like mindless sheep." Jae's brows furrowed. "They must learn to think for themselves. To set their goals and make good choices."

He turned to look at Dule full-on. "This is about the soul of Aldierra's citizens, both individually and en masse. It's time for your world to grow up, Major. They'll be happier – and freer – as adults."

The grimace appeared again but remained as Dule met Jae's gaze. "I'm in. I'm a loyal officer, but my true duty is to my people."

"Glad to hear it."

"I have ideas about who else should be involved."

"Very good. Let's get started."

– – –

THAT AFTERNOON BACK IN HER TENT HEADQUARTERS OFFICE, Lina ported Legionnaire Mimik in from Sarastor as Jae stood waiting. Mimik had caused Lina trouble and embarrassment in the past… but maybe she'd had good reason in her own mind. The insectoid Legionnaire arrived in male Aldierran civilian clothing of a businesslike Reydan style and carried the usual Legion duffle. That duffle was held with one of two hands instead of her usual four. Had she pared herself down to fit the clothing? A largish syntho box accompanied her.

"We have minimal quarters ready for you in this compound. If you need more room, we can provide that."

"Not necessary, Speaker."

"Do you have special needs? Food, medical, transportation?"

"I'm good."

Lina frowned at the Legionnaire. It was almost impossible to read her as anything but mulish. A while back Lon had confided how close and valued a friend Mimik was. "I can play you Lon's 'Aldierra is violent' warning speech if you want," Lina added helpfully.

Mimik nodded inscrutably. "Not necessary, Speaker. I studied it prior to coming here. Neutrino?"

"I think you can call me 'Jae,' Mimik."

That earned him a nod as well. Lina waited for an invitation to informality. Legion rules. Mimik turned to her. "My name is–" and she gave a stridulent chirp with a blip of a drone inserted within it.

Oh. Well, that was a friendly step. She should be thankful and acknowledge it in some way. For a moment Lina stood silently to ponder the sound. The thingie inside her and all the Starharts' heads that instantly translated language didn't seem impressed by it, not in enabling Lina to form the word herself. She decided, "I hope you don't mind if I call you Mimik."

"Perfectly fine."

Lina observed with a questioning expression as Mimik shifted to take on the aspect of a male Aldierran, one of average height and medium orange skin. Jae escorted her out of Lina's office, toward his office tent.

– – –

THE TWO WATCHED A SERIES OF VIDS featuring Majority Army General Nover Kettite. Mimik cocked her head and stared in that ultra-focused way she had of studying people.

"He has a slight accent different from the majority of officers around him," she said and before Jae could reply she added, "No problem. I'll be able to do him if needed."

"Let's hope you aren't. I haven't finalized my plans yet, but his assistant seems to be more of the proper target. Things are still loose though. Let's also look at Major Dule. He's not entirely certain about allying with us," Jae told her, "but he's ninety-five percent there. I'll convince him through the rest. He'll be close to the action, so he might be injured at some point, and we need his presence for this to work. He's already supplied me with his private and army personnel information. I let him set up your identity. Bracken confirmed that the data he came up with will pass scrutiny."

"Sounds committed to me."

"Lifelong loyalty runs deep in some people. If he turns on us, we'll have to deal with him. I want him at 100% before we begin our true push," Jae insisted, and Mimik nodded.

She glanced at the uploaded folder on her padd. "It will take me a few days to get through all this."

"We won't begin until you have a firm command of your parts." Jae paused. "You are fully in?"

She let out a whistly snort. "I wouldn't be here if I weren't. It's not like it's official Legion business." Still she held her breath a moment before letting it out. "And Lon doesn't know?"

"I'll bring him in on this when the time is right, when we see it's progressing in a way we can utilize."

"He's my Team Leader. I was appointed Acting Team Leader in his absence."

"This does not conflict with Legion business. I think," Jae said. "All he knows is that you've applied for personal leave. He won't be expecting you here, and I doubt Lina will mention it. She knows you're not here for any obvious reason. Who's taking over in your stead?"

"As Acting Team Leader, Stargust. Boroh's coming over to temporarily fill Lon's non-command team seat. With Lon out for this Three Worlds mission and now me as well, we can't have two members gone at the same time. People were wondering why I'd leave. I gave a vague personal emergency excuse that I think will hold them. For a while."

Thoughtfully Jae nodded. "Good man, Boroh. Lon has always considered him a trusted friend. And of course, few come better than Stargust." He heaved a sigh. "I feel better about this now."

A beep of alert came through Jae's earring and he listened to the message. "That's for me," he told Mimik. "I'll have Bee Termon show you around here. I've told him you're undercover. We can trust him with that much. Your name as this–" he nodded at her disguise for the Compound– "is… is…"

"Ibbiov Legentine," she improvised.

That made Jae laugh. Legentine was the subject of a particularly ribald folk tale in the AffSys. Quickly Jae brought up a list of common Sha-Green names. "Let's make it Iteov Battletine," he said.

"Iteov Battletine," Mimik confirmed. "I'll let you know when I'm prepared."

— — —

KANTI CLOUTIER, LINA'S CHIEF OF STAFF, Mace LaFayette, their head of LGBT+ matters, and Wicker Greenweave, the Three Worlds' PR coordinator, sat waiting for Lina to port into her office.

"To what do I have this pleasure?" she asked sweetly but with a hard shiver as she divested herself of a parka crusted with snow from Sha-Green's southern Master Range. She swept the ice out of her hair as she shivered twice more. What must she look like? She could *feel* the redness of her frozen nose, which she had to blow twice. Her assistant, Tidda, followed her to set a mug of hot tea and some energy cookies next to her usual conference table place.

"Thank you," Lina said as she sat. She motioned for three minutes of heat to be focused on her by the room's systems. Ah, there it was. She tried to soak it in through sheer willpower, but a few more shivers helped. "Don't mind me," she said as she reached for the cookies. Ooh, the tea was blessedly hot. "I'm not sure when I last ate. Can we get you something?"

When all were settled, Kanti and Wicker called up screens. "Someone's promoting a campaign against the Worlds," Wicker said and allowed a short stream to play.

It was a cartoon. A worried man stood amid a landscape that soon became filled with scribbles representing overlapping background voices, which increased in number and volume. The cartoon showed the man under stress, perspiration streaming from him, and that stress getting greater and greater until the scribbles crushed him.

A voiceover talked about the chaos of life since Three Worlds had arrived. Instead of solving problems, the Worlds were just making them worse. Forcing people out of their homes. Destroying cities. Encouraging gays. Teaching women to rebel. Grabbing children from their families to be used as slaves elsewhere. Subverting the justice system as innocents were thrown into prison.

There were three other similar presentations, those done with live action, interviews with men feeling the unbearable pressure of their current life.

The same male narrator in each stream provided the closing comments before a card came up: "Stop the Worlds from destroying our lives! It's time to stand up to them!" The card held a button for anyone, illiterate or literate, to utilize to talk to… whoever this was.

"Why isn't the real info getting out?" Lina asked.

"We'll have our first answers to this campaign ready by end of day today," Wicker assured her. "We're airing interviews with people who've been helped so far."

Kanti nodded. "Formerly homeless people. Those who were dying, but who got help."

Lina murmured to herself. "We can't show them women who are getting back on their feet in our shelters. The men of Aldierra would have a fit."

"Maybe we can't," Kanti said slowly. "But we can show them the kids who were saved from abuse. That is–"

"Do we exploit kids?" Lina mused.

"Use the ol' black-bar-across-the-eyes effect to hide their identities," Mace suggested, and Lina nodded.

"Hate to do that, but we need to show everyone, especially kids thinking about getting out of their homes, that they'll be going to safe places."

Wicker pushed some info padds her way while signaling for a new stream. "We were thinking about following a case," he said. "Maybe two or more. Show someone – Londo maybe – stopping a crime, pulling the perpetrators away. Now we see them taken to prison, but show that they get a fair trial first. Then show them at their punishment, not an execution."

Mace said as the AI-created suggestion played for Lina, "We interview displaced people, show them moving into their new homes. Which they like. Show the gays in their new communes, safe at last and actively contributing to society."

"This may irk many men," Kanti said, "but maybe we should show the women, before and after, in their shelter communes. Just as much as the kids, the women need to know."

Lina grimaced at herself. "I was caving in to the men. Can't believe I did that. Somebody hit me. I don't want to be surrounded by yes-men! Yes-people! Tell me when I'm wrong.

"Yes, let's show women definitely, and to hell with the pushback! We'll ask them if they want their faces shown or not. Black bars and mosaics will be an option."

"The children definitely get black bars," Kanti said. "As for the women, we get some who are willing to show their injuries and how they've been healed since arriving in shelter. What they're learning. How their stressors have been removed. How they're helping their kids by providing a healthy home."

Lina read three pages of their proposal and motioned for an audio call. Before she could say anything, Jae's voice came through. "Yes, we can afford this. We aren't anywhere near the point where we need to worry about it. When we are I'll tell you. But if it comes to it – and it won't – Aldierra gets every penny we have. Copy me and Lon on these proposals. We'll add to our press releases and public appearances."

"All right." Lina said. "I hate propaganda. We'll just be telling the truth in these spots, right?"

"Absolutely," Kanti swore.

"Then make it so."

YUSUF RUBBED HIS TIRED EYES. He had been studying reports for four days. And thinking. Time for a break.

Indeed he could break. This cabin they had given him had a door to the outside that he could open and leave through during daylight hours. It was no prison cell. Much.

Plus it possessed a View. Home to a small, established village, Santara Island held an adjacent tiny research encampment, not made of Quonset huts but rather a couple handfuls of linked houses with pointed roofs. His was separated from its neighbor by mere inches that weren't readily visible from any distance.

"Call it insulation," Valiant had told him as he was moved in. "It's not much because you're on your honor, being here. This is just in case your ethics suffer a hiccup. Which I'm sure they won't."

Valiant. The man who'd captured him when Yusuf had been at his height of power on Earth.

There were likely all sorts of electronic systems set up around Yusuf's cabin, set to protect the neighborhood from him in case he went rogue. He couldn't see any sign of them but was certain they were there.

Valiant hadn't pleaded with Yusuf to be on good behavior. He'd treated him as if he were a new member of his team and was expected to perform well and as ordered. Though there hadn't been any orders yet, just map after map: ocean temperatures. Atmospheric temperatures. Temperatures over time. Migratory patterns of sea life from centuries ago, before global warming had begun. He had five days to settle in and study before his tasks, whatever they would be, began.

The cabin overlooked the beautiful, rocky bay. A short pier was being built for his use, and a red boat with quite un-Terran technology was tied up to one of its pilings. Santara Island's rocks tended to be a bright red that complimented the boat. The lichen that grew upon them was brown and an iridescent green that glowed blue in the twilight. Now and then he'd spot a sea creature that seemed noticeably smaller than a whale but which also came up every so often to breathe.

They were perhaps the size of killer whales, which were actually large dolphins. When he got time he might look them up, along with the birds and rodents of the area.

Unlike the rest of the world, the overcast wasn't as great up here by the north pole. To be sure, a constant haze of high clouds impeded nighttime star viewing, but surface visibility was about two-thirds of Earth-normal. On clearer days the murky ocean stretched far into the misty distance, dotted with greenish-blue chunks of ice.

There were gentle tides though Aldierra had only two tiny moons. Likely they resulted from the sun's gravity, but again Yusuf would check if it became important. Which it might soon, since weather also relied on the sun. More information concerning that would arrive this evening.

Neutrino had sat down with him to show him the intricacies of the Internet here and what the best weather resources were to study so he could develop a plan to cool Aldierra's poles safely.

The Speaker had communicated via that Internet, frankly telling him that her husbands and staff had ordered her not to visit in person. She had introduced him to Aldierra's weather experts, plus those of Earth and of the AffSys. The latter were familiar with weather control, but the Worlds would be stripping this world of that soon.

And that would create all sorts of new problems.

Yusuf spent time each day sitting on rocks, gazing at the ocean, and thinking. The energies of this world oscillated around him, in tune with its winds and tides.

Earth and its laws no longer held him in confinement. In fact, he could forget Earth, forget his life before this if he wanted.

He could begin anew.

What would that entail?

They'd signed him up with a therapist first thing, and in the introductory online session he'd been asked: if he could live the life he wanted, free from the horrors of his childhood and the horrors he had committed as an adult, what would it look like?

He'd had no idea. This was a foreign concept.

His therapist, Voreezer, suggested that he begin to make a list. That list could be adjusted as time went by; it wasn't set in stone.

Well, it only took a few moments a day. He began the list and within hours around his research it started to grow. He crossed some items off and combined others. He didn't have to forsake the powerful vortex of control he'd been on Earth.

But was that what he wanted?

Yusuf put his list into the bottom drawer of the desk they'd given him. It was a good-sized one, manufactured from natural materials and holding designs that were similar to those of the village buildings. He had a conference tomorrow with some Weather Control bigwigs from the AffSys. He forgot which planet or planets it was. He'd research later. And apparently Tuesdays were the time when Valiant, Neutrino, and the Speaker, as well as another mega they called Nesh, met to coordinate plans. Others often popped in when needed, but now he was part of the central hub of megas working on Aldierra. He would do his meeting via something akin to Zoom and not in person.

"If you have an idea of a technique you'd like to try, please give a yell and I'll find someone to help you run computer models about it," the Speaker had assured him. "Is your bed comfortable? Do you have the medical supplies you need? Are you warm enough or too warm? Is your food all right? You may be aware that we're trying to increase the quality of food here. You're getting the new scanners in your rations. They can run good Terran burritos a tight race.

"Have you met any of your neighbors yet? They might be waiting for you to make the first move." A window popped up on his screen. "Here's their community calendar. They're not all scientists. Some of the Houses have been there forever. The scientists have brought their families with them, and some families from the mainland have moved here to help with services."

She was an odd one. By the time their conversation ended, he knew the names of her cats, most of whom had climbed all over her during their conversation, demanding attention. They did that in most of the public interviews he'd seen with her, and in each one she introduced the cats to the audience and told some personal nugget of info about them. There was one, a very old black cat, who didn't climb on her but rather slept against a shoulder. That cat had an odd name, but the interviewers all knew it and oohed and aahed about it. Bizarre.

Yusuf knew that the Speaker referred to her new home being built as "the Monstrosity." Others weren't supposed to overhear that name. She didn't want to insult Valiant, who'd seen it rotting away on the other side of the world and brought it there for his family to live in. Yusuf had an open invitation – after Valiant and Neutrino gave their okay – to visit. There was going to be a pool, the Speaker gleefully informed him.

In turn, he might have told her about his mother and the dishes he recalled her making in his childhood.

That was the part she took hand notes about. "Let me see if I can track down some of this for you," she told him.

He wore a necklace that filtered the air, and outside that smelled sweet like cold air always did. Free. It riffled his hair as he looked around.

Down the roughly paved street a door opened. Dressed in a bulky coat, a figure stepped. It was that woman who had been assigned as a guard to him. Reen Elikal. Yusuf could freeze her in her tracks, but what would be the point?

He'd been told she was from off-world, that she – and the young brother she'd brought with her – had some immunity from ultra-cold. They were both paras. It might be amusing to see how far that went.

If the situation warranted.

Instead he stepped back inside and put on the coat he'd been issued. He didn't need it, but it would help him fit in, not look so odd.

10

With growing excitement, Londo listened closely to the committee from Reyda. They were located south of Drape-Tessay, one of Aldierra's three capitals, and they had been diligent in their research. They also had top-notch architects at their disposal, it seemed.

"These are beautiful plans," Lon said. Now, *this* was what he'd had in mind for the new buildings and city sectors he was building. These structures not only incorporated traditional design elements from before the bland, featureless designs modern Aldierra encouraged, but they also contained Lon's suggestions.

Central House courtyards were common, but the designers hadn't forgotten that they were also to encourage community areas where House inhabitants could gather with their neighbors. Cafes, microbusinesses and community centers filled the lower stories, and two of the plats contained small parks planned for recreation, gardens, and general greenery. Walkways slowed traffic down to human levels. Facades held curving lines, partial columns – even a true column here and there, with none of the overtly phallic symbology – and archways, mosaics, and were punctuated liberally with lively colors.

"These are based on historical styles?" he asked.

Opiserk, the speaker for the group, assured him they were. Then he made an apologetic grimace. "We've adapted them because our traditional buildings were never used with these kind of multi-purposes in mind," he said. "But these–" He pointed them out. "These are absolutely true to the historic style. This is a copy of what was once a very famous theater. We thought it might be used again for that, as well as community services."

"Excellent," Lon enthused. He wanted to study these plans at length. Learn from them even as he discovered so much pleasure in what these designers offered. Though he had a degree in engineering, he'd also earned a license for architecture. Buildings fascinated him.

"We saw what you were trying to do on Malcone, but we wanted to emphasize it more, really play on the idea that Reyda has a long, distinguished history of our own."

Lon nodded, his brown eyes bright. "That's precisely what I'd hoped to get from these groups. If you don't mind, I'm going to show these plans to some others to demonstrate what they could do. I'll make sure they don't copy."

Imagine the new designs going up everywhere. Lon had made only the merest fraction of changes he wanted to make on this world. Now he pictured the process as it should be. He'd have a hand in these neighborhoods, boroughs, cities; even conurbations and megalopolises. They'd also be so much more genuinely Aldierran. This was what he'd imagined.

The picture grew in his mind: such groups coming to him for advice, and he being able to work in a more defined way with them, now that he'd seen these. Others would come up with unique ideas of their own. Together they'd make Aldierra a showplace. A good home for everyone.

Everyone deserved a home they could love. These Aldierrans were such talented, conscientious people.

"The continents of Aldierra have very different histories of architecture," Opiserk assured him.

"And we'll show them all– Oh, Excuse me."

Londo blanked the screen, holding the connection. "No!" he shouted, reaching to the side of his control console. "No!"

Molly squatted over Lon's *draway*. It was a very good print copy. "Molly, no!" He brandished a water bottle and spritzed the long-haired yellow cat.

She looked up defiantly, hissed at him, and quivered in her nether regions as if about to loose a day's worth of whiz.

Another spritz, water output on high. *Name, command. Immediate punishment if needed.* "Molly, no!" and Londo lunged.

But she was quick. Maybe not as quick as Lon, though, for he signaled the room's services to dry up the *draway* before it could be damaged. It had only been subjected to water from the spray.

Lon couldn't go after Molly now. He reset the screen, apologized for the break and for looking anxious, and got back to discussions about things that truly mattered.

He and Molly needed to have a showdown. Soon. Show her who was boss.

But after this meeting he had a mysterious errand to attend to.

– – –

LONDO MET THE MEDIUM-SIZED SPACECRAFT with curiosity as it materialized out of hyperspace directly into a mooring at the Drape-Tessay Spaceport. Someone was showing off their piloting skills. It sat precisely in the center of the landing spot. Neither Lina nor Jae had known exactly what or who it contained but three days ago Lon's mentor, Chimrin Dinar, aka the Legion's Psyche, had informed Lina of housing and office needs. This was a group of people to do… what?

Chim herself was first out the door. She stood by a parade of twenty-some disembarking passengers, all wearing different colorful costumes. The lavender-skinned telepath in famous gold and green uniform cocked her head at Lon. She'd been Legion Commander when both he and Jae had first joined the Legion, and had guided the boys through rough teen years.

Her sharp eyes took him in. "Surprise," she said in a monotone. "We invited ourselves. I figured you three were too proud to call on major help. At least not at this point. You'd likely wait until the last minute to howl for more hands. Well, here we are and there's still time left before your Deadline."

The passengers formed themselves into two crisp lines ready for inspection. Three stood apart: team medics, to judge from their uniforms.

"Legion Support," Chim explained. "They're all volunteers, are prepared to stay through Deadline and beyond, and will be getting job experience that they wouldn't otherwise be able to acquire."

Lon assumed his famous scowl, which these… would you call them recruits? would be expecting. Support was, in effect, one of the waiting lists for Legion membership. Make a good impression while in Legion Support, and you stood a better chance to get in when the next slot opened.

On the other hand, he'd seen a few of these pull stupid stunts in order to stand out from the crowd.

"Support," he said in a loud voice, to draw their attention. He bowed his head to Chim. "Psyche. We are grateful for this help in our mission. Have you just accompanied them, or–"

"I'm commanding the unit," she told him. "Ah." Her expression became expectant.

Lina appeared next to Londo, a little out of breath. "Got it. Oh." She took in the scene even as she handed an info crystal to Chim. "Ah?"

"Support troops of the mega–"

"Some of these are top paras," Chim corrected Lon. Lina would know that clever top-level paras could hold their own alongside a megapara.

Londo nodded. "Of the powerful variety. They'll be here for a while."

Lina tilted her head this way and that at the troops, taking them in, likely fitting the new data into her personnel charts. "Okay," she said. "Okay then. Welcome to Aldierra. We have quarters and vehicles for you," she told the troops. "You'll find general information on contacts, armies, culture, food, entertainment, all in your quarters. I'll send more specific stuff now that I know you're Legion."

"Legion-adjacent," Chim corrected, and Lina nodded.

"I've split you up into two groups. Hope that was okay. All Chim, I mean, Psyche, said was two groups of about twelve each, to be placed on opposite sides of the planet from each other."

Lon glanced at Chim. She'd told Lina more than she had him. Or Jae. He chewed on his lower lip a moment and then addressed the troops: "Anyone here have any weather-related powers? We'll be getting rid of weather control in a few weeks."

Two people raised their hands.

"That should be fun," Chim said under her breath.

"Plus if y'all know of any weather people on other worlds, please tell us," Lina said.

"Also people who can grow vegetation, clear contamination," Londo added. "If you've been assigned here you will have researched our situation. We welcome the manpower you bring. The first thing to remember about Aldierra is this: it's a violent world. Riots and wars can break out at any moment."

"I've played them your 'Aldierra is violent' speech, Valiant," Chim informed all as two aircraft flew by overhead. Wind rifled her short, pale green hair. "We've concentrated on dealing with mental health encounters. It's a good skill to master."

"You're going to run into that a lot here. Plus we have psychiatrists available for you whenever you yourselves need them," Lina piped up.

Londo eyed the group. "And you will. You will." He felt like Yoda warning a young Luke Skywalker.

Their spacecraft disgorged four vehicles from a long bay door. "We brought our own flitters," Chim explained. "Easier to pack our equipment in them rather than make multiple trips for everything." She eyed the crystal and tucked it into her Legion Array wrist band. A screen popped up in front of her and she read it. Then she returned it to Lina.

"Very good," she said of its contents before addressing her troops. "We'll coordinate with Valiant and Neutrino's divisions for orders, though I've also sent through suggestions."

"I will check those immediately, Psyche," Londo said. He would need to coordinate with her and Jae to see how these troops could best be utilized. There was so much for them to do, even if he wasn't sure what their powers were. Yet. "And remember: everyone reports through the Speaker's section at some point or another."

"I'm supplies and support," she explained to the crowd.

Chim ordered the group to their respective vehicles, and they quickly left to their new stations.

Londo looked at Lina. "I'll tell Jae when he gets up. By then I'll have a preliminary action plan. We all need to be on the same page."

"Do *not* say that we don't need them," Lina warned.

"I might have, a month ago," Lon said before heaving a sigh. Then he smiled at her and wrapped an arm around her waist. She knew him so well now. As she ran a hand up his chest, he motioned for his Legion ring array to display the list of what the powers of these Support personnel were. "Now… We'll find them work to do. Essential work."

– – –

ERIK EMERGED FROM A DOCTOR-PATIENT CONFERENCE ROOM in Legion Medical on Sarastor as Lina walked toward the staff section. How nice to see him! He looked well.

He gave her a surprised glance. "Taking some time off?"

"Building up bonus points by attending a Spousal Meeting," she confided. Required Legion Spousal Meetings were a royal pain, but she kept the wrath of Ms. Yency at bay if she attended one now and then. "Plus visiting Dinah. She's not doing too well. She's refusing psychiatric help. I can't figure out why. Could you talk with her when you have time?"

"Sure. Happy to do that."

Lina's good friend Dinah had been abducted, tortured and severely injured during the Mind Control Tour, when agents from the Yanist-Glory Empire had mistaken her for Lina.

They chatted a moment more. Erik revealed that he hadn't been studying psychic work even though that quick war on whatever world it had been – so many worlds, so many names to keep track of – had revealed him to be a budding clairvoyant and telepath. "Chimrin is a real taskmaster!" he whispered to Lina after he'd glanced about as if she might be hiding nearby.

Lina chuckled. "She doesn't have to be here to hear you," and she tapped the side of her forehead. As the Legion master of telepathy, Chim had made noises about training Erik.

Still, it was interesting that Erik was referring to Chim as "Chimrin" and not "Psyche," her official Legion nom de guerre. That was good. The Legion had so many rules about propriety.

Lina left for her true mission: a personal meeting with Dr. Riz Gorgeon, Chief of Legion Medical. Some things had to be done face to face.

"I'm suggesting that the workload is not letting up," Lina told Riz. She tried to sound reasonable, though she wanted to shout in frustration. Riz had been so kind to her. She'd saved Lina and Jae's lives. But still she was, well, Legion stubborn. "It's getting more expansive, more difficult. We're hiring people all the time, but it's never enough. I'll be needing stims soon."

Riz refused. Lina tried a different approach, and Riz refused again.

"Twenty billion people, Riz."

The doctor looked as sour as Lina had ever seen her. She made a disgusted noise. Lina perked up.

Riz made another noise and Lina could feel the extreme reluctance behind the next statement: "I'll contact your personal physician there. Absolute, all-out, imminent death only. What's their name?"

Lina told her, thanked Riz for help, and tried to make her exit not look furtive.

This would not do.

Riz would see that stims would be rationed. Lina had overdosed a few months ago – for the best of reasons; she'd been saving a galactic sector. It had only been these past three-plus weeks that she'd been allowed even rationed caffeine. And of course Wiley had come through for that one emergency, but she doubted he'd be so easy to convince next time.

Nope, this would not do at all.

She ported home to Aldierra. Deadline approacheth. Lina knew her limits. She could sit here all day and fill more and more jobs to help her with the workload, but in the end the person that everyone turned to for explanations and supplies and general problems was Lina Starhart. There was a reason she'd been given this position.

And in the future – likely the near future – she would need the occasional stim in order to get the basics of her job done. A job that was often an emergency. Not only were a few immediate lives usually in danger, but in the end, it was twenty billion people who relied on just how well she'd be able to operate.

Riz and the Legion-related doctors here who looked after the highest Three Worlds staff would insist on going through paperwork and permissions before Lina could get the stims she'd be needing. That would take time.

That might involve people saying "no."

Lina grabbed her office chair, turned it to the screen hanging in the air before her, and then gestured.

Legion and even Sarastor weren't the only places one could get stims. There were lots of other planets in the AffSys she could contact.

After an hour-plus and three cats jumping up onto her lap to be petted, she had five sources contacted from disparate points along the far edges of the con-federation. Wasn't it nice that the pharmacists all recognized her as the mega who'd solved the problem of Mind Control for the sector? Of course they could supply her, especially when she explained that it would be for the people of Aldierra, who were working so hard and had little access to stims. Only a few people needed them, not the entire population, and the occasions would be a very limited basis.

Along with the preliminary supplies came information about the drugs. Lina studied it, and then placed orders for variants of the mainstream kind, because studies had shown that alternating the type of stim allowed for fewer side effects in those who had to use the stims for prolonged periods. Though she'd try to avoid using them too often, that might happen.

There were warnings that she'd have to look up. Do not use with… and the labels listed drugs she'd never heard of. They all warned about mixing with al-cohol use. That was easy enough, since she hated alcohol. Besides, the stuff always put her to sleep. If she were taking stims, she didn't want to sleep.

She bookmarked more in-depth studies for further reading and made sure she included instructions on proper administration of the various types.

That done, she breathed a sigh of relief. No stims yet needed, but she knew the day would come. She'd try to avoid it as long as possible.

In the meantime she hurriedly ordered the more mundane items on her list of needed supplies, and ported them to the usual places. For the few stims she or-dered now for emergencies she had to clear out one shelf of a corner of her office floor cabinet. She double-checked the stims' storage requirements and stacked the doses there, behind the semi-forbidden boxes of powdered chai mix she loved. Tidda knew about the caffeine and how it was there only for Lina's use. She wouldn't invade the space.

CHAPTER

11

Rei-Gone Siekesh was Senior Advisor in the Office of World Security for the Intelligence Echelon, or IE. He was of medium height for an Aldier-ran, and his skin was somewhat brighter orange than the median. Gray patches streaked the bristle of his military hair, and his eyes were a piercing brown. His aide, Tipton, escorted Jae into Siekesh's office, silently oozing curiosity and trepidation. Jae appraised him with a surreptitious glance. Someone else to pay attention to? That's right; he'd seen him a few weeks before, enough to take notice of him.

Jae and Siekesh bowed to each other before taking their seats. Tipton set hot drinks by their sides and then, after Siekesh nodded to him, left the room.

Jae's sensors showed Siekesh had a listening device that, upon Tipton's exit, linked to an office outside. A crook of Jae's left thumb traced the connection and showed the trail on a screen only Jae could see. Tipton was listening. No one else was.

Interesting.

"You wanted a private meeting, Minister?" Siekesh asked.

Jae sipped the drink. It had a decent amount of alcohol in it. It wasn't enough to inebriate, and would allow him to concentrate on the matter at hand.

"I've told the Patriarch that I wanted to meet with his most useful officers," Jae said. "I asked for privacy because, especially in these times, one doesn't want to lose the advantage that security provides."

"And yet Three Worlds proclaims their activities are transparent." Siekesh settled back in his chair.

"To an extent. We do have a world to save. Sometimes transparency becomes an impediment. Tell me, why does the Patriarch think so highly of you? Are you a great leader of men? Can you keep secrets better than others? Are you brilliant at cyber security? Can you force secrets from people more efficiently than anyone else can?"

Siekesh took a moment to consider. "I have been in this position for almost ten years now. My predecessor was assassinated. So far, I haven't followed in his footsteps with that. In this profession, that's an important skill to possess."

"You have your finger in intelligence operations around the world. I've read your file," Jae summarized. "Several times you've managed to expose major embedded schemes that might have brought down the government."

Modestly Siekesh bowed his head.

Jae kept the conversation to a comfortable level for three minutes before he began digging beneath the superficial. He asked about specific operations from the past. How had this one plot been designed to work? Why did Siekesh feel it had to be exposed so thoroughly?

"If you'd exposed only half of them," he mused, "that might have left an opening for you to take over the Limbernie continental intelligence sections. From there you could begin to undermine that of the Green Army, or at least the Red parts still absolutely controlled by the Patriarch."

"I, ah, don't know what you mean."

But the man's eyes had sparked. Perhaps Siekesh hadn't revealed the entire operation, as Jae had suspected. He had inserted feelers into the system, hidden anchors that would allow for a later operation, possibly of a larger size, to be triggered.

Oh, how lightly Siekesh tiptoed around that! He diverted the conversation to discuss two other operations, both of which had scored successfully for Siekesh and Lupoff. Jae nodded approvingly.

"We need to keep track of those who would subvert our Three Worlds operations," he told Siekesh.

"The Patriarch has already signaled that the Majority Army should do all it can to help in this business," Siekesh said.

"Has he?" Jae swirled his drink for a few seconds. "Or is he moving to sabotage it? Sabotage our building plans, our eco-plans?"

Siekesh didn't say anything.

"Twenty billion people," Jae reminded Siekesh. "I will not allow this world to die. If anyone has a system, or the beginnings of one, already in place that we can utilize to help our efforts, they would be thanked profusely for helping. Maybe even rewarded."

Siekesh didn't say anything.

"And perhaps their aide would be as well," Jae offered. "We could work with them quite secretly, as long as we could rid this world of the negative forces that operate against it. We too are developing our own information webs."

Siekesh pressed his lips together.

Jae tried going one step farther than he'd planned. "Whoever would do this would work directly under Bracken," he said.

That brought Siekesh's head up with a start. He began to repeat the name and then shut up. He glanced around the room.

Jae motioned to his screen, which became visible. "I cut off all listening devices that were in here five minutes after I entered, except your line to your aide," he explained. "What the others have been listening to has been a general patter of minor intelligence info between the two of us, AI that I programmed." His lips lifted into a small smile. "I read where you like to joke when you're at ease. I inserted two rather witty but pithy stories for you into the mix."

"Perhaps I should get Tipton in here," Siekesh said.

"If he's to be trusted, I'd be interested in his thoughts on the matter as well as yours, Advisor."

– – –

LINA LOVED WATCHING NESH WORK. The fairy-like ex-Legionnaire danced through it all, joy in every aerial movement. It made Lina slightly envious, that this was all Nesh had to do so of course she could play in her work.

No, that was unkind. Nesh didn't have the same work requirements Lina did, but Nesh made sure she was attending to her duties almost every moment of her long, long days. Just like Lina. They both worked until they dropped. Well, Nesh might stop before that. Exhaustion couldn't feed the goal that Nesh had to create.

Perhaps the dancing was an essential part of Nesh's power.

But watching Nesh lifted Lina's spirits. When Nesh seemed to pause, as if she were about to move to a new spot, Lina cleared her throat. "Excuse me?"

Nesh turned, and smiled to see Lina there. How sweet.

"Speaker. I mean, Lina."

They chatted about what Nesh had just done here, urging the new plants to grow in health, and she brought up a video map to show where she'd been, where she planned to be.

"I had an idea," Lina told her.

They discussed it before moving to the next location. Nesh paused in the air above the small patch of newly-planted land and looked to Lina expectantly before beginning. Lina held out her right hand and her amazing golden Flute appeared in it, its engravings of vines catching her attention more than normal today. They were fitting for this.

Help me, Aldierra, she asked the planet. She needed a song of growing and nurturing and safety. A green song. A tune came to her mind. She listened to it, and then, hesitantly but then with more confidence, began to play.

Nesh cocked her head to take it in but nodded. Then she began her dance of joy, this time moving to the rhythms of the song, both on the ground and in the air.

Around them the seedlings began to twitch, their branches and vines reaching out to claim more area they could fill as they grew.

After an hour, the two women stood in wonder to view the fruits of their handiwork.

"You are always being recorded, am I right?" Nesh asked.

"Yes."

"Could you send this to Dr. Mem-Bazer, please?"

Lina chuckled. After all this, Nesh still had a problem with familiarity. "Call him Wiley, Nesh."

"He has not invited me to use his familiar name."

"I am now." Wiley's voice and then a projection of himself appeared alongside them. Lina hadn't sent out an alert. How often did he listen in? "You are important to this project; you've become an important personage in your own right. May I call you 'Nesh'?"

She blushed. "Yes, of course, Dr. Mem– uh, Wiley." She said it as if tasting the word.

Wiley didn't notice. He was checking figures and measurements on the screens they could see around him. Now and then he touched points on his many rings, as if inputting data. "What have you done here? Was this your normal time spent on one spot?"

"Yessir."

Lina said, "I'm sorry if I overstepped Legion etiquette, Wiley."

"Mm. Not important, but thank you. Look at this. It's difficult to tell for sure, since we have five species of plants here and… it looks like another five at least of seeds that have sprouted… But growth rates are some twenty… maybe even twenty-five percent greater than your usual, Nesh. Did you feel any extra strain or exertion of your power as you were doing this?"

"No sir. Everything seemed normal to me, except that there was music."

"Ah."

But Lina's mind had been racing. "Nesh has the entire world to grow." She grimaced at Nesh. "Well, it seems that way to me. I know you're operating in selected spots. But still… Would it be worth it for me to stop what I do and accompany her with the flute?"

Wiley held up a finger to the both of them. "Let us try an experiment. Are you rested enough to try another location, Nesh?"

– – –

THE RECORDED MUSIC STOPPED as well as Nesh, and the two women actually on Aldierra waited breathlessly for Wiley to look over his notes. At long last he looked up at them. "Same results, or close enough. Just playing the music as a recording seems to produce the same acceleration."

"It's a matter of frequency," Lina said. "Or at least that's what *they*—" her spirit guides – "say. The source doesn't matter. Well, it came from the Flute, but the results won't change depending on if it's being played live or replayed."

"This could be utilized in many ways," Wiley said slowly.

"That tune was good for here," Nesh put in. "Will it work the same for different plant material? Different terrain?"

"How about I tag along with you today and you show me a variety?" Lina suggested. "I could record different songs for different situations." An idea came to her. "I wonder if I could record some songs for hospitals, for medical situations. I've used the Flute and it's helped people. D'you think recordings could as well?"

"We will experiment," Wiley declared.

Nesh called down her flitter and climbed in, gesturing for Lina to join her. Wiley's image floated in as well. "You can spare today?" Nesh asked Lina.

"For this, I can spare a day, maybe more."

"We'll just take today. For a start," Nesh told her. "I will call upon you later if the need occurs."

"And I'll begin making inquiries among the medical personnel on Aldierra," Wiley said. "We'll put you on that tomorrow, Lina, see what you can do for a variety of medical conditions."

"Might take some stims to make it through," Lina warned.

Wiley nodded, though he seemed to be paying attention with most of his minds at his data. "For this, we will allow a few stims."

CHAPTER

12

Utilizing the Legion Array that had been granted her after she left its ranks, Nesh Inagar flew over today's landscape. *Her* landscape. Increasingly she was feeling a growing sense of possession, of belonging, to this lonely world. The Starharts were working with its structures and cultures, but she worked with its soul.

Satisfaction oozed from her as she surveyed the growth she'd nurtured. She saw the creeping battalions of mostly women who dug and operated small machinery to sculpt the soils in arid places. Their projects would attract and hold water that would allow her plants to flourish. Good, good.

Those damned giant bulldozers that had been so out of position were now where they should be. She'd had to call upon her Legion training to assert her normally quiet self and order them away. They wouldn't stray from procedure again!

She laughed to herself, finding that attitude funny and, if she dared admit it, a bit thrilling. She would have to explore this potential more, especially since she now held so high, so important a position. She'd have two other worlds to oversee as well, with new landscapes and cultures to learn. Assertiveness would come in handy. Mustn't rely on the Starharts to have to handle that for her.

She landed lightly in the center of a shallow valley in order to plant line array speakers. There were not many; technology could easily handle an area this large and make sure a balanced sound came through. Then she triggered the tape of Lina's flute.

With a languid leap, she soared high above the valley in order to record plant reactions to the music. She made her own notes about how she felt they were doing. Then she raised her arms and called more Life to the area, reinforcing the work she'd already done.

Ah. She could feel the difference. When she finished, she saved the readings as well as her own thoughts on the matter. Then she sent the results to Dr. Mem-… No, he was "Wiley" now, she thought with a smile. Wiley would want to see these. Lina would as well and would know who else to send them to. Nesh herself sent them to mentors she'd studied under through the years. They would also have their own contacts.

As she finished, she saw messages pop up. There were two in particular, from a close cousin and one more distant. Yes, they had minor plant powers as well, although Cousin Maggie referred to it as a "rapport." It was just like Maggie to think that way.

They were both excited to come to Aldierra and at the very least, check things out enough to see if they might be able to make a difference.

Good. Nesh signaled the Speaker's Section about the arrivals so things would be ready.

Then she gathered her array and took off again, this time in a new direction with a skimmer that could handle long distances, to territory she'd not yet attended to here on Sha-Green. It was along the Great Duktiv Divide and relatively near the capital of Soshe, though mountainous enough that it was considered uncomfortably distant.

Whatever, it was a different kind of terrain than she'd been working in. Eagerly she consulted her notes and only looked up when her security alarm went off.

She was entering a sensor zone. Odd.

She slowed her skimmer and checked her instruments even as she cautiously redirected the vehicle to bank southeast. She tried to plot a course that didn't look like she was reacting to anything on the ground. This might be important.

Aldierra was dangerous. Londo had made that clear. Tuesday team meetings had revealed dark plots that Bracken and the Worlds had countered again and again.

She sent out tiny drones to scout the area and then settled back to be patient even as her flight path took her farther and farther away.

Something. There. It showed up electronically before the visuals spotted it.

A camp. A rather large section of land with temporary structures on it. The land was being graded, dug into. Flora had been stripped. Structures were being built.

She consulted Lon's plans for Sha-Green construction. No, nothing for here. A small river ran nearby through the mountains, but it was not listed on Jae's mission lists.

She sent out more drones and called upon satellite investigation.

And sent them all to… Whom? She decided on Jae. Not his section, but Jae himself. Jae had shown particular interest in these Aldierran plots.

He'd be interested in the building of a large, secret army camp.

— — —

YUSUF'S FLITTER HELD POSITION only fifty feet above the ocean. Jae and he studied temperature readings from the past month, and Jae brought up charted accounts of the life under the waves.

"I've been working in small patches," Yusuf told him. "Large ones are not only more strenuous, but in terms of cubic acreage I can get more done quicker by working in small chunks."

Jae nodded. "You'll be disturbing the sea life less doing it that way. They'll have a chance to relocate to temperatures they prefer, rather than be suddenly trapped."

"There is undersea life that isn't that mobile," Yusuf pointed out.

Yes. Life connected to the floor of the ocean. Life that merely floated using currents and had little ability to self-propel.

"I'll get a crew out to follow you," Jae proposed. "Give us a couple days to research, make some surveys, and they'll start moving what needs to be moved. Maybe the spots can fill in with the proper life as the ocean gradually cools. I'll get Nesh in on this as well."

Jae's warning system beeped at him, and he motioned for Yusuf to take the flitter down to surface level. The waves lapped at it on the calm sea, and Jae let Yusuf check the area monitors with him.

Ships.

The computer didn't recognize their call-signals, but the ship classifications were all of Green Army naval stock.

"You have a rogue navy," Yusuf surmised as Jae's demeanor went dark.

"We have more than that," Jae replied.

"Ah." Yusuf straightened, to dig his hands into the rear pockets of his pants. "Something to do with Lupoff? Do you have a mutiny going on, Minister?"

Jae motioned for the flitter to increase its altitude to just above wave level, but to return to home base. "We do. Keep it under your hat."

Yusuf's eyes widened. "It's all right for me to know? A prisoner?"

"You're not a prisoner here, Yusuf. You're a man with a second chance in life. You make your own decisions." Jae shrugged. "We do keep an eye on you to make sure you're not deviating too far from where we'd hope you go, but so far you've been impressive here."

Jae paused to consider. "Do us a favor?" This might help.

Yusuf looked interested.

"Start dropping a hint or two… nothing much. Just a couple. To outsiders you might come in contact with, Aldierrans. That the Patriarch is looking a little… stressed. Or pale."

Yusuf's gaze was considering. "I can do that. Just a word?"

"Or two. Off the cuff, maybe after you see something, a picture or video of him, that could be used as a reason for your mentioning it."

"I'll see what comes up." He lifted an eyebrow and the side of his mouth twitched. "Intrigue."

Jae gave him a nod and small smile. "Your guard has been sending in good reports. Rather glowing ones. I think she's surprised by you."

"She's rather surprising herself," Yusuf replied. "She brought her kid brother along with her, did you know that? They have a day care thing set up so she can keep track of me. Even so, she wasn't pleased that you had taken her place today. She says it is an honor to guard such a fearsome criminal as myself. Then she laughs." One eyebrow twitched. "But she keeps her gun ready."

He straightened his neck and stretched. "Haven't frozen her yet. I was tempted to, once. Maybe twice. Good behavior. I'm giving it a try."

"We award points for that."

Yusuf's lips curved into a small smile as he examined the waterscape around them before he turned back to Jae. "So. In my reports I'll subtly include surveillance of these mystery ships in polar waters?"

Jae scratched the side of his neck, then his upper left chest through he wore some kind of body armor. "Yes," he decided. "We'll add satellite to that, but you'll have a unique viewpoint. Though we want your ocean cooling to be the highest priority."

"Of course, Jae. The native people on Santara Island, they've lived there for generation upon generation. They always tell me how in the old days it was very different. They braved the ices in their small boats and before that, canoes. They have legends of heroes who are now stars in the sky – stars they can't see because of the overcast – and want them watching over them again."

"We're trying," Jae said with a sigh. "Tell them that we all – and that includes you – are working hard to return that world to them. It will be better than before, though."

Yusuf laughed quietly. "Equality for all, health services for all, education, peace…"

That was rewarded with a smile. "You've been listening to our broadcasts."

"Who can escape them, even up here? The nights are getting longer."

"Anytime you want to do your own broadcast, contact me. Or Lina. We'll have Wicker Greenweave set you up with some camera crews. People are curious. Not only about what you're doing up here, but about you yourself. I think you have a lot you can tell them. Give us a call when you're ready."

Yusuf nodded, his expression thoughtful.

– – –

"HONEY," LINA'S VOICE SOFTLY CALLED Jae from the next room, "can you come here? No emergency."

No fast moves. Don't raise your voice, she warned him as he neared.

In the main living area, she stood with Moose cradled in her arms high against her chest. He gazed up at her adoringly as she scratched his black belly. With one paw he touched her chin. With the other…

He's got a claw through my nose, she explained.

Jae caught his breath even as he saw. The idiot cat still held the same loving gaze, not even bothering to glance at Jae as he arrived.

"Good Moosie," Lina cooed. "What a good boy you are." And in the same tone she added, "Just take his paw and press gently on it. He shouldn't retract the claw; it should lengthen. Easier to extract."

"Good Moosie." Jae joined the quiet chant. He moved as smoothly as he'd ever done, and indeed a press on the paw pad made the claw stand out farther, straighter, so Jae could slide it out.

"Isn't that a gooood boy," Lina told Moosie, who closed his eyes in ecstasy. He stretched his front legs out so Lina's scratching could move to his arm pits.

Then suddenly he flipped out of her arms, landed on the nearby couch, and trotted to the kitchen.

Lina breathed a sigh of relief. "Didn't want to scare him. His attention span is not long. He could have ripped out a corner of my nostril. Thanks, honey."

Jae examined said nostril. Just a hole. "Do you want a nose ring?" he asked his wife, and she smiled.

"No thanks. There's antiseptic creme in the–"

"No need." Jae touched the spot and commanded the darker matter that had been on Moosie's claw to cleanse itself. He reverted the toxins to pure carbon and hydrogen.

"Done," he said.

"Thanks again." Now Lina touched the spot, and he could feel her linking in with the astral and etheric planes where her body existed as a plan, an energy diagram of how it was set up in the material world. **This,** she reminded it, and it remembered how the cells were supposed to work, their shape, their attitude…

The hole-began to close.

"That is very cool," he told her. "I want to learn."

She stood on her tiptoes to kiss him, and he bent to receive and prolong it. "Umm, that's so nice. I will teach you after we get through all this. I'd like to learn how you do what you do. If that's possible."

"We will give it a try," he promised.

--- --- ---

ONCE MORE, THE BITTER RIVER in central Sha-Green had been targeted. The dam that was in place to control spring flooding had crumbled, luckily a few weeks before the typical time of peak flooding. The engineers who greeted Jae had their excuses: "Unexpected. An accident." Lon would see to rough preliminary repairs tomorrow.

Snow-topped foothills of the Master Range rolled into what distance Jae could see, since pollution limited visibility. The clear near-distance was dotted with ponds and swollen streams that fed into an increasingly wide river.

"How odd," Jae said ironically to Kettite, the Green Army Major General who proudly wore a red uniform. Big-eared and bony with the beginning of drooping jowls, he was a distant relative to the Patriarch and really shouldn't be milking that position with the red in an attempt to increase his already significant standing, but there it was.

"These things happen," Kettite told Jae. "Last year's inspections showed shocking deterioration of the southern side."

"Yet nothing was fixed, or even scheduled to be," Jae observed.

"These things happen."

"Is this the kind of situation the Patriarch wants?" Jae asked. "Destruction of important infrastructure? A good leader doesn't allow for foul-ups along the way that might distract, much less impede large plans." He side-eyed Kettite. "I've seen last year's inspection records of the dam. It was certified in excellent condition."

Without skipping a beat, Kettite shrugged his medal-bedecked shoulders and frowned. "I would say that if I were Patriarch, I'd make sure such 'accidents' didn't happen. I'd save my energy to handle the real needs of the Majority Army."

"I see none of your units have been assigned to assist in the repairs here."

"They are too busy working on the new…" He paused uncertainly.

Jae gave a grim smile. "Army base. Yes, I know about that. Lupoff keeps me apprised." Lupoff didn't, but Londo did after he'd investigated Nesh's report yesterday. "If Lupoff wants to assert his power on this continent, he needs to be attending to all of his facilities and making sure he provides for his troops."

"Weaponry," Kettite declared. "You don't need many men if you have the right weapons."

Jae made a play of considering that. "What kinds would you think best?" He tilted his head as if going through different scenarios. "Stringers… There are several manufacturing plants that are still capable of switching back to making those. Hydards… More complicated, and the plants would have to take more time to re-converting themselves for the task. But you are heavily invested in two of them, aren't you, General?"

"They're making agricultural equipment now." The disappointment in Kettite's voice was evident.

"But if you were… Patriarch…" Jae ventured. "You might be able to speed things along."

"I would never dream of–"

"Lupoff gets in our way far too often," Jae said. "Sometimes we… or maybe just I… think things would go much smoother if he were… no longer participating in decisions, shall we say."

"I–"

"You are in charge of at least four divisions and support troops."

Kettite managed to look humble. "I had a fifth added to my duties last month, Minister."

Jae nodded and then gazed thoughtfully into the distance.

Into that silence, Kettite said, "What kind of backup could the Worlds provide if, say, I wanted to increase the scope of my command?"

———

"WILEY!" LINA EXCLAIMED at him over the monitor. "I've just got to have a stim. It should last three hours; four hours, tops. But I need it now!"

"No," Wiley calmly told her without even stopping his rearrangement of a data table on his screens.

Another screen popped up next to those. Lina's schedule. Next to it ran a list of riots breaking out, along with critical requests that she make public announcements to contain them.

Wiley brought up Lon and Jae's schedules and current positions. Lon was halting a small war in Orchin. Jae was tackling a flood in Sha-Green, though it was far past his scheduled rest period.

"Please, please!" Lina begged.

Nesh wouldn't be able to do this, not the extent that Lina Starhart could. "Okay." Wiley set his mouth in a straight, disapproving line. "Port over here. Four hours and not a minute more."

"Thanks, Wiley!"

"This is the absolute final time, though. Even if Aldierra's core begins to, I don't know, explode. No more stims."

"Absolutely. You're a lifesaver. Literally."

CHAPTER

13

Opening the door, the military aide announced Jae to Dule. Inside the expansive, bright office, Dule stood up to greet Jae, his stance becoming more wary.

The door closed to give them privacy. A Majority Army officer had accompanied the Minister. Jae said, "May I introduce an operative. Lieutenant Novrin Muvvik."

Mimik in Muvvik disguise, stepped forward to click the heels of her boots together and crisply bow her head.

"Operative?"

"This is the one I told you about."

"I do not recognize you. What army–"

Mimik said, "I am not a member of any army. I am not from Aldierra. I am from a few sectors to the west of galactic center."

"She is a fellow Legionnaire," Jae said.

"She? Oh. Yes."

Muvvik's form shifted, becoming taller, slimmer, with longer arms – four of them – until she stood in Mimik's true insectoid form, her Aldierran clothing slumping on her.

Dule stepped back with a short gasp. His orange skin had turned pale and golden.

"I am a shapechanger," Mimik explained as she took her human form again. She tucked it and its uniform into position. "I have unlimited security clearance through the Legion. I am one of the chief undercover operatives that organization uses when we need such."

"I–"

"Mimik is on temporary leave from the Legion as she works with Three Worlds," Jae explained. "As I said before, I thought you could use her. I'm having difficulty utilizing administrative means to dig down into the various army networks to see who is who and who is not loyal to whom."

"I can disguise myself as lesser officers," Mimik explained. "I can embed myself here and there, as needed to investigate at lower levels than you can comfortably reach."

Dule motioned for both of them to take seats, and he joined them in his private conference area.

"But you are truly a female?"

Muvvik shrugged in a very human way. "Only approximately. My race has four genders. 'Female' is a fair estimate."

Dule turned to Jae. "And she is adept?"

"Let's not refer to Muvvik as 'she,' Major. Get in the habit of Muvvik being a man. A fellow officer. Perhaps another aide to you?"

Dule leaned back, giving Muvvik a full inspection. "There are times I wish I could be in two places at once, especially with this… operation going on. Could you imitate me? Credibly?"

"I have been studying you, Major Dule." With that Muvvik gradually changed into another Dule. He gave a Dule nod with a brief lift to his eyebrows, the sort of half-smile he had when he favored the left side of his face, then cleared his throat in a Dulish way. "All officers will report to me first thing after final lunch chime!" Muvvik's voice and inflections were Dules.

Dule blinked a few times at this. "I do not usually study my own self, but that seems… very good."

"Dule" changed back to Muvvik. "I am a Legionnaire." His voice was confident. "I am the best shape-changer known to the AffSys." With a twitch to his lips he added, "Of course, they don't have much communication with the worlds of my home sector. There may be better ones there, but they have not been trained as I have, especially with human conditions."

"Mimik is the Protector's lieutenant on his Legion team," Jae mentioned. "He doesn't know she's here. For the duration, she is on personal leave and has left very fine replacements to fill both her and the Protector's places."

Jae leaned in, meeting Dule's gaze. "You can trust her. She will communicate Three Worlds info only to you and to me. She goes by another name, another form, while she is at our headquarters. The Speaker knows she's here but–" Jae gave a brief chuckle – "there are a lot of off-worlders, including Legionnaires, coming through to Aldierra these days. Most stay only a short while and sometime take regular transportation back. The Speaker has too many things on her agenda to worry about where one person went. She knows Mimik came at my call and that I am responsible for her."

"But the Protector does not know."

"That can change if situations warrant," Jae assured him.

Dule was still making up his mind, his fingers slightly steepled in front of him as he thought.

"I assume you will want to test me," Muvvik said.

The discussion continued.

– – –

LONDO PAUSED IN HIS ROUTE from the Great Shit Flats to Kristith, one of the sea cities off Orchin's east coast. He set his protective suit to auto-clean and when that was done, he folded it to deposit into a special pocket in his vest, one sealed not to let any remaining atoms of odor out.

Then he dropped down to the floating city below. These things were marvels of engineering, set upon great pilings that could move up or down in storm conditions, holding the city level and solid.

Canals ran through neighborhoods and city sectors like the veins of a leaf. Of course they were clogged with smelly scum. Over there a number of Jae's water-based teams were working with both equipment and by hand to clean one. But over here…

He gentled his descent to land lightly. The teen boys who worked here had varying skin tones. Some were the orange of native Aldierrans, and others were the peachy browns of Terran stock.

"Valiant!" All the boys looked up at his arrival to point and draw the attention of their fellow workers. "It's Valiant!" Some of the Aldierran boys referred to him as "the Protector."

Londo greeted them with a smile and strolled through their area, asking what they were doing, how the work was progressing. What were they proudest of? Did they need help or equipment?

He nodded as he walked around, talking individually to them. When he came to one, a tall teen with curly, light brown hair tied into a queue, he dropped his voice so no one could hear.

"How's it going, Drew?"

"Valiant. See? I didn't call you 'Uncle Lon.'"

"Very good. No one suspects?"

"No one."

Londo nodded at Lina's sister's older child. Lon had arranged for him and a small group of other juvenile delinquents to be sent to Aldierra, as a type of learning experience detention. "You've been doing all right? No undue stress?"

"My shoulders and back hurt." Drew quickly added, "But the medics check us if things get rough. They're great."

"Read any good books lately? I haven't heard that you've been missing sending reports."

"Oh no. I wouldn't do that. Besides, there are some really good ones on our shelves. And I'm way ahead on my school schedule."

Lon couldn't resist giving him a grin. "I will tell your parents if they don't know already. Any subjects you think you need that you aren't getting?

Excitement made Drew's thin shoulders tremble. "I'm watching the psychic stuff. We all are. Or most of us."

"Psychic–?"

"Aunt Lie's got a channel with all these people teaching how to become psychic. I think it's beginning to work. I just feel… Well, it's really interesting stuff."

"I will tell her that. She says that becoming psychic makes you up your vibrational level or something. That the more you learn and do, the better a person you become." Lon gave a brief frown. "Jae says it's not about being a better person; it's because you're tuning into your soul purpose."

"Soul purpose?" Drew cocked his head at his uncle.

Lon dug in a vest pocket for his padd to check. "Here it is. Jae's posting lots of Feithi philosophy, theories about how the world works. Apparently we're in a simulation, a matrix that we've all created in order to grow our souls."

"Huh. Philosophy?" Drew peered at Lon's screen.

"Here. And here. I think you'll find these interesting. You might have your friends here watch as well. I'll send them–"

"Not to me directly."

Londo nodded. Good for the boy not to want to be found out. "I'll send them to your group."

"Thanks, Un… Valiant."

"Okay." Lon turned to the rest of the group. "What can I help you out with today? Pick a big job, one you were dreading. Hup-hup!"

The boys all cheered.

– – –

"SPEAKER, WE HAVE A PROBLEM," the county manager told her.

There had been fights about the park planning, whether the space should be allotted to community vegetable gardens, flowers, green space, or activities. Normally Lina would refer him to Lon's section or Nesh's, but both were unavailable and this man had irritated people from all sides waiting on screens. Apparently Lina's staffers weren't important enough for these citizens to listen to.

Spring was approaching. They had to know now. They'd listen to the Speaker.

"Give me two minutes," Lina told him. She truly was making an effort not to rely on stims as much as she could. She double-checked herself; questioned herself as to who could otherwise do the job at hand.

She was the Speaker, the person who had directly communicated with every one of the twenty billion people on this planet as Aldierra issued her Ultimatum. They knew her.

Using her magical Flute to energize herself had worked. Three times already today. But this last time hadn't been as thorough, as if the Flute were telling her it was time to knock it off and get some rest.

She couldn't afford that right now. A quick port to her office, a tap of a medium-strength stim to her arm, and she was ready to talk this community through their arguments. She took another stim with her in case discussions ran long.

- - -

JAE PEERED AT THE FLOW CHARTS on his counter-mounted monitor even as other monitors floated in the air around his office. Down he scrolled, through a maze of interconnected military directives from several armies.

Senior Advisor Siekesh had handed in a very thorough compilation of what he'd been able to dig up these past few years. Now AI helped Jae extrapolate from that, but intuition from his career of behind-the-scenes Legion work had him looking in more unlikely places.

Mimik was pursuing other possibilities, but she was doing that in person and under disguise.

AI eked out password permissions, utilizing the best of Wiley's cryptoputers, but AI took time, even with Jae nudging it.

Jae had almost grown up in Wiley's labs, helping the genius in so many areas as Jae hid from the rest of the Legion. They'd had long conversations over the clacking hiss of Wiley's more esoteric experiments. He'd been so young, so terrified of the universe and what it had done to him. Wiley had not only taught him the intricacies of AffSys tech Jae found useful, but also reassured him that not all non-Feithi were untrustable.

Then-Commander Chimrin had visited the labs often, keeping track of Jae's psychological needs without digging into his mind and privacy with her telepathy. Jae had respected that and watched closely to see how she accomplished her leadership. Non-Feithi could esteem other beings; that was one of many lessons he learned from her.

This Aldierran rot ran deep. It held little esteem for others in it. The armies had been ensconced as a part of Aldierra's very foundations for centuries. Over and over they had built upon what existed as modernization forced them to change, which made the pathways even more labyrinthine.

Number one, these armies needed a complete reorganization. Get rid of this mess and restructure it for efficiency, if nothing else.

Number two, the armies lacked focus. No wonder one had never been able to win the world definitively.

Number three, the armies were all dedicated to requiring more and more equipment and supplies each year, and to support more and more of a workforce as the population grew. That was their true focus, and they accomplished that goal handily.

Jae instructed his computer to diagram the more important paths he'd decided upon, and then leaned back in his chair as it compiled the data. He took a sip of *valbing,* which his Chief of Staff, Walker Sentristone, had recommended he try. Good stuff, but strong. He'd have to make sure not to drink too much. He needed his mind alert to do this work, though he also needed his nerves to stand down from the constant strain they were under.

The angled screen on the counter in front of him focused into a web of color-coded lines. Much better. Jae puzzled out the connections, especially the overlaps between armies.

And the paths that led from the Patriarch's office.

He followed one of those two, no make it three levels downward. That would be where the interesting communications would lie, the ones that might utilize looser security regulations enough to let some truths through. Maybe to disclose some names that might otherwise hide in obscurity.

Then again, the egos at the top of the ranks could be complacent and slip the most amazing bits of info into unclassified communications. Jae double-checked those as well.

These people. Jae compared conversation logs to get a feel for them before he began to program AI to help. AI had a tendency to be blatant; this required

Jae to tone down its search. Make it subtle. Give it branches so if the hacking came to light, others could be blamed.

With Jae's practiced touch, his hacks shouldn't come to light.

— — —

BY THE END OF THREE HOURS, Jae had a list of twelve well-placed officers who needed a visit from the Minister. Some seemed like honorable men and might join his efforts, while others were blatantly working for their own gain – or had been brought into the Patriarch's deeper plots. A personal conversation and telepathic prodding might lend some light to their statuses.

Whom to report these to? If anything happened to Jae… Lon and Lina had to be kept out of this. Best that Jae's own staff remained ignorant until things got to a stage when they should be brought in. The fewer people involved in a plot like this, the better.

Jae composed a message in Legion code, Security Level Unlimited, and sent it to Mimik.

CHAPTER

14

"A re you ready to call it a day, Lon?" Lina asked as he flew down to her. He was always so graceful as he did so, like an angel in black softly dropping to the ground.

The construction camp was filled with hundreds of men milling around. As the sun set, their day was ending as well. Most stood in line for the food tent. Three men squatted off to the side of it, doing their business out in the open, though there were plenty of portalets at hand.

Should she? Privacy. Oh hell. "Hey!" she shouted at the men, but Lon rushed to block her view and yelled at them for her. The men hurriedly pulled up their clothing and shambled to the latrines.

"Wash your hands before you eat!" Lina called.

Lon closed his eyes as he ran one hand through his hair. "You think you've got them civilized and they keep pulling this kind of thing," he sighed.

"We'll get them there," Lina declared. "Maybe we need to do another educational video."

"More like a dozen." Londo's shoulders sank. "For real, though I don't know if many people are watching those things. Or maybe if the people they're aimed at are. I'll send a note along to the propaganda team." He gave Lina a quick kiss. She came back for more.

"You should wash up too," she told him. He was covered with mud and gray dust.

"Still got some work left to do. Tell you what," he offered. "You grab something from the mess hall and get enough for me too. Go ahead and eat. I'll eat when I get done and have a shower."

"We'll have time to… talk? when you're done?"

"Maybe no… talk tonight. I'm kind of tired."

"Raincheck then." She gave him a small, wry smile and added so he wouldn't feel guilty, "Me too."

He took to the sky again and as long as she was here, she got in line for the food tent. No Lon tonight. No Lon for many nights now. The same for Jae, damn it. She knew they got together often enough, but their schedules were more closely matched than hers. This was dinner for him; lunch for her. Still, she was indeed tired.

Nothing to be done about it, except stims. No. No stims. She was taking too many as it was, and those were for emergency situations. Here was no emergency: dinner. She'd set aside Lon time that now wouldn't be used. Well. She needed to sample the food their people got. This was efficiency.

"Do you guys want to eat here?" she asked her ever-present squad of guards, who lurked not-too-distantly on the sidelines, watching everything.

"We'll eat when we go off duty, Speaker."

Okay. The men in line urged her to go ahead of them. Politeness or fear? Likely more fear than anything.

She felt so odd being the only woman in the crowd. There were women in some adjacent tents, entertainment women whose jobs she shuddered to think about, but she'd made sure they were volunteers and were being paid *very* well for their services. Also, that they had doctors looking after them, and nearby guards they could call upon in case of trouble. But they ate separately from the men.

Lina needed to be seen doing things with men and not just women. Three Worlds was not an apartheid operation.

She tried to engage the men in conversation as they subtly pushed her forward. When she came to the immediate chow line display she asked the men around her what their favorite foods were as well as which things they didn't like.

"It's army food," more than one man told her. It was what it was.

There was liquidy glop and glop with a crust on it, both of them grayish in color. She deliberately stayed away from the new scanners that everyone else went for. What else did they have to choose from? On second thought, she requested four scanners for Londo, which was a bit much even for him. She'd steal one if he said they were good.

The other offerings certainly weren't.

Sitting at a table among the men, Lina gagged just a little at the dry, so-called edible square on her plate. "Is it supposed to taste like this?" she asked the man who'd dared to sit only two seats away from her.

"It's *bitzy*," he told her. The word clicked in her brain: a common fast food.

The soldiers told her that bitzy came in variations around the globe, but mostly bitzy was bitzy was bitzy, especially army bitzy.

"And you live on this? It sustains you?" she asked wonderingly. The man shrugged and spooned up some crusted glop to go along with his bitsy. She noted that it took a lot of beer to deal with the meal. "Do they ever serve anything with, well, taste here?"

Another shrug.

They talked of their living conditions, whether they were being worked too hard, if they got enough time to communicate with families and friends, what kind of entertainment they'd like added to the current line-up. Were there things they wanted to learn? Where did they want to be in, say, five years? What did they require to get there?

Five years. The men exchanged dark glances with each other. Finally one said, "Doomsday is soon."

Lina frowned. "Doomsday is not guaranteed; only Deadline is."

Grumbling. Mutters. "Like we're not all going to die."

"I get it," Lina said. "Why should we work so hard if it's all for nothing?" she asked them.

Their expressions as they gazed at her were puzzled, questioning.

"I mean, if the worst does happen–" she gave an exaggerated shrug – "no one's going to be interested in any improvements we've made anyway. But if your world doesn't end…"

The men's blank expressions told her they hadn't considered this.

"Then all you're going to have is a world that's a bit better than what it is now. Maybe even a lot better. And getting even better from there."

As if they'd choreographed it, the men all began chewing on the harder choices on their trays, as if they could divert their minds with digestion.

Lina squared her shoulders. "Four minutes a day," she declared with some volume. "When you first wake up, when you're taking a break, whenever. Four. Minutes."

Bless him, Strayer asked, "To do what?"

Lina didn't remind him that she'd made videos about this. Maybe there were too many videos, too many choices. Too little entertainment to entice them to watch.

Maybe the three of them were doing too much lecturing.

"Four minutes a day, you sit down. Or lie down. And imagine a wonderful world, somewhere you'd like to live with things you'd love to do and visit in it. People you'd love to know. You're practicing this every day, so you don't have to tackle the entire vision at once. Just take it one pleasant chunk at a time."

She nodded at the man three seats down, who was working on a chunky stew.

"Put yourself into that picture. Imagine you feel excited, loved, fulfilled, intrigued by whatever it is you've dreamed up. Try ramping up that feeling, really letting it run to the max. Enjoy it! You might even want to add a minute to your visualization. See the details. Feel the feelings, in as much detail as you can summon. And when you're done, send a message to the Great Beyond: 'This or better.' The universe hears you. It's better at imagining than you are, and it knows you better than you know yourself. Trust in it.

"Keep that vision or emotion going with you throughout the day, if you can. If you can't, you'll do it tomorrow. No sweat. Don't worry about how this will be accomplished. Don't think about that at all, unless you see something pop up in your life that might help lead you to that future. Take that path. But until that happens, just visualize once a day, four minutes. Many of my home world's philosophies teach than thoughts become things. This is basic manifestation, and it is something everyone can do."

"Just… think?"

"Imagine. This dream or vision isn't for anyone else but yourself. Think you can do that? I find it one of the more refreshing parts of my day."

She smiled to herself. "So far I got the 'better' part. I got my wonderful husbands. Believe me, I never ever dreamed them in my life, but here they are! I got to come to Aldierra, where I've met so many wonderful people and made new friends. And I've received the chance to help others in a larger way than I could ever imagine."

Strayer began to nod absently at her, his eyes unfocused. His dream was beginning.

Around the room Lina noticed others who were obviously taking their four minutes now. She let out a sigh of contentment and matched the gaze of two men on her left who were more interested in the moment at completing their dinner.

"Tell me," she asked them. "Another teaching from my world is that the best way to a man's heart is through his stomach. Is that true here?"

She had to explain the concept and the men wound up with equating "heart" with "loyalties."

"Okay, we'll start there," she told them. Batt had asked for a list of upcoming food contests, so they could give people around Aldierra more time to prepare. Armies certainly operated on their stomachs, even when they worked with the Three Worlds. "Now tell me: what are your favorite foods? What would you like to see served here, and who makes it the best?"

– – –

AGAIN, IT WAS JAE who went to Lupoff and not the other way around. This time they met in the Patriarch's offices in Soshe, on Sha-Green continent. The offices held an arresting view of a very large lake surrounded by considerable hills. Oddly for Aldierra, those hills had been allowed to remain undeveloped in many places, but there were still far too many stark buildings crowding the landscape for it to be truly picturesque.

Even so, Jae told Lupoff, "Remarkably beautiful location. Is this your favorite headquarters?"

"It's near Soshe, so it allows easy transportation for government officials," Lupoff replied. He wobbled around the room, an aide discreetly following him.

Something wrong with Lupoff's hips? Still, he made the effort to sort through a pile of info padds on one table before gathering two to keep.

Jae nodded, making sure his features portrayed appreciation of all he viewed. "And you manage your entire world's affairs without seeming to be stressed by any of it." With a small laugh, he accepted the offered chair in a seating area, as well as an alcoholic drink. He needed one. "We've been here only a short while, been able to address just a few problem areas, and we're stretched to our limit. How do you do it?"

Lupoff joined him, and the serving woman who was attending them discreetly vanished along with the other men. The Patriarch set down his info padds to take up a glass of liquor. "Discipline. I grew up in an army household. My father and his father before him were army through and through."

"As are your brothers."

"Yes."

"Yet you have managed to rise above them all. You took over the Red Army and then the Greens. That is impressive leadership."

Lupoff couldn't mask his pleasure at the compliment.

"That's something we could use," Jae told him. "Leaders like you. Leaders who know what they're doing, as well as how to utilize the vast amount of manpower you command."

"There aren't that many."

"You're the best." Jae sipped again at the drink, which had an acidic undertone to it. His Array would have warned him if it contained any poisons. Still, he could feel the alcohol calming him. He needed this. "I know we could never convince you to work for us–"

Lupoff let out a small snort. Jae set down his glass and leaned forward.

"But in the past the Legion – you know about the Mega-Legion, don't you?"

Lupoff nodded warily.

"The Legion has operated, shall we say, under the table and procured major deals with such powerful men as you. We offer reciprocity. You scratch our backs, and we scratch your army's. Mutually agreeable. I see Three Worlds operating the same way."

Lupoff's eyes narrowed.

"Of course you are worried that after Deadline things might not be as comfortable for you as they were before the Ultimatum."

The Patriarch couldn't hide his sneer. "That might have occurred to me. I can see changes even in the short time you three have been here. Maybe too many." He began to sway in his chair, left and right.

Jae leaned back to regard the ceiling. "In this case, my partners might not agree with me. I was thinking the scratching might be adjusted to more than usual. More a *quid pro quo* that no one has to know about. Say… You scratch my back and I scratch yours? We leave the Protector and Speaker out of this. They will never know. I can assure you, my own powers and contacts are considerable."

He could feel the panic he tried to keep at bay deep inside. No. Aldierra would not wind up like Feith! As long as he was alive, its people would be too. Jae quashed the emotion away from himself and took another slow sip.

He gave the Patriarch a slow, sly smile. "If you wish, I can furnish you my more, ah, unpublicized work history. I am often sent undercover by the Legion, and I have made some missions personally profitable. Though the Legion doesn't have to know that." He took another sip and watched the Patriarch consider.

Lupoff seemed wary. His emotions were so strong that Jae could feel his mind darting back and forth, as if he were considering many angles.

"I wouldn't mind – after Deadline that is," Jae mentioned, "having a world of my own under my thumb. I think I could mold it to something very interesting." He shrugged, took another sip. "Then again maybe I wouldn't need an entire world. Maybe… half would do."

Lupoff's eyes widened and he sat straighter in his chair.

"Quid pro quo," Jae reminded him. "My partners don't need to know. They're worried about our schedule, which deals with surface concerns. Air, water, migration routes, ho hum. Not about government or military policy."

A slight quirk lifted the edges of Lupoff's lips. He leaned back to listen.

– – –

LINA HELD UP A HAND to halt the reporters' exits. They'd crowded around her when she came out of today's organizational meeting to combine, simplify and modernize the governments of the small continent of Reyda. "Just one more thing, nothing to do with this but I keep hearing… rumors."

She took a breath. "My husband Jae first told me of this Aldierran tradition, where y'all schedule an important contract to be signed, and then you grab a nice-looking woman, paint some of her parts gold, and then have some kind of public sex ceremony to metaphorically seal the deal."

She glared into the cameras aimed at her. "No. Let me say that again so I will be clear: no!"

"If there's an important contract or deal to be made, leave the sex out of it. Everyone dress up nice and sign or do whatever you need to do to make things legal. Maybe have a party afterward. But we've already told you that from here on out, all sex needs to be done only by cheerfully consenting adults in full possession of their faculties. We are extremely serious about that. You see your laws changing to accommodate that aspect.

"If you want to have an orgy after the contract is finished, make sure no one is impaired to the point where they can't make a sober decision, and that everyone – everyone – and I mean they'd all better be legal adults too – is willing to participate. Then go wild, and let everyone fingerpaint everyone else. Whatever. Just not all over their bodies, as skin has to breathe.

"Got it? No more 'goldens.'" She paused. "Of course, what you do in your own bedrooms is your own business. Just make it personal, not contractual."

– – –

LONDO ARRIVED AT THE NEW WHITEFERN COMPLEX, where crews from that House should be dealing with the final finishes. The House of Whitefern was due to move in when it was done.

But there were no Whiteferns here.

Whitefern was one of the larger Houses, but still within norms. It had about 1500 family members living in one targeted compound. Houses averaged in the 1000 – 1500-person range. They would usually take up a large city block with an interior courtyard. Some Houses couldn't afford that acreage and wound up in a thrown-together stacked chawl situation. Any associated courtyards usually involved latrines, as the chawl interiors didn't have plumbing.

Part of Lon's building process was to make sure these new buildings and even city sectors were partially designed and okayed by the people who would be inhabiting them. Lon's staffers had met with this House. They'd been fairly enthusiastic, though loath to leave their original location.

That location, like others, had been smack on a major migratory route for local wildlife. Had to go.

They'd moved in with an associated House in an existing complex not marked for renovation, the Plaidblackwalls. *Ç'a pas d'allure*, the names these Houses had. So many were about location, because once they struck a claim somewhere they were by god going to keep it.

He called the House, and the head of the Whiteferns came on screen.

"No one is here," Lon stated the obvious, gesturing to the echoing room behind him. Only three men seeing to the last of the plumbing were present, doing their job. Independent contractors.

Shelken Whitefern shrugged. "It will get done in time," he said. "We worked hard to move and now you want us to move again."

"So Plaidblackwalls House is comfortable? They've made you welcome?"

Another shrug. "As good as could be done in such short time."

"But you're comfortable there? Moved in?"

"Well…"

The man looked around his surroundings and sneered. Actually sneered in full display. Lon could see the House there was stuffed with extra furniture from where the two families were cohabiting. Frou-frous had obviously been piled on top of each other and not stored in the temporary facilities arranged for them. Boys with flailing arms ran screaming through the house. On camera, Lon watched one knock an expensive-looking something from a shelf. It shattered on the ground, spilling some sparkling contents, and the boy screamed with delight, then reached for something else to destroy.

Behind him, a man hurried in to scold and protect the possessions. The boy finally ran off to destroy something somewhere else, and Londo called out to the man.

He looked exhausted. Did this kind of thing go on all the time?

"Mister Plaidblackwalls?" Londo surmised.

"Do you want to speak to Head of House, Protector? He's out right now, but…"

"No, no, you'll do fine. How are you and your people managing with the sharing situation?"

Warily Mr. P eyed the Whitefern man beside him. "We have only a few more days of this," he decided to say, and bowed his head. "We are glad to do anything we can to help this project. Soon we will have our House back and all will be as it was before."

Lon rubbed his nose. "Tell me, Mr. Plaidblackwalls…"

"Reyin."

Lon gave him a relieved grin, happy to be given that informality. "Reyin. Have you seen the plans for the new Whitefern compound? Are there elements in it that perhaps your people would like to add to your own?"

Reyin's eyes lit up. "Are there! We've all been trying to figure how we can adjust our home to be more like parts of their new place. Our House is an old one. It's grown in population through the years, so we're bursting at the seams. And now there are the new ideas about giving the women better spaces.

"The Whitefern plans are so spacious and organized. Even their women have a fine place in it. Ours were all talking about it. Perhaps it's time to give them a better space of their own. We're wondering if our structure can support another story, or if we should build into the courtyard."

"And you, Mr. Whitefern? Are you excited about the new place?"

Shrug and small nods. Sourly he said, "We are excited to be moving out of here. It's much too crowded for two Houses. We overestimated the amount of room we'd need during the transition."

"Did you put *any* of your possessions into storage?" Lon asked.

"We're keeping it here. Easier to keep track of. Don't trust those storage units Three Worlds arranged."

"I see. No wonder it's so crowded. Are you caring for the possessions of your hosts? I just saw some things destroyed by boys that I think are of your House."

"Those?" Whitefern gave a snort. "They are unimportant."

"They are – were – ours," Reyin corrected.

"Well. They can be replaced."

"Are you replacing them, Mr. Whitefern?" Londo asked. "Your people damaged them. You should replace–"

"The Plaids are our hosts!" Whitefern retorted. "We do not pay when they are hosting us!"

Londo looked from one to the other. Then he told Reyin, "I would like to speak to your Head of House, please. Could you ask that he contact me immediately?"

So it was that Plaidblackwalls House instead moved into the new complex, after a few extra changes had been made. Most of the work was accomplished by the entire Plaidblackwalls family, working tirelessly on those adaptations as well as the finishes to meet Lon's building schedule. This way, Londo explained, the Whiteferns wouldn't have to exert much effort in moving yet again. They could remain in the old Plaidblackwalls place.

The Plaidblackwalls people seemed quite happy with the switch.

– – –

IT WAS JUST A LITTLE THING. The end of a long, hard day, fourteen hours so far. Lina was ready to skip dinner and hit the sack. There'd be little enough time between now and the start of tomorrow's day.

But Londo had somehow rearranged the first duties of his schedule. He had almost an hour before he needed to report in.

He wiggled his eyebrows at her as she made her daily journal entry.

He looked good. So sexy. That's right; they were married.

Too often it seemed that they were mere co-workers. Occasionally they glimpsed each other, maybe even had a chance to say a few words. Tuesday team meetings were about Deadline and hardly anything else.

That was not good. They both needed to give their relationship attention, and "sexy" was one of the things she'd signed up for.

Yeah, sexy. Hot. Steeeamy.

That constant yearning in her lower gut that she kept lashed down surged so powerfully that she had to catch her breath: Londo! Londo!

"Give me five minutes," she told him.

He nodded and bent down to pet one of the cats before strolling to the bedroom. Lina ported to her office. Corner shelf on the bottom: the stims.

She reviewed the instructions and warnings, and gave herself just enough to last about seventy-five minutes. Seventy-five wasn't that long to worry about. Then she searched in her mind for that deep blue lingerie that Londo loved, ported it on. She ported to him.

After he was asleep with the echo of a satisfied smile on his face, she still had a few minutes of wakefulness in which she could rearrange those equipment shipments near Kristith so they wouldn't interfere with Lon's new sea-city build.

Cut down on the stims! her guides insisted.

But first an emergency call came through from the Legion. She was always on standby to port a Legion squad to some dire situation. They usually didn't take long. If she was efficient she'd have some time left to attend to the Kristith shipments before the stim wore off.

CHAPTER

15

I n the dead of night, Yusuf heard a sound.

It was a small one, just a "tik," but Yusuf knew his house/cell was airtight. No rodent could make its way in.

The front door hadn't opened, nor had any of his windows. Locked from the outside. In an emergency he could open them, but he hadn't called for that.

So. There was Somebody Here.

He eased up, wondering how long it would take Whoever to come into the bedroom. He gathered the coldness that always lurked in potential around him and slid his feet to the floor.

He could feel no warmth, no human presence in the other room. No further sounds betrayed an intruder.

He pulled on some pants and a shirt, slid his feet into shoes, and wandered out without turning on a light. Still no pockets of warmth out there. Nothing but him acting as any non-structural heat source.

Ten feet into the living room, when he'd slunk as silently as he could, a glow appeared over his coffee table. It brightened slowly, as if not to alarm him.

It was some kind of monitor. A communications one, to judge from the menu on its screen. It floated almost immaterially over the table at eye level to himself.

"What do you want?" Yusuf demanded.

The glow became the three-dimensional head and shoulders of a man, looking as if he were there in the room but cut off along the edges of what might be a cube. As Yusuf shifted, he could see the side of the man's head, but it was still cut off in even, cubelike form. He peered at Yusuf, looked offscreen as if someone else were there, and then returned his gaze to Yusuf. "Yusuf Joshi of Earth," the man identified him.

"And you?"

"You don't need to know my name… yet." The smirk on the man's face created slow anger in him.

Yusuf stopped himself. "Anger is not your best way to deal with the world," his new psychiatrist had told him. Many times. "Acknowledge it. Ask it if you can handle things differently. What would serve you best? What would get you what you want?"

In this case Yusuf wanted (1) to maintain his physical safety, and (2) to discover why this man was contacting him. Logically, it must be something the Three Worlds would not approve of. This man wanted to strike a bargain, one that would counter the Three Worlds' mission.

Yusuf triggered his personal video system. He didn't have to send a record to his jailers, but he would want to revisit this interaction to parse it.

"I'm listening," Yusuf decided to say. Interesting how his mind remained fairly clear without the cloud of anger forcing it this way and that from fear.

"We are an army," the man said. "We respect the power you have as well as what you have accomplished in your life."

"I accomplished winding up in jail."

A nod. "Granted. But Earth has unusual paras who were powerful enough to capture you."

"Aldierra has Valiant."

"And he is often distracted by this Three Worlds work. Plus he won't notice you if you cooperate with us. We have worked out a way you can help us counter this Doomsday plot. You help us and we help you. We can return you to Earth. We can set you up on a non-affiliated planet near the AffSys. We can get you to the Yanist-Glory Empire. They would welcome you there."

"And all I would have to do is–?"

"Help us sabotage what the Worlds are doing. A little here; a little there. Nothing to bring attention to you."

"But won't that mean that Deadline becomes Doomsday?"

The man scoffed. "It's all a hoax," he said. "The Speaker or perhaps the Minister – he's Feithi, and who knows what those people could do? – have set us up to glorify themselves. Once Doomsday hits and – miracle! – the population lives, they can declare that they are the heroes. They should be worshipped."

"Hm," was all Yusuf elected to offer, so the man went on.

"We pledge ourselves to our world and our Patriarch. We have armies at his command, armies that can take control once they leave."

"Will they leave?"

The man laughed. "Of course they will. Aldierra's only a stepping stone. They've already announced that after Doomsday they'll be off to Earth and Sarastor. Sarastor – You probably don't know this, Earther, but it is the capital of a vast, rich star confederation. It's full of human-friendly planets with lots of land area and resources. That is their true target, the AffSys."

"That… would make sense," Yusuf said, drawing out the sentence. "But you realize this is all abrupt. I don't know you. I don't know your people or army. I need reassurance that this on the up-and-up, that you people can do what you'll say you can."

They talked for over an hour more before the screen disappeared completely.

Yusuf wasn't familiar with this world's technology. For all he knew, other spyware was in place, embedded in his house.

He waited until the next morning, when Reen Elikal came to release him from his quarters. She greeted him like a human being, he was pleased to note. As she always did.

If Valiant and Neutrino had hired her, she would be top-of-the-line trained.

They went out for a morning walk, ostensibly to pick up one of the warm drinks the local bar offered. It wasn't caffeinated, but it contained something that made his body begin to hum with eager energy for the day.

"I need to speak with the Minister. Neutrino," he said in a low voice to her as the bar crowd's voices increased around them.

Her eyes widened for only a moment and she gave the slightest of nods.

They left the conversation at that.

– – –

BUT LATER THAT MORNING came a flitter with the Three Worlds logo on it. Out of it piled two guards and Neutrino. The hero made a show of meeting with Reen and checking schedules. Then he walked with Yusuf.

"Make a point of having an argument with something." Jae waved his hand monitor at Yusuf, who shook his head and pointed angrily at a line on it.

"You can't expect that amount of work!" he said loudly. "Not all in one day!"

They faked the disagreement, with Yusuf embellishing it with what seemed like righteous anger. He pointed to the screen, but it was the part that held an icon about monitoring his house.

Yusuf tapped his finger on it in a way that didn't trigger the program.

"I will put in a decent number of hours, Neutrino! No more! But no less." He lowered his voice as if retreating from anger.

Neutrino and he talked longer, this time in a discussion about how much work Yusuf would be expected to accomplish, and where he should concentrate his efforts.

Finally, Neutrino and his guards left.

— — —

THAT AFTERNOON, JUST BEFORE SUNSET as Yusuf was sifting through some cultural data about Santara Island, his station lit up.

For a moment Yusuf thought it might be That Man, and he tensed.

Instead it was the Minister. "We've double-checked your house," Neutrino told him. "We found a bug. It's now getting looped input and doesn't register our current conversation. But do be careful in the future until we can retrieve it without alerting the other end.

"I know of the man who contacted you," Neutrino continued. "It makes sense. I'm investigating a mammoth conspiracy within the Aldierran armies, but I'm not sure at this point whether they're on the Patriarch's side or on a side we aren't sure of yet. Knowing who this man is helps us figure that out. Thank you for contacting me."

They set up a code word that could be given to Reen that would bring Neutrino here or set up clandestine communications that the other side couldn't intercept.

"You've declared your loyalties," Neutrino observed. "Will you stand by them?"

Yusuf let out a huff. "Better you people than them," he said. "In the end, I don't think they have any loyalties at all."

– – –

EVENTUALLY THEY LOOSENED THEIR HOLD on him, but Yusuf's schedule was so packed there was little time for freedom or world exploration. However, when the invitation came to visit the Three Worlds compound, Yusuf cleared that schedule. He was curious. And he'd never met Lina in person. Like Jae, she called him three times a week to check in, and he'd appreciated the momos and thukpa she'd added to his rations.

The person he met first was Maximus, who was visiting Aldierra on a low-priority basis. Yusuf tried not to tremble, then resisted the almost overwhelming urge to grandstand, maybe attack. He'd battled Maximus before, just not man-to-man. Maximus would have won, of course, so Yusuf had always kept whatever distance he could from him or his son.

Now Maximus and Yusuf strolled down the gravel walkway next to the Starhart tents. Above them, past the Monstrosity's force fields, a patch of sky peeked out in a lilac shade, surrounded by high masking clouds while a tide of dark clouds threatened to roll in from the west.

Yusuf didn't refer to the large building as such. He'd gotten the impression that the Speaker – Lina – wanted to keep that designation to herself. It was also Londo's baby, and Maximus was Lon's father. His real father, his bio-father, as it turned out. Yet through all the family lies, Lon's father had always stood by his side, supporting him. How unlike Yusuf's own father!

Harsh, loud sounds of construction blasted from the Monstrosity, with workers yelling at each other to make themselves heard.

Yusuf preferred his quiet village.

Maximus' attention was focused on the sky. "I don't think it's my imagination. The skies look much clearer after just a few months. By the way: fine job you did on that albedo whazzis."

"Albedo improvement project," Yusuf corrected. "Another way of saying I'm forming a layer of reflective ice over the northern polar areas so the seas don't absorb as much solar heat. We'll see how the coming winter adds to the ice cover."

"Yeah, that," Maximus said. "Good job. I admit, I've had my doubts about you."

"They've asked that I switch to the south pole, even though the northern ice isn't as thick as it might be at this point," Yusuf said. "I wonder if I should stay and do more."

"You have dozens of experts running computer models. Still mighty impressive," Maximus said. "And I like what I've seen of your media interviews. You seem honest. That has a great impact on people who need to be inspired."

Yusuf stared at the hero who had just glancingly called him "inspirational."

"Here we go," Maximus motioned ahead of them as they walked beyond the tents. "Someday this is going to be a fantastic view."

"I like the view of my bay," Yusuf countered. There was a wider space ahead with grass browned from winter. Definite view to be seen: land stretching out below them beyond the sudden edge. Rolling hills with higher ones in the far distance.

"Well, here's another. Their old cat, Fafhrd, likes to come out here and look. They've got the bench there heated especially for her. Let's see if she'll let us join her."

The black cat didn't stir at their approach. "She looks dead to me," Yusuf said.

"She always looks dead. That's the game she plays with everyone." Maximus drew up closer to take a chair, and stopped abruptly in mid-squat. Yusuf looked at him.

Maximus was staring at the black cat.

"Uh oh," he said.

CHAPTER

16

They lowered the cardboard box into the deep hole prepared for it, just downslope of the bench. Lon shoveled dirt on top of it. "Rest in peace," he decided to say.

Lina used up yet another stack of tissues, trying not to sob so hard and not succeeding. "I ignored her," she hiccupped.

"You did not. None of us did," Lon told her.

Jae nodded into the top of Lina's head as he held her close. "She was content. She knew that she was loved. The entire world loved her." He chuckled for Lina's sake.

"She always seemed to find a way onto your shoulder when you were giving an interview. She has miles of messages in the system. Some from before, telling her that they adore her and asking where they can get a cat just like her. Some from Earth, saying that they adopted a senior cat because they liked her so much. And lots and lots of messages to us as well as to her through Three Worlds, saying how much they will miss her."

"And that she was a good cat."

"The… The best cat," Lina sniffled. "She taught me what a cat really was. She showed me how to treat the rest as they joined the family."

"Empress cat," Londo decided.

Hal cleared his throat. "Fafhrd was the reason why the Egyptians worshipped cats," he pronounced as an epitaph.

"Though I never saw her catch a mouse," Lina admitted. "Cats protected Egyptian granaries from rodents. She was already well past that stage when I got her." She wiped her eyes again. "She had been a day from being euthanized at the Durham shelter. They told me, 'You don't want that old cat,' but there was no way I was going to leave her there."

Jae gave her another squeeze. "She got so many more years with you. And a family. Every Starhart cat knows she was their queen mother."

Lon nodded to his father. "Any cat could go up to her and she'd give them a bath. I even saw Moose drag himself to her when he was having a bad day, and then bow his head so she'd lick it."

"Fafhrd." Lina sighed. "I am going to allot more time to playing with the herd. No matter what." She frowned at Lon and Jae. "I might have to take a couple grains of stims now and then to do it, but they're going to get fifteen more minutes a day than what they've gotten so far."

"No st–"

"Here you are."

The new voice came up from behind them. Dr. Mart approached from the office tents. He was handing his prothesis well now since that awful night. His left arm swung with his movement in the same way that his natural right arm did. Legion Medical was growing him a new one, but it would still be a few months before it was ready for transplant.

"They told me you'd all be here." Mart nodded to Hal. "Maximus." Then he nodded to Lina. "My condolences on your loss."

"Thank you." She rubbed a tissue over her nose and then said, "Well?"

"It's my first time on Aldierra, much less outside," he said. "Give me a moment." He looked around, saw the freshly filled grave before he drew a breath and looked up at them. "There were some minor, very minor issues, but the entire group is now enjoying excellent health."

Lina sank against Jae's shoulder and Londo put his hand on her arm. "Oh. Oh."

"It was only a cursory check, but anything major would have stood out. We'll wait for that equipment to be shipped here after I'm fully certified as a… veterinarian to give them complete physicals."

"Thank you, Mart," Lon said. He motioned to the place, the vista. "This is Fafhrd's Bluff. Originally I wanted to call it Faf's Overlook, but she bluffed us so long about whether she was dead or not, I thought that was more appropriate."

Behind her tissue, Lina nodded.

"A very nice place," Mart said diplomatically. More cats had followed him to ramble about as their examinations had concluded.

"Can you tell what she died of?" Londo asked.

Lina flinched. Jae shook his head. "She died of a long, happy life. She had accomplished what she wanted to do, had influenced whom she needed to. She made the decision to return home."

"That," Lina said. "Yes. There are lots and lots of cats on the Other Side who were so happy to greet her. Her larger family. They're playing like they're kittens, flying through the air and batting at each other and playing tag. Having a wonderful time."

"So why are you crying?" Lon asked.

"Because I'm going to miss her like hell! And I feel so guilty for letting her be sick."

"Shh, shh." Jae enveloped her.

"I'm sorry I'm taking so long to learn veterinary," Mart said.

"You're fine," Londo hastened to reassure him. "We're glad to have you on this."

Jae crooned to Lina, "Be calm, be quiet, and you'll feel her when she comes to visit. Give yourself time to grieve. But give her some time, too, to celebrate with her friends who are on the Other Side."

Lina nodded. Lon glanced at his father with raised eyebrows, and Hal glanced at Mart.

"I'd like to have a discussion about the cats' diet," the doctor said. "Is this a good time?"

$- - -$

"DINAH!" THE CALL HAD JUST COME THROUGH. Lina had made sure Dinah was on her top contacts for her staff to send her calls in.

Dinah Stewart was a close Terran friend, a student of Sue Taylor's psychic classes of a few years ago, whose members had remained in contact. Dinah was such an impressive psychic that she'd been invited to join the Mind Control Tour as an assistant instructor.

There Rikli-En, heir to the Yanist-Glory imperial throne, had mistaken her for Lina. He'd kidnapped and tortured her.

They'd gotten Dinah to Legion Med as soon as they could, and she'd undergone medical reconstruction for over two months. To Lina's dismay, she'd refused almost all psychological therapy. "I can set myself straight," Dinah had insisted. "I'm not some psycho."

Lina wasn't sure how well that was going. The effervescent Dinah now seemed closed off from the world, certainly from her. "How are you feeling?" Lina asked.

Dinah put on a peppy expression. "Fine," she lied. "Getting over it. Getting out into the galaxy, you know. Seeing what there is to be seen."

Help her. Help her. her guides urged.

But how? Dinah was putting up a big wall about this. Lina couldn't imagine what kind of hell she'd been through. Bad enough to cut herself off from the world.

Lina had done that for years. How did she manage to break it down? Londo. He'd done it. She wasn't Lon and she and Dinah were not in the kind of position to do anything like that.

Today's to-do list was as mammoth as usual, but Lina disregarded it. The two women chatted as Lina tried to find a way to get to some true communication.

Then Dinah said, "The Tishana want me to visit them."

"As instructor or lab rat?"

Dinah gave a small smile at that. "Sue said it was okay, not to be frightened. You know she's teaching there, right?" Lina nodded. "But that Doctor Mem-Bazer guy found out and told me it might not be a good idea. He said I needed a shrink and without that, the Tishana might… do things to me."

Lina frowned. "I've been told the same thing by Psyche. She's one of the Legionnaires, a telepath. She's from Tishan. I don't know if she was born there, but she's been through the best of their programs. She told me that the Tishana can be quite tricky. And powerful. Apparently you've got to be on your toes if they think you know things they don't."

That made Dinah's mouth work as she shifted in her padded medical chair. "I'll keep that in mind. I've also received offers to do some more Mind Control instruction. Accompany the lessons as people watch them."

"Oh, that's a great idea. You'll get a nice tour of the AffSys as well. Take lots of pictures and send them to me, if you would. Hey, you might want to do a whole YouTube thing, the AffSys for Terrans. They'll love that. And I'll arrange a personal guard unit for you, if you choose that."

"I can afford it."

"So can I. I *know* more people than you, Dinah. These days I have a little more clout. I can get you the best of the best. My treat. Have you asked your guides about that?"

Dinah's guides would certainly be able to help… *if* Dinah listened to them.

Wait. When was the last time Lina had had a long talk with her own guides?

They tentatively settled on that option, and Dinah specified she wanted a 50-50 mix of men and women in her guard unit because she didn't want all men with their underlying male threat ("Not all men," Lina tried to convince her) and she didn't want all women because well, she hated to admit it, but she didn't think women were as competent in those areas as men.

Lina chuckled. "I think you'll be pleasantly surprised," she said. "Now you take care. Give a yell if you start getting heebie-jeebie vibes from anything. And please, please just try a therapist. One time. It doesn't hurt but it helps an awful lot. Plus those AffSys people can accomplish therapy in a hurry. It doesn't have to take years."

The response to that was a vague one. As Dinah signed off, Lina reached under her desk to cross her fingers.

Then she went to tuck a stim pack into her pocket. She had a lot to do today.

— — —

"GRIGACH, LINA, ARE YOU STILL UP?" Jae squinted at her when he arrived, as if checking her condition. Then he gave her a kiss.

"You worked during my sleep period," Lina lied, and hoped he couldn't tell. The stims sang through her blood. She had another hour and a half before she'd require another one. She'd already had two. Better work fast.

She ported in filters and portable dams directly from the AffSys to river cities that had reported sabotage and flooding, and tried not to breathe much as she accompanied them to target. Even with her personal air filter, the sewage smelled to high heaven as it seeped everywhere in the seasonal heatwave, trying to over-run the city sectors.

"Lessick and Glidepath should cover the bridge on Summit Boulevard," she told Legion Support, some of whom had come to the flood zone to continue their training. "Danica Prime, can you solidify some of this, make it easier to haul away? And we need some muscle here to lift these old buildings out of the way of repair crews. Their foundations are crumbling."

She was needed to help the evacuations, to calm the panicked residents. They trusted the Speaker but not so much her staff. City managers consulted with her even as she hugged wandering kids and found their House families. One of her body guards, Paglash, fell into the worst of the mess and she had to port him to Decontamination. Everywhere hoses were spraying fairly clean water to chase the stuff into the drains or off surfaces, so Lina and her bodyguards were soaked and miserable in the heat.

"Do not tell anyone where you got this from," she told the rest of her guards as she administered stims to them. They nodded and kept their mouths shut.

CHAPTER

17

Londo shouted over the roar of the site's machines and pointed at three bulldozers and the accompanying crew on foot. "Quitting time! Back to camp!"

He could see the relief in the crews' eyes as they shut off their equipment and climbed out of the cabs, as the others gathered their tools and brought them to the rolling trailers that accompanied this mission. Only then did they remove their sound-dampeners.

He thought he saw a spring in the soldiers' steps as they trotted to the meal hall. The new scanners from their contest had appeared at dinners recently, to great approval by everyone. Tonight's dinner would include various local sweets that should lighten spirits.

The Legion had never taught their Team Leaders the importance of using food to increase morale and team energy. Once he got back in that game he'd spread the word. Mission rations shouldn't be met with sighs of surrender.

Lon went over his schedules with his own primary deputies. All held military backgrounds, and he allowed those who wished to wear their uniforms though they also had the option of adding a Three Worlds alteration or vest to them.

Ungerloggen was a dour but amazingly inventive man who'd been right-hand man to the right-hand man of the commander of the Majority forces of Orchin, Aldierra's largest continent. Crafty Drogon used to be a high-ranking clerk from a major communications center, coordinating messages from around the world. Tcherid dealt directly with the various city managers in keeping them informed of what was going on, when, and where. He could always find the right contact at the right time.

Lon had three lesser assistants on this shift as well as duplicates of their positions for other shifts. So far it was going well, but he wondered just how much was being leaked to the military… and beyond. Leaks were occurring like the one that revealed that women's shelter.

Lt. Twofence was a backup PA, on this later shift. He'd started out as Lina's reluctant assistant and had been eager to switch positions. Would he do such a thing?

Lon couldn't quite trust Tcherid, but he was damned good at his job. Lon was keeping his eye on him. As was Twofence. Lon chuckled to himself. A bit of envy was making Twofence a better employee and less of a suspect. Knowing that he was around, Tcherid was upping his game as well. Win-win.

They all joined the final meal shift to eat, and dutifully filled out the food surveys that Lina insisted everyone get. Londo wondered if just having something in front of them that they could consume and keep down was enough for most of the men. Still, he'd heard comments from some who'd been impressed that the Worlds were concerned about furnishing food they would like.

The men also like the improved conditions. Their camp was urban but composed of dozens of sleeping barrack tents pitched on various pavements. All had air filters, and filtered water served it as well. Mattresses were comfortable. Hot and cold drinks were always available, and there were usually a dozen or so men standing in line outside the medical tent.

They were so much better than when Three Worlds had first arrived on Aldierra. Back then a day didn't go by without a crew showing up drunk, or completely without the skills needed – or both. Fights had broken out regularly.

Now– not nearly so much. In fact, such events were rare exceptions. The men even seemed more energized when they worked. Better food? Or better attitudes?

There were entertainment tents for table, video and wrestling games, and one that they were trying out an old Aldierran comedy movie in. Lon had sent out queries for live comics to do some shows, like he'd heard they had on Earth during World War II and other conflicts. Good for morale.

Another tent allowed privacy for video meetings with therapists or friends and a quiet spot in which to meditate along with video instructions on how to do so. There was always a good number in the gym. The men settled down for the night, awaiting another day of hard work.

Londo usually made general announcements every day, televised on a screen in front of a camp's central tent for all to hear. The next morning he, Jae and Lina showed up at this camp in person for such. The men stood in front of them at attention or at least at rest, their air filters hugging their faces.

Lon took center stage. "I just want to say what a fine job you all are putting in. If you get a chance at lunch, we'll have a holographic map set up so you can see just what it is you're accomplishing and where we're going next.

"As you probably know by now, we're having to move more people out of their homes so we can make room for the animals and plants of this world to thrive. We're using Aldierran studies as to where those corridors should go, which also indicates which Houses need to move. Then we have to figure how to fit the moved Houses into areas where other Houses already exist. Minister?"

Jae stepped forward. "You've been at this for ten days now, and we're ready to hit the accelerator somewhere else. As usual, the Protector manages the massive work, because that's what he does, and then we'll need cleanup crews to come after him, because that's what he doesn't do."

The men liked that and laughed.

"So we're going to be repositioning you troops as well as bringing in more. If you want to switch jobs, now's the time to register to do so."

They watched a video enumerating needed job postings.

"We'll give you a half-hour to think about it as you get ready to begin work for the day, your last day here. If you change your mind later, just notify your chief and we'll see what we can do, but at that point we don't guarantee anything." Londo pointed at a minor assistant, who nodded and activated the cheery all-male vocal music camps liked to listen to in the morning. Jae and Lina ported out.

"Five minutes to input your decision," Londo told the crowd when the time came. "Make it now," he instructed. "We'll have you sorted out by lunchtime, and we'll move the camp at end of workday. Keep up the great work, everyone!"

– – –

FROM THERE JAE TRAVELED to attend to more covert duties. His fame made it impossible to operate secretly, so he utilized a work-around: creating false paths; utilizing a variant of his public self in these more private settings. Make himself to be a hypocrite.

As if a Feithi could be such.

It went against a nature that was DNA-deep, that his parents had subtly reinforced as they guided his growth.

But the Legion had taught him that some situations required subterfuge.

He was Feithi. He could handle it.

He'd developed new expressions: sly agreement, quiet co-plotting, harsh command, approval so that the recipient would add suggestions to their plot, even one that was "I'm not getting involved with this nonsense."

At age 16 he'd begun to drink occasionally.

It was all right. He could drink people under the table – a true espionage skill – while neutralizing the alcohol within his own body. He learned a wide range of drugs so he could recognize and deal with them even as they were ingested. He didn't like getting high, and it was rare that he let himself get drunk.

Here on Aldierra, as in so many places, alcohol and drugs were handed out regularly on a social and business basis. These people had mental problems. They faced ethical and social predicaments that often didn't percolate to the top of their consciousness.

In his job infiltrating as deeply as he could into secret military maneuverings, Jae found himself accepting these mind-altering substances. Mustn't make himself stand out farther than he already did. Had to look like one of them, not something apart. He was careful to neutralize everything while faking hits and boorishness... and stupidity.

It was the stupidity that truly got people to open up to him. Truths blurted so easily. True, sometimes those truths made no sense as the minds behind them blurred. And sometimes Jae could operate right in front of the person he was talking to, lean over and check their puter, then dig deeper while their personal security protocols were still open. They were too far gone to notice. Sometimes

Jae increased the efficacy of their drug to make his job easier, but he always carried a medical scanner so he wouldn't go too far.

Often he'd call up the person the next day and make a joke about how they both had gotten really wasted. "Haven't done that for a while," Jae would "confess."

Thus he sealed bonds that needed to be deepened so he could explore farther.

When he saw a promising situation, he contacted Mimik. Together they gathered a good bit of security secrets that allowed them deeper access into systems that should have thrown them out fifty levels ago.

The rot ran deep.

There were military plots, but also political ones and those of society. Men wanted to climb in social standing. They wanted the prestige. They wanted the wealth and the women. Better protection could be secured at higher ranks.

Jae didn't feel protected from himself in these types of dealings. They went against everything he'd been taught, been born to… or had taught to others. He was a hypocrite.

So he began to drink more than usual, and not neutralize it all the way.

He wanted the sweet safety alcohol brought, the haze that all was well.

It wasn't that much; just now and then. He needed it.

The Majority Army had ten major factions plotting to take over, plans firm enough and utilizing personnel important enough to be able to accomplish them when the time was right. There were hundreds of minor ones active, but many of them paused to discover which way Doomsday would fall.

Violets, Oranges, Golds, Blues, Reds… even the Yellow armies were determined to bring everything down when the right circumstances and personnel presented themselves. Luckily, only a handful presented a true danger.

But those dangers were frighteningly real.

Jae's staff took over most of his ecological duties. He told them he was working on something of more immediate concern, and they took him at his word because it was true enough. He showed up when his powers were required. He himself was still needed for public announcements, but they'd made the majority of those earlier in their term here on Aldierra. He hired good people from Earth and the AffSys to produce the instructional and inspirational videos he'd been making up to now.

He and Mimik often met along secret Legion lines of communication.

Luckily, Lina and Londo's schedules were more than packed. Jae having to call off meetings or even bowing out of their after-Tuesday-conference meetings, was seen as just a matter of Deadline looming and things to do.

True enough.

Still Jae drank.

– – –

THERE WAS A BREAK BETWEEN MEETINGS THIS MORNING, and Lina ran to grab some caffeine and whatever was left in the breakroom. Kanti was already there, emptying crumbs into a compost container, a cup of freshly made coffee in her other hand.

"Morning. What does your team think of the Plarmers' landsharing ideas?" Kanti asked.

Her team. Kanti meant her spirit team.

A physical shock ran through Lina. Good heavens. She hadn't talked with her angels today. Squinting her eyes at her own memories, she tried to recall the last time she had.

When had she meditated? Day before yesterday? Last week? What day was it anyway?

And what about Aldierra? Yes, the world liked to keep her thoughts fairly closed during this process, but had she ever run *silent?*

"To be truthful," Lina said slowly, "I haven't had the chance to ask them today. Been a little busy."

Kanti gave her a "what are you thinking?", tilted-head, raised eyebrow stare. "Remember what we pay you for, Speaker." A slight chuckle took the sting off the statement.

Lina smiled ruefully. "I'll get to that right away," she said, and sincerely meant it. Plus her angels were owed huge apologies. Aldierra deserved being groveled to. Derelict in her duties! In her relationship with the spirits who watched over her! Lina was appalled at herself.

A little voice in her head – surely not coming from her Higher Self – wondered if the stims were interfering in her abilities. It seemed a good possibility. A balance had to be struck.

She saw that the next meeting wound up with due haste and then began to make her way to quarters, where she could have a few minutes of peace, meditation and communication in the sheltered corner she had there.

Her earring beeped.

"Legion emergency," Tidda told her.

Lina needed to respond asap. Another Legion emergency? People's lives would be in immediate danger. A squad must arrive to their mission as quickly as they could. Lina ported.

CHAPTER

18

Lon lay there, counting the number of port calls he'd gotten during Lina's "night," which was only tangentially matching up with his at the moment. He stayed awake until Lina was back from the latest and in bed. Finally asleep. Though he'd been checking plats and plans when she'd hit the sack it had seemed to him that it took her some time to fall asleep. These days when Lon crawled into bed he immediately fell asleep, exhausted.

There they were: three calls, fifteen to twenty minutes apiece. Coming out of the hours scheduled for sleep, interrupting the dream cycle.

Lina wasn't around when he woke in the morning but his breakfast was prepared, waiting for him in a foodkeep. Likely Jae hadn't done that. Should he call Kanti or Tidda to get their opinion of how she was doing? Were they her mother? Was interference from him an overstepping of husbandly authority?

La chier avec ça.

"Stoan, it's got to stop," he told the Legion's commander from Aldierra as Lon came in from his morning rounds of the planet. He'd taken that time to work up his decision… and his nerve. "I'm sorry. At least during Lina's sleeping hours." He shared the notes with Stoan that he had made about the Legion ports.

Stoan studied it. He reached over to signal his own puter and compared calls with it.

"This is piled on top of her Aldierra duties," Londo reminded him. At least five times a day Lina was called upon to port to Sarastor in order to then port a Legion team to their emergency. That plus night ports?

"I can see where some of this might become too much of a stressor," Stoan said slowly. "But we are the Legion. It's awfully difficult to make sure that emergencies only come up during Lina's waking hours." Stoan's voice couldn't keep out the sarcasm.

"Not so difficult to figure out what time it is and not call. Nothing less than thermonuclear war," Londo told Stoan firmly as he took the padd back. "Do not call during her sleep periods. I don't want my wife dead by the time she's thirty."

It was by some miracle that Lon saw movement out of the corner of his eye and managed to grab the spray bottle. "Molly! No!" He gave a hard spritz, accelerating the stream with his parabreath. The cat galloped out of the room.

"That cat, on the other hand," he confided to Stoan, "is free to pass away. The sooner the better."

Stoan sighed and sat on the side of his desk, thinking. "It has become very handy," he told Londo, "to get a call and then be able to be on the spot immediately. Our teams and the worlds they service have become used to it."

"So let them get unused to it again," Lon said. "Give Wiley the task of figuring out porting top priority, so anyone can do it. If we only cancel night ports, I doubt if criminal activity will increase; they'll never know if the Legion will answer immediately or come through hyperspace."

"She'll get paid less. Fewer ports, less pay."

"Damn the money!" Londo hissed. "She doesn't care about it. I certainly don't."

"Let me think about this," Stoan finally decided. "Let me talk to Wiley, see what he thinks about being able to get on this porting thing. Last time we talked, he said that he had no idea whatsoever how something could travel without going through space, much less how the actual mechanics of it worked."

"Jae says he's almost got it figured out."

"So we'll use him when he does," Stoan said.

"Until then?" Londo asked.

"I don't know. Like I said, let me think about this. What if we just ask for a night port? She might be awake; if she's not, you could refuse for her..."

"Lina doesn't refuse if someone asks her for help."

"Listen, Londo, there are times when I need to get a message through to your wife – not a transportation message – and I can't even get her attention because

I'm not on some kind of priority list that they keep at that receptionist desk of hers."

"Not on The List?" Londo fished his notepadd out of his vest and opened it. "I can't believe that." He scrolled down, cross-referenced and read, then put the padd back in his vest, smiling a secret smile. "You're on the List. Don't worry about it."

"But they told me..."

"Lina's got a way of joking sometimes. You're on the list. Anything that you tell them gets sent immediately to whoever needs it. Any of us."

"But I have to argue with that secretary of yours..."

"Of Lina's. She has a couple handfuls of them. If you don't want to argue with them, then just leave a message and shut up. It'll get through. If it's an emergency, they'll bring her in to talk to you directly."

Stoan made a strangled noise deep in his throat. "She talks to my receptionist. She got some food recommendations from him last time she was here. I can't have her bribing my people..."

"I wouldn't call it a bribe, would you?" With a chuckle, Londo shook his head at Stoan. "She was just being friendly." He paused. "Was it vegetarian food? She's got a kitchen trying to replicate Terran and Sarastoran food for our people, using Aldierran produce."

"I couldn't say."

"Guess I'll find out soon enough. Rand— I don't believe I'm still using that name. No more night calls. *Starhart* out."

— — —

JAE WANDERED WITHIN THE WESTERN MALCONE MAJORITY ARMY OFFICES. He'd spent hours in the past few days, studying the lines of conspiracy that showed different secret operations. Sometimes those lines touched. Intersected. Sometimes an officer was playing two games at once.

There had been a few in such intersections that now showed as deceased. Someone had discovered the double agent and disposed of him. The ones who remained would be smarter.

Some might be working on private counter-plans of their own. By meeting them Jae could better determine their true motivations.

Captain Highhill had an impressive resume, and had demonstrated his loyalty to the Patriarch many times through the years. He was also involved in two possible insurrection groups.

"How are things going here?" Jae asked him from a corner of the M-Staff offices, his voice hushed. He raised one eyebrow and leaned in to give the proper body language of a conspirator.

"We are within upper percentiles of projections."

"I've spoken with Katurch," Jae murmured, citing an officer high in an insurrection cell, and Highhill's eyes widened. "How are things going *there*?"

Highhill's response came slowly. As Jae reinforced his information with what he'd already gathered from his research, Highhill confirmed more. Included data in a direction previous unnoticed.

Jae nodded and then upped his volume. "Very proud to see the Patriarch's plans moving along," he said so the closer people could hear. "The looming Deadline has interrupted far too many of his important projects."

When he left he went to other locations and planted an idea here, an idea there, along both insurrection lines.

By afternoon of the next day, Highhill was reported as having suffered an unfortunate medical event.

Jae read the news on his monitors and reached for a drink.

– – –

LINA RECALLED HOW SHE'D PULLED all-nighters in college. Easy-peasy. It had been just a few years ago. Her now being in her mid-twenties didn't mean she'd achieved geezer-hood. She could do this.

And she had these wondrous stims. Her ankles had been swollen yesterday but she'd switched drug types and today they were just fine. She was a bit constipated though. The last time she'd tried to sleep she'd been surprised. Usually when stims gave out, so did she. Bonk. Out like a light. Whenever it was she'd last lay down – when had that been? Hard to think – it had taken effort to relax enough to let sleep take over.

But this new kind seemed to work. There was another type waiting in her office for when these started to give her trouble.

As she always did, she triggered a testing program she'd found. All she had to do was roll her eyes left, then right at its camera, and then do some finger motions. It gave a pleasant chime; her mind was clear.

She didn't know what she'd do if it told her it wasn't.

A couple cleansing breaths focused her enough to concentrate on the crisis at hand. She coordinated the entire northeast quadrant of Orchin. Today the people there had decided to go crazy en masse. Reports were coming in about fake news that had stirred them up. Were they so stupid that they believed it? Wouldn't they double-check info like this?

Wicker and Batt alerted their entire staffs and contacts to the problem. Lina gave interviews and insisted that Jae stop whatever it was he was doing to reassure the public. Londo dragged himself out of bed to do some as well, and then flew off to kick some common sense into Orchiners. Orchinites. Whatever. Lina couldn't think what they were called.

And she couldn't hear her guides. Guides didn't like the stims. There were no clinical trials on psychics who used stims to determine why she couldn't operate as such. Likely the stims lowered her vibrations, Lina reasoned, thought she wasn't precisely sure what "vibrations" meant from a medical point of view. It would be a temporary thing, she reassured herself.

Whenever the stims stopped, her full psychic abilities should reappear. Until then she'd have to come up with work-arounds.

When was the last time she'd meditated? When was the last time she'd had time to do so?

This crisis would have to end at some point and she'd hit the sack and not use stims for a long, long time. She'd be able to talk to her guides and Aldierra again.

CHAPTER

19

An uneasy ocean held the ten small ships, crammed with equipment of Aldierran, Sarastoran and Terran make. Wind whipping his hair, Jae squinted at the next boat over, and the one beyond it, everyone in position.

Surely someone else could have done this. He had so many important things to do.

Of course many cameras focused on him. Fortified by a modest drink beforehand, Jae turned to them with a concerned smile and welcomed the home audience. "This week high school and college students will be assisting the efforts to monitor antarctic conditions. Yusuf Joshi is using his powers, as he has for weeks, to lower temperatures at the Aldierran poles. We're running experiments today to see how he can best do this: by concentrating power on a small area, or by spreading it out over a larger area, which will have less immediate effect. We'll also be testing whether spot-placing icebergs into the ocean works better at lowering temperature than cooling the air."

Wiley checked in by monitor from one of the ships, looking a bit greener than his usual blue. "I think I'll use my Array to monitor from above the ship," he told Jae.

"I can get a medic over there."

Wiley rolled his eyes. In unison. "I waited too long to see them. Their cures will kick in in a little while. I'll use that time to take some atmospheric readings."

As if all the lacy antennas decorating the ships weren't doing that already. Plus Jae could see sparkles in the air, indications of meteorological equipment flitting about. Beneath them sensors were keeping track of ocean depths.

Just last night Wiley had decided he needed to be assigned Temporary Additional Duty. He and Stoan had discussed it and come up with a compromise: two of Wiley's minds would remain connected to sensory ports in Lab 1-A at Legion HQ, and the other three would come with Wiley's body to Aldierra.

Wiley had a way of letting his minds sleep in rotation, so this way at least one mind at Legion HQ would always be on duty. In case of emergency, of course, he could reconnect to 1-A's resources.

Lina had given Wiley a tent in their compound. He'd arranged to share one of the major labs in Plegerit. He'd brought two of his assistants with him (also housed in the compound) and had hired three Aldierrans for the same type of positions.

Lina had received permission through Legion Subcommander Andri to begin to bring in Legion-affiliated medics as well as guards. Jae wasn't sure where they were housed, but he knew that before their schedule finished the job of releasing Aldierra from weather control, there'd be a lot more paras on Aldierra helping out, many of them at least partially Legion, and they'd need guards specifically trained for para needs. Lon's branch was furnishing them with mission specifics and equipment.

So that panic that rose again and again in his guts should be satisfied and go away. Jae told it so, even as he tamped it down yet again. Wiley in person was a huge measure of more help. So were the occasional shots of liquor, which he neutralized in his body before going on duty. Usually.

Aldierra would not fall. Jae clenched his eyes shut and gritted his teeth. Not while he had a breath in his body left would Aldierra lose this fight!

But damn, he was here for fluff news when he should be working on his undercover project. Lupoff and such cohorts could so easily bring this whole thing down. Jae had trained his staff to take over in these water-related cases that didn't involve his powers. Jae wasn't like Lon, needed for physical labor no one else could do. All he was here for today was the cameras. PR.

Patience, Jae-Jae, Mama's voice murmured in his ear. *Patience.*

Jae forced himself to relax. He'd been taught by so many psychiatrists over the years to do so. Now he chatted with the journalists on board primarily utilizing Expression #1, and then went around to contact the research teams. Men on the *Honor Tide* were demonstrating control panels and monitor data to teen students, who listened closely.

After a while Jae flew over to the next ship, which was "manned" by all-female researchers and students. Those students had been given intensive condensed lessons in what needed to be done, and why. Some Sarastoran teens were mixed in with the Aldierrans, as were two Terran ones. On top of everything, the offworlders had had to learn the language. But in addition to helping gather this valuable information, they were also setting an example to the women of this world.

Jae stopped to converse with some of the Aldierran women and girls. They rehearsed how they'd be interviewed, and then actually did so in front of cameras, where they came off as confident in their skills. By the end of this mission they'd be true experts.

"Where do you want me now?" Yusuf swooped in on the flying platform that he'd been using these past weeks. He wore a large, flapping overcoat which mainly protected him from wind and rain, though his hair was coated with frost.

Jae and he peered at a map of the area as Wiley joined them. Finally they decided to begin with the construction of a good-sized iceberg.

"Might take over an hour," Yusuf warned. "Something this big…"

"It will give us solid results," Wiley said.

Jae nodded. "Let's get you started then."

— — —

LON STOPPED WHAT HE WAS DOING and flew off as fast as he could. He disregarded his own rules about flying at such speeds within atmosphere.

Lina was screaming.

He left a divot in the ground under their tent with his landing, and ran in. She was writhing in bed, screaming with her eyes clamped shut, and when he leapt to her, to hold her in his arms, she didn't awaken.

"Lina! Lina!" He reached with his mind only to find chaos.

"Lina, I'm here! Wake up. Wake up!"

Delicately he probed her mind until he found her, cowering deep inside herself. Fear. Desperation.

"I'm here, *chérie*. Here I am."

At last she recognized him, and began to wake. His arms enclosed her. "Shh. Shh. I'm here. Here is safe. Here is home."

Her entire body vibrated with shivers.

"Let me call the medics."

"No. No!" She shook her head as she inhaled deeply, then deeply again. "It's just nerves. Things I saw. The last few days have been rough. The Gray Army and the mountain Houses of Limbernie. Ghastly. I'll call Carrie."

Pink blotched her cheeks and lips, atop pasty skin. Her eyes were shadowed and puffy. "Are you sure?"

"Valiant!" They could both hear the call from his earring. "We need you back here. Now!"

No. Lina was more important.

She took another shuddering breath and shook her head. "You go. I'll be okay. I'll call Carrie right away."

He disagreed but she convinced him. As he rose from the bed to depart, she said, "I love you. So much."

"So do I, kitten. You call Carrie right now, *tu comprends*?"

Lina meekly nodded, still looking like hell, but there was another emergency so he left.

— — —

IN HER OFFICE, Lina wrinkled her nose as she tried to hear the Limbernie civil governor on the screen. "Sorry," she finally had to tell him. "Give me a second."

Again – for the fourth time – she told the family tent's enviro controls to switch on the noise dampers. This time she added a gesture that meant, "no foolin'," and hoped that would work.

Jae was banging away on his rialla in the tent's music section. It seemed he was using every subinstrument the percussion provided, and at top volume. Lina hoped he had earplugs in. He'd cancelled her previous requests for lowering volume, negated her command for dampers.

He was in a mood. He was drunk. He was displeased with something and wanted the world to know.

Well, he had a shrink who could help him while Lina had critical problems facing her from every direction. Lon was on the other side of the world this afternoon but she had no doubts that at some level he could hear the racket. Likely he could smell the alcohol as well.

Before they'd married Jae had assured her that he wouldn't get drunk. Had that been a promise?

With her on so many stims, could she demand such a promise from him?

After a blessed moment of peace, the pounding began again. Again Lina apologized to Governor Stonyford and begged for four minutes. In that time she got on the interstellar Internet, ordered a wireframe soundproofing igloo, and ported it in.

The cats, who had all gathered in her office tent, breathed their own feline sighs of relief as Lina quickly released the system into place so it created a dome outlined in circuit systems inside her tent, and switched it on. Blessed silence reigned.

"Sorry about that," she told Stonyford as Obi and Bran climbed onto her lap. "We're having… construction problems here."

The governor nodded understandingly.

– – –

"NEVER GO AFTER THE MAJOR PLAYER," Mimik explained to Jae in his office, late at night.

She was dressed as Iteov Battletine, the anonymous Green Army soldier who on occasion visited the Starhart compound.

She laid out her materials before Jae. "We want Kettite and his operations for sure," she told him. "Here's his aide. In-Donez–" she tapped on the image of a middle-aged Aldierran, pert and rather blank-eyed in his uniform –

"accompanies the Black Box wherever Kettite goes. It holds the codes and communication outlets for the most destructive weaponry the Green Army possesses."

"He's in the background," Jae mused.

"But always there. Unobtrusive." Another series of determined taps. "He's our target for impersonation."

They discussed pros and cons. Escape routes to be used if needed.

"And what if something goes wrong?" Jae asked her.

"They won't."

"Famous last words." Jae scratched his upper chest. "I will begin to work on something after we return from Earth this afternoon. It's from one of Wiley's recent inventions. I think I can reprogram it to suit our needs."

Battletine's mouth twisted. "I look forward to seeing what you can come up with," she told the Legionnaire. "But I hope you don't mind if I come up with some ideas of my own. I've been in the disguise business longer than you've been a Team Leader."

"Absolutely." Jae's eyes looked haunted. "We may have to bring Wiley in on this. I don't want you harmed. And I want this operation to be a success. Aldierra must *not* die."

– – –

AMID THE NOISE AND CROWD that the convention center's security guards kept from them, Londo checked his watch. "Not to hurry you, Wiley, but you know our schedules are pretty crammed these days. As long as we're on Earth I should hit Starhaven to check on the work there, and then go to Montreal to see what the new HQ needs. The plans haven't been finalized yet, even though we broke ground on the project two weeks ago. Do you really need me here?"

"Yes, to explain some of the tech. If you would."

Wiley had provided them with so much help in this and many other matters. He deserved a little treat now and then. Now he crouched to examine the tires of the car on the platform next to him. A ceiling filled with spectacular lighting –

for Earth – cast purple and blue shadows over them, so dramatic in contrast with bright highlights.

"Las Vegas," he murmured to himself.

"Yes, famous for glitz and glamor," Lon told him. He checked the signage. "This is a hybrid, gas and electric, but it says it can set speed records." He paused to admire the model. "Looks good, too, for a hybrid." Lon looked around. "Lina needs a new car. Her old one is *skurny prax*. Ancient *skurny prax*."

"Maybe you can find something suitable here," Wiley suggested as he made notes of the car's structure. For a moment, glowing blue lines traced the real-world supports, and red mapped the electrical systems. They disappeared into the rings that wrapped around each of his fingers.

Wiley had a thing for various methods of transport. Once he'd discovered Earth's recent rapid technological growth in that area – still so far from where the AffSys stood – he'd been spending much of what spare time he had checking out every bit of Terran workmanship that contained wheels. He stood and took stock of the hall, with its attention-grabbing displays, flashing lights, and barely-clothed female models. "Perhaps over there," he pointed.

Lon glanced all around the show, beyond barriers that would have blocked others' views. Nice car over there. Near it was a car that practically announced, "Here is a Starhart." A car that Lina might–

He caught his breath. "Is that–" He hurried over to the other car he'd just spotted, not fast enough to knock over norms, but fast enough. "It's a Pagani Drago 888," he breathed.

The blue-black car crouched on its platform, barely reflecting any of the glitter. A garish red bow had the affrontery to sit on its sleek hood. Lon peered inside the windows. At the engine. In the trunk and behind the front seats.

"It's… not just a Drago 888," he told Wiley when the Legionnaire arrived, "it's *the* Drago 888. The 888 DLX. Dragonlord's main vehicle. It was totaled about seven years ago. Wiley, I *lusted* over this thing. Dreamed about it. Who restored it?"

This was perfect. He'd had a poster of it on his bedroom wall in his Legion apartment up until a couple years ago. When he'd been in his teens he must have talked about it nonstop, even to his Legion cohorts. There was no way… "Or is it a copy? It's an excellent one."

Suddenly black balloons waterfalled from the ceiling, followed by scads of colorful confetti.

Then the auditorium's sound system began to play "Happy Birthday."

People crowded in to see. Lina and Jae ported in. So did Hal, using ParaNet systems. And Mama Ruth and Papa Mike. And Else.

A group of caterers rolled in a cake that must have been three feet high with a big, rainbow "30" on its top. Behind them were carts carrying tiers of matching cupcakes in case the crowd devoured the main offering.

"My birthday's not until next week," Lon managed to say before Lina caught him in a hug and kiss, followed by Jae.

"As if we could keep a secret any longer," Jae laughed at him. Hal clapped him on the back.

A Drago… 888… Lon checked the car closer. LSX, not DLX. LS for Londo Starhart.

This was his. His dream car. He had never driven a car before, but by god he was going to learn. And learn combat defensive driving, yeah. That would impress. It was going to be a *great* year! But now he had to design a garage good enough to house it. More work.

He couldn't wait!

— — —

THE NIGHT WAS STILL inside most tents of the compound. Lina had had to purchase more stims. She'd planned for the trip to Earth and Lon's party – oh, that had been such a success! Londo had really been surprised – but not for the three emergencies that bookended it. She was exhausted. Couldn't use the clinics she'd already bought from; her paper trail was likely fairly blatant because of her notoriety. Had to research to find new sources. One place had a new kind of stim. Not much info on it, but stims were pretty standard, weren't they? A different type meant that she didn't have to put up with the side effects that were cropping up faster and faster as she switched the usual kind.

Playing her flute in "wake me up" mode only worked a couple times a day. Maybe three if she were lucky. She had to make sure not to play it around HQ, as people's sleep periods were diverse and she didn't want to wake anyone in the affected area. As for her own sleep period, it was getting harder and harder to sleep when she had actual time to do so. Harder to hide these things from Lon and Jae, or her bodyguards.

But at least she was getting important things done by being awake.

CHAPTER

20

She accomplished her orders and shut them out of her thoughts before Chim's arrival time. They had agreed to begin immediate planning of duty stations for the upcoming weather switchover. Chim was actually out of her regular uniform and relaxing in a loose-fitting kurta along the same lines as Lina's costume. This was a pretty blue pattern and covered her up without being the skintight fashion that was usual Legion costuming.

They discussed possibilities and supply needs in front of geographical and computer-predictive maps of the various continents. Chim pointed out where the members of her team could best be utilized.

"We'll need to place the extra medics," Lina began to explain.

AUNT LIE! AUNT LIE!!!

The volume and power nearly knocked both back.

Drew, where are you? Lina asked even as she said aloud, "Computer, give me the location of–" She hesitated a moment as she reached out in her mind. "Got it."

Both she and Chim appeared in a flat city. Very flat. It was one of those floating cities. Lina whirled around, searching–

"Aunt Lie!" Her nephew's voice cracked in its shout. He pointed ahead even as he ran across a plaza. "There! There! Get Uncle Lon!"

"What–?"

Drew barely bothered to point out the offender behind himself as he reached a murky canal's edge. "That man just threw in a baby! A baby!"

With that Drew dove into the mess.

Chim darted into the air to view the water from above briefly before diving after him.

Londo! Please hurry!* Lina called.

But wherever he was, Lon was carrying a partial building. He'd need to set it down somewhere before he could come.

Again and again both Chim and Drew's heads appeared above water as they gasped for breath.

"Medics needed!" Lina called on her comm line. She couldn't get a sense of where the tiny life was.

The blare of emergency vehicles combined with shouts of dozens of bystanders as they tried to help from the banks. "I think it went in there!" "No, there!"

After ten minutes Lina ordered her nephew and friend out. Chim helped haul Drew up as he swiped at his clenched eyes. Chim's were redly swollen, streaming, and squinting as well. Without her Legion uniform, she'd had no protection from the elements.

"Polluted water," Lina instructed the medics, who swung to their jobs. Quickly they fastened eye irrigation units to the two and began to check for other injuries.

Londo swooped down from the sky. Lina pointed at the canal. "Someone threw in a baby," she reported. "It's been… too long."

He gave a pained look and dove in. Within only a few moments he emerged from some few hundred feet further down than the would-be rescuers had looked. Lina had a small blanket to receive the poor little corpse.

"No chance of revival," he reported unnecessarily even as he looked up.

"I know. She might already have been dead before he tossed her in." Lina rubbed his back and neck as he nodded in sorrow.

A police vehicle approached and stopped. "We got him," an officer told them. "He'll be at Johency central jail, awaiting you."

His partner added, "Many people helped in the search. Houses together, Protector. Houses together."

Lon nodded and tried to give a small smile of thanks to the man who had repeated the call that was becoming so prevalent. They needed every bit of good news they could find. Then he saw to Chim and Drew.

"How you doing, kid?" he asked around the ring of medics.

"He's doing like a hero, Lon," Chim replied from behind her own slathering of medical equipment. "Dove in immediately. Didn't stop to think. I bet you could hear his call back on Tishan, if there was anyone tuned in. Who is this?"

"My nephew," Lina told her. "My wonderful, brave nephew, Drew."

"He's been studying the psychic stuff on TV," Lon told them.

It was impossible for Drew to talk. He'd swallowed some of the muck, and the medics were bringing it back up as carefully as possible. It didn't help that he was bawling.

"That will help flush the eyes," one medic commented helpfully.

– – –

"A BABY! She was just a baby!" Drew exclaimed back at their tent. The rings around his eyes had turned purple, along with circles around either side of his mouth and nostrils. "Why? Why?"

"Because some people are just turds," Lon told the damp teenager. Both had been through showers.

Chim sat in a chair, wrapped in a dry, fuzzy robe as she sipped tea thoughtfully, a Legion medic hovering behind her with instruments. Her face bore similar chemical markings to Drew's. "And some people are blessedly different," she mused. "How long have you been telepathic, Drew?"

Drew's confused expression changed to confusion of a different flavor. "What?"

Another medic disconnected monitoring equipment from his arm. One of Lina's Aldierran psychic readers, schooled on the Three Worlds videos, sat nearby in a thoughtful pose, as if she were testing the vibrations of the area. Three of Lina's, plus one of someone else's, guard squad had taken equidistant positions, now silently watching a member of the cleaning crew dusting around the tent's walls, accompanied by a small robot. Two of Wiley's crew peeked in, saw what was going on, then hurriedly backed out.

"We heard you," Lina explained to Drew. "You yelling at top volume."

Chim shook her head. "Very interesting development. They'll want to see you on Tishan."

"What, they want to dissect him? Study him?"

Chim shrugged as she made a face. "They won't do that with you people as relatives. Not overtly at any rate. No, he needs to be trained. They always told me that I could be dangerous unless I could control myself. Now I think… Well I think they like to study people for their own purposes." She glanced at Lina's shocked look. "Not vivisection, at any rate."

Lon looked at her with one raised eyebrow, and she caught his thought. Jae was asleep. During all this. The raised eyebrow meant: *drunk*. Not again.

Lina took in the expressions of everyone in her dining room. Of course the table was now set with morning snacks and pick-me-ups. There were company and personnel here; she had social protocols in place.

"Okay," she decided. "You're going to be all right," she repeated to her nephew. "You too." To Chim. "And you're all going to talk to your favorite therapists about dead… babies. Oh shit, dead babies. I'm so proud of you, Drew. We'll call your parents later. You can talk with them. It's past midnight there; we'll let them sleep. I've already notified your probation officers."

But Lon was rubbing his nose. "You got this from the video courses, Drew?"

"Well, yeah. I guess."

"I want to see those," Chim said. "I've glanced at them, but…" She heaved a sigh. "I need to talk with Jae when he wakes up. And you." She pointed at the startled psychic. Then she targeted Drew in her gaze. "You should go to Tishan. Within the next few days."

"Drew is under probation," Londo informed her. "He finishes it as ordered. He's learning all manner of things. One of which we witnessed today. It really was powerful, Drew. We will discuss this with his parents." He took a moment to think. "You could be in on that discussion," he granted Chim.

"I insist on it."

"Tishan…" Drew's eyes moved so he could check Lina's reaction.

"Let's just say that Chim here said it could be a dangerous place," Lina told him.

"Not that dangerous," the ex-Legion commander told him. "Not like Aldierra, and not for someone your age, someone with your connections. Unless you're really stupid."

"I'm not stupid!" Drew exclaimed.

Chim laughed. "Kinda got that idea. You've surrounded yourself," she took in the immediate group, including herself, with her gesture, "with people more intelligent than average. That bodes well."

— — —

WHEN HAD SHE LAST MEDITATED? When had she last talked with her guides?

Could she have saved that baby this morning if she'd been more on her game?

Was the silence from Aldierra because the world was keeping things close to her vest, or because Lina's frequency was so low because of all this endless work and all the stims, that she couldn't match frequencies with her to hear her?

"I'm sorry; I'm sorry," she told her guides sincerely, knowing they could hear her even when she couldn't hear them.

What was a Speaker for the Three Worlds if she couldn't Speak?

At least she could still port. It took effort to focus though. Focus on the clairvoyance involved, trying to picture the landing point in a way that she could just switch the perception so the porting was accomplished.

Even if Lon hadn't been carrying a building, she couldn't have ported him in time. She'd been too shocked. Too out of tune to focus.

She should have been able to stretch her mind to reach outside the box, outside the bonds of accepted science. Space and time had no true meaning. They were just there to help humans deal with the matrix we'd all helped plan, the matrix called The Universe.

Right?

Would trying to reason it out make it more difficult to do it? Once Lina could port, it was just as natural as breathing. She didn't consider the mechanics of lungs and gas exchange in order to take a breath. Her biofiltering was a bit of a trick, but she only had to do that with interstellar ports and she mostly left it up to the places she ported to to consider what they'd let in. Still…

What if her ability to port or biofilter conked out in the middle of biofiltering? Or even just the port? Someone would be stuck in hyperspace or wherever it was – forever. Or she'd loose a plague on an unsuspecting world.

She'd have to put out feelers about cutting down the number of those ports until things calmed down and she could regain her psychic footing. At least it seemed as if things in the AffSys were cooling down. The Legion hardly called her any more.

Oh– Was it just at night they did so?

In the meantime she'd try to fake her way through. She could claim she was talking with her guides and such. Who would contradict her?

Ugh. Lying.

Ah, maybe she could go through the psychic groups she'd set up. Ask them for their opinions, what their guides were telling them. If what they said made sense, she'd agree.

What if they were wrong?

Tarot. She had cards of her own she could use. And dowsing or divining rods and a pendulum. They could bring messages through, though not clearly or not as quickly as direct communication. Return to the basics. Old school.

It was a plan.

Now: when had she last slept?

CHAPTER

21

L ina looked up as Kanti strolled into the room. Was it time for a meeting? If so, she'd missed it on her schedule.

She began to sweep the cards in front of her off her desk, but stopped. She was getting at something here. "Just a moment," she told Kanti, and continued the spread.

It hadn't been all that long since she'd last used tarot, but it seemed she was exercising stiff joints as she puzzled out the card meanings as they pertained to this. Tarot was about opening the mind to possibilities it hadn't considered, not locking it into book definitions.

She tried to ignore Kanti looking over her shoulder.

Finally Lina tapped on the warning card, with Strength under it. Ariel, an angel associated with Nature, was depicted as the main Strength figure. The King of Pentacles sat as its adversary. "More sabotage, this time in Reyda," she announced. "Definitely Lupoff's energy behind it. Let me grab my dowsing rods. Kanti, could you stand beside me instead of behind?"

Lina had Kanti align her foot with hers so they touched. Kanti then had to state that she gave her body permission to work with Lina's in this.

Lina brought up a map of the continent of Reyda and displayed it on her desktop. As Kanti ran a straightedge on it from top to bottom, Lina watched the two metal rods she held. Now and then they suddenly splayed out.

"Computer, note latitude," Lina instructed.

Then they did it left to right on the map. "Note longitude," Lina said as the rods reacted.

When Lina released Kanti, the computer coordinated both axes to show spots on the map. Lina tapped them. "We'll have Jae and Lon investigate immediately."

Kanti was looking at her like she was nuts. "Since when–"

"You cannot tell either of them." Lina's voice was absolute. "I haven't been sleeping lately."

"You've been taking stims," Kanti accused. "I've seen your log-ins on the schedule. No human could possibly keep that–"

"Just a few stims. Only when it was necessary. I'm following directions and switching between varieties so I don't get the side effects, but–"

"But you can't sleep."

Kanti's features were sour and accusatory.

"Occasionally I'm out of touch with things." Lina made gestures toward what might be ethereal forces. "I'm making sure I have back-up systems."

Kanti sat in a chair with a thump. "So the Speaker can no longer Speak."

Lina shrugged. "We've been training our own psychic circles. You've seen. And I have these."

Kanti looked at the colorful cards and the metal rods.

"What makes you think I won't tell the Boys?"

Lina stuck out her jaw thoughtfully. "Because it hasn't reached emergency yet? Because we just hired a slew of new personnel who will potentially free up my time so I can sleep now and then?"

"Personnel who haven't been fully trained." Kanti's voice was sour.

"They will be."

"But in the meantime…"

"In the meantime we have these." Lina tapped the rods.

Kanti could hear the beep in Lina's ear as easily as she.

"Problem in Reyda," Tidda's voice reported.

"Speak of the devil. Give me the location," Lina told her, signaled the guard unit for that region, and ported out – at least that was still working – before Kanti could argue with her.

– – –

DARN IT, ALL THOSE STIMS made Lina's back prickle and strain, even though the three of them were now on Earth. Clean air; lush greenery considering the cool season. She should be ecstatic and relaxed.

She'd managed a good four and a half hours of sleep last night, though not without problems falling asleep. She'd laid awake for far too long, gotten up to do some work since she was awake, and then returned to bed. Rinse and repeat a few more times before the four and a half hours kicked in. Maybe it had been three.

Sending Wiley back to Sarastor for a day so he could coordinate some kind of equipment system for the Legion, seemed more difficult than usual.

The more stims she took, the more tired she was. Were they interfering with her sleep? That made no sense. She really should investigate more different types of stims. Maybe that medical school on Lennox could help. She'd been dealing with them about sending people to Aldierra to complete medical residencies there.

Jae and Lon had finished meeting with province building officials at the site for the main Three Worlds HQ in Montreal. A couple of local mayors and such had been there as well. Three Worlds would shift traffic patterns and upset general living conditions for the area. She'd check in there once there was more to see besides a few stakes and strings. This morning she'd been smoothing out some problems at the call center before porting south.

Lon took off on a quick trip to gather Earth equipment. As he collected it he was double checking that the Terran electrical connectors he'd managed to get Sarastor wiring to accept, were enough to service it and the, well, warehouse of supplies that had been unloaded here, ready for a different kind of travel.

A good-sized Signet Starlines cargo ship materialized from hyperspace into the spot allotted for it at Richmond International Airport.

Jae stared at the logo on its side. "How did you arrange that?" he asked her. "I thought Wiley handled our interstellar transports."

Lon landed with a largish box in hand in time to check it out as well. A cargo hatch opened and began to disgorge ship-loaders that took positions nearby.

Rows of forty-foot metal shipping containers filled with merchant goods had been parked nearby to join the Starharts' equipment.

Ship personnel emerged to check and calibrate.

"Wiley transports personnel whom he either recommended for the project, or who are doing studies about it that interest him," Lina explained to Jae. "That's an awful lot of people. I think even his finances will be strained if he keeps up this kind of thing for any length of time." She nodded toward the ship, rather stunned by the size of it. "I got Dari and her son out of a kidnapping situation once. It was back when you had arrested me."

"Oh yeah." The far-off look in Jae's eyes registered. It probably reflected how angry he'd been that she'd slipped her confinement orders when she was under his command just before the Sarastoran Invasion.

Lon just sucked on the inside of his cheeks, considering. "She gives us a discount," he surmised.

"A massive one. It's taken quite a load off my schedule. She's been ferrying non-Wiley personnel between Sarastor and Aldierra, and on occasion has sent a small ship here."

Now this very much larger one sat expectantly on the tarmac.

"She's also beginning to deal with Terran goods. This one is already loaded from Sarastor, for Aldierra. We're still trying to figure what the AffSys will allow Earth to take. Prime Directive and such. She consented to make a more roundabout route this time for us, and to try some Terran merchandise to see what the market wants, on both Aldierra and Sarastor."

From Richmond it wasn't far – just a nanosecond, if that – to Fort Gregg-Adams at the Naval Culinary Specialist School she'd researched. Its kitchens were massive and varied, dealing in main courses to breads to desserts to… anything edible. They specialized in preparing their troops to deal with the eating needs of thousands at a time, in a way that garnered genuine tastebud enthusiasm.

The three took turns shaking the hands of ten Naval officers who'd volunteered for this duty.

"We're all up to speed on the language," Chief Warrant Officer Sangretti assured them as the group stood in front of their luggage. "We've been shown your 'Aldierra is violent' speech, sir," he added to Lon.

"It's famous," Jae put in. "And by now it's a very thorough orientation."

Lon gave a momentary grimace of irritation. "*Ch'tedi*, it *is* a violent place. A little less polluted than it was when we arrived, but still far from pristine. Your quarters and workspace on Aldierra will provide you clean atmosphere and water."

Sangretti nodded, as well as the culinary specialists next to him. "We'll take care of the rest. We are bringing a large shipment of food to counteract the amount we'll be eating and cooking while we're there. We were told not to put Aldierra in a deficit, no matter how small."

Lon nodded. "Plus appearances are everything. The people will see that you're not stealing from the planetary supplies. Standard onboard quarantine will make all your foodstuffs safe within a few hours of hyperspace travel."

"They've had a few Aldierran foods to experiment with for three weeks now, the common basics," Lina told her husbands. She sighed and shook her head. "It sounds so silly, to have you all come out to help, but–"

"Food is what keeps the forces working," one of the specialists blurted.

"It's of primary importance," another said. "Food is energy. Food is health. Eating food forms comradery."

"I like that," Jae said.

Lina had to concede. This was her idea after all. "We've been having food contests, but that's been one food at a time. It's not enough of a complete diet with which to feed our own troops. And despite us trying to drill it into them, all too many of our mess halls aren't up to cleanliness code. Too many people are literally falling ill to bad practices."

Sangretti laughed. "We'll have your people up and full-on running in sanitary conditions within two months. Our training is seven weeks. We'll be working with your established culinary sections to bring them up to speed even as they bring us up to theirs. It will be an… enlightening experience."

"I hope it will get our people looking forward to mealtime," Lon said. "I've been hearing whispers of mutiny because of the workload, even though Three Worlds is starting to be known as the place whose workers get the best meals."

Lina ported them all to Richmond, where the military personnel boggled at the spaceship. Within moments though, they began to attend to their duties.

Jae trotted off with some of the specialists to doublecheck the food supplies and their needs. The spaceship would have industrial foodkeeps, which needed special connections with which to handle interstellar quarantine. There were also scores of individual equipment and battleship crowd-sized food prep machinery to deal with. Londo loaded it all on the ships, the two double-checked everything, and then a small mechanical army began to load Dari's merchandise containers for their nine-day journey. The specialists and a portion of the personal equipment they felt they could not live without for those days, Lina ported directly to their new quarters on Aldierra.

Lon brushed some equipment grease from his hands. Behind him trucks growled into position as robotic cranes tended to the ordinary loading. "Rest of the day here is small jobs," he said. "I've got at least ten stops to make. And I want to check on my car, make sure it's comfortable where it is. Give it a few kisses. Jae, can I give you a lift?"

"I'll take the flitter." The new Starhart vehicle also sat on the tarmac. "There are some people in South Africa whom I'd like to speak with. And one in India. I'm arranging videos and conferences."

Lon nodded and looked at Lina. "You're not too tired? I think we should stay here tonight at Starhaven. Get some rest before going back."

"That sounds fine. I am a little tired. I was going to–"

"You text me what you need and I'll do it. You go rest. Take it easy. Watch some *Star Trek*." He gave her a lingering look.

Lina wondered if he could see how tired she was. She tried to brighten up for him.

"I might phone some people," she told him. "I'm still not sure we have some of our emergency housing units staffed right, and we're looking into a major medical need in the middle of the Orchin grasslands. I told some people they might hear from me today."

With all that decided, they took off to their various destinations.

— — —

LINA SHOULD BE ENJOYING being home after all this time, but it was all she could do to make those calls. When had her energy deserted her?

Lon had shooed the construction crews out of Starhaven so they could sleep there tonight, in their future residence. Lina was able to walk around, see the improvement since the last time she was here. She tried to imagine what it would be like when it was finished, but couldn't summon the wherewithal to do so.

She brought in the cats so they could get used to the changes and maybe wouldn't be so spooked when they all moved here for good. Litterboxes, cages, food… These new purchases would be needed here as well as Aldierra. She'd have to get some for Sarastor eventually.

Port port port. She should be thankful she could still do that. She was.

She should have taken a few minutes to admire the fading autumnal mountain view and blue Terran sky while the sun was still up. She should peek to see if maybe the moon was up with her familiar moon face. See the stars. Smell the air and the green forest all around.

Instead she paced the house. Her legs seemed to move on their own accord, which was a good thing. Without that, she'd likely have stood in one place and stared at an unfinished wall. Londo was gone somewhere, to his people in Montreal or maybe the ParaNet. Lina couldn't recall. She couldn't recall so many things these days.

There was something she should do, but she couldn't figure out what it was.

Jae sprawled across a sofa in front of a floating screen, watching some droning sports show from Sarastor. He was drunk. He'd been drunk an awful lot lately. Should she complain? After all, here she was secretly on stims. Pot shouldn't call kettle… something.

"Sit down," Jae slurred. "Sit by me."

That much she could do. She leaned into his shoulder and prayed for sleep to come. As usual, it didn't.

Had she done her stim brain check today? She couldn't recall.

Instead Lina rose to stalk the room. Jae snored lightly, spreading across the sofa. Ember crawled to his side and assumed a compact sleep position there. Moosie took up residence on the back of the sofa. Obi and Bran-Bran confiscated the warm spot where Lina had been.

Pacing didn't help. She didn't feel sleepy. Instead Lina decided to hike. Moving was the only choice she could make any more. She began at the lower level of the western wing and dragged her swollen feet (oh no, another side-effect) across the house's interior acreage until she came to the eastern wing. Then she hefted herself up the stairs, up to the family room where Jae was.

No, not sleepy at all. Exhausted; not sleepy. Why did there have to be a difference? But Jae was truly out.

A half-empty cocktail glass of amber liquid sat next to him on a side table.

Booze made Lina sleepy.

Of course.

But she was determined to sleep in their bed. That's what beds were for.

It was too much confusing trouble to port Jae to the bedroom, so she went alone by foot. Once there she took the glass, wrinkled her nose at it, and downed it. Three swallows. Ugh. How could he stand that stuff?

She crawled expectantly into bed.

– – –

LON ROLLED ONTO HIS BACK without opening his eyes. Something was different. Hm. No Jae snuffles, but there was another body in the bed. His mouth curled into a smile. Lina. Lina was still in bed. Last night he'd found Jae asleep in the family room – the smell of alcohol was strong on his breath; he'd have to talk to him about that as Jae was drinking too much lately – and Lon had carried him up here and tucked him into bed next to snoozing Lina. But Jae had some kind of interview this morning, right. He must have gone to that.

It was odd that Lina was still here. Wasn't she supposed to be checking in with HR at the call center complex? This was very nice but strange.

Lon moved carefully so as not to wake her. The morning light was bewitching; she almost glowed in it as she lay on her side in the bed, his golden goddess.

She must have had a couple of cancellations this morning and decided to take advantage of it. But still, maybe she'd like to take advantage of him as well.

He glanced at the clock. Lina made most of her appointments in hour-and-a-half blocks. The big ones were always in the morning, while she was still fresh. And here it was, coming up on the end of a block and she hadn't even gotten out of bed yet. That meant that they had at least an hour-plus before her next appointment. Maybe two.

He showered quickly, humming and then singing to himself. Great day, great day! What to wear, what not to wear? Hm. Meet her under the sheets. Quick, efficient, and she couldn't get away from him. They could play pirate, his favorite. Nice and slow. She liked it slow and they hadn't done that in ages. A full hour, plus. He'd insist on it.

He ran a final check of his hair and then decided to muss it a little. Baby liked it mussed. Just a little splash of cologne. He darted outside, south a thousand miles to collect some wildflowers, and then returned to ease into bed.

"Kitten…" he called to her softly. For too many weeks he had missed watching her wake up, and now brightly looked for the wondrous signs, the feelings as her mind rose to the surface. But no, she was deeply asleep.

"*Chérie,*" he urged. "My empress." He let one of the daisies tickle her nose, but got no reaction. "Lina. Wake up. Lina?" He reached to brush her hair back from her face...

CHAPTER

22

Stoan happened to be in Wiley's lab, trying to make sense of some test results there when the screen unrolled from the ceiling. "Riz! Wiley!" Londo was in bed, barely covered with a sheet, holding a limp Lina in his arms. "Tell me she's not dying! Riz! Lina, *mon coeur*, wake up! Wake up!"

"I'm here, Londo," came Riz's voice from her connection elsewhere in Legion HQ. "Checking data. Trying to coordinate through that earring of hers."

"Wiley!" Stoan shouted. "Get over here now!" But Wiley was already running to the screen.

"Londo, what's happened?" Wiley asked. "You're on Earth?"

Riz broke in. "How long has she been like this? Get me some readings! You must have a medikit there somewhere."

Lon looked lost for a second and then eased Lina down on the mattress. He swiveled to rummage through the drawer in the night table and came up with a health sensor, fastening it to Lina's wrist as his own hand shook.

"How long has she been out?" Riz's voice came.

"Riz, help us," Londo cried. "How long? I don't know. She was sleeping– I thought she was sleeping when I hit the sack last night. I woke up just a few minutes ago. She's missed her first appointment this morning. She won't wake! And look at her–!"

Lina lay there limp, barely breathing, her skin a distinct yellow. There were purplish blotches under her eyes, around her mouth, along her collarbone.

"Get me a blood sample, will you, Londo?" Riz asked calmly through her own shock. "There's no way to port her here, is there? Grigach." Riz's final mutter was to herself.

"She's not going to die, is she?"

It was all Londo could do to fumble the sensor clip onto Lina's earlobe so it could prick her and relay findings.

"She's not going to as long as I have something to say about it," Riz growled. "Now calm down, Legionnaire. I know you want to panic, but we can't have it, not when I can't reach her from here!"

Wiley was frowning at the readouts. "It's stims," he surmised.

"Of course it's stims," Riz retorted. "At least she's breathing. The girl has the stamina of a *kamzan*. Anybody else would be dead by now. What kind of medical supplies do you have there, Londo?"

"Um, um, standard Legion issue." Londo searched the area for his duffel and grabbed it, not caring how much Riz saw of him. He opened it and dragged out its medikit to add to what he'd already unearthed.

"Well, that's a start," Riz said.

"Kidneys and liver have shut down," Wiley said.

"What?! Oh god, oh God!"

"Very good, Mem-Bazer, alarm him if you can," Riz said. "Where's Jae? Is he on Earth?"

"Yeah, he's here. He's on his way."

"Make him hurry. Who let her have alcohol?"

Londo looked blank. "Alcohol? Lina doesn't drink."

Riz shook her head. "There's alcohol in her system. Everything's skewed bad enough – this would have happened anyway, although maybe not so bad – but she's been drinking. I need the CNE, Londo."

Lon fumbled his way through the medikit looking for it.

Wiley pointed at the drink still sitting on the nightstand. "Whose is that?" he asked.

"It's probably Jae's. He was..." Now was not the time to mince words. "He was drunk last night. I had to bring him to bed before I was called away. But… I didn't bring the glass with him."

"Give her 8 units into her liver," Riz ordered.

"It was probably hers, then," Wiley surmised as Londo administered the shot through Lina's nightgown. Its whiteness made her look even more yellow.

"Hang in there, *cherie*," he crooned to her. "What next, Riz?"

Riz frowned at her readouts. "Whatever we do it's going to have to be subtle, at least until Jae arrives. She's overrun with chemicals as it is. We don't want to fill her with more."

As if on cue, Jae flashed into the room, coming to a dead stop as he saw the scene in front of him. "Lina!" he cried, and dashed to the bed. "She's not..." Grateful tears sprang from his eyes as he spotted the tenuous rise and fall of her chest. "What happened? What can I do?"

"I need you to get her liver and kidneys working," Riz announced crisply. "You must do it gently; there can be no shocks to her system right now. Bring her around slowly."

Lon lifted Lina up as Jae slid under her to cradle her in his arms. "She was acting weird last night," Jae said. "Really spaced out. Wandering all over the house."

"So you gave her some whiskey to calm her down?" Londo asked sharply. "What else, Riz? Give me something to do! How could you, Jae?"

"All right, Lon, find some iddi points," she instructed.

"Iddi points. Iddi points… What will those do?" Lon rifled through his kit, then his duffle, searching.

"It will keep you from distracting Jae. Jae needs to concentrate, not listen to you berate him for whatever happened."

Jae's normally placid expression was wracked, Lon saw. He'd been passed-out drunk. Maybe he hadn't realized what he was doing. No excuse!

Maybe that glass wasn't Jae's, but Lina's.

He squeezed his eyes shut. Too many possibilities. Too many ways drunk Jae could have almost killed Lina without realizing it.

But he could feel Jae forcing his mind into sharp focus, diving deep into Lina's body, into her thick etheric net to speak to the biological devas there. He was confused by what he found and had to slow, slow…

"Slower," Gorgeon instructed. "Can you hear me? Even slower than that."

Londo watched, searching for any sign that Lina's color was getting better or that she was breathing deeper. **Come back!** he cried to her.

"Londo," Stoan said from the other screen.

Dazed, Lon looked up at him. "She's going to be okay," he said. "We won't let her die. We won't."

"That's right, Londo," Stoan told him. "She's not going to die now. Take it easy."

The room was spinning around him, but Lon still lurched to his feet and sought his robe, tying it with a jerk around his belly. He rubbed his nose. What to do? What to do? Jae was caught up in the healing process, and Lina didn't look any different than before. The flowers were strewn across the bed. Lon gathered them up, then threw them in the trash. Damn him for trying to push Lina when she should be sleeping! Damn Jae for giving her that drink! Damn them for not helping her out more!

Lon touched his earring. "Trey, cancel all our appointments for the next two days at least. Three days out, give 'em warning that we may not make it. Tell Kanti. Lina's out of the system for... at least five days."

Trey's voice was anxious. "Is she hurt again? Is there anything I can do?"

"No. No, thanks. It's just that you were right. The stims finally got to her. She's going to live, but we've got to get her to Sarastor. We'll have to take the long way." Damn himself for not learning how to port yet! "So we'll be out of communications for eighteen hours. We're leaving as soon as Jae can stabilize her."

"*Darkeer prague.* I'll be praying for her, Londo. Tell her that we're all praying for her."

"Thanks, I will. I don't need to tell you that we need to keep this secret. Tell people that we're called off on an emergency; it's close enough to the truth."

"Yes sir. Are you taking the cats with you, or should I arrange for a pet sitter on Earth?"

"The cats..." Londo looked around. Obi was silently observing from the top of his dresser, despite the hubbub. "We're taking the cats with us. Don't worry about them. Starhart out."

Getting the cats' things together would give him something to do. He packed for Lina first, as well as for Jae and himself, and notified the Network to stand by for emergency transport to the hyperspace bay on their satellite. Maybe he should push the ship to Sarastor; they'd go faster that way. But he should be realistic. He didn't think he could bear to stay outside the ship away from Lina when she could be drawing her last breath.

No, the ParaNet had cocoons now. Lina could go into stasis.

Jae was speaking to Riz. Apparently Riz thought Lina was barely well enough to take the ship, although everyone hated the thought of being out of communication for that long. Jae wouldn't be able to work while she was in a cocoon, but for now Jae eased out from under Lina's sleeping form and gazed down at her as both Wiley and Riz compared their data.

"They say the whiskey was what triggered it," Londo hissed.

"Whiskey..." Jae reached for the glass and sniffed it. There were still some drops left in the glass. He held it for a moment–

And then savagely threw the glass against the far wall.

"Clean it up," Londo pointed to the shards. They would come back, all of them, no coffins, "and let's get out of here."

— — —

LONDO PACED IN A TIGHT OVAL around the unreflecting black capsule on the floor. Lina's body was inside, held in stasis and thus unaffected by time or anything else until they could get to Sarastor.

Eighteen hours travel time.

He wanted to shout his frustration, anger and worry, but that would likely tear the warpship apart. Jae was curled into a ball on the living area's couch, his arms encasing his head. Occasionally he'd break out into new bouts of weeping.

The cats had crept into hiding in the next room. Now and then Moose and Bran gave little yowls of distress from there, as if they knew what was going on. Maybe they were just afraid of Lon's anger or both of their humans' misery.

All the Rands would be following in Hal's private ship. The staff on Aldierra would keep things in hand. They'd proven themselves before.

Lon paced, his hands clenching into fists and then out. Fists and out.

On top of everything he was so furious with Jae! How could he have given booze to Lina? They'd suspected she was on serious stims, even though neither of them had guessed how much. They'd needed her working. But how could Jae have been so irresponsible?

Because Jae had been drunk. Jae was a drunk.

"I didn't… I didn't give her alcohol," Jae groaned.

"You just left it out for her."

"But she doesn't drink. She hates liquor. How was I to know?"

"You could see she wasn't in her right mind."

Jae's voice increased in volume as he looked up. "So could you. It's not like it happened all at once. Why didn't you say something?"

"Why didn't you? Were you too drunk these past few days to notice?"

"I wasn't–"

"How often have you been drunk on duty lately, Jae? You've been drunk when you've come home. It didn't come upon you suddenly. You had to begin in your office. Don't we have a policy? A rule? And that's just for business. Now you're falling-down drunk on private time?"

They didn't see the cats crowd close to each other in the next room, watching them through the doorway. The animals relied on each other for safety in this suddenly unsafe environment, this atmosphere of abject torment.

The men shouted at each other. Brought up old sins and arguments. Jae pounded on Lon's chest while he batted at Jae's until Jae said, "Ow."

"Sorry."

That made them pause.

But the back-and-forth accusations began again. They dragged up major events, minor events, events that both had thought they'd forgotten and even forgiven, but appeared fresh again.

And they wept. They held each other tightly as the tears flowed.

Then there was silence.

"I would take it all back if I could," Jae finally whispered. "Every drink I've ever taken. I'm never going to drink again." His gaze pierced that of Lon. "I vow."

Lon closed his eyes. He wanted… He wanted… He wanted to tell Jae just how he should run his life from now on. How it would be easy enough to stop drinking. Jae should stop behaving like a child and grow– Wait.

Maybe this was one of his therapist Adam's "Stop, shut your mouth, and explore past your first reaction" lectures.

To take that moment, Lon returned his attention to the black capsule on the floor. Right now, right in this moment, this was the most important matter.

"She'll be okay," Londo said softly. "We must have faith."

"Yes. But we have to see to Aldierra. And–"

"Find out who gave her the extra stims."

"Wiley wouldn't do it."

"Wiley would give her some, I bet. If he didn't know she was getting more from somewhere."

"She's tricky. You know how she's always after something that will keep her going."

"We'll hire more people."

"She already has dozens helping her within just her own office. Maybe hundreds."

"We'll get more. We'll insist on spreading out the duty."

"Everyone wants to talk with the Speaker."

"So we'll do more of that." Lon gritted his teeth. "We need to recruit more paras so we'll have time for it."

"We'll track down her pusher."

"She probably uses people who don't know that she's already taking. Ah. Money," Lon decided. "She had to pay for those stims. There'll be a trail."

"She could have stashed the actual drugs anywhere. I'll get our accountants to find the payments." Jae thought further. "She'll wear a bracelet through Deadline. A monitor."

"I bet Riz already has one waiting."

"Yes."

They sat in silence.

"How long do you think recovery will be? Should I take off on my own to go to Aldierra?"

"Don't be stupid, Lon. You'll worry yourself sick – literally – by the time you arrive. We don't need another one on the casualty list."

Slowly Londo nodded his head. "Maybe it won't take long before she can port one of us there."

"We go easy. We don't rush her."

"We follow Riz's instructions. To the letter."

"So. Do we yell at her?"

"At Lina?"

They considered.

"She needs yelling at."

"I bet all the money in our account that she thought she was doing the right thing."

"She needs to talk with us."

"When do any of us have the time to sit down and talk any more? Not about Aldierra, but this kind of thing?"

They both heaved sighs.

"Up her psychotherapy sessions."

"And ours too, I think. Lina's just showing more symptoms first."

Lon rubbed his nose. Jae scratched his jaw.

"Yeah, maybe."

Then they told each other of the stresses they had found hardest to handle these past weeks. They discussed solutions, but also confessed how it made them feel. Then they brought up AI therapists to delve deeper.

CHAPTER

23

By the time they arrived at Legion HQ on Aldierra, the animals had been well-petted, fed and comforted, Jae and Lon had rested their eyes though neither had slept, and they had formulated a plan of action well enough that they could place all their attention on Lina and getting her well without worries about their jobs interfering with their focus.

The med staff left the two men alone in Lina's room after they had finished preliminary treatments and settled her in her bed. Her skin still held a golden stain as she lay deeply asleep against the white pillow. Monitors lined the room, and two intravenous lines attached to her arms, disappearing under the sheet.

Jae brushed her hair with his fingers as he sat beside her. "She swore to me she was only using them a little, under Wiley's supervision, just until things calm down."

"She lied." Londo heaved a sigh. "How could she have used so many? What did she need them for? I know she's busy. She'd need stims now and then but not all the time. She mostly has appointments all day long, just sitting while we're out there doing the physical work." He thought a moment and shrugged. "Porting too, but that's all mental."

"She says it feels like work. It tires her physically if she ports too much."

Lon grunted as he paced. She should try what it felt like to tote city-building equipment out of hyperspace and into position on the ground. Still…

"She's lying to us," Jae growled. "She can't do that."

"We don't lie to each other," Lon affirmed.

Jae retreated from Lina's hair and gave his husband a cutting look. "You lied to her about me. You lied about Aiko."

Londo sucked in a breath. Then he said, "I withheld information."

"Important information. Like she did with this. She doctored it, made it seem less than it was. 'Oh, Wiley knows what he's doing when he gives me stims.'" Jae imitated Lina's voice.

Lon's expression turned into a scowl. "After we came clean about the marriage–" and keeping that secret had been his order – "I said I'd never lie again. Not on the important things. This is important. She should be held to the same standard."

Jae sat back. He extended his legs straight in front of himself, rising in his chair to clench everything from his waist down and then release, as he considered. Then he clenched everything above his waist. Release. Three deep cyclic breaths. "Three Worlds is having us do strange things," he decided. "We're stretching ourselves in ways we've never done before. We may have to… embroider on the truth or withhold information from each other if the occasion warrants."

Londo grunted and took a seat on the other side of the bed. He laid his hand on Lina's covered arm.

Jae said, "Lina is new to all this. Really, really new. How much has she been through so far?"

"I don't like this. I don't like having to watch either of you in a hospital bed. I won't have it, not ever again."

That made Jae give a wan smile. "We have dangerous jobs. We will try our best not to die on you, Lon. But Lina hasn't developed the coping skills we've been trained with."

Lon's jaw worked. "We will hire someone to tutor her. And get her that training Chim is always nagging us about, self-defense."

"Time for that after Deadline," Jae said. "Until then, we watch out for each other. If we can't help her carry her load, we get some of our staff, her staff, to do it." As if in afterthought he added, "And we keep watch on the condition of our staffs."

"What does Lina do so much that she needs so many stims?"

She did make a lot of human interest videos, flitting around the world to show Aldierrans what ordinary people were doing to help out. She reminded them of the Three Worlds' suggested "to-do" lists. She met with quarreling Houses and made them work together. And of course she was in charge of keeping supplies and transportation routes for those supplies running. But Lon and Jae were out physically rescuing people and cleaning and building things; *that* would wear someone out.

Londo tried to remember what she'd said she had on her schedule for a normal day, day before yesterday, and then realized that she'd been gone when he got up.

"We need to check her schedule," Jae told him. "Fix it as much as we can while she can't argue."

"Hmph." Lon didn't like to argue with Lina. Too hardheaded. So was he. That didn't make for efficient arguments. His therapist said they should begin marriage therapy to help them with such.

"Feithi marriage therapy," Jae said, reading his mind. "For Triunes."

"Okay. Maybe she just doesn't know how to budget time efficiently. Or delegate."

Stoan had assured him she was on minimal porting duty, so any Legion requests must have been serious emergencies indeed. You didn't turn those down. Too many lives were at stake.

Jae snapped his fingers at him and pointed. Lon reached over Lina to the padd that was on the night table, and together they checked her daily schedule.

"Jesus," Londo said.

Breakfast, check, plus clean laundry would be ported in from Sarastor, then the dirty stuff ported back. Cats fed, check. She kept a record of playing with them; they all did just to make sure.

But a few of those play dates had been crossed out this past week, with guards penciled in to fulfill the duty in her stead. Meetings and emergencies had overwritten the cat times.

Both Jae and he made a questioning noise at that.

Lina had begun with allotments of time for the both of them, individually, throughout her day, but as they scrolled back and forward again they discovered that more and more those were crossed out and Three Worlds-related appointments penciled in.

Lon almost complained until he saw the subjects of those appointments. They were needed.

Then she'd been coordinating those constitutional talks on Reyda. AffSys experts had been adding their opinions and help to the Aldierran talks, sometimes in person, which sometimes required porting. Plus there'd been something to do with the Flute, either with Nesh or some medical centers; Lina had been making experiments and recordings.

Then dealing with the public. Making videos. Checking in around the globe with all kinds of people. Make that globes, plural, as she had regular contacts on other planets from whom she was receiving vital information.

Staff meetings on numerous levels.

"Great orb, are we employing the entire population?" Jae muttered as they went through them all. But it seemed to Lon that Lina was delegating as much as she possibly could.

He compared to Kanti's schedule. Also packed, but Kanti got in at least seven hours of sleep a night. She was sending out frantic memos to HR to hire and train as many as possible.

Every hour of Lina's unreasonably-lengthed days was filled with essential-looking meetings, and judging from the names involved, Londo didn't think that anyone else could handle them.

Five hours a day for sleep. Sometimes less. Every Tuesday, their official team meeting day, held the notation in large letters: NO STIMS.

Lately that had been crossed out.

"Stims," Londo said thoughtfully. "That often."

Jae tapped the padd to reference a goals chart that tied into the schedule. Knowing Lina, there was one.

"Cat sitter to pay attention to cats" had "security risk" written beside it. "Needed," was also noted.

"I can't believe she'd consider having someone look after the herd," Lon murmured.

They scrolled down the list. Londo reached to take the padd from Jae, but Jae kept it away from him. He took the stylus and went back to the schedule, to the next day. On the yet-uncancelled and unsplit block labelled "L&J", he wrote:

"family meeting." Londo snorted approval, and Jae handed him back the padd to replace on the night table.

CHAPTER

24

"Demerits." Lina heard a voice that took her more than a moment to recognize. It was Subcommander Andri's.

She must be at Legion HQ in the all-too-familiar Med section.

"Big, big demerits for this."

Lina shuddered and tried to look unconscious.

"Faker."

"Your actions have also resulted in Dr. Mem-Bazer receiving demerits."

Stoan. Lina's eyes snapped open. "Aw, f–," she blurted. The shock of the expletive didn't hit her until a moment later. Then she noticed the sudden silence of people in the room. Well. Nothing to be done about that. She could claim she wasn't in her right mind. It didn't seem like she was entirely conscious, so maybe that was correct.

"Wiley didn't do anything," she managed to say. She wasn't sure the words were recognizable. "It was just a couple times."

"If he's administering medicine, he'd better check the condition of his patient first," Stoan retorted. "He will not be giving you any more stims."

Riz stepped forward.

"Sorry," Lina said. Had she caused a ruckus? Why was she here?

Oh right. Stims. They were making her wonky.

She must have wonked out big-time. What had she done?

"I am the only one who will be giving you stims in the future," the chief of Legion Med declared. "Me or one of my staff, on my orders. But I think it will be a long, long time before you'll be allowed, even if you need them."

Lina tried to raise herself on her elbows, but had to drop back the few millimeters she'd accomplished to the mattress. Too much work. No energy.

Where were–? Ah. Behind these Legion types. Londo and Jae. Their expressions were inscrutable. Lina shied away from reading their feelings.

They were probably so disappointed in her. She'd messed up royally this time. All her fault. How had they gotten her to Sarastor? How could she help Aldierra when she was like this?

They were probably thinking about divorce or separation at least. She'd shamed them.

How long had she been out? "Aldierra?"

Londo spoke. "Our staffs report everything is as secure as one can expect."

A weight sloughed off her shoulders. "Oh. Good. Wanna sleep." As she closed her eyes she added, "Critters are hungry."

"Your 'critters' have escaped," Stoan said darkly. "We're trying to capture them."

"Cat traps," Lina thought she might have whispered as she sank into a deep drowse.

———

"CAT TRAPS?" Andri asked Stoan. Then she turned to the man who stood just outside the doorway: Wiley. "Cat traps?"

Wiley rubbed his cheek next to his mouth. "They make metal ones on Earth. Painless ones that need to be baited."

No one had noticed Londo turning to the doorway. "Boxes. About cat-sized, maybe a little bigger. Constructed of a soft but fairly sturdy material. With flaps that can be closed when the trap is full."

Wiley scratched his head. "I'll see what I can find."

"We have at least one cardboard box in our apartment," Lon told him. "I'll replicate it and scatter them around. Someone should keep an eye on them, close them once a cat gets in."

———

THE SCREAMS PIERCED THE HALLS of the medical section at Legion Headquarters and went no farther, but there was a sudden swarm of headaches throughout the enormous complex. Sleeping personnel were also reporting nightmares when they woke.

"At least she's sleeping fairly normally," Riz said in front of her observation monitor. To either side of Lina's bed, Londo and Jae held Lina's hands.

Stoan watched, too. "You call this normal?" he asked.

Riz shrugged.

"Grigach."

"The girl has guts enough for three Legionnaires," Riz reported sourly. "And sometimes I think she's got the sense of a rock. Stim overdose! Running herself so hard she collapses! I hope you're satisfied!"

Stoan turned to her, his arms crossed. "She's not dead."

"No thanks to you! Londo confessed that he's let a few nighttime Legion calls go through to her. How many others have you had her doing?"

A screen scrolled down and Stoan glanced at it. "Have you gotten all those creatures yet?" he asked Boron.

"Not yet, sir," Boron replied, a trickle of sweat running from his brow. "They're so small. And they're skurny quick. Smart, too. All I could find was this one." He held Bran-Bran up for the viewer to see, and the young cat twisted loose in his hands, jumping down. "Grigach! Catch it, catch it! But don't hurt it! The Speaker will have us chopped up for dinner if we hurt it! Aw, shit – catch the door before it–!" Boron turned back to the screen. "Correction," he reported. "All six are now on the loose. But at least none have gotten outside headquarters."

"Do what you can," Stoan said with a defeated sigh.

– – –

"CRITTERS SPOTTED," came a report.

Lon rose to grab the small pile of cardboard boxes he'd replicated. "I'll handle this," he told Jae.

"You need help?"

They made a quick plan to cover adjoining floors of HQ, and then flew off.

Andri and Wiley watched from monitors. The act of setting cat traps did not seem difficult: Lon and Jae chose hallways and tossed boxes every fifty or so feet, their open sides facing up.

Stoan tuned in in time to see one cat amble down a hall only to spot the box. It made some playful feints around it and then hopped in. The box had small holes in the side and the cat poked its paw through some before settling down to gnaw on the top.

Sorbens flew in high in the hall from the direction the cat wasn't looking. At the last moment she swooped down to close the flaps. "Target secured!" she called.

Another Legionnaire flew in, this one with fasteners to strap the box shut.

– – –

ACCORDING TO THEIR RECORDS there was one remaining cat left on the loose. Searching Legionnaires reported in: no sign of it. For some reason sensors often gave conflicting readings when it came to cats or wandering toddlers.

"We'll find it eventually." Stoan groaned. "Starharts." He glanced at his office monitors to check Lina's Medical Section room, with her in bed.

A cat lay across her chest.

– – –

"IT'S NOT TUESDAY HERE, but we need to have a talk," Jae said. He'd pulled a small table up next to the bed and had some writing materials out on it, as well as two screens hovering above. Londo was seated by his side so Lina could see both of them without moving her head too much.

"We are going to get some basics straight," Jae told her.

The screen rotated so she could see it as well. Her schedule. Mealtimes and sleep periods were now highlighted in glowing red.

A popup flew out of the screen, its surface undulating gold with neon stripes. Something about her earring containing new sensing circuits. It would be monitoring her use of stims and similar substances, as well as her sleep and eating habits.

Three guesses what this meeting's agenda was.

— — —

"OH NO," SHE SAID when she woke again. Was the "We're not angry; we're disappointed" lecture over? No, Lon and Jae weren't seated by her. They were here somewhere though. As were a lot of others. "Not again." She pulled her blanket higher to cover herself to the bridge of her nose.

Privacy? What was privacy? A crowd of people had gathered in her room, most of them staring at her. She couldn't place just when, but once she'd awakened just to Mama Ruth and Papa Mike. They were so sweet. They weren't here.

Her mouth felt like she'd swished it with a thick glue. Tasted like glue, too. Blech.

"I thought I was the fourth Three World." Wiley's voice held distinct disappointment.

Apparently there had been a discussion around her bed. Lon, Jae, Hal, Riz, two medics who were trying not to listen in, and Wiley stood there, with Kanti and Wicker Greenweave on screen and various cats in various arms of the people materially present.

"Unh," Lina managed. Yeah, that would impress them. The Speaker speaks.

"Tell them," Wiley ordered. "They've given me demerits."

Lina was about to form better words when Hal piped up. "No, I am."

"You two are mistaken," Kanti said, a pout on her expectant face as the monitor screen that held her image hovered beside Hal.

Lina smacked her tongue around her mouth, trying to get rid of the glue. "You all… are the… fourth Three Worlds," Lina told them. "And Bracken. And Andri. And Riz. And every last one… of the med staff here and on Aldierra. With special commendation roles awarded to Nesh and Yusuf. Mace too. Probably Erik as well by the time we're through Deadline. Chim has been a lifesaver." She paused. "And our therapists. Good lord, our therapists."

Londo crossed his arms over his chest. "We will send out certificates after Deadline."

Jae seemed to be silently discussing the situation with gray Ember, with whom he looked eye to eye as she raised up in his hold before laying her head back on his shoulder.

Kanti glared at Lina. "Tidda found your stash. We have stored it where you cannot get to it. We have sent out… gentle reminders to your suppliers."

Couldn't get to it? That would be a trick, Lina thought, but her next thought was that perhaps she *should* swear off stims unless someone was watching her. Apparently she had no self-control. But emergencies…

Lon piped up, "Emergencies will not signal an automatic release of any stims. Not any more. You will go through channels."

"But–"

"We will arrange for those channels to operate quickly."

"Otherwise, no more stims," Jae said and the way he said it seemed very final indeed.

– – –

LEGION SOUNDPROOFING COULDN'T ENTIRELY MASK THE SCREAMS. The legendary Olympia, aka Demi of Earth, paused at the closed doorway, seated on a floating medichair. A familiar orderly approached.

"Don't worry about it," he told her. "That's the Speaker's room. She's detoxing from stim overdose."

"Is anyone with her?" Demi asked.

"An AI attendant. She's been doing this a lot since she arrived. It doesn't seem to be fatal, if that helps."

Demi snorted. "Stims? Why did she overdose?"

He shrugged. "Overcrowded work schedule. You know she's got that Three Worlds project."

"Doesn't she have a staff?" Demi protested, then waved the orderly on his way. "I won't keep you. Thanks for the information."

She returned to sit at the electronics console in her own room, where there was now so much less medical equipment than when she'd first arrived, months ago. In those days she hadn't been able to see beyond a blur, hear beyond muffled noise, and the pain had wracked her no matter how many painkillers they gave her.

Now she was within sight of a full recovery. Oh, they'd told her she had a few months to go before they'd release her from this chair, but in her mind she didn't think they knew how resilient she was, how Scythian techniques could speed healing, prolong life, and empower. That was, if a person practiced them enough.

She'd been wondering why during this past month she'd chosen to learn Farrani, the common language of Aldierra. Likely: boredom. And because she knew the next phase of the Three Worlds project would be beginning soon. The worlds would be working together, and she was an important player on Earth. She'd need to know the language.

That is, if Lon and his spouses carried this off. If not there'd still be paperwork and histories and videos that would likely come up in the aftermath and be dealt with. This way she'd be prepared.

But perhaps in the meantime there was something she could do from this chair.

CHAPTER

25

The Speaker's Chief of Staff sat in the screen's picture, her eyes wide. "O… Olympia!" she breathed.

Ah, hero worship. Demi smiled into the camera. "Chief Cloutier," she said. "I am glad to meet you. You've been partnering with Lina to keep this organization functioning, haven't you?"

"Uh. Yes, Olympia. We–"

"And I hear great things about how you've managed during these periods when Lina and the others have been unavailable." Demi frowned. "Sometimes through their own stupidity. Like now."

"Oh no, Olympia," Cloutier quickly protested. "Lina was trying her best. There are things only the Speaker can do, situations for which the population will only accept her help with. I can… see how…" Her words slowed.

Demi closed her eyes and nodded. "Yes. She had the best of intentions and though from what I understand she did a lot of research on stims, they got away from her. And now she's here."

"Yes."

Cloutier slumped in her chair. Dark circles ringed her eyes. Her shoulders and chin drooped. Demi could hear the slight office noise behind a door: busy people having important conversations. There might be some panicked words in there, to judge from the occasional exclamation.

Demi cocked her head at Cloutier. "And how are you holding up, Chief Cloutier? You had your own job pressures before, and now–"

"If I must be truthful…" She didn't look as if she wanted to. "Things are beginning to fall apart. The upper echelons of the organization have held numerous meetings. About the Deadline. It's coming fast. About Lina not being here. The weather operation is right around the corner. And of course Londo and Jae are worried sick about her. Their attention is split from the program. They can't be here until she can port safely again. Interstellar, that is."

As an afterthought she said, "Legion Med's going to let her do that sometime tomorrow. For Lon and Jae, not for her. In the meantime she's sneaking calls in when she thinks no one is watching her. I've been monitoring to make sure she doesn't exert herself too much." She gave a strangled laugh. "I have to end those calls because she falls asleep on them."

"Then let me ask. I've been around for a while…"

Cloutier's face broke into Worshipful Mode. "Since the Crimean War," she said breathlessly. "I grew up reading about you. I read your biography before enlisting in the Canadian Army. I think I've seen all your major speeches and read all your books as well, though I might have missed an essay or two."

"What an honor to me that you've done that," Demi said smoothly. She'd heard that kind of thing so many times before, each time giving her spirit a lift. "Over the years I have developed some experience in world affairs, as well as dealing with people at odds with each other. With women and gays and the general undertrodden. You know how Earth is. Could you use some help from me in those areas?"

"When could you arrive, Olympia?" Cloutier immediately asked.

— — —

"DO NOT SAY ANYTHING," Lina commanded behind a pointing finger as Woody came into the hospital room.

She'd ported Lon, Jae and the cats to Aldierra yesterday afternoon (doing it in two jumps to take things easy), after Wiley, Riz, and The Boys had given their approval. Demi – Olympia! – had hopped onto a hyperspace ship to make the journey at a more leisurely pace of three days. She'd been accompanied by medical personnel that Three Worlds was supporting to complete her recovery. Kanti had quarters "fit for a legend" ready for her. For a few moments Lina had thought that Mace would wet his pants in his excitement to work with the storied hero.

By the time he'd hung up she was surmising that he was planning a raucous welcome party for her.

Today Lina was propped into a comfortable sitting position in front of a video screen wearing a new bed jacket. It was modelled after Aunt Bea's frilly concoction from TV. That was the only bed jacket she'd ever seen. Since *The Andy Griffith Show* at the time had been in black and white, Lina didn't know what color the original was. This one was a spring green to match her usual uniform. It made her feel less exposed and the tiniest bit more professional than her hospital gown, despite all its ruffles. No boobage exposure with this!

So she managed a few short interviews for the outlets that had been begging for them these past weeks. When had she become so blasé about being in front of cameras? Since the Mind Control tour, cameras of every technological sort had been shoved in her face whenever she appeared in public. People had shouted questions at her.

Her first interviews after she'd married Londo had been horribly frightening. She knew she'd looked like a terrified rabbit, trying to hide behind Lon. Now… For better or for worse, the Worlds had her. Take her as she was.

Lina chatted with the services who wanted a soft interview, and gave more serious answers to the journalists. She allotted five minutes to each.

Dr. Woody arrived – why didn't Legion Medical add the "doctor" to their names when these people were addressed? Some kind of elitism on the Legion's part, Lina had always theorized – to check on her and then nag her about relaxing and getting more sleep.

By now she was sleeped out. She was almost pretty awake, and made a point of taking a nap about every two hours, Sarastoran, which was every three or so, Terran, so the docs would be impressed. Plenty of sleep.

"I am entering this as part of my report," Woody retorted.

"You do that. Now, Kanti, you were saying…?"

Because Kanti was on her screen, filling her in as to the goings on on Aldierra and how they were being dealt with.

As Woody hovered around her bed and its readings, Lina listened closely to her Chief of Speaker Operations. Staff were doing follow-up calls where they should, finding out especially what the Houses who were moving in to new residences still needed. What the ones being moved out and their hosts were finding difficult to put up with.

Others were circulating at hospitals to speak to those victims of domestic violence and neglect that Lina had been sending their way. The thousands of plushies they'd ordered were being funneled to the kids who needed or wanted one. Some adults were also requesting their own; Lina made a note. Children and women and gays were being counselled at the special homes that had been set up to serve them. Instructive videos were being broadcast to handle emerging problems and fears.

Mace and his section had spread themselves out not only to handle the LGBTQ sector, but these others as well. They were also concentrating on reeducating the cis population. He was working closely with all kinds of Terran and AffSys folks to learn the latest approaches to transform bigotry to acceptance; domestic violence to anger management and safety.

Lina also wanted to learn that, but… after Deadline. Priorities.

Lon and Jae's people worked with her own to make sure supplies made their way to where they were supposed to go. Their troops would not go hungry or exposed to the elements. Famine had not spread in the Starharts' absence.

As a result and even with Jae and Lon finally showing up, everyone was overburdened.

HR was hiring and training as quickly as they could.

"Are you ready for this call?" Kanti asked her, looking hopeful but also giving Woody the side-eye.

Lina didn't hide her wary perusal of him. "What level security are you?" she asked the doctor.

"I'm Level 5."

As he looked up from his equipment his expression betrayed curiosity. He checked out Kanti before returning his gaze to Lina.

"You do not hear any of this," Lina informed him, and he nodded.

Lina made a face at Kanti, and she added a new screen.

On it a group of four moderately blue-skinned people sat around a table to face her.

"We are from Drimmon," they told her. "Thank you for seeing us, Speaker. Drimmon is just outside the AffSys. We run considerable business and social interaction with the AffSys, but we are not members of that confederation."

"I understand," Lina told them. "You will not be held under AffSys laws and requirements."

"Yes, Speaker. We know you are deep within your mission on Aldierra and wish you the best outcome with it, but..."

The next person at the table spoke, "But if it does not turn out the way you would prefer... If Aldierra kills all its humans..."

They waited a few moments for the idea to sink in. Lina needed them.

"We were hoping that you would turn ownership, in whatever legal fashion you name, over to our world."

"We will continue your ecological efforts," the first person quickly assured her. "For the past century we have been working hard at improving our own environment. We have equipment we could add to help you achieve your post-Deadline goals faster."

The third said in a sepulchral voice, "We will help clean up the bodies and dispose of them. In a respectful eco-friendly way, of course."

"We have a large population on our own world as well as a few neighboring ones who are in close coalition with us, that would like to spread out, have more room. We do control our birth rates and prefer small families, but time has..." The center woman shrugged her shoulders and tilted her head to the left. "Our birth rate has very slowly increased. We are working on bringing it back down, but are left with a population we would like to keep living fulfilling lives."

"Ours would be a world of four or five cultures. Over the years we have learned respect and admiration for each other. We would be continuing your ideals of inclusion..."

The talks went on, and Lina came up with some intelligent questions to ask.

Wiley arrived halfway through, and Lina allowed him to ask questions of his own, even as Lon and Jae chimed in her mind.

These guys were organized. They did indeed have excellent plans.

"We will consider what you've told us," Lina assured them as they finished their presentation. "I am impressed. If we do survive Deadline–"

The Drimmondi immediately wished only the best for the Deadline.

"We will hire some experts to find you all a suitable planet or planet-sized structure that you can use instead."

Where to do from there?

"Thank you for your presentation. Please know that it will be Aldierra herself who makes the final decision."

"Of course, Speaker." "Of course!"

When the screen had cleared, Lina took a long breath and checked to see how Wiley was taking it. He looked more thoughtful than usual. Kanti came back on to ask her how it went.

"It was interesting," Lina finally summarized. "And terrifying."

Kanti nodded before her brows set in a frown. "Aldierra will be saved. You can count on that."

— — —

RIZ PERSONALLY ARRIVED the next morning to note that Lina had completed a full night's sleep with no repercussions. "I want you here for three more hours," she insisted as Lina tried to eat everything on her prescribed breakfast platter. "Just in case. Then you may return to Aldierra."

Neither Jae nor Lon bestirred themselves to protest Riz' commanding tone. They were busy on Aldierra, the jerks, while Lina sat here doing next to nothing.

She waited until Riz had left. Wiley was not going to make another appearance until they were ready to leave for Aldierra. The health attendants had left her alone.

Lina looked up a contact within Jae's files and called them.

"Ms.– Speaker!" The smartly-dressed woman reared back from her desk in shock at seeing Lina on her screen. From behind her, a man and woman ran into the office, adjusted their clothing to perfect order, and then sat beside her trying to look as professional as they could.

"Sorry to bother you without warning," Lina said pleasantly. "But you all are listed in your company as heading the section that oversees Three Worlds' funds. You're in charge of our money. Is that correct?"

"Yes," said the woman who introduced herself as "Lafeedrin." "We've only had them for two months now. It's an enormous task, to keep amounts of this kind in order."

"Much less wisely invested to garner interest," the man next to her added.

Lina had been instructed not to worry about her money. Well, she'd heard too many horror stories about wives who left the finances to Hubby.

No matter how well-intentioned Hubby was.

The financial institution had split itself in two when Jae had hired them. This division, which was quickly getting to be as large as or larger than the entire thing had been before, was devoted solely to managing Three Worlds' funds, particularly the wad that Lina had earned during her Mind Control Tour of a few months ago.

"There are immense problems with currency conversion," Lafeedrin confided. "We have worlds from across the AffSys, plus worlds outside of there, paying into the fund. Plus the AffSys as a whole has added to the payments. They are grateful.

"Then you three are operating on three worlds, two of which are outside of the AffSys entirely. Earth has few if any interstellar connections. Aldierra has a few, we've discovered, but none particularly helpful."

Lina made sympathetic noises, utilizing most of her energy to not zoning out as she usually did whenever finances were discussed. These people had begun by dividing all the money into three, one part saved for each world, but as the Aldierra crisis continued and they began to understand the scope of the problem, Aldierra's pot was made much larger than the others.

When they got past Deadline and into "normal" operations, whatever the heck those might turn out to be, the company would look at things again and re-allocate.

Jae and Lon's wages as paraheroes within various organizations were going into the family funds, which included Starhaven and the Monstrosity, and whatever they'd wind up living independently at on Sarastor. Plus a host of other things, like personal guard units and guests and food and shelter for same. Starhart stuff, not Three Worlds.

It all seemed very logical – and these folks seemed quite stressed by the scope of it all. Glad she wasn't the only one.

"Thank you," Lina told them and made sure her gaze included all three. "But… Could someone just tell me how much money we have to work with? In total?"

The figure came on the screen in AffSys monetary units. By now Lina had a good idea of what expensive equipment cost, what AffSys personnel required as salary.

But this figure…

It had a starting number that then had zeroes filling space to its decimal. She tried to name their places: Tens, hundreds, thousands, ten thousands…

Lots and lots of zeroes.

Lina blinked in incomprehension.

"At the current point," Lafeedrin explained, "we also have a large portion from all worlds' funds set off just to grow in interest until needed. Compound interest," she began to recite, but Lina stopped her.

"Compound interest is financial magic," she said as Lafeedrin gave a small smile. The final few figures of the amount were clicking a few dollars or credits or whatever down as she watched. Then they'd click up. Then down again. The money was pulsing in its work. "You start off little, and end up big if you wait long enough. And don't spend it in the meantime."

Lafeedrin's partner on her left nodded. "In a nutshell," he confirmed. "We will keep as much in that interest-accruing account as possible."

"So." All those zeroes. "This should last a while? This will allow us to do…"

"You should be able to accomplish amazing things, just with the money alone," Lafeedrin assured her.

"And you'll let us know if we… Is there a way to run this figure down to zero? If we start approaching zero?"

That made them all chuckle. One even snorted.

"It's going to take a lot of world building before that can happen."

There was going to be a lot of world building in their future. Who knew how long the overall project would take?

"You should have no worries, not with us at the helm," Lafeedrin told Lina. "We will manage your money well."

With visions of financial decimal-holders whirling through her brain, Lina signed off.

Only to find there were two more requests from different worlds asking about adopting Aldierra should Deadline go wrong.

CHAPTER

26

Londo walked beside Chim and Wind Master, one of the Legion Support team, as they made their way through the tent city to the home cluster, which included upper-echelons offices as well as the Starharts' quarters.

Legion Support was accomplishing some fine things all around Aldierra. Chim reported that they were working well in their teams, and training hard for the Weather Control event in two weeks. Very good to hear. Lon was spending a lot of time gathering paras and megas to help out. Having people who were already used to working together was a godsend.

The path was pleasantly cobbled, which gave it a non-industrial feel while not offering impediment to those with mobility problems. Low greenery of a clover type was beginning to spread along its borders, despite the cool season. Signage directed visitors, and Lon noted that Demi now had a directional sign to her office. She'd been working in Lina's for a few days as things were rearranged and Lina healed enough to go back to work.

But a new sign sat next to those:

"No cursing area ahead. Violators will be fined."

Chim and Lon paused at it, and Wind Master pulled up behind them.

Chim turned to Londo. "How much?" she asked.

"*Aucune idée.* This is new." He rubbed his nose. "I don't think this is from Jae. He cusses almost as well as I do. Lina doesn't like bad words. I've never heard her use one of the really bad ones, except… once. She was pretty drugged up at the time. Bad language is probably something to do with lowering vibes or something."

Chim was nodding. "Language influences personal frequency," she confirmed. "I can see the reasoning."

"But how much, sir?" Wind Master piped up behind him.

"*Euh...* Say one credit for every..." Lon stepped back to just before the theoretical line that marked the sign's official effect area. "'Frickernen' or derivatives. 'Kicking.' Maybe 'blat' and its permutations. I shall sit down and make an official list when I get a spare minute. Things like 'grigach' and grigach-related, oh, half a credit. Those aren't too vile, are they?"

They continued the discussion before they split to proceed to their own destinations.

— — —

"BOTHER RECUPERATION!" Lina grumbled. "It takes too long!"

The ruffles on her bedjacket fluttered as she floated on her hoverchair into her office. There sat Chim and that guy, uh, Wind Master, at her desk, with a screen showing Wiley from his Aldierran lab, and Andri from Legion HQ on Sarastor. Demi had just wandered down the passageway in front of her, to duck into that new tent of hers. Demi on Aldierra. Lina shook her head in wonder. And gratitude.

But whose office was this anyway? "I need some surface area," Lina told them irritably. She couldn't work up the energy to be polite. This was by-golly *her* office.

She could feel Lon was in his own taking care of business that didn't concern these people. Okay then, but he might have let them use the conference tent, unless that was busy. Jae had mysteriously requested a month ago that his office be By Invitation Only. Well. Jae was Jae. Or was there a different reason?

Oh hell, this office was just as convenient and as far as these folks had been concerned, empty. And equipped with security features on the things that mattered that they couldn't get to, so there'd be no harm done. Well, maybe Chim, who was Unlimited with the Legion, could get through, but Wiley had added some Three Worlds refinements to everything. Lina let it go, but determined to maintain her own boundaries.

"Take your business over there." She pointed to the seating arrangement on the other side of the room and settled at her wide desk. She shoved the few items on it far to the side.

"Why aren't you in bed?" Chim asked.

"Because I need to be here." Lina ported in a favorite tarot deck and then changed it to the classic one, the Smith-Waite version. Its messages wouldn't be as gentle as those of the ones she more often used. Her post-overdose state left her peckish. She asked Archangel Michael for protection. She felt his sapphire blue energy and thanked him.

You're welcome, dear child, he replied.

So good to hear the angels again! Old friends were so welcome!

She began to shuffle.

"I'm calling Gorgeon," Andri tattled, her screen in its original position.

"I'm just playing with cards," Lina retorted as she cut the deck three times and rearranged it. "How fun is this? It's a game. La la la. Go away." They didn't.

Lina laid down a pattern of six cards and frowned at them. She muttered sounds no translator could have made sense of. Then she picked four cards out of the remaining deck and laid them face-down to the right of the others in a column.

She turned them over, bottom to top.

"Shit," she said as the first revealed itself. She let out a "sss" of a breath as the second one was turned. No sound for the last ones.

Chim hung over the back of her chair, examining the desktop display. "This is divination?"

"Yes. Tarot. Dammit."

"That might be a credit penalty for you, both words added up. I'm not so sure about English. So what does this tell you?"

Lina frowned deeply at the cards. Then she signed words into her comm system's DMs: "Londo: come immediately, no danger. DON'T TELL JAE." Aloud she asked, "Wind Master? What's your security rating?"

Lon arrived as Wind Master assured Lina that he had a fair rating, so they reluctantly let him stay.

Lon checked the cards. "Oh no, high woo-woo. Sometimes I forget you're into this fringe stuff." Still he frowned as he puzzled them out from the pictures, which had a lot of what seemed to be extraneous detail on them. "As I understand things, there must be a question asked. A specific question."

Lina nodded. "All these weird things, outside what we're doing. The sabotage. The bad press, not the normal bad press, but the lies being deliberately spread. The return of the Blue Army. The problems we're having with the naval fleet. Some rumors I've heard. Vague comments from the phone lines and my psychic groups. I've had time during my recuperation to root around in places I wouldn't ordinarily go."

"You were supposed to be resting," Lon chided, but his heart didn't seem to be in it as he tried to puzzle out the images.

She laid her palms against the table under the six central cards. "There's a major plot involved, very organized and involving top Aldierran echelons, mostly military but not all. It's separate from our plans. Dark. Contracts made. And here's the Emperor card, behind it all."

"Emperor Yanist Glory?"

Lina shook her head. "That's my card for Lupoff." She tapped on it and lifted a corner to more fully reveal the card below it, the Devil.

"Not only the Devil, but the Devil reversed, which makes the card super bad news, pure evil," she reported. "I asked what Lupoff was up to."

"I don't like the looks of this other card," Chim said of the seven of Swords next to it. A man on it was sneaking swords away from a war camp.

"Trickery. Deceit," Lina said and looked up at Londo. She pointed to a card with a heart that had three swords skewering it. "I also want to ask what Jae is up to. Betrayal. Treason. You know he's been keeping something from us."

Londo glowered at the spread. "This would begin to explain things. He could be plotting against Lupoff. Maybe with Lupoff, but… in order to betray him?"

"But not telling you?" Wiley asked from his screen and vigorously shook his head. "No. We can't have that. This mission is in a tight balance. We can't afford–"

"We will sit down with Jae at his earliest convenience so as not to tip anyone else off, and find out what, if anything, he's up to," Lon declared. "Bracken's been pointing out oddities among the Red and Green Armies. We'll bring him in on this once we know what's going on."

"Let's keep Nesh and Yusuf out of this," Lina counselled. "We'll brief them when we have a clear picture, but they don't need to be distracted from what they're doing."

"Agreed."

Chim regarded the paper cards. "Does this really work?" she asked Lina, who had gathered the cards and begun to shuffle again.

"When you're in the Zone, it does. The cards can help get you there. They open up the mind in non-linear, unexpected ways. It makes it easier to catch the ideas floating around in the ether."

"Hm. Some of my teachers have said that a detachment from expectations is required for precognition."

"And clairvoyance," Lina told her. "With tarot you focus in on different levels or meanings of the pictures and go from there. Different decks have different pictures, to be used in suitable situations. I have a Guardian Angels deck that's all sweet pictures, so I can tell clients la la la, here's how your granny is looking after you from the Great Beyond. That deck's not suitable for this."

"You haven't done much woo-woo in some time," Londo observed. "I'm not used to it."

"For a while there I couldn't hear anything." Lina tipped her chin and rolled her eyes to indicate her stupidity.

"Not even Aldierra?" Chim asked.

Lina's lips thinned but finally she nodded. "I kept telling myself I was going to schedule time to meditate and get back my mojo, but…"

"Emergencies came up," Chim guessed, and again Lina nodded.

Lon's expression went dark. His eyes burned accusingly into hers.

Had she forgotten to tell them?

Lina cut the deck five times, shuffled some more, and then began to lay out a different-patterned spread of seven cards. She shook her head at it.

"Three of swords again, this time in the past. Gotta be Feith. This is rooted in the loss of Feith," Lina declared. "See, here Jae's working with others on an intricate plan. Here's another contract. A partnership – yep, with Lupoff. There he is. Plans that face out to sea. The water cleanup? Factions in other continents? But I'm doing a worldwide view here. So that means water cleanup." She laid down an arcing line of more cards over the existing spread. "Ah, see all the cups: here, here, and all through there. Water. They began with Jae's projects, screwing up the waterways. Sabotaging them." She peered at the cards. "Did he help them?"

"Would Jae do that?" Chim asked.

"To prevent Aldierra from meeting Feith's fate, he would," Lon realized. "How is he doing this? What does he have planned to correct it?" He rapped his mighty knuckles a millimeter from the surface of the desk. *"Câline,* we don't even know for sure if this is happening."

Lina pointed at a final card. "With the present energies, this is the projected outcome. I'm hoping that means Lupoff," she said of the man lying on the ground, impaled by ten swords through his back. "It might just indicate the Deadline, the end of the cycle."

"We aren't going to have that kind of result at Deadline," Londo vowed as Lina began to gather the cards.

"If that were the World card – Major Arcana – I'd definitely assign it to Deadline. But it isn't. Minor Arcana."

"Let's see what the situation is in the real world," Londo said. "We'll sort through it – if there's anything to sort through – and get back to those who need to know."

Chim frowned as Wind Master squinted at the remaining cards. "You'll keep us updated as well."

CHAPTER

27

"J ae."

With a start, Jae broke out of deep sleep. Who? What?

Londo sat beside him. He could sense Lina on his other side and turned his head to see her on her floating chair.

Grigach. Their thoughts.

"It has to be done," Jae began. "I decided–"

Lon's gaze bore right through him. "We do not keep things from each other. We do not keep secrets. First Lina with the stims, and her not telling us she couldn't even talk with Aldierra any more."

"What?" Jae was suddenly entirely attentive.

"I can hear them all just fine now," Lina retorted. Then she corrected, "Well, it's getting much better."

"Now you're the one holding secrets from us, from the rest of the operation. Jae. No. We all are involved in major decisions like these," Londo countered, his voice edged with anger.

Jae turned over to lie on his back so he could see both of them at once. "No," he said. "First *you* decide we're going secret on our relationship, even to Lina, and then on our marriage as told to the worlds. *Then* we get to Lina, then to me. Let's get this in the right order."

"You're trying to distract," Lina murmured.

Lon frowned at him, visibly holding in harsh words. Finally he said, "Just tell us what's going on. In detail."

"I'll set up an Eyes Only folder," Lina offered, and Lon nodded at her.

"What do you know?" Jae asked them. "So I don't go over information you've already covered."

"Mimik is in on this," Lina said in a rush, as if it had just occurred to her.

Lon looked up, startled. "Mimik? My Mimik?"

Lina nodded. "I ported her in some time ago. She has quarters here but is rarely in them, and when she is, she comes in disguised as an Aldierran man. Military clothing. I haven't ported her out yet, but there have been plenty of ships available to take her back to the AffSys. Haven't checked lately to see if her quarters are still being used." She scratched the back of her head thoughtfully. "I should probably do that."

"She's still here." Jae sighed. "She's a major operative in this. The 'personal business' excuse for her taking leave is Aldierra." He added, "Bracken's been working with me as well."

Lina and Lon took that in.

"None of us want Aldierra to fail, Jae," Lina told him. "This isn't the same as Feith. Don't equate the two."

"How can I not?" Abruptly he threw off the sheets as best he could around Lon, then wiggled out of the bed. "I couldn't do anything about Feith dying. But I am in charge of the Aldierra situation. If I see ways to eliminate plots against our mission, I'm going to take them."

"And if Lupoff is a major problem…" Londo began but answered himself. "He is. He and those who follow him, even while smiling at us."

"Yes! And people like him. Govrle Kettite in particular. I'm rooting them out, discovering their networks. They have so many contacts. So many moles and sympathizers, mostly within the armies."

"Red or Green? Or–?"

"All of them. Lupoff got to be Patriarch because he held the goods on them all, even the armies who barely poke their heads above ground every few years. They live in fear of him and do his bidding, in hopes that if they kiss up to him, he'll elevate them into power – or at least not destroy them.

"Kettite's got something big on him, enough to keep him under control. Kettite's rearranging things as he can, positioning for a final battle. He's waiting for Lupoff to make a mistake so his people can step in. He wants to be Patriarch."

Jae wrapped his robe around himself and sat at the neighboring desk, where he could best signal screens. He found Lina's new folder within ultra-secure depths of their main database and transferred his files to it, wiping them from his own local systems.

One opened file traced various routes of information throughout the planet. It was color-coded as to armies, with civilians noted with a handful of colors of their own to designate their area of expertise.

Lon and Lina studied the chart, scrolling through it at their own speeds, which the system split up to allow them to do.

"I've met an awful lot of Aldierrans," Lina said as she scrolled. "Is there a secret way I can link my list to this? So when I come upon them, I know?"

Jae showed her. It always amazed him how much she organized her world. Ever since she'd come into the AffSys, and especially since Wiley had hooked them up with their sensory earrings, she'd programmed her own system to keep track of her contacts and note facts about them she felt were important, so if she ever met them again she would be able to put them in context and follow up on whatever matters they had brought to her attention.

Wiley was signaling him. "Later," Jae responded. Wiley would certainly give good input, as would others. Maybe it *was* time to loosen the seals on the plan, let others in. He truly couldn't operate as a solo, not when the entire world of Aldierra was at stake.

"I may have made a mistake," Jae admitted. "You probably should have been brought into this from the start." He huffed. "But you're both such awful liars!"

"I am a very good liar," Londo grumbled as he continued to follow the chart to see what actions had been taken so far. Mimik's path through it was a deep-reaching one.

"How much danger is she in?" Lon asked and was only partially reassured by Jae's answer. People were assigned as security backup to Mimik, just in case, though they knew her only by her disguise.

Jae expanded the screen to show his operations journal, and his spouses leaned forward to study it. They spent the next hour and a half discussing its major points as Jae and Lon called their Chiefs to have them rearrange their work day. Then they began to plot possibilities into the future, things that were able to change and expand now that they knew.

After that, they brought in Wiley, Chim and Demi. Jae sent Mimik a quick code to inform her of the new Three Worlds conspirators, and she relayed that to Bracken.

That awful, heart-squeezing panic Jae had been trying to restrain was still there, but in lesser form. He didn't relax, but he could now catch a full breath. Others shared the load. Others would stand behind him to help as he led the way to make sure Aldierra lived.

Still he wished he had a drink in his hand.

– – –

AS IF THINGS WEREN'T BUSY ENOUGH. Londo juggled his schedule, going all-out on the physical duties he had to do, like tearing up cities so Nesh and her crews could come through to landscape animal migration routes and natural areas. Overseeing the doubling-up of Houses as one would be moved out of their ancestral home to await new quarters that were updated but in unfamiliar territory. Stopping the fights that usually proceeded from same.

Coordinating with police departments and the armies. Lon thought people were going crazy before but now, as Deadline drew closer, they were absolutely insane. Screaming in the streets. Running around with weapons that they utilized freely, thinking there'd be no consequences. The police were overwhelmed. The parts of the armies that weren't put on peace-building, Londo directed to backing up the cops.

He had thousands of people now whose sole job was to visit various sites, especially the ones that required precision construction, to make sure workers were not only sober but qualified as to their jobs.

And now he added serious time talking to high-security experts in army movements and the history of political coups. What should he be looking for? What had successful coups done that made them successful? What kind of people participated in overthrowing a government?

It didn't take him long to realize that was exactly what he and his spouses were doing. Their actions were primarily in the open, though. If they were going to counter this insurgence, he needed strategies that could be… not as blatant. Let Jae operate undercover.

He also took the time to exploit his goodwill with the armies to subtly question people who had popped up on Jae's lists, then track down others who might be associated with them.

Valiant was not an unobtrusive personage, so he left the subtlety to agents his own staff recommended. Soon he had an investigative network that was almost as far-reaching as Jae's and explored areas Jae had chosen to ignore.

— — —

"JUST CHECKING IN, MAJOR GENERAL," Jae advised Kettite and the few other soldiers working in the area as he sauntered into the war room. Lighting was kept dim so the screens lining all surfaces could be better seen. "Making sure things are keeping to our schedule." He gave Kettite a Significant Look, reminding him that he was participating in a darker plot.

"The Patriarch is keeping a close watch on operations this close to Deadline," Kettite said.

"We have to get past the weather control reconfiguration next week," Jae responded. "I wonder if the Patriarch realizes just how much that will shake things up. It doesn't help that he's not… looking in the peak of health lately. I hope the stress is not getting to him. We have megas and paras training to contain the chaos as best it can be."

"Yet widespread destruction is entirely possible."

The lesser staff picked up at the conversation, obviously straining to hear everything above the low murmuring between officers, even as they attended to their jobs.

"We are doing everything we can to ensure as little destruction as possible," Jae replied. "Here, Aide-Major… ah, Muvvik." Jae indicated the maps on monitors in front of him. "Help me add the latest personnel assignments to these, if you would."

"Certainly, sir." Mimik rose from her controls to join him and they both leaned over the surface monitor. "Things are tense in this division," she – no, he should think of her as a male, Muvvik – told Jae quietly.

Across the room General Kettite worked with his small cadre of aides and assistants, plus two colonels, to address the latest orders Lupoff had sent down. They involved troop repositioning.

From what Jae could guess, the new postings would back up protections at Duktiv Keep. If any attack came from nearby Soshe, those troops would be perfectly triangulated, providing easy counter measures.

"Sir, are you expecting unrest in Soshe during the reconfiguration?" Muvvik asked Kettite. She pointed at the Warder River, south of the city. "A better position might be here. So much equipment is transported on the Warder. It would be best to secure it if anything would happen." She paused a moment. "Besides, water transportation is subject to many more variables than land or air."

"Air transportation will not be possible during weather reconfiguration," Jae put in. "It might be two or even three days afterward before that will be safe again."

Muvvik nodded. "Perhaps we should ask Major Dule his opinion. He's very familiar with the area and its tensions. He stood a tour as logistics chief there early in his career."

Kettite walked over to join them. "Major Dule has had a long career. That part of it was well in the past. I'm willing to bet that he'd hardly recognize the river as it stands now."

"Wroppie and Taltrene are currently filling the highest positions along that river," Muvvik told him.

Kettite nodded. "Then they would likely be the better choices to get to coordinate."

CHAPTER

28

Londo tried to ensure that Lina spent most of her days in her office instead of out on the road. She loved talking with the people to see what they needed but they could do that via screens almost as well. Communicating from her office was not only more efficient, but allowed her staff to keep better track of her hours.

True though, Bart had positioned journalists to follow her as much as possible. Lon had to admit that footage of the Speaker interacting with the common folk of Aldierra was gold. It not only endeared Lina to the public, but to their mission as well. The audience could see projects being done by Houses and even entire city sectors, and might choose on their own to accomplish something along the same lines.

A dizzying number of unexpected projects was being done around Aldierra, not under Three Worlds direct supervision. People were stepping up, working with each other. Those to-do suggestion lists Lina's offices posted were getting a huge amount of traffic.

She had an army of assistants, most of whom were now up to speed. Some helped her in office and supply matters; most others accompanied her outside or had matching missions of their own. The security force expanded to protect them as they went out into the world.

Lina had been talking with many people today, it seemed, for she floated into his office on her medichair, which she hardly used any more. She must be tired. This time there was an additional excuse for it: cats. Katie had spread herself on one chair arm, surveying their journey as if she were the chair's navigator, while

Obi and Bran-Bran snoozed in Lina's lap. One didn't disturb cats when they were settled.

"Lon," Lina said. "Honeybear…"

"Uh oh." He turned to her. "Honeybear" meant she was piling on the sugar. "What is it, *mon chou chou?*" he asked warily.

"Um. I know you're busy – super busy – with rebuilding Wovo-Nik and all."

Uh oh times two. She wanted to interrupt his work. He, Jae, and their staffs had been working so closely with the people of southern Limbernie, dealing with that minor Shit Flat that fed into the Scaly River. He'd torn down a good fourth of the megacity there, and rebuilding units were working as hard as they could, while the Aldierra Corps – and various prison facilities' populations – were dealing with the excrement. They'd made good progress in both areas.

Now Lina wanted to interrupt?

"There's a problem," she explained as her chair glided nearer his desk. With two gestures she brought up new screens showing central and southern Orchin just across the Geonie Sea from Limbernie.

Migratory patterns, check. He was familiar with them. Much of central Orchin was desert or semi-desert, mountains along the east coast, with western grassland steppes to mirror the more vibrant steppes of eastern Limbernie. Then there was some truly awful scrub forest in the south. Very thin subsoil; lots of rocks. Nesh was trying to come up with a good attack plan for that alone.

For such a populated world, southern Orchin's population density was scarce. Relatively speaking, that was.

Aldierra's average was about 130 people per square mile. He rubbed his nose, trying to remember statistics. Central Orchin… something like thirty? per square mile? Or had he been researching with kilometers? Of course the average greatly varied per local terrain. Still, that desert was damned empty. The only thing it was full of was abandoned mining sites.

Lina was going to be getting at something, Lon surmised. He shifted in his chair so he had a good view both of her and the maps.

She pointed. In the middle of nowhere: a small region.

"The people here, 'the Wastes,' some call it – Well, they may not like the place; don't know why they stay there but maybe there's nowhere else for them to go, or maybe it's a heritage thing; I haven't researched that part. Anyway, the important thing is that here in particular there are no medical facilities. Zero.

"There are extremely few facilities in the entire Wastes, or the steppes.

"Mortality rates are high for a number of reasons. The food we're supplying has helped a lot, but there are still diseases, bad if any water, and the awful physical conditions that only Aldierrans can give themselves."

"Because they don't care."

"Right. Well, we're helping with that, aren't we? They seem to have a hopeful spark in them when I talk with them."

She continued, "You *are* talking with the people, aren't you, Lon? And not just you but Jae as well, and not just to your troops but the average people, the people who make up most of Aldierra. Aren't you?"

He hadn't, not that much. "On occasion," he admitted. "I don't make a habit of it like you."

"Well, try it. At least ask some of your troops to introduce their families to you."

He nodded and then glanced to the maps. "Orchin?" he prompted.

"Look."

Another map appeared to show medical facilities on the lower continent. On others he'd expect to see a view covered with dots. Here: only a sparse handful. And the dots there were, were small clinics. Many of them were noted as not accepting female patients.

"That's not good," he murmured as he motioned for more info.

"We were thinking," she said. "And when I say 'we,' I mean they've been talking about this for a while, in specifics since we arrived. They need a central hospital, a big one. It would have to be huge, to serve half a continent. Or maybe three or four, spaced out, still pretty darned big. But here is pretty central for these Wastes people. It's a good place to begin. Most of them have little access to long-range transportation which is what they'd need to get there."

"Roads?" Lon asked. He tried to imagine a network.

"Eventually. We also need a network of lots of smaller clinics for everyday problems, spaced out according to population density. But for larger problems, for long-term problems, we need a real hospital. Better more than one, but…"

"A starting point." Lon rubbed his nose.

"Yes. Right now I was thinking maybe a fleet of supersonic ambulances from the clinics to it, with buses or maybe trains available for non-emergencies, or to haul families who want to be with their relatives or friends."

Lon began to doodle on the digital notepad he kept on his desk. "There'd need to be hotels for those…"

"Hotels and restaurants and entertainment facilities and nursing homes providing after-care, plus educational establishments both for the children coming with those families and for, say, medical personnel who would want more training. Facilities for support and business personnel on everything. They've already gathered a list of interested parties, and we've been helping them. There are more people than you'd expect wanting to reach out to help. It's so encouraging. The discussion has been there all the time, but–"

"But cultural attitudes."

"They didn't think there were enough of them to assume enough power to get it done. We're helping with that. Now there are organizations in place, movements across the entire continent, even places that aren't in the Wastes." She looked up at him with a expression of amazement. "They're saying 'Houses together.' Isn't that wonderful?"

"*Oui*." Lon had been hearing that. He pursed his lips as he regarded his maps. "You're talking one hospital. And an entire city."

Lina's head gave a quick, emphatic shake. "Town, Londo. Not an Aldierran-sized city. There used to be one, Li-Poor, right there a few hundred years ago. There are some nice ruins people could tour in their off-hours. We'd need guards. Preservationists."

"Water systems… Do they have ground water there? Enough for a small city?" Lon brought up more maps and linked in Jae's Chief. Some unit recently had surveyed aquifers. A major one ran underneath the site, which explained the ancient city. Not too deep but not shallow either. With a city drawing from it, it would need to be replenished periodically. Hm. Pipelines could be run from both the Geonie and South Spratly Seas. They'd have to desalinate; no problem. "We could do a decent municipal septic system. I've been looking at some variations.

A drain field could offer large recreational facilities on top, if it were done right…"

"We'd need more hospitals in the future," she reminded him. "This would be just to start them out. They're working on plans for others."

Lina was looking at him with adoration. He liked that, and smiled back at her.

"You're wonderful," she told him. "Can we really do this? Do you have time? I could port some megas and paras in to help, I think. There are a bunch who'd love to volunteer for something like this. You know all the municipal planners. Three significant Houses – say, five thousand people – are willing to relocate to work, because Li-Poor is their ancestral home. They'd be returning to their original Houses and allowing their overflow to remain in the existing ones. Allied Houses would likely come with them."

"We'd have to buy new tessercranes. Batchers. Print boxes," Londo mused. "Wait. I've been wanting to get a really large set because dammit, this is an entire planet and we still have a long way to go. We could put the oldest set we already have to use here."

C'a été donc Li-Poor. They were building a brand-new city. Lon gave a firm nod to himself and the project. Starting from scratch, showing them how it was done right.

"Get those Houses together," he instructed his wife.

"The affected ones have already had lots of meetings," she told him. "They stand ready for your direction. Regional Houses have been working hard on where to place the clinics so they serve both the people and the land."

He nodded. "Give the potential residents my plans for…" Lon checked his completed projects… "Hormu. The west side. Not for the buildings; just the traffic and business patterns. I'll give them plans for quarters and businesses that are working well. I need input for the area layout, so they can adjust for how they want things best positioned for what they need to do. You've probably got people standing by with possible hospital plans?"

"I do. They know what kind of things they need to deal with."

"*Bon.*" Hm. He rubbed his nose again and Lina waited. She was quivering in her chair with eagerness, and the cats were beginning to stir. Yeah, this would be interesting. Different. And none of the same ol' that established Aldierra liked so much. "I want to play with some building plans. Give me some contacts, both for the Houses and the hospitals and clinics. Let's make these different. I still want to see what has been there historically, but let's try something new."

In their enthusiasm they might have used up more of their scheduled break than was wise to congratulate each other. They might have scared the cats in doing so, but they didn't mind. They both returned to their duties a while later with lighter, satisfied hearts.

— — —

JAE'S PRESENCE AT FORT IRONWOOD at the mouth of the Warder River did not go unnoticed. Alongside his presence alone, Jae had made sure he'd be noticed by altering the heels of his boots so that they would make a satisfactory click on military flooring.

Beside him, Mimik moved comparatively in silence. Between they two, they maintained constant communication through their Legion Array rings, which vibrated directly into their bones. The vibrations created a sound that only they could hear.

The Majority Army's secret plots wouldn't be found on normal channels. And often higher-ranks wouldn't be involved. People of lower rank were often more easily manipulated or persuaded. They had the most to profit from an insurrection.

Even so, Jae split off from Mimik to pay his respects to Commander Wroppie. As soon as Wroppie's aide ushered him into the commander's office, Jae could sense the tension in the room.

There were listening devices: there, there and there. Odd for so many to be present. Did Wroppie know of them all?

"The Patriarch sends greetings," Jae said. "He wants to know the preparedness of Fort Ironwood. Is it ready?"

For what, Jae didn't specify. He waited for the response.

After a moment, Wroppie said, "Ironwood is almost there. The last pieces are being arranged even at this moment. Personnel have been trained. Equipment has been installed. It's only the final programming we lack, and that should be done by end of day tomorrow."

"Excellent." Jae turned in a partial circle to take in the room. Each day brought word that Lupoff's plans were larger than he'd suspected when this all began. Lupoff's machinations could foul everything. "I have technology that can speed things up, if you need it. Expand your range."

By an iota, Wroppie relaxed as he must have realized he'd made the proper conclusions. "We would welcome that. Is it AffSys tech?"

"AffSys and a little more," Jae replied. "Enough to handle both events in good form."

"Both?"

Jae set his expression at puzzlement. "Two events," he said after a pause. "You've been told of the first, but not the second?" He nodded to himself. "That sounds like the Patriarch being careful. I'll inform him that you need to be in on the plans. Or… I can inform you myself. His Excellency has been advised to slow down for his health. Too much stress, you know. We can take the pressure off him."

Wroppie indicated a chair, and Jae took a seat on it. "Please, Minister. No time like the present."

Jae nodded. "Time is slipping by," he confirmed. He motioned and a dark privacy screen surrounded them. A map of Sha-Green shimmered into the air. Diagrams and bulleted points covered it. Mimik, Bracken and he had taken a lot of time to work this out. "Make your own notes. Don't put this in your systems."

Then he talked, careful to make note of what Wroppie knew even as he fed him misinformation.

$$- - -$$

MUVVIK APPEARED AROUND THE CORNER as Jae emerged from Wroppie's offices. The disguised Legionnaire subtly pulled some skin into place, adjusting her semblance to correctness. She must just have been impersonating someone else. Her changes, like Jae's powers, took time to complete.

Wroppie walked at Jae's side. "Taltrene is not on board," he told Jae quietly. Jae gave a small nod and looked to Muvvik.

"Shall we continue our tour?" Jae asked her.

Up the Warder River, Fort Drill-Burridge was not nearly as large as Ironwood had been, but its personnel were industrious. Maybe they'd been warned that Jae was in the area. Maybe they were merely attentive to their duties.

Col. Taltrene was every inch the attentive officer when he met Jae. Jae could sense his indecision: which side was the Minister for Aldierra on?

"Let's check out your preparations for the weather changeover," Jae told Taltrene. "It's in less than a week. We don't want your base damaged."

Taltrene nodded vigorously. Nervously. "Command has indicated that it will sustain level seven destruction."

"Sustained," Jae agreed. "But there will be places we cannot pinpoint where for short periods it will go up to a level nine."

"Nine!"

Jae stretched his neck and shoulders as if this had been a tremendous burden. "We can only go so far in our projections," he told Taltrene. "This has never been accomplished before. We must be prepared."

"Yes sir!"

The two toured the fort, with Muvvik excusing himself to widen the inspection, accompanied by officers of less rank. Jae pointed out possible problems. He had no wish for people to be hurt by the coming operation. The tour showed him places where Fort Drill-Burridge had realigned various weaponry systems recently. Jae examined them on the excuse of the weather changeover.

Taltrene and his aides took copious notes even as they pointed out other newer systems that had not yet been battened down.

Lupoff was definitely gearing up for some kind of military coups, likely tied to the changeover. It would be a time when attention was rightfully directed elsewhere as the Three Worlds' plans worked around the planet. There would be widespread damage that would have to be dealt with as it happened, and leftover storms would combine with secondary disasters that would have to be combatted.

It would be a perfect time for someone to take unethical advantage of the situation.

Among this group Jae received no indications of loyalty to Aldierra and not Lupoff. His Legion Array amplified a conversation on the edges of the crowd of aides that spoke of "Worldstorm," which as it progressed sounded like a code-word for a covert operation.

When they reunited after the tour, Mimik added the word to her notes.

CHAPTER

29

This seemed like something out of some old British period soap, Lina mused. Veddy prim and proper with an extra serving of olde-fashioned etiquette. Still, it needed to be done.

You can do this, her guides told her.

She stood to greet the four women, all Lupoff's wives, as they arrived from the security checkpoint outside the Starhart tent. "Pelzire."

Here was Asma, Patriarch Lupoff's most senior wife. She was of medium height, Aldierran-slender build, and dyed dark hair under a satiny snood. She was slightly stooped with age, but she was still here and not dead. A long life, compared to most other Aldierran women. She was… something like fifty? Her eyes looked older than that, with deep creases to either side, matching the ones around her mouth as if she spent her life frowning. Makeup had been thickly applied, likely covering the evidence of some illness or another. Maybe of violence.

"I'm so honored you could come," Lina enthused as she led the small group from the foyer. She took them on a short tour of how the Starharts lived, and Lina could feel the women contrasting and comparing with their own home. The cloth walls alone should have been a new experience for them. Still they were visibly shocked when Lina let them peek into the main bedroom, explaining that all three Starharts slept there.

In a front room – not their real dining room – a cozy dining area had been assembled, dressed with warm carpets and some impressive bits of Jae's collected bric-a-brac. Of course they'd put a picture of Lupoff on one wall.

They took their seats. Three other women had come with Asma, ranging in age though no one of these could be over, oh, forty years old. The youngest was barely twenty. And married to a geezer like Lupoff. Ugh. Visibly pregnant.

They all wore a new style of air mask, which mimicked a veil that draped across their noses. It was actually rather pretty. Lina complimented them on it, and they preened.

"I do have some influence with fashion," Asma confided.

"That's nice to know. In this complex our air is filtered, so you don't need them. If you wish, you can take them off."

Hesitantly for the youngest, Shanza, they set their veil masks to the side of their plates and looked curiously at the settings. Some of the women were missing teeth and didn't open their mouths much either when they ate or spoke. Their gums did not look healthy. Lina had a female aide pour tea for everyone, and appetizers appeared soon afterward.

They talked of their homelife with the Patriarch. "How is His Excellency?" Lina asked. "Is it my imagination – everyone is under stress these days – or has he been looking a trifle ill lately? Paler than usual, certainly."

They assured her that Lupoff was as well as ever.

"I suppose I'm just sensitive right now." Lina chatted.. "I had a bad spell there myself," she told them. "Lon and Jae and all the doctors said I had to slow down a little." It was just a few days ago. She pointed at her right earring. "This now keeps track of my sleep and meals, in addition to communications and recording and such."

"And what happens if it doesn't like what you're doing?"

Lina sighed. "Then I bow to my computer masters, grab something to eat, and take a nap. We have a deadline that is more important than my ego, thinking I can do everything and no one else can help."

Which made a good segue to gentle inquisition as the main part of luncheon arrived: were they working in any fashion to help their world's situation?

"We have people who do what needs to be done," Asma assured Lina.

The others did not talk much unless Lina directed a question specifically at them. She learned the regions they'd come from – mostly Reyda and Sha-Green, and they were all familially related to Red and Green Army members.

Each had married young as a result of agreements and treaties between political and military powers. Krusta had been the first, but she was dead now. There had been another wife, also dead, through complications of childbirth. Lina might look her up if she turned out to be important.

Asma had been sought after by many because of her family ties. So had Chio, the second-youngest. The youngest, Shanza, might not have had as many offers because it had been clear from the start that Lupoff had his eyes on her. She had been handed to him with little legalese involved.

Hunuhe and Chio were of mid-level importance in their female household and silent, though their gazes took in the room, the food, and especially Lina.

None had been formally educated beyond what any average Aldierran female achieved. That was mostly education in how to run a household (without letters or numbers), how to please a man. There was some kind of internal political structure with the women of a House that had to be learned and adhered to. A senior wife was often the Woman in Charge. Shanza smirked when Asma told Lina this. Shanza must be plotting a coup of her own.

They were astonished as Lina revealed her own background. Curious about how she and Londo had gotten together. "I was always mesmerized by him," she admitted. "A member of his fan club, with no pretentions to ever meeting him, much less anything else. We were thrown together – not accidentally, it turned out – and fell for each other. Then he told me that Jae was part of the deal, and by then I'd already become uncomfortably infatuated with Jae.

"Before I could tell Jae that I needed to take some time from him so I wouldn't be tempted, I found out about him and Lon. They'd been a twosome for years, though they couldn't do anything physical in that time. They offered the threesome." Lina hefted her shoulders with a guilty smile. "It was… quite odd at first, but I was a new bride and even that was odd." She chuckled. "And I was so crazy about both of them that it seemed the right thing to do."

She paused and raised her eyebrow at the ladies. "Though I did have to insist on some basics before we made it legal. They countered; we discussed, and came to mutual agreement. Then we had a…" she sighed with another smile… "lovely wedding. At Starhaven. That's going to be our main home, on Earth. Our witnesses were the cats and some close friends."

"You bargained? With men?"

Chio elbowed Hunuhe, who shared a Look. "She is the Speaker; she gets to do what she wants," might have been the message.

"I was an equal party in the deal," Lina said. "I had a say in the matter. This was the way marriages were decided on Feith. I was not going to be walked on in any way."

She cut some more vegetables on her plate. "The Triune is a balancing act. We are distracted by Deadline and our outside duties. It's extremely difficult to find some alone time for each other, but we try to take at least a few minutes every week to discuss our relationship. We don't want things to go south before we have a chance to truly get this marriage up and running. We're trying to deal with the bumps in the road before they become hurdles. And we keep very much in mind the idea that there's going to be a honeymoon when this is all over."

"Really." Asma's face twisted as she tried to digest the thought. She glanced at Hunuhe to share.

"After Deadline we're going to up our meetings with an AI Feithi marriage counselor. We want our relationship to be a healthy one, one that allows us to grow as people and support each other without feeling demeaned. Oh – sorry. Is that an insult? I didn't mean it to be."

Oh, the conversation after that! Each woman now had many questions, and there were hints of domestic violence. Sexual danger from the men passing through the household on army business. Danger from the men assigned to guard them.

And from some of the dark looks passed along the table, danger from Asma.

Those questions allowed Lina more freedom to interrogate them over chocolate and more tea. Lina asked about the men whom they were frightened of. Who'd been visiting Lupoff lately? Was there another way the women could protect themselves from them?

Oh, they'd met Siekesh and Dule? And some fellow named Kettite? Another: Cone-Sycup? Had any of them been meeting with Lupoff much before Deadline had gone into effect, or was this only after the Deadline had been announced?

God, she hoped she was being subtle.

"THERE ARE AIDES to the highest-ranking military," Lina reported to Lon and Jae afterward. "They will work undercover for the wives if the wives put in a good word to Lupoff for them. Cone-Sycup's aide was mentioned more than once. Everyone in both directions insists on extreme secrecy, though. A wrong word can mean death or worse, dishonor."

Bracken, Liten, Walker, and Kanti were all present as well, adding their comments to the description of Lupoff's hidden power structure.

"Why did Lupoff allow one daughter?" Jae asked. "That's bothered me."

Lina nodded. "She was Asma's. Daughters in the Lupoff family were forbidden up to then, but Lupoff thought he could get away with it. He was powerful enough and thought this was a new avenue to more power he could explore.

"The wives explained that they'd been allowed to live because their families thought they'd need something extra in order to form power alliances. Having a beautiful daughter who was the member of a powerful family was sometimes a good thing, a solid bargaining chip."

Liten nodded. "Absolutely."

Lina went on, "Chio had a sister whom she loved. When Chio was twelve, the sister was ten, the family deemed the sister not pretty enough to support a reasonable alliance. She'd had an illness that left scars. She was killed."

Kanti and Lon sucked in air.

"Chio blames that trauma on why she has been… dissociated emotionally from others. She didn't say that aloud. She was shouting her anger internally." Both Lon and Jae nodded. "She has learned to put on a good show. Pandering works; she's made it an art. It's what brought her to Lupoff's attention. Now she relies on drugs to get her through her days. Our equipment showed that Hunuhe was also pretty out of things during the meal."

"But they utilize military aides?" Jae prompted, and Lina nodded.

"Asma's daughter was allowed to live. The first wife – Krusta – didn't like it, but Lupoff kept the daughter as a possible bartering chip. Then Lupoff held a Goldens ceremony when the child was only ten."

Gritted teeth from the non-Aldierrans in the group. Golden ceremonies involved sex acts that "sealed" contracts.

"The girl was married off to one of one of Lupoff's top enemies, or maybe competitors, in the Blue Army. Krusta arranged it. After the Goldens ceremony, the man had orders not to have intercourse with the girl until a year after she entered puberty. That's pretty liberal here. He didn't wait; the girl ended up pregnant when her body couldn't handle it, and she died. The beatings she had suffered at his hands could not have helped matters but she was his property.

"That husband died three weeks later from an ambush. Lupoff and his top cronies had public alibies. These things happen. But everyone knows that Asma had arranged it, through the aides she used. She hates the Blues." Lina paused. "Quite unexpectedly, Krusta died a few days after that. Asma became senior wife. She is a force to be feared."

Lina told them that the wives sat around most of their days, making themselves beautiful, taking drugs, and fighting with each other and other women in their compound. "Now that three of them are post-menopausal," Lina said, "they aren't utilized by Lupoff as much. He often hands them off to men as a reward."

"I don't think getting Asma or Hunuhe would be much of a reward," Kanti muttered, and two men's grunted agreements echoed her.

"I asked if that were so, did they at least get a choice of who they had to sleep with," Lina said. "They reacted as if they'd never considered that idea before. I think they do now."

"Other matters: we need to encourage the aristocracy to utilize their free time to work with the mission," Bracken said even as he researched some of the names that had come up.

"I'll get PR to address this," Kanti told him. "Make it a prestige thing. Show people looking up to those who work for the cause."

"Better a poor excuse than no excuse," Jae agreed.

"We will shape them into new habits," Walker declared.

− − −

LON SCRATCHED HIS HEAD, pulling his hair into complete disarray. These plans. These blueprints of his. No, no, no. He rubbed his nose. The entire town of Li-Poor would have to be built underground. That way the arid environment and harsh sun – well, it would be harsher once they cleared the air more – would be made bearable. But there was something terribly wrong, and he just couldn't put his finger on it except that he knew something was at fault with some of the basics. Not the entire concept? *Peut-etre.*

If someone had asked him if he wanted to live in one of these housing units, he would have told them where to go. They were... Sarastoran, that's what they were. Or maybe the type of underground housing Earth was beginning to build. Machinelike. The human equation was relegated to afterthought.

Instead of closing off from Aldierran culture, the city should make it come alive, reflecting the long history and many peoples of southern Orchin.

This was what he'd always wanted to do: design an entire community from scratch, with his distinctive fingerprints all over it. His style. Oh, it should have a thick veneer of Aldierra set upon it, of course. Well, maybe Aldierra should form the foundation, and his fingerprints could be applied liberally as a veneer.

Everything should be underground. Yes. Like some of those post-apocalypse movie cities.

Why couldn't he do this?

It was the kind of thing he'd danced around for years, designing buildings here and there. His designs – in teamwork with hundreds of others – now housed entire cities that had been reconstructed individual sector by sector.

But not all at once.

Two beeps from midair. "Vet appointment; Molly," a voice said. Was it time already? And *marde*, Molly.

Lon got up and stretched. He needed a break. Clear his mind. But… *Molly.* It was time for her annual checkup and shots. Lina was busy in the Magna sea cities still; she had been afraid that her appointments would take longer than she'd thought. No need to pile this onto her schedule. He strolled into the home tent's storage room and picked up a cat carrier, a hard plastic box with a metal gate over the front opening. Put a towel in it as a cushion, Lina had said, and he got one.

Mart was on Earth today, doing some final veterinary study. He'd assured Lina that he'd be prepared for the appointment but that he couldn't make a house call. He still needed oversight from the vet school. Molly would have to come to him.

Now. Where was Molly? Hellcat.

"Molly!" Lon called. "Molly!" There were Moose and Ember, but when they saw him, they turned and ran away. No, it wasn't because they saw him, it was because they saw The Box.

Lon put the offending item down and quickly walked in search of the hellcat. There she was outside, a great ball of long, orange fur sunning herself near Fafhrd's Bluff. He tried to be nonchalant. "Molllly! Come here, Molly!" She perked up her head suspiciously. She could be a biter when cornered and didn't enjoy not being able to bite him without hurting herself. The other day he had found her running around with one of his socks in her mouth. She'd settled down in a corner, staring death at him, and had unsuccessfully tried to shred it to pieces, growling as she did so.

Last night he'd been cuddling up to Jae in bed when she'd jumped up with them and sunken her claws about six inches into his butt, through the blankets. Him letting out a howl had not been a good idea, and jumping out of bed and running after her down the hallway as she fled had not enamored him to her at all.

He tried to make his voice sound sweet. "Come on, Molly. Molly-Wolly. Come to Papa." He rubbed his fingers together to attract her attention. "Psp psp psp." She looked at him and lay her head back on the ground, closing her eyes as if she were asleep. He knew she wasn't.

"*Okay d'ac*, we do this the hard way," Londo grumbled to himself as he retreated to gather equipment. Then he glided soundlessly over her. She raised her head and looked around to see if he'd gone. "Right here," he chortled, and she looked up, letting out a little cat *meep* of surprise. He grabbed her with padded gloves before she could bolt, and held on as she fiercely tried to break out of his unbreakable grip. She yowled, louder and louder, and bit at his vest, scratching at it instead of his skin.

"Easy, girl," Lon said, but she started to hiss. He held her with one hand as he opened the gate to the cat door and pushed her in. Or tried to. She extended both hind feet to either side, straddling the box; she wouldn't fit the opening. Lon considered, and then grasped both back feet in one hand while holding onto the rest of her with the other. She hissed and spat at him, and he stuffed her into the box vertically, clapping the gate closed. Hoping he hadn't broken any of her bones.

She yowled. Yowled and howled and tried to claw and bite the metal gate. He picked up the box and called Lina for transportation.

"Port, Molly, port," he said firmly as a warning before everything turned black.

Two long minutes later he appeared inside a modest Terran Vet School office, right in front of the appointment window. The assistant there looked up from her screen and gave a little jump. Molly howled from her cage, a great hooting, yodeling sound of distress mixed with anger and fear.

"Do they always carry on like this?" Lon asked helplessly, bringing the cage up to eye level. Molly spat at him before she yodeled again. "She's not going to break her teeth on that grate, is she?"

The assistant had to laugh despite her awe. "Not if we get her out of it quickly, sir," she said. "I take it Molly's not in a good mood today."

"Molly's a spoiled little brat cat," Londo growled into the cage. Hate spilled from Molly's eyes.

"You're not helping things," a male voice said from behind Londo. He turned to see Mart. "May I?"

Londo handed him the cage, and the doctor looked in. "Hi, Molly," he said softly in English. "Remember me? We're here to make sure you stay well. Let's take you back to examining room number two, so you don't scare all our other patients, shall we?"

Molly's volume decreased to a low growl as she clawed, and Lon followed the doctor back, nodding at the other people who were here with their pets. In this case, he didn't care if he were getting preferential treatment.

He closed a room door behind him, and the doctor let Molly out of her cage as two assistants or perhaps vet school teachers looked on. She wouldn't come out. She stopped hissing, but she wouldn't exit.

"I've seen a style of cloth bag used to transport small Terran pets," Mart mentioned. "I think the idea is new. Reports are that they're easier on both owner and pet."

"We will get six." Londo reached in and pulled out Molly as she bit his shirt, gnawing on it fiercely.

"She doesn't like me," Lon said.

"Still? You're still not used to your cats," the doctor said, amused by the parahero. "Tell me, have you been feeding them?"

"For the most part I have. Lina was in charge of Fafhrd's medicine, for obvious reasons. I would have accidentally ripped that poor cat in half if I'd tried administering it. I was put in charge of feeding them as my schedule permits. Everyone thought it would make the cats love me. Didn't work on this one. We got off on a bad foot."

"The way to a cat's heart is through her belly," the doctor intoned, patting Molly on her own belly. "Speaking of which, yours is getting a little large, Molly. Been eating a lot, have you?" He lifted the cat up to a baby scale, but Molly darted off. Lon caught her with one hand.

They had to have Lon hold her while he stepped on some scales in the back room, and then they weighed Lon alone.

"That's okay, Molly," the doctor murmured to the cat. Molly seemed calmer when the doctor held him. "Good girl."

"So what's the trick?" Lon asked when they were back in the office.

"Have you had the time to play with her? With any of the cats?"

"I'm required to check off twenty minutes a day for that. Obi and I play with his track. Katie's so independent, she's almost always out hunting around; she comes in and takes her nap and then she's gone again. She'll walk with me sometimes. Bran likes to come over and be petted; he doesn't care who does it. Ember's Jae's cat now, and puts up with me because she knows that Jae's my partner. And Moose… I never know how to play with him. He has moods. He's either acting crazy or, well, missing. We pay attention to him when and if he shows up."

"Moods," the doctor mused. "Quite a few cats have them, I'm told."

"But Molly hates me with a pure and vicious hatred," Londo said, eying the yellow cat.

"Then I'll get someone else to help with this," the doctor said, and one of the observing doctors stepped forward.

They took Molly's temperature rectally, and Molly squirmed and growled and tried to bite. Lon held up his hands. "See?" he told Molly. "I'm not doing it. They're doing it."

She spat at him and he sighed.

"Try to think like a cat," the supervisor suggested. "Look at her body signals and figure out what she's saying or what mood she's in. Molly's one of the more excitable cats, but according to her records she's usually been in a good mood or afraid. She's a sweetie, isn't she, Molly?" she sing-songed, and Molly stopped growling to look at her. "Yes she is, a liddle shweedie baby."

Lon and Mart looked at each other.

"Thanks, Ginnie," Mart told her. "How's about getting me three shots for our Molly? Or should I do that?"

"I'll get them," the other doctor or nurse, Chase, volunteered brightly and closed the door behind himself.

Londo watched as Mart gave Molly her exam, listening to her and palpitating her. She took it stoically, and both Mart and Ginnie kept telling her what a good cat she was. "Even if she isn't, she might think that she is if I tell her enough," Ginnie confided to Londo. "Animals understand a lot more than we think they do. Like babies. Babies understand speech long before they try to talk."

Mart concurred. "There's a lot of body language to learn. Tail language alone, and then there's how she holds her ears and what posture she assumes. You can tell a lot just by watching a cat. Just a bit more, Molly."

Chase returned to arrange the shots on the examining table and watched closely as Mart administered them. "Very good," he remarked. Then Londo opened up the gate to the cat carrier and Molly zipped in all by herself, rolling into a ball in the back, her butt facing the front.

Lon paid, thanked the doctors and Mart, who was staying on Earth for two more days, and was about to signal Lina for transport when he saw that there was a small arts and crafts store next to the vet. He carried the cage like a briefcase and visited it.

— — —

NOW HE SAT IN HIS HOME OFFICE with his blueprints, technical requirements, and topological surveys on the computer screens. A very large mound of clay sat in front of him. Underneath it was a solid reproduction of one area of the proposed town, done with the 3D mini-sculptor. That area was already a basin and might warrant filling in and then covering over for his underground city.

He'd given the clay mound that would become the city structure the preliminary shape of a beehive with the bottom cut off, a cone with an opening on top. It was just for roughing in, a shape that allowed for sunlight to enter. The city couldn't be dark. He peered down into the opening as Molly ran up and down the fabric walls outside the office, *free at last, free at last!* An occasional happy *yow* reinforced her mood.

She ran into the room and circled it at top speed.

"Out, Molly!" he yelled, and she zipped out of the room to run up and down the hall again. *Mow, mow!* He'd been told this was called "the zoomies."

He didn't want this project to look like a hive stuck in the middle of the undulating landscape. In geological times, southern Orchin had once held a huge lake. Now it was primarily high mesa, modifying into parched gullies, buttes, and canyons, most of it set upon a type of sandstone as the area extended across the lower continent.

Okay, he'd put sloping sidewalks into the underground city like the Guggenheim on steroids; that seemed natural enough. Those would be easiest for non-ambulatory patients. Occasional terraces to break it up, let people rest. But people needed natural light to function best. How often would the sun be directly overhead to shine down the well? Would it still be too hot? He pressed another package of clay into a hollow mound shape and put it next to the first, squinting at the effect. Breasts. Pert big breasts in the landscape. They could call it Silicon

City. Or Boobtown. He sculpted two nipples and set them on top of the mounds to complete the effect.

Molly came scrambling in again, hopping onto the table that was on the other side of the room. Her landing made her slide on some paper, scattering sheets every which direction.

"Molly!" Londo bellowed. Defiantly she ran twice around him and before he could react, she was up on his table, heavily landing on top of the one mound, poking her feet through the clay shell, sitting down on the second mound and scrabbling as she couldn't free her feet.

"*Câlisse!* Molly!" Controlling himself Londo carefully picked her up and stopped. Waitaminnit. The mounds were squashed now, lumpy as if they'd been hills and not constructions. There were still the major lightwells, but now they were organically tipped and shaped, not just round, and there were minor wells here and there, scattering light inside in a pleasing pattern, or one that could be if they were placed right. The larger ones were tilted to the south, not the sun's direct path across the sky. That would permit a fair amount of light without so much heat. And one entire side of the mound could be higher than the other. It would give variety, let more people have a windows out the sides of the city for their living quarters...

It didn't have to be so equilateral. He could landscape the inside of his mounds as well as the outside. Natural lines, flowing lines, quiet pools where the lines gathered, straighter lines when he wanted to direct the flow to a faster pace. These interior clay support walls were now waves. They looked like…

Until just a few centuries ago, most people of the Wastes were nomadic. They'd lived in tents that were broken down and moved to their next encampment. The Wastes were proud of their history; he'd noticed romantic media entertainment that hearkened back to it, the nomadic chieftains heroes in their stories.

Treat the walls of the underground city as if they were the sides of tents, blowing in a desert wind. Undulations. Natural, with occasional formal Orchin architectural elements breaking it up for interest and utility. Tiny perforations dotting the roof like Molly's toenails cutting through the clay, creating dappled light for the heretofore shadowed corners. An oasis or two to brighten things. Yes. Yes.

He could clearly imagine people wandering through this city when it was finished. Smiling. Talking with each other. People with disabilities not being seen as oddities but as part of the community.

"Londo Starhart designed this city," they'd remark to each other. And, "Isn't this the nicest place to live? It's perfect."

"Londo Starhart is a genius!"

Yes.

— — —

WHEN LINA CAME HOME from her appointment, she found Londo in the kitchen with Molly sitting on the breakfast table. He was hand-feeding her flakes of nutri-treat straight out of the tube. "Yer a widdie sweedie, Molly," he cooed to the cat. "Papa's golden baby girwl."

She purred as she munched.

CHAPTER

30

Jae strode into Advisor Siekesh's inner office. "Why aren't the armies able to accomplish anything?" he demanded loudly as the door closed behind him.

Siekesh stood up at Jae's entrance. "Minister," he said. "Are we…?"

"Protected," Jae announced with a slight squinting of his eyes. He could also feel a vibration: Mimik noticed the action, from her position to Siekesh's left, disguised as Muvvik. Jae nodded at her. "Muvvik," he acknowledged.

The glance Siekesh spared her was one filled with uncertainty.

"Muvvik asked me to come here to reassure you about our plans," Jae told the Intelligence Advisor… and his aide, who would be listening from his office. "His word is to be trusted, absolutely."

"In my line of work there are no 'absolutes,'" Siekesh countered.

"In mine, there are."

Jae called up screens showing troop movements, camp enlargements.

"I knew about the one in the Jezarun Hills," Siekesh said.

"There are also these others that Muvvik has discovered."

Siekesh shook his head slowly. "I have a very large net of informers. I don't think that some of these plans could have slipped their notice."

Muvvik stood. "I have my own ways of discovering information," he said… and began to morph into a copy of Siekesh.

He couldn't summon breath for long moments as both Jae and Mimik watched him.

"Muvvik is a teammate of mine from Sarastor," Jae decided to tell him. "A mega with unique powers."

"They let me infiltrate areas others might not be able to access," Mimik told Siekesh.

"I… I should say so." Siekesh sat heavily, his face dazed.

"Muvvik has a big job coming up," Jae explained. "He will be taking the place of a soldier who maintains an important job. This soldier is always in the background when any large operation is happening. We'll need her to be able to make the switch while ensuring she stays alive."

"'She'?"

"I mean 'he,' of course." Jae gave Muvvik a small smile.

Muvvik reverted to her Muvvik disguise and placed his right hand on his chest. "Muvvik must exit the stage. Advisor, you need to start making aspersions my way. Not colossal ones, for I don't want to be arrested or worse before I can make this switch. Enough so that when the time comes in a few days, we think during the weather reconfiguration, I can be branded a traitor in a limited space, which the Minister here will control."

Muvvik pushed a small padd toward Siekesh. "This contains some questionable actions I've been involved with these past weeks. At least the ones I allowed witnesses to. Alone, they don't account for much, but taken as a whole…"

Siekesh's cheeks puffed out as he eyed the screen. "Apparently you've been plotting against the Patriarch for the benefit of another," he surmised. "Who is this…?"

"Flimmettre," Muvvik told him.

"We're going to tell people that he wants to be the new Patriarch," Jae said.

Siekesh's lips moved to the side in a half-grimace. "He does. In time. He's not willing to assassinate to achieve the position."

"You know that. And we know that. But it seems Muvvik here–" Jae cocked his head toward his friend– "has been told something else and is operating on that information. On Flimmettre's orders."

"I've faked some older assignment papers from him for Muvvik and buried them in the system," Muvvik told him. "They'll probably come to light… soon?"

Siekesh chewed on that. "Yes, soon."

"Hold before you unleash everything you've got," Jae said. "We have the day for the switch chosen, but the precise time is still in flux."

"Not by much," Muvvik countered, and Jae nodded, straightening his back. "I dislike putting colleagues in danger."

Siekesh palmed the padd before depositing it into an inner pocket. "Danger comes with this job. Contact me as soon as you have a specific time and I'll be sure that whoever you need to know this, knows."

"It will be Kettite, sir."

That name deflated Siekesh. "You aim high," he decided to say.

"Deadline is less than three weeks past our switch-out date. We must accomplish this in the little time we have left."

"Yes, Doomsday…" Siekesh breathed.

— — —

THESE NIGHTS IT WAS HARD TO SLEEP. Jae was restless as he slumbered lightly, his breath pungent with alcohol. Lina tossed and turned, groaning, sometimes whimpering from within her dreams, and there was nothing Londo could do but lie awake and worry, going over and over what they were accomplishing. What else could they be doing? How could they do it better?

He could sense her earring was about to beep, but he used his own to intercept. "I'll handle this," he told whoever it was on duty in the Speaker section.

He rose from bed and summoned a hush curtain as he activated his Legion Array ring. "No," he said simply.

"Londo, we need a port. It's an emergency." It was Stoan's voice.

"No. No more ports. She needs her sleep."

"We wouldn't have called unless it was an absolute emergency," Stoan said tightly. "Thousands of lives could depend on this."

"And twenty billion lives definitely depend on this. I'm sorry," Londo's voice broke, and he bit his lip. "I'm sorry."

"Londo!"

"I'm sorry. I hope you can manage this emergency, but do it on your own. No more Legion porting, day or night, for Lina until the Aldierra deadline is passed. We need her here. We need her rested. Starhart out."

Ten seconds later Jae's ring beeped. He twitched in his sleep, and Lon reached over to draw the ring off Jae's finger. He walked down the short hallway, Molly rose up momentarily to get out of his way, and Lon went into the kitchen to its small breakfast table. There he placed Jae's ring before taking his own off to put next to it.

Jae didn't say anything the next morning when he went to find it, and Lina didn't mention seeing the rings there when she had fed the cats earlier. They both knew what must have happened, and Lon's grim visage did not encourage questions.

– – –

THEY WERE FINALLY DOING THIS THING. Lina was terrified of the idea.

It was so *big*.

And it absolutely, positively had to be done.

Across Aldierra, earthquake monitors were registering mini quakes. The planet was trembling with excitement.

People across the world had been preparing: inventorying infrastructure, repairing and replacing what they could. The Three Worlds helped on the large projects, but couldn't do everything. Communities and sub-cities had stepped up to pitch in as they could.

Lina's staff had scheduled this for three weeks before Deadline. Get it done. A few days for things to settle, then clean up the aftermath. Take another week to look around to see what they'd missed. Another week to finish what they could…

And then Doomsday.

"Call, Speaker."

Lina jumped when Tidda's voice sounded in her ear. She wouldn't have interrupted for anything but an emergency or…

It was Asma Lupoff, the Patriarch's wife.

"I want more protection!" she shrilly demanded as her screen popped up.

"We're busy here," Lina began.

"And we are in danger! All of us! He hasn't done anything to reinforce our quarters. Our people, our servants, are going crazy with fear!"

Her face was white except for the purple rings under her eyes and around her mouth.

"You've had lots of warning. All cities have safety shelters for this. Use one of them."

"With the common people? I want—"

"Then all I can advise is to shelter in inner rooms, like we've told everyone," Lina said to the woman.

"We need better than that! We are Lupoffs!"

"Everyone," Lina repeated. "Shelter in inner rooms. Stay away from windows. If you have time, move to a location that is built sturdier than your home, though your compound should be one of the most protected places on the planet."

"Not good enough, Speaker! I *demand*—"

"Then demand it of your husband," Lina said brusquely. "We have important work to do here."

"I am wife to the Patriarch! How dare you—"

Lina clicked off her screen.

She had to close her eyes then take a deep, deep breath. Inhale. Count to four. Exhale.

"Let's do this," Lina muttered between gritted, determined teeth. Then louder, so communications could hear her: "Let's do this. Status. Central Control?"

One by one, the stations checked in. Global monitoring stations reported their readiness. Orbiting weather observers began to recheck their readings.

One hundred Legionnaires waited on the surface. Two hundred Legion-adjacent paras held their positions, with over a score of non-Legion types joining them. Yusuf called in from the South Pole. Hal and three ParaNetters stood ready, assembled near where the operation would begin. Wiley; Kanti, with Deputy Chief Ardy Wavewatch, Kanti's backup; and three heads of various departments sat next to Lina along with assistants also watching just this first phase, in front of a long bank of monitors. Demi was here to oversee the first hour or so. After that she was scheduled for sleep, and would take Lina's place at the helm of the operation when Lina left for her own sleep period.

The assistants would trade off as their sleep periods kicked in. One of Wiley's minds was asleep and would switch with the others as the operation proceeded. For this day only, four of his minds were devoted solely to the Aldierran mission.

Some personnel who could not be substituted had been assigned their own medics who would administer stims. Lina was not on that list.

Jae and Lon were the last to check in. They hoped no one would notice when Jae dropped out of the main mission. He'd help at the start and then leave – supposedly to rest – as things moved to Sha-Green. For him they had stims ready if needed.

"Are we really sure we want to do this?" Lon asked the assembled. That produced a few strained chuckles here and there.

"Remember," he told everyone, "it took Aldierra's people over fifty years to complete installing their weather control systems, and they've been tweaking it ever since. Our programs tell us that a simple way to take it down will take ten months.

"But we don't have that kind of time. We're going to do this in one day.

"There will be unforeseen problems. There will be destruction, both that we've foreseen and ways that we have not. We thank everyone who has agreed to help out, from our Aldierran citizens, to paras and megas from across the sector and beyond, members of many organizations and independents. You are all needed.

"Pay attention to your section officers. On occasion you might receive orders from Speaker Central. If you notice a looming problem, report it immediately so we can deal with it before it becomes… disaster."

He looked around at his varied screens, beamed to how many people? Certainly all news networks were picking it up as well. "We will meet again in one day, after we have accomplished this essential goal. When things go south, and they certainly will at some point, keep that in mind: for the most part, this will be over tomorrow. Speaker?"

Lina smiled at the cameras, trying to look brave. She took a deep breath. "Aaand… *go!* Commence dismantling of Aldierran weather control. We can do this. Everyone be careful. Report anomalies before they can become problems. Well, *bigger* problems."

Part of their sensor network consisted of thirty teams on Earth armed with pendulums and large maps of Aldierra. Tishana were scattered across those teams, having been training for two weeks in the skill. AffSys personnel had joined them to coordinate their findings to Aldierra.

But the brunt of all this would rest on the shoulders of those with weather-related powers. Chief among these were Erik, aka the Legion's Sunstorm. In their group were also two people who could control oceanic movement; stop a tsunami should one generate.

A planet of Aldierra's size held a shallow atmosphere, but it exerted formidable force upon the surface. It was an ocean in itself, capable of terrible storms and destruction. It could operate across wide continents or concentrate in tornados.

"Starting at the Limbernie Steppes," Erik reported. His family were receiving special feed about this, as they'd want to worry along with him as things happened. Others were hooked up similarly so they wouldn't have to wait for official reports.

"Planetary weather control transmitter networks one through ten – Shutting down now," Wiley told them. "One through ten, offline."

CHAPTER

31

They'd timed this to take one full day, keeping all operations in daylight as much as they could as the world rotated. There'd be a significant rest period for most once they'd cleared land forms and had only the Ocean of Wadentach to watch.

Londo had declared he was absolutely certain that everything he'd constructed would withstand whatever storms resulted from this, but pre-existing buildings and possibly even entire cities… Maybe not.

He'd been particularly concerned about one category of city. They'd secured the sea cities so they could ride out any storm without crashing onto their respective shores, but could their very structures withstand this? Locals had worked hard to determine and repair weak points. They'd demolished or rebuilt as they could before this. The population all knew how to reach lifeboats quickly and hopefully, safely.

Londo crossed his invulnerable fingers.

"Whoa!" Erik exclaimed from the speakers. "Wind. Lots of–"

"One hundred twenty kph," Wiley reported. "Squalls."

"Yeah, big gusts!" Then Erik's sound feed stopped. The dot on the map that was him flew in a zigzag pattern around the front.

The crew began to chase the pattern of dissolution west across the continent. Once thunder began in the background of their communications, it rose to the point they had to shout to be heard. Sometimes it was so loud it knocked people over just by volume alone.

And it never stopped. It followed the work around the globe.

"I can feel the strain ahead of us," Erik told them as his communications came back. "Not so much to the north. We're on it."

Kanti directed personnel to the upcoming west coast of Limbernie, drawing them down from equatorial regions.

— — —

CAMERAS AT LIMBERNIE'S MINOR SHIT FLAT showed impenetrable dust storms barreling to the west. They had to turn the sound of howling turbulence down so they could hear each other.

"Wind speeds dropping above the steppes," Lina read off the maps. "Down to eighty kph." A converter told her that was about 50 mph. How much of the land would that scour? The thought made her skin itch.

"That's as good as you're going to get right now," Erik told her above the shrieking gale. "I'm moving to the next southern focal point. That's the mountain range foothills. After that we start moving into the real mountains."

"Kinesis, I'm going to port you into Sunstorm's group. We want you to do what you can to slow down the winds where they're at their worst. You ready?"

A voice replied. "Ready for port, Speaker." The Legionnaire gave a thumbs-up signal to the camera as he appeared at his new location, then zoomed off into the blackened sky.

Erik asked, "How's the northern hemisphere going? Nothing up there but water."

Chim's voice came on from her station on the other side of the world. "Focus on your own hemisphere. We'll inform you when you're needed up there. Thunder Breeze, please coordinate with Sunstorm."

Others reported in. Lina had trained in Legion communications, how to say "Copy that," and some codes and such, how to address the heroes clearly, using the terms they were used to working with. The people who had trained with them these past days and weeks had learned the same.

The entire room quietly chattered with people checking statuses and locations. The occasional voice raised over the normal gale-inflicted volume indicated a problem that was quickly attended to.

Lina was checking on the line of paras west, who would be facing the next wave, when pain sliced through her. She grabbed her midsection.

"Augh! Hurts – Something's wrong!" She curled tightly over it, trying to breathe.

"Medic!" Kanti called, rising from her chair. As quickly as she did, she resumed her seat to take over command. The first thing she did was to cut off Lina's transmissions.

Wiley spared one eye's direction to look in Lina's direction even as two doctors rushed up and he kept his gaze on the maps with the other eye. Over her monitors, Kanti nodded as if reassuring herself.

"It's .. it's all twisted," Lina managed between pants. "Into itself. Out of balance."

Ten seconds later: "Out of control!" Erik's voice howled through the command center. "Something's wrong. Can't… handle it! I need more help here. We've got three – no, five big storm centers that suddenly appeared right over, right beside each other. The mountains aren't helping things. This feels unnatural. It doesn't obey me. The winds are fighting. Chaos! Chaos!"

"Should I port?" came Kinesis' voice.

"No!" Kanti ordered. "Maintain your position. This is a systems problem."

"Where?" Wiley asked. "Which systems?"

Kanti gave him the locations of the redline points. But which in particular?

Lina gasped, "It's conflicting orders. One station's doubling up or something. Pulling the atmosphere in opposite directions. Grabbing instead of releasing– augh! Augh! Gorob. River. Source, just above it. Please! Aldierra says make them stop! Make them stop!"

Wiley's hands flew as he gestured to the computers. Behind her agony, Lina could hear some of the several brisk conversations he was having via audio inputs.

Wall screens showed the Gorob River: the water standing up like crazed columns, leaving its riverbed empty. On its banks, buildings were shredding. Swarms of materials swept up at lethal velocities into the clouds. Two lone people holding on to each other hunched next to one disintegrating structure, then scrabbled across city streets to get to shelter.

"Pain killer?" the medic asked Lina.

"No! I have to be able to… To… There. That's it, just a bit. Wiley, whatever they did, it helped. More of that. Need more. Hang tight, Faun… Aldierra. We're with you."

She snarled against the pain. It was like someone had reached inside her and tightly twisted a muscle in her ribcage around their finger. No. No!

Lina signaled to return to the broadcast conversation. "Erik needs backups. Who's available?" Lina fought for breath as she sent her mind out. "Be prepared for port, everyone! Not sure who–"

There were three people that her guides pointed to. Eyes clenched shut, she ported them with their air vehicles to Erik's location. On the ground. She had to steady the one. Winds were trying to blast it sideways.

Someone affixed an oxygen mask over her face as she squirmed in agony. "It's still…"

"Releasing!"

Lina fell back against her chair in relief. "Better," she managed to say even as the medic reached to undo her blouse. It had been obvious where she had clutched herself. When she looked down she could see the large, blackening bruise on her skin.

"It's not quite loose yet," she told Wiley. "They're close, but they didn't get it all– ack!"

Her face contracted with pain. Something somewhere was adjusting in the wrong direction.

"Opposite!" Wiley yelled into his mic. "Minus sixty, not plus sixty!"

Within long moments the pressure disappeared. Lina gasped. "Okay," she said. "Okay, that's… yes, that's done it. Yes, Faun. Yes."

"Stupid technicians," Wiley muttered. "I know what to look for now. I'll be prepared if it happens again."

She drew a deep, shuddering breath and then added three more to it. She couldn't see those civilians on the screen any more. Hopefully they'd made it to that building that was still pretty intact. "How's everyone doing out there? I think I wasn't the only one–"

"Glidepath went down," someone said. "That added to the problem. Medics are here. He's going to be okay."

Lina nodded. "Copy that. Can we get everyone to check in with their status? Those along the Magna Channel: let's get this straightened out before we have two close continents and mountain ranges stretching north and south to worry about."

They'd begun with Limbernie, because that continent had only the Terwick Ocean above it. All ocean vessels had been recalled for this event, to avoid the possibility of running into wild sea storms.

But Erik's mic revealed groans. "I can… handle it," he told them. "It's rough. Thunder Breeze is going to need help after this. Be ready. Can you get someone else to back us up?"

Lina checked the status of the megas and ported three more weather people – this time giving them two moments' warning – to points along Limbernie's western coast.

Five minutes later Erik reported, "Yeah, that's good. More power to handle the chaos. Can we continue doing it this way? Concentrate our power where the change is happening, or just about to, instead of having fresh people standing by doing nothing. Let's take a chance that we can handle the long-term mission. We'll need stims."

"I know where to get some," Lina said sourly, which actually produced a chuckle from both Erik and Wiley, though Lon growled in her mind. "They'll be there. Massages and unlimited rachets for everyone once we get through this."

– – –

LON AND JAE, accompanied by Nesh and with Hal alongside, kept their armies on the move just to the east of the atmospheric battleground and following the end of it. Structures had suffered damage; terrain had to be set back to rights.

"Not as bad as I'd feared," Jae told his husband as they began.

"Bad enough," Lon muttered, "but *oui*."

"We can do this," Nesh assured them.

Lon had helped clean up after many a natural disaster, but the scope of this one was what frightened him. All across the world people had been reinforcing structures. Some buildings had been buttressed just to accommodate people safely, holding them until it was safe to return to any homes that still stood.

Some valleys missed the full brunt of the winds. Others had been scoured as if targeted.

The people and animals came first. Nesh whimpered at the state of some landscapes, but her duties had been focused on areas where programs thought things would survive. For these desolated areas, she could return later and work.

Lon and Hal scraped up the worst of the debris and the infrastructure that was beginning to collapse. They piled the materials to the side, out of transportation routes and away from residences. Lon set up a windbreak in one valley where several herds of animals huddled as they could.

Then he spotted Toisenmarch. Most of the sea city had been flattened by winds roaring in off the Battle Mountains to its east. The southern half tilted into the ocean. How hard had those winds hit?

There were hundreds in the water. Thousands trapped in collapsed buildings that were rapidly filling with sea water.

"Hal!" Lon cried. "I'll take the city. You get the civilians." He called on two heroes who could shape earth, and Lina ported them in. The two began to build a huge circular wall of dirt on land that overlooked the shore.

Rain pelted him as he grabbed fallen framework. Massive bolts of lightning flashed from horizon to horizon, almost instantaneously accompanied by blasts of thunder. Cobbling together a massive net of rugged materials, he caught up a sinking section of the city and lifted it out of the crashing waves. He deposited it near the wall. Then he went back to salvage another neighborhood.

Hal's form was a streak in the sky as he returned to the wall again and again, groups of people clinging to him. Nets began to appear on the ground, and Hal snatched them up to use to gather more survivors from the sea.

From the south, three battalions of what was once the Violet Army raced along the beach. The wind knocked their hovercraft about so their paths looked like balls caroming on a pool table. But they made it to the wall. Companies deployed sections of a roof over the walls and interior supports the paras had also seen to, with others coming behind to seal the gaps between them. The roofs were secured in place, and as winds threatened to free the moorings, more men streamed to hold them fast.

Jae flew above the worst of the clouds. There was madness here; devic spirits unleashed after being chained for so long. Their intent to be a part of a healthy environment had been stripped from them long ago. Now they were left with emotional release. Jae spoke through their distress and confusion. He tried to point out that yes, they were free and yes, they needed to shake off the last of their oppressive binding energies, but they should strive to calm themselves. Be what they'd been pining to be. Merge with the fullness of the whole.

In his mind he could hear whispers of other worlds who knew how far away, those who did not have weather control. How did Lina talk with worlds? He tried to link that feeling to these winds and currents. *****Help them heal,***** he begged them.

— — —

FILLED WITH UNFAMILIAR NAMES AND SYMBOLS, the map Lina had devised quickly told her which mega had what powers, and to what extent.

"Vine and Lessick, I want you to go to Control Point thirty-five," she instructed. "Ur-Rael, you and Ephny should help out at thirty-seven. Doan-Te, Tamers, and Paseed, take up stations to the east of the line. We're getting more backwash than had been projected. Danica Prime and Haley, plus all the people stationed over Orchin, start moving to Sha-Green so you can relieve some of the troops along the lines there as needed. Limbernie people east of the line, move to Malcone for similar purposes. Don't forget the islands."

"I've operated on worlds with severe atmospheric storms," a voice said behind her.

Lina whirled to see who it was. A Ruby Guard! Of course there was the automatic stomach clench, but these two – two of them! – weren't Granger. They made the "pelzire" motion to her.

"Welcome!" Lina couldn't hide her relief as she returned the gesture. "We are honored to have you here. Uh, who can I…? Not Wiley. Not Stoan." Stoan had a group of newbies to manage. "Andri? Can you link in? We have some powerful help who just arrived. Treat them well."

Andri and the two Guards conferred for less than five minutes before Lina ported them to separate positions. Their rubies primarily shaped gravity in intricate ways. They might be able to shape the storms to a calmer formation.

Kanti was trying not to be distracted, but it was obvious she'd never met a Ruby Guard before, and had wide-eyed the both of them even as she directed the ground troops. "How are we doing on supplies? I want reports: medical, housing, clothing, transportation, and food needs before they become a problem."

Bracken reported in that the Majority Army was backing local police and relief efforts to take care of the citizenry on both sides of the battle line. "Remind them to be gentle, Bracken," Lina said with a sigh of resignation.

"Always, Speaker." There was a chuckle in his voice.

Four hours of intense action crept by as the longitudes now contained two continents, with little tempering ocean.

"There may be a blizzard forming over Malcone," came the report.

Lina checked the world map. Wiley also peered at it.

"Four hundred years ago, that would be normal for this time of year, though–"

"Maybe not at this intensity."

"Yusuf, can you handle a blizzard?" she asked into her mic.

"I can operate at its heart," he quickly replied. "I can interfere with its energy engines, break it up a bit."

"You're hired. Unless you've got an emergency down there?"

"Brek and Drake should be able to modify the storms here to not-quite-Armageddon levels," he assured her.

"Right. Prepare for port. I'll set you in a weather control station near the center of the pending storm, so you can see what's going on."

Lon and his people swept through the district around Soshe. Its structures had not been as resilient as they'd hoped. A few thousand people were saved and sent to refugee centers.

"I'd planned on redoing much of this once we got past Deadline," Lon told her. "Guess we'll have to step things up a bit. As long as so many locals are in their shelters, can we get them to decide on designs?"

Lina conveyed the request to his sections.

Jae studied the effects of the changeover on the Terwick Ocean. There had been a handful of incidents there, but they had been minor compared to the hundreds of crises over land. Using their systems, he coordinated with the megas and controllers overseeing the Ocean of Wadentach. They conferred as to what might happen there and how best to control it.

Jae gave a nod to his Chief. Then he unobtrusively left on his own mission.

Nesh and Lon kept up their conversation as if he were still embedded with them, so anyone monitoring them might not notice.

CHAPTER

32

Even protected by Duktiv Keep's thick shielding, the gathered three Green Army soldiers, plus Dule, Muvvik, Jae, and Kettite reared back as winds from the leading edge of the oncoming front pummeled the walls outside.

Occasional crashes and thumps against the ramparts were reminders that conditions were more violent than predicted. Equipment within the keep that should have been better secured, wasn't.

The room was plain and of medium size, larger than the group required. It held two long tables and ten chairs, plus the usual array of electronics and screens. A large one mapped the progression of the squall line against a map of northern Sha-Green. There was only one door to the outside hallway, and one wall contained a door that led to a small utility room. A ceiling light blinked unnervingly from power fluctuations.

Jae's nerves flickered as well. He used his Legion equipment to check the environs, knowing that Mimik was doing the same. She, as Muvvik, made a final calibration on the disguise equipment she had brought. Wiley had designed it to be the size of a small bug that would adhere to clothing. Jae had been amused that Wiley had programmed it with three possible disguises: not only Muvvik, but those of Kettite's aide, In-Donez, who was targeted in their plans… and of Dule.

"Even this plan can go awry," he'd told Jae.

Every man except Jae started anxiously at each bump, as if they might sense how much structural integrity the walls still held. Dule sat at one table, a tablet with notes beside his work surface, and Muvvik stood protectively behind her superior.

Feet spread apart and arms crossed over his chest, Kettite surveyed the room. He glowered at each bang as if accusing the walls of collaborating against him. In-Donez accompanied the famous Black Box. It was that color with a surface that seemed to absorb all light. The size of small luggage, it rested on a hidden and silent air curtain.

A small enough object to carry the possible fate of a world inside.

Before he'd begun today's mission, Jae had added another "just in case" disguise to the bug: that of Kettite. Kettite was the one whose info they were after, so it seemed unlikely they'd want Mimik to disguise herself as him. Still as Wiley warned, they couldn't be sure everything would work. At this uncertain point Jae was tempted to make a disguise program of himself. If it were needed that would mean that Jae had been killed. It was a possibility. But there wasn't enough memory available for the complicated programming. Jae told himself that since that was the case, he had to live through this.

Whatever it came down to, this switch-out would have mere moments to complete. Jae signaled the addition to Mimik on his Legion ring. He hadn't had a chance to talk with her since they'd arrived. She gave him a slight nod.

Dule needed to reveal Mimik as a traitor. They'd set up enough subtle proof that led to a warren of dead ends with a few true traitors mixed in. It had been funneled to Kettite in the bits and pieces normal intelligence usually provided. If not, Siekesh had sent Kettite more information this morning, per their schedule. Would he have read it by now?

Certainly Kettite was eyeing Muvvik enough, so he must know. But he also directed glances toward Dule. Had Siekesh double-crossed Jae? No. Jae was almost certain of that.

Jae would trigger a fake holo battle, and Mimik would disguise herself as In-Donez while Jae would knock Donez out, plant the program on him so he'd morph into Mimik as the traitor Muvvik, and they could dispose of Donez, hopefully without bloodshed.

Thus would Kettite's office have a major mole in it to report back to Jae. Operation Worldstorm was scheduled to take place somehow, somewhere, during the time period directly following this weather reconfiguration. They needed specifics.

Kettite reached inside his uniform jacket for his phone and said, "Get some men out there. Secure the base."

"No," Jae quickly interrupted. "All personnel to remain inside until these storms are over. No need to send anyone to their deaths."

"We'll get damage we could have prevented," Kettite argued, the phone line still open.

"The troops secured the base as best they could before we began," Jae told him. "They won't be able to accomplish any more, not with any efficiency. You'll have to repair damage, period. But not until things calm down out there. Inside, everyone is as safe as they're going to get. Worldstorm will proceed per schedule."

Kettite flinched as the code word was pronounced even in these secured quarters, but he let it go.

Even with Jae's reassurances, Mimik as Muvvik flinched at the particularly loud noises. She was sensitive to sound, Jae recalled.

With reluctance, Kettite countermanded his orders and closed his communications. He leaned close to Jae. "We need to make sure the Patriarch is in optimum position for the next two days. In the meantime I want to report current conditions to the Patriarch on a secure line," he told him. "This room doesn't allow synched frequencies. He'll be expecting my call. I'll be back in a minute," he told the others.

Optimum position. Kettite hadn't informed him of the planned coup being quite so imminent. Well, it wasn't as imminent as this operation.

Just before he left the room to the hallway outside, Kettite glanced back at Dule, a small smirk on his lips.

"What was that about?" Muvvik asked as the door closed. Unconsciously her mouth mirrored the same smirk.

"I have confirmation: Lupoff is in the underground bunker of his Soshe offices," Dule told them as he closed his puter screens. "He wanted to be as far removed from the mayhem as possible."

"At this point his security is minimal," Muvvik reported. "He thinks HQ is secure."

"It's as secure as anywhere on the planet can be," Jae said and added, "That may not be too much."

"A possible problem," Muvvik said.

Over a frown, Dule asked, "How long does it take for him to make that call?" Kettite still had not returned.

Jae wanted to know as well. They had a tiny sliver of time in which to do this. The storm front would be past them soon. The more confusion and fear, the better this would work.

A glance to his side and his personal holographically-aimed screens indicated that the effects show he'd programmed would be tracking everyone. Mimik's image held a target. That's where the imaginary weapons fire would be aimed.

Kettite burst through the doors – finally! But an unexpectedly large squad of his own guards rushed in before him. "We said to keep this minimal," Jae barked at him, but received a glare in return.

All was proceeding as suspected, if not hoped for. Kettite would accuse Mimik and then… Jae set about neutralizing the arming mechanisms of the guards. It would take time.

"There is a snake here," Kettite roared. "A traitor in our group!"

He whirled to point at – Dule.

Not "Muvvik."

"Who? Me?" Dule gave an excellent pretense of innocence.

"I have proof," Kettite said. He brandished a padd that projected documents.

Jae squinted at them a moment then returned his attention to the weaponry in the room. The evidence Kettite showed wasn't what they'd set up. This were different, showing Dule communicating to their ring of moles. Names, ranks…

Dule also gave the list a long look as the room leveled their guns at him. Without reaching for his own gun, he raised his right arm… and pointed at Mimik. "There is the true traitor!" he announced. "I've been investigating this man for a week. His work history doesn't check out. Look him up; look at the details! He's a mole for the Yanist-Glory Empire, a conspirator!"

Some guns swung to point Mimik's way. Jae strove to finish the neutralization as quickly as he could. His power needed time to work, time to convince the devas of machinery to respond to his commands.

The lights blinked.

Jae's mind raced. Then he made them blink again and again, even as a terrific pounding shook the building. "Switch now," he signaled Mimik through his ring. "To Kettite."

Then he cut power to the room. Something crashed against the outer walls. Amazing that it could be heard so thunderously in here.

Jae took it as a godsend. The guards shouted conflicting questions to each other. What was happening? What were their orders? Should they obey Dule?

Jae triggered the effects: Mock laser fire. Moffer blasts. Shouting. No one could figure what was going on – except for the two Legionnaires who activated their infra-red goggles. The systems tracked the useless weaponry of the soldiers, projecting images to match targeting blasts as if they worked.

Then, weaving between the lines of fire as the bright, focused display disguised him in relative darkness, Jae shoved Kettite to where Mimik had stood. She planted the bug on his chest and an illusion instantly formed around Kettite of Muvvik. She rose to her feet… almost in his image.

As the real Major General fought him, Jae cut his body energy levels to almost zero.

Kettite went down like a collapsing pile of laundry.

"Cease fire!" Mimik shouted in Kettite's voice as the guards did as well. "Someone see to Dule's safety!"

One light flickered on again. They needed more time. Giving Mimik a heads-up, Jae summoned his Staff and struck it against the floor. "I have the turncoat!" Jae yelled above the body of Kettite as all attention turned to him. Not to Mimik, whose transformation was filling in to completion. "He tried to kill Dule!"

"The traitor!" Bless her, Mimik raised her voice to impressive levels so that the ones whose attention was beginning to turn from Jae's face, now turned to her. They missed Jae cutting Kettite's arm crosswise, which left an impressive blood path.

Dule caught Jae's gaze, and Jae gave the smallest of chin-nods at "Muvvik" on the ground, then at Mimik as Kettite. Dule's lips formed an "o" before he clamped them shut.

Jae began to drag Kettite away from the guards, toward the inner utility room they'd held ready. Finally, the illusion was complete. He'd have to talk to Wiley to give warnings that these things weren't instantaneous.

"Kettite?" Dule asked through the darkness, which was still flickering and dim. "Are you well? I thought he was targeting you."

"I'm just roughed up," Mimik as Kettite replied. "It appears you were right. Let's get full lights in here. Now!"

Two guards ran outside to see to that.

"Anyone else hurt?" "Kettite" asked in a gravelly voice. Mimik make him appear shaken, a little wild-eyed, even as he "recovered" from the attack and stood straighter. The guards regrouped as the lights came on and Jae partially closed the utility room's door behind the blood trail. He scuffed his foot in it to give it more width, make it look like the victim might have sustained several hits.

Dule asked for full status report. "Kettite" requested Dule and Jae aid him in questioning the prisoner. They pointed the guards away.

"We will question him. This could involve classified information of higher security than you guards can hear," Kettite growled.

"He'll need to be taken to hospital first," Jae told the crowd. "I've already called for it. I believe he has serious wounds, maybe even fatal." With that, Jae returned the guards' weaponry to normal operating conditions. The reinstatement of elemental structure took just as much work as the first change did.

"We'll have to question him quickly then," Dule said. "I'll download the files I was gathering about him. There seems to have been a widespread conspiracy, deep within the Majority army and others. It couldn't have been just him, to get by all our security. I've only had suspicions about him for a little over a week now. He seemed completely loyal until I broke into his files four nights ago. Couldn't believe what I was finding."

"Good job, all guards," "Kettite" declared. "Lives were saved by your actions. Very possibly the life of our Patriarch as well."

The men looked proud and allowed "Kettite," Dule and Jae to exit into the inner room.

They waited until the storm outside had abated enough that it was deemed safe to travel in Jae's flitter. In-Donez never noticed any difference in the box he'd been guarding and the one that was now by his side. He brought it along with Kettite when that group left, even as the real one resided in the side room, to be picked up later.

CHAPTER

33

There weren't many reports at Headquarters for problems with the various animals of the world. Either Aldierra must have warned them to safety or people just didn't notice. Wildlife biologists had taken shelter like everyone else. Even so, crews of both megas, paras, and norms swept the areas behind the main front to do what they could.

It couldn't be called anything as civilized as controlled chaos. What everyone all over the world did was to hold things together until the worst of the maelstrom was passed, then tend to the aftereffects.

The day stretched unendingly. Everyone took their sleep rotations and meals according to schedule, as it was possible. Lina reluctantly left. Chim took a stim to help Demi when she came in. There were enough personnel from the Speaker Section to coordinate between both the other sections and the mega help. Plus Kanti sneaked in two stims for herself to make sure things went as smoothly as they could.

But the exhaustion roughened everyone's faces. And powers.

Lina returned to duty early and ate breakfast at her station as she could between porting dozens of megas here and there and then back here again, as the situation demanded. Equipment was broken and had to be replaced. The injured had to see medical help quickly.

The wide Wadentach was cleared. Then came the large islands that formed the Joice; Reyda, and then the huge continent of Orchin. Over the course of this day they had quickly learned how the process could go so very wrong and were able to discover similar situations before they could form completely.

There were a few unique exceptions, of course, but the heroes found their second wind to tackle them.

Then they were back where they began.

"Where are we?" Lina called.

Wiley was the one to respond first. "AffSys monitors estimate three days of relative chaos until things truly settle, but we're over the worst. For the most part. There will be pockets of extreme turbulence for a while."

The various troops checked in. Lina couldn't port any more; she was too tired, but they had the planetary porting system available and now they knew how to keep up with the fading front. They could anticipate it. Thousands of Aldierran families and companies had loaned the effort their aerial vehicles. They made use of them.

The front had become far-ranging eddies of warring weather. In some places it lost the energy to make it fearsome. In others it remained strong. All weather control was officially off-line.

Finally what remained was merely the considerable backwash of a planetary event. The atmosphere still sloshed around, catching on landforms, butting up to opposing waves of wind, shrieking across plains and oceans. But it was steadying.

In her mind Lina could hear Aldierra shouting with the joy of regained freedom.

Surely this would count in their favor for Doomsday?

— — —

AMID THE PLANETARY CONFUSION as civilians of the world began to emerge from their safe quarters, the small group of loyal officers awaited their Patriarch. Monitors around the dim room displayed maps of the world with glowing red lines connecting military and political centers. Strobing blue lights pinpointed major weapons installations.

Three World activity was depicted with an overlay of green symbols and grids.

"Begin," Lupoff ordered.

— — —

LONDO GATHERED HIS EXHAUSTED FRIENDS around him: green-skinned walking fortress Boroh, the sharp-eyed rising leader Andri, both from the Legion; and his good friend Gary, aka the Bolt, and mischievous Russian Forte, both from Earth. All could bring the power when needed.

"Glad you could stay another couple days," Lon told them as they searched the skies.

"When will the first strike of this Worldstorm operation happen?" Gary asked. His leg had completely healed from the last time he'd come to Londo's call. He looked eager to run as only he could.

"Are you sure they won't use many missiles?" Andri asked. "It's stupid for them not to."

Lon scanned the horizon and beyond. "I've already destroyed much of the aerial warfare systems," he told them. "Plus the satellite ones. They'll primarily attack with ground troops."

"They certainly have the numbers for that," Boroh noted.

"I've destroyed an awful lot of gunnery," Londo said. "Not all of it by any means."

Boroh nodded at his hand monitor and brought up the picture for all to see. "Here they come."

"Remember, we'll approach each venue as if we're surprised," Lon told them. "We aren't supposed to know their battle plans. We're reacting."

"We are actors as well as warriors." Forte chuckled as she smashed one fist into the palm of her other hand. Standing in the open small fighting flitter, she was ready for this. "Prepare the Oscars. Chill the champagne."

"Don't get cocky."

"Yes, Captain Solo."

— — —

WORLDSTORM'S FIRST BATTLE was fifty thousand black-uniformed soldiers versus five megas. The reason it raged for almost two hours was because the heroes didn't want to kill too many.

Trucks and military personnel were standing by to truss up the defeated and haul them off to prison camps. For the next few days they'd be separated so as best not to reform their ranks. Eventually some would begin to confess to their captors some interesting stories. Jae's people were standing by to sort through those.

"Warder River just began," Andri reported. The planetary transporter units kicked in, depositing the quintet on Sha-Green continent near that river, where an army moved toward Soshe.

That battle took only an hour, as the army apparently hadn't counted on bad weather and coastal marshes slowing them down. Also it seemed as if their new weaponry was suffering from faulty programming. Targeting had to be reinstated manually. The remains of that army were mud-covered but not much blood joined it. Angry birds and amphibians hissed at soldiers as the fell in their habitats.

Bracken's troops hauled them away.

The Worlds para crew broke for showers and a leisurely lunch before the battle of the Gulf of Byssa, because somehow the Black Army had mis-communicated the location and attack time to its troops.

"Funny that," Boroh commented as he reached for another sandwich.

— — —

THEN CAME A THIRD ATTACK, and a fourth, but the fifth and sixth, situated on both sides of Blood Bay, saw the troops surrendering as soon as Londo's squad appeared.

Operation Worldstorm was over.

"Everything under control?" Lon asked his more specialized Division services.

Bracken reported only a few escapees. "They won't make trouble," he told them with confidence. "They'll find very deep hidey holes and stay there. Maybe for years."

"I've had services preparing meals and beds for a week now. Jae's gotten together some tents."

"More than enough," Jae told them cheerily.

"Nothing like an efficient war."

Forte nodded at Andri's words as she knocked clods of mud off her own hair. "Time for another shower and the champagne."

YUSUF LOOKED SOURLY at the new building intruding in his arctic village. "Seems secure enough," he told Londo.

"I believe it is. The guards assigned to this will make sure of it. They're good."

"Aldierrans?"

Lon let a slight snort loose. "Not going to trust any Aldierran with this, Yusuf. These are AffSys security guards, the best I could find. In case Kettite gets through them – and he's just a norm – I'm relying on you as backup."

Yusuf nodded and only then wondered at himself. He was helping Valiant. Valiant trusted him.

How the world changed.

"Please tell that husband of yours that I appreciate not having any more nighttime visits from… our friend."

"'Our friend' is now in solitary confinement. He proved a big help for us, uncovered a nest we hadn't been aware of, except around the edges.

"In my opinion, Jae should have told you from the beginning. Not that I'm taking sides."

Lon grunted. "Right now Jae is treading water hard trying to deal with the other conspiracies. There's a lot of them, but we're unraveling them as quickly as we can. Some are drying up on their own."

"Good. But not all, I'll wager. I'll keep my own ears listening, but I don't get much random info up here."

"*Pas de trouble.* No problem."

Yusuf chewed over this newest information and the building. "So this is a big-wig army general?"

"Biggest on the planet, except for Bracken. Right now we have a double in place so we can put the rebel army to more positive use, shall we say. Lupoff was counting on Kettite to lead his army for him. He didn't know that Kettite was ready to take Lupoff down and take his spot on the Great Council."

"A tangled web. So. After Deadline – how will you deal with Kettite?"

They turned to stroll the village street to the pub that also served as a community gathering point. "The man – in this case, a woman – in Kettite's place is gathering evidence of his own traitorous plot. Once Lupoff is forced to step down – and he will be – we will inform the real Kettite of what we have. He can either take honorable, silent retirement, or be exposed. Traitor to Lupoff or traitor to Aldierra – he won't want either scenario." Lon opened the door to the pub for Yusuf and the two entered the airlock of the cozy place. "He'll retire and stay quiet. We might even suggest a nice AffSys world where he can do that, never to be heard from again. Maybe he and Lupoff can be neighbors. Buy you a drink?"

– – –

JAE WANTED A DRINK. Wanted it badly. Instead he signaled the medic on duty and got a stim.

They were getting down to the wire. Deadline was next week. In his communications Lupoff smiled and smiled, revealing no defeat from or existence of Operation Worldstorm. Instead he claimed how well he and his armies were following the Worlds' requests, though so little had been accomplished by them. Yesterday just an hour before it was supposed to happen, Mimik had discovered another sabotage plot, this one including mass murder. Bracken and "Kettite" had both worked feverishly to quash it.

The follow-up investigation had uncovered levels of insurgents they'd never guessed at. By now there were only a few left to gather, imprison, and question. Jae wanted them all.

Here were two of them, on Jae's own fleet of ocean-cleaning ships. This one was cruising the Terwick Ocean performing a regular cleanup as well as an accompanying one taking care of the weather control transition debris.

Over the past month Jae had increased the number of unobtrusive cameras across the world especially in mission points. They'd caught at least five major attempts this past week alone.

Now Jae checked the cameras. He had good men on the *Torat Norsel* and would alert them as soon as any action began.

There they were, the two traitors. Cupper and Rownin had signed on as volunteers. The boat's mission was to collect the top ten meters of ocean debris for recycling. The weather changeover had turned many ocean areas into a soup of *cremda* and plastics. Robotic vessels worked tirelessly beside the manned boats.

Cupper and Rownin were belowdecks. Jae's instruments picked up the signal they received through implants that hadn't been detected when they had signed up. They'd been assigned to gain control of the ship and throw all but absolutely essential personnel overboard. To make the job easier, there were guns secreted in four spots around the ship. Jae had already neutralized them. He watched as the men looked at each other. "Insurrection" was the word the transmission used. Also "rightful revolt."

"Here we go," Rownin whispered to Cupper as he set down the long hook he'd taken out of Supplies. He turned to the stairs, where he could get to their quarters and hidden weaponry.

"Wait," Cupper said. "Wait."

Rownin paused. Jae watched curiously, holding back on giving the "go" signal to his own people on board.

"Are we sure we want to do this?" Cupper drew Rownin into an open closet. "I mean… We could… say communications broke up. Or that we were being watched."

"It's our duty."

"To whom? The Patriarch is crazy old. I heard someone say the other day that he looks sick. He won't last for many more years. That is, if we have those, if we aren't all killed at Doomsday. Won't Aldierra punish us for not, well, changing our ways?"

Rownin snorted. "Aldierra."

"Yes, Aldierra. You've seen the newscasts–"

"Propaganda."

"Probably, but only to an extent. Could the Worlds have altered all the news?"

"Yes."

Jae made a mental note to try to show their broadcasts more transparently. Difficult to do when an undercover operation of this size was going on.

"The weather– Something big happened here. Something, like, historic. Look at all the interstellar megas they brought in. *Darkeer*, I saw a Ruby Guard! Would they all be fooled?"

Rownin considered.

"They are heroes in their sectors. I've heard of a bunch of them."

"Yeah, I saw the Ruby Guards." Rownin nodded slowly.

Cupper leaned in so his words would be clearer. Jae's equipment picked it up easily. "Look at us. They've given us good food. They've given everyone good food. They pay us on time. We have clean beds. Medical care." His mouth quirked into a small smile. "I like the therapist they assigned me."

"They freed the women and slaves."

Cupper granted him that with a shrug. "Well, maybe that will change in the future. But with them I think we actually have a future. With the Patriarch… Well… Doomsday is next week. Even if we win with this crazy plot–"

"It might mean we're still toast." Rownin's jaw moved right, then left as he thought.

"I heard Aldierra that day. We all did. She was f-ing clear."

Rownin couldn't argue with that.

"So what if we stay here and do our job and ignore the Patriarch? Aren't we better off?"

"Unless someone in the insurrection comes after us."

"Shh! We're in the middle of the Terwick Ocean. It's going to take a long time for them to find us, if they ever do. And if Doomsday comes and we're all still alive, it will be partially because we're working here."

Rownin still appeared to be undecided.

"Scanners for lunch," Cupper urged. "I hear they're trying something new at dinner. Plus tonight's sing-along and line dance. You enjoy those. I've seen you laughing."

Rownin scratched his chest. "Laughing's not… manly. Men shouldn't be so… together unless they're in a real army."

"Those Terran men certainly seem to stick together, even when they're relaxing. You watched that 'movie' the other night. Men jumping all over construction equipment – acrobatics – and singing. Plus they each got a woman all to themselves. That's what might happen here."

"Maybe we can wait a few hours," Rownin hedged. "I'll keep an ear out as to what's happening in Limbernie, or Malcone."

"Scanners for lunch." Cupper grinned. "Soft mattress tonight. Houses together." He reached to take hold of his hook again.

Both men proceeded to the upper deck and worked hard for the rest of their shift.

Maybe Lina had been right about giving everyone good food, that that would make a difference. Maybe Lon was right about all the entertainments they offered.

Jae scratched his chin before changing to different cameras in a different part of the world.

– – –

PR HAD BEEN ADVISING LONDO to do what he could to meet individuals and their Houses. Otherwise he often came across as distant or overly commanding as he stood too far from the people. Jae did lots of videos about spiritual theory and being understanding of each other. How did Aldierrans connect with that more than with what Londo did? Lon was *building*.

Of course Lina made a point to meet everyone. *Eh bien*, maybe that just happened for her and wasn't a designed approach. She was everywhere, dealing with everyone, whereas Londo had specific missions to accomplish, with limited spacial scope. He did enjoy talking with people about building plans. And he very much liked dealing with kids.

Kids were special. They were innocent, or close to a time of innocence. If "Protector" was his title, then that innocence was a good part of what he was protecting. When he'd been a powerless child himself, he'd watched as other children had been tortured by his side. They'd been killed.

Well, he wasn't powerless any more.

Too many of the boys of this world were growing into bullies. Others were victims. And the girls – Lon always tried to show them that he treated them just as well as he did boys.

Houses were another matter. They were worlds unto themselves, most of them, observing isolationism in hundreds of thousands of neighborhoods around the world. Lately he had begun to hear "Houses together!" as a rallying cry. That was hopeful. People working together, getting away from the binary thinking, or "us vs. them" viewpoint that so many held.

Was this a sign of Aldierra improving?

He planned to bring the matter up at a dinner he'd been invited to. It was a celebration for Fencehill House, who had won a significant continental sports championship. Londo liked dinners, even ones with Aldierran food. If worse came to worst, he could eat solid acid and give a smile to the cameras.

These days he'd gone vegetarian. Much of Aldierran food was such, but meat was included at fancier dining venues. This would be such an occasion. His hosts were aware and assured him there'd be no problems.

He'd cleared an extra hour and a half for this, which would be publicized through channels that didn't often include him. A sports championship. He'd looked it up: Gui-Po, a tough field sport that looked a lot like rugby but with more violence. There was a playing ball but also several bats involved, and lots of body contact.

Well, Aldierra was a violent world.

Did the winning team have a mascot? Lon liked shaking hands with mascots because kids often gathered around, their laughter brightening the occasion.

The sizeable banquet hall included a good proportion of the winning House's population – all male, of course, with many enthusiastic boys attending. Londo didn't see anyone with disabilities. Oh, Aldierra. A long table had been placed on a platform with the Head of House and other dignitaries gloating on it. Lon was included as Honored Guest, looking down from a superior position to reinforce even an in-house binary mindset.

The winning team also sat on the platform. Londo could tell who they were, though they dressed in the same formal dress as the others. These men were horribly bruised and battered, their orange skin mottled with dark brown and purple injuries. More than a few had limbs in casts. It seemed to be expected for Gui-Po.

The food was Aldierran. A couple of good dishes; Lon made a note for the Three Worlds kitchens. Most was rather blah. Appetizers. Soups. Then there was some kind of parade as the main meat was presented on tables rolled out from the wings.

The crowd exploded with cheers.

There, on the first table, was displayed a large roast to be carved – and the severed head of a young man.

"Vizmoden!" "Vizmoden!" the crowd jeered, offering some choice personal insults to the late Gui-Po player.

That roast's shape was…

Londo blinked. It must be a theatrical prop – No. Real. Human flesh. The head's eyes had been propped open to regard its conquerors.

Vizmoden had been the captain of the opposing team at the final playoff.

Ceremonially killed as recognition of House Fencehill's superiority. Kill their opponents. Show them who was boss.

Hastily Lon excused himself to the nearest restroom, where he was thoroughly sick. He threw up even after his stomach had emptied, blinking back tears of frustration, fear, and disgust.

Lon? **Londo?** Jae and Lina's presences gathered around him for comfort. As he explained, twitching in his revulsion, he felt their own shock.

Both also vomited their consternation, and desperately he tried to shield them from his own feelings.

It was a long time before Londo could drag himself from the helpful toilet and back to the "festivities." He excused his absence by saying he'd had an emergency call that had to be answered.

By now the diners were making their way through dessert and drinks before the speeches began. The first two were about the tournament, and how Fencehill had thoroughly trounced their inferiors. Fencehill was the ultimate House of Aldierran sport!

The crowd cheered and banged their tableware. Some jumped on tables to stomp victory dances. Two men picked up the head of Vizmoden to display it over their heads as they danced around the tables. They attracted a short parade of Fencehill men behind them, and from somewhere a small band played a jaunty, triumphant tune.

Kids gleefully witnessed it all.

It was into the dregs of this that Londo took his place at the speaker's podium.

He congratulated Fencehill for their hard-fought victory, and the hall erupted into more cheers.

Then he pointedly regarded the head of Vizmoden, returned to its display on the main meat trolley. "I am relatively new to Aldierra," Londo began, "but I am very familiar with many different sports that people delight in this side of Galactic Center."

He went on to describe some of the more interesting ones, including his own beloved hockey, the sport where men strapped metal blades to their feet and propelled themselves across ice, using long sticks to hit a small puck into goals. It could be a bloody sport, whether from violence or accident.

"In each of these arenas," he told the crowd, "the idea of competition reigns supreme. Too often it becomes 'win at all costs,' but I think even with that mindset, sportsmen honor each other. They may be jealous of another team's prowess. They may scheme to trade loyal team members in order to strengthen their own.

"But this competition is seen as a way to hone their skills. To make themselves champions or at least better athletes through being tested by honorable opposition."

He took a breath. "They do not kill their opponents. They do not celebrate their deaths. They know that, often but for fate, defeat might be theirs."

The hall was silent.

"I don't know how you kill them, but I'm willing to bet there is some ceremony involved, some kind of overwhelm by force that they cannot defend themselves from."

"It… It is a Guard of Honor, Protector," said the man sitting next to him.

Londo nodded. "A Guard of Honor. 'Honor.' An execution squad to overpower an innocent person and kill him. Because he was great, but not quite great enough. That is a crime here. It is an all or nothing mindset."

Londo's hard gaze swept across the tables. "Instead of honoring your opponents, you honorably kill them. Instead of celebrating your superiority until the next round of competition begins, you eliminate them. It seems as if you're afraid that if you don't kill them, they might rally to defeat you the next season. Your honor is based in fear."

He shook his head.

"We must eliminate that fear. To see ourselves in our neighbors. In our opponents on the sports field. Sometimes we work together and sometimes we stage entertaining and exciting competitions that measure how well we have trained. How our skill levels are progressing. How we can train the next generation of sportsmen. And yes, how we represent the Houses and organizations that sponsor us.

"Sports are a unique to celebrate the fact that we are here, in human bodies that can perform astounding feats. Yes, we'll celebrate winners. We will glory in them. Perhaps we'll develop a system like Earth has, awarding first, second and third-place honors." Lon used his Legion Array to project an Olympic medals ceremony with the crowds cheering behind the winners. "We will introduce a concept called 'sportsmanship,' which encourages cooperation and encouragement even while competing.

"I have these hopes for you. For all of you."

CHAPTER

34

Deadline – Doomsday – was so close! It had taken some time for Londo to return to normal duties after that sickening dinner had concluded. So much left to do! He could almost literally see the wire they were down to. There were a few hours left before his rest period. Should he call Jae or Lina so he could get a stim?

The Legion Support team filed out of Londo's office, leaving just Chim and Londo standing there, gazing at the wall screen filled with operations that had yet to be done. Must be done. Before Doomsday.

Even prioritized, the list scrolled on and on. The new items scrolling up were every bit as important as the ones at the top of the list. Londo couldn't think. He couldn't recall how the programs had been set to rank importance.

It was all important. Deadly important.

"Too much," slipped out of his mouth.

In his mind that severed head still stared at him.

Chim stood behind him, silent.

"Even if we had every mega from five sectors around, even if we had every last Aldierran doing their best, we can't accomplish all this."

"So just do the most important items."

He spun on her as if she were attacking him. "Which is the most important? Every single one of these items holds lives within it. If not lives now, then lives in the future. Billions."

"Londo–"

He clapped his hands to cover his face. "We can't do it. I can't do it. It's impossible."

His chest heaved. He felt sick. Nauseous.

"We get the world to take one step forward and when we stop to take a breath, it slips three strides back. This will kill Jae. It'll be another Feith. He can't take it. No matter how we support him, he won't be able to–"

"He shouldn't have been able to survive the trauma of Feith, years ago," Chim gently told him. She placed a hand on his shoulder. "He's survived. With the help of hundreds of others and you. And Lina. And me," she added with a forced lift to her tone.

Behind his hands, Lon shook his head. "It won't work this time. We'll lose Jae. Lina's so invested in everyone. I think she's met as many people as she can. They're family, she keeps saying. For her it will be like Jae losing Feith that first time."

"And what of you?"

Slowly he lowered his hands to meet his mentor's eyes. "I… don't know. Without Jae, without Lie… I'm not sure how–"

"Contact your therapist. What's his name? Colam?"

Lon nodded. "Adam Colam."

"Get him on the line, pronto. Start taking care of this now. And Londo…"

He looked at her.

"Remember that this is just Step One of your duties. Even if you mess up on Step One, there're still Earth and Sarastor. You'll need to suck it up and move on. Take what you've learned here and apply it to those. They aren't as badly off as Aldierra is. You won't have a deadline."

"But–"

"Londo Rand Starhart, you haven't lost the war yet. Don't give up until the final battle plays out. This world may surprise you. You've done a fine job. A mammoth job. No one else could have done so much as you. Or your two co-horts. Whichever way this shitshow falls, you cannot blame yourself for a negative outcome. This began long, long before you were even born. Aldierra wants it fixed, in essence, in less than the amount of time it takes for her to snap her planetary fingers."

Londo drooped at the table while Chim stood behind him, her hands on his shoulders "What outcome do you think we'll have?"

"If Valiant is in the fight," she replied, "I always place my bets on him."

"But I'm only…"

"Uncle Lon?"

He looked up at the newcomer. "Drew?" The teen stood hesitantly at the door to Londo's office.

And he'd called him "uncle."

"What are you doing here?"

"I got special permission. I told Mr. Bloodtree, told him that I thought I needed to come here. Something's pushing me. Like a guide or something. I don't know much about guides."

Lon couldn't look weak in front of this boy. He had to set an example. Slowly he straightened his spine.

"Guides are a strange concept to get used to," Lon said.

"I'll say," Chim put in. She tilted her head at Drew. "But you think it was?"

"It was a feeling of urgency," Drew told her before turning back to Londo. "I watched something last night. Uncle Jae was streaming online. I kept feeling – really strongly – that you needed to see it."

Not now. This was not a good time. The world was in chaos, though there were still many megas who had stayed a while longer to handle emergencies. He shouldn't be abrupt with a young man who was trying his best not to trip through life.

Londo had tripped through too much of his life.

"What is it?"

Drew came further in, glanced at the electronics of the room and seeming lack of them to everyday Terran eyes, and gestured. Londo's main screen came up. More gestures; a link to something Drew had on his own systems.

Then a holographic Jae stood before them, smiling benevolently as he did in his instructional videos. "It all comes down to choice," Jae said.

"I don't think that's the beginning," Drew said in confusion. He began to make a gesture to return to that, when Londo waved him down.

"Choice," Jae said, "is what it's all about. Free will. How do we explore our world in a way that is not only unique, but valuable to us and our soul journey?'

Chim took a seat beside Londo to watch.

Jae gestured on screen and showed a check list graphic. "First you decide what it is you want out of life. What kind of person you want to be. What you want to explore. You make different lists: for the coming week, the coming month, the coming year. Ten years. Twenty. These aren't set in stone. You can change them as your wants and needs change."

Londo ran his hands down his face. "We've made all kinds of lists. Priorities."

But Jae continued onscreen. "This way you can see the choices Life presents you more clearly. One day you come to a point where you need to go in one of two directions. By knowing your goal, you can choose the path that's best for you if you want to achieve it.

"Sometimes that path seems awful. If so, the other path will look worse. Choose the least-bad path. Don't worry; you'll be offered something better soon. All you have to do is to make the decision to notice it when it comes along.

"Sometimes you'll see two good choices. Look at them carefully. Does one have more heart to it; is the other darker in some fashion? You will probably like the heart path better. Ask for spiritual help in finding your path if you think that will aid you. You will receive it."

"I thought we'd been walking our best path," Londo murmured.

Chim motioned onscreen Jae to silence and exchanged a look with Drew. "In that case, Lon, you shouldn't punish yourself. Have you done your best?"

Londo considered. "There have been times…"

"Shush. Brief hiccups don't matter. You've done your best. All of you have done so, even when that crazy wife of yours OD'd. She was trying to get things that needed to be done, done. Even when that insane husband of yours–" she gestured at Jae's image– "went off more than half-cocked that only he could disrupt Lupoff's plans."

"We got help," Londo said tiredly.

"Help arrives not only in spiritual form but from other people," Drew said. He seemed surprised he'd said anything out loud but then shrugged. "That's on another bit of the video."

"We have received a tremendous amount of help," Lon acknowledged. "More help, perhaps, than any project this galaxy has ever seen."

"And you have tried your hardest to follow the right path," Chim pointed out. "You've set yourself straight, Lina and Jae as well, when you've wandered. You've pulled out every stop you could to accomplish this Aldierran mission. You have nothing to be ashamed of. Except one thing."

With an effort, Londo raised his head to meet her regard.

"You have forgotten that this Three Worlds project is not Londo and his spouses at the helm. It concerns changing the people of those worlds. It is they who are in charge, Lon. They who must change. You just show them some paths they might choose to follow. You lend a hand to smooth that path. But it is the people who make the final choice. It is they who accomplish the task in the long run.

"It is not all on your shoulders. Let other shoulders help bear the ultimate responsibility."

Londo's gaze was bleak. "I'm not sure I can accept that."

Drew scoffed. "You may be Valiant, Uncle Lon, but you're not God. And Aunt Lie and Uncle Jae keep talking about the importance of free will. You've used yours."

Chim put a hand on Lon's. "Now let the population use theirs. From what I've seen, the vast majority of them are working, changing their lives in the right direction. The bad ones get publicity because their behavior is odd. It stands out because it's the minority. It will take generations to get out from most of this sludge, but from what I've seen, it's night and day from where you started."

"But is it enough?"

Chim's mouth formed a grim line. "And that is Aldierra's free will, her decision to make."

"Aunt Lie says thoughts become actions. Uncle Jae says negative thoughts are what keep us trapped in our own egos. I'm not sure what an ego is. Not exactly. But we should think positive thoughts."

"I should make up a lie about how everything is going peachy-keen," Londo sneered. "Keep saying it and–"

"Use your imagination," Drew countered. "The imagination opens the inner mind and connects to Source."

"How many videos have you watched?" Londo asked Drew, but he said it with a small smile.

"Maybe too many. I like them. They make me feel good."

Chim considered. "Perhaps what it all boils down to is to visualize an excellent outcome."

"With emotion," Drew said. "You've got to inject some to drive the visualization home and excite the energy around us. Oh – and always add 'or something better,' because the universe has a longer view than we do."

Londo drew a shaky breath but nodded. "I will do that. If it doesn't work, it won't have hurt anything, will it?"

"Keep track of any results," Chim told him. "Wiley will want to know but I will as well."

"Okay." He heaved a sigh. "I will visualize. I will, what, repeat affirmations. 'Or something better.' I will finish this job."

"We all will, Uncle Lon."

CHAPTER

35

Though they had a set appointment, Lupoff kept them waiting twenty minutes. Jae glanced at Bracken, then Dule, and then exchanged knowing glances with "Kettite" as they sat in the waiting room. Lupoff's secretaries and assistants eyed them curiously – and nervously – from their desks in the adjacent room.

Finally they were admitted. In addition to his large monitor array, the Patriarch's office held two sofas and some chairs around a table. The three officers saluted Lupoff smartly as they entered. Making the pelzire sign, Jae bowed his head to him. Lupoff grunted as he rose from his chair to move to the central one in the conference area, the one with extra girth and height.

"We are increasing the manufacture of all-terrain vehicles in Limbernie," Kettite reported. "Men are being trained on all aspects of the process, since there are not enough civilians to handle the more technical parts of it."

"Ah?" Lupoff's face was puzzled. "Did I order that?"

"Yes, five days ago. You sent orders for two platoons to begin retraining," Kettite told him. "I sent both to Limbernie since they have the large installations at Wovo-Nik.

The other officers reported on the battalions that were being redirected to work that didn't involve warmaking or even sustaining such.

In an astonishing motion, Lupoff jumped to his feet, his face turning into flaming amber. He shook his fist. "No. I did not order this! Any of this! What are you all trying to pull?"

He looked to the door, as if expecting someone nearby to hear him and come running.

But Jae pointed to it, and a dark shield faded into view.

"Soundproofing," Bracken informed his Patriarch.

"Excellency," Jae said in a soothing voice that was not bereft of irony, "you look tired. The failure of Operation Worldstorm must have been a disappointment. Have you been forgetting other things lately? Have your doctors examined you?"

"Worldstorm!" Lupoff exclaimed. His face turned pale, then dark orange with anger.

"His skin is flushing. See the left side of his face, how it sags," Kettite added helpfully. "Could be a minor stroke."

Jae strode to the Patriarch and laid his hand on his shoulder.

"Ouch," Lupoff said with a start. "What was that? What did youuu dooo?"

"His words *are* slightly slurred," Dule offered.

Jae shook his head in sorrow. He patted the shoulder. "So sad to see such a magnificent career cut short."

"Short? Isss this–? In…surrebb… ec…tion!" Lupoff managed to bellow.

"See, he can't even raise his arm very high," Kettite said *sotto voce*. "I've seen that in stroke victims."

Lupoff's next shout was incoherent.

Dule seemed nonplussed. "It can be cured, if treated quickly enough," he commented. He rose from his seat to walk toward the door. The shield there began to fade. "Let's call some medics. Get the Patriarch to a hospital."

"One that specializes in stroke victims," Bracken said as Lupoff began to roar in short bursts of syllables. He joined Dule at the door. Assistants had already begun to move in their direction.

"Get emergency medical services in here," Bracken ordered. "We want to keep this as unobtrusive as possible. The Patriarch seems to be having a health emergency. Possible stroke. He is not making sense."

Two of the assistants immediately retreated to their desks to begin arrangements.

"Stroke," Jae could hear one calling an emergency line. "Hurry."

"Private," the other told whoever.

"Your Excellency, please sit down and relax as much as possible. You're just making it worse," Jae pleaded for the audience's ears.

$$---$$

JAE APPEARED BEFORE PLANETARY BROADCAST, relating the news that the beloved Patriarch had been struck by a major stroke or possibly a series of more minor ones. He was undergoing treatment, and doctors reported that he should recover… in a few months. If nothing else went wrong.

The others broadcast to the troops to inform them that those that had reported directly to Lupoff were now being reassigned to Dule, Bracken, and Kettite. The affected divisions should immediately begin preparations to relocate or absorb troops, as needed.

They should coordinate with Three Worlds to facilitate the process.

They gave the troops two precious days to adjust to the new situation. Four days until Deadline. Then:

"Attention, all personnel! Attention!"

In every army camp of every army color, the giant screens appeared overhead, as well as interrupting normal broadcasting on everyday monitors. Only essential services were left unaltered.

The screens let out whoops that woke the sleeping as well as those awake, and summoned them to their communications.

Jae stood in full, regal Neutrino uniform against a wall emblazoned with both the Three Worlds and the Starhart emblems. Bracken, Kettite and Dule stood at attention behind him. Jae's jeweled staff materialized in his left hand.

He struck it on the ground.

Attention all across the world riveted upon him.

"As of this moment we are reassigning all our armies. No longer will any work for war. There is no war. We are one Aldierra, one people, and we work together. We help each other. We are helped by each other."

The three officers' expressions brooked no nonsense from the audience. They too listened raptly.

"Orders are being issued right now as to your new duties. For the most part, ranks and seniority will remain the same. New duties may require alterations in hierarchy here and there. There will be no reduction in pay or benefits. In fact, you may discover you have more now.

"You work for Three Worlds. Three Worlds works for Aldierra.

"Instead of fighting each other, you will focus your energy and skills to building our world. New cities, new roads, new terrains, new oceans.

"The armies of Aldierra are renowned for their prowess, but not their ability to stop war and aggression. That last changes now. We will be the best at showing all galactic sectors around how much we can get done… and how well. We will change the world even more than it has already been changed!

"When you are old you can tell your grandchildren how things were in the days before Deadline. You can tell them how bleak and frightening the world was. How people lived for power and riches instead of honor, community and mutual regard. They will be mystified as to how people could have existed like that. And they will be so proud of you and your efforts now to right things.

"If you were awakened by this message, go back and get what rest you can. There is much work to be done tomorrow. Everyone: this day will see you stretching yourself and your abilities beyond the limitations you thought you had.

"You will join in the effort to save your world."

In turn, Bracken, Kettite and Dule stepped forward to give orders to their own divisions. They had split the remaining ones that had been directly under Lupoff's command, scattering them so they could not form quick alliances to collude with each other. Diluting them would more manageably merge with the regular armies.

From there the broadcast went to more local levels, and Jae, Bracken, Kettite, and Dule quietly signed off.

They all gathered in Jae's office to check his monitors. There were reaction charts to be glanced at, but mostly coordination schedules to be meshed with those of the Speaker and Protector. Batt and Wicker reported in to speak of how various sectors of the population were taking things. As findings came in, Bracken's adjutant joined with reports from the armies.

Bracken nudged Jae. "Before this is over, we may need those stims from your wife."

Jae nodded. "We might. But dosages will be strictly governed. And she, of course, doesn't get any."

When the non-essentials had left the web conversation, "Kettite" peered at the upcoming schedule. "There." She pointed at a time slot in the day before Deadline. "That is where I shall disappear."

The others bent closer to see. "So soon?" But they didn't argue. Instead they moved a few minor operations around it here and there until all were satisfied. Bracken muttered about the impending Deadline.

"Will it be death or exile for him?" Dule wanted to know of the real Kettite.

"No unnecessary deaths," Jae told him.

"Either way, none in his family will much miss him. They'll miss the reflected influence," Mimik said. "Even so, I'll subtly prepare them for a shock."

Jae raised an eyebrow at her.

"No one is more subtle than I," she insisted, and he nodded.

"We don't want him to return," Bracken said. "One death out of twenty billion…"

Jae frowned at the schedule. "We'll see how things are panning out," he decided. "Plus we'll let Kettite have a vote."

"YOU'LL WANT TO TAKE THIS CALL," Kanti called to Lina from her office.

Lina hesitated at that. "What–?"

"It's Asma Lupoff." Kanti's eyebrow raised significantly as she peeked around the doorsill that separated their offices. "He's escaped; making a break for it. Leaving her behind in the process."

Lina signaled Lon, Jae and Bracken as she answered. The entitled wife of the Patriarch of Aldierra, who usually presented herself as the epitome of society and polish, stood aghast, part of her hair standing straight out of her head, her makeup patchy as if she'd been caught halfway in applying it. Instead of a posh dress, she wore a simple house robe.

"He's gone!" she sobbed in a furious, slobbering shriek to Lina. "He's gone and he's left me! He's going offworld!"

"Don't worry; we'll nab him," Lina assured the woman.

Just got the call, Jae's telepathic voice told her. **Someone was planted in Lupoff's hospital room. He and several staff disappeared two hours ago. Current location unknown. Hospital staff injured; two dead. We're tracking it.**

Lina nodded to the man who couldn't see her. "Did he just leave your House?" she asked Asma.

"He came back from wherever they had him. He took Shanza–" the youngest wife – "and three of his sons!"

"He's in a small warpship," a report came in from one of their spies via Jae. "Correction; a warpflitter. It just left Tentaeve."

Asma was a mess of sputtering, tears, hopelessness and rage. She screamed wordlessly.

"I don't need this right now," Lina said. She notified police, Aldierra Corps people, and the press, and let them see the message so far. "Number one, he can't escape any Deadline Doom. Aldierra will get him and any other natives he takes with him, if she decides against us."

"And if her… her decision is to save us?" Asma blubbered.

"No worries; we'll catch him. Anywhere he goes, even in the Empire, we will locate and retrieve him."

Londo cut in from wherever he was. "That's if he can make it offworld," he growled. "He won't. Warpflitters can't achieve hyperspace until they're above the gravity well of a planet. Ah. Here we go." Lina could see the flitter in his mind as he spotted it.

Kanti came into the office to trigger newsfeed that showed their first reports, and after a few minutes, coverage of a small warpflitter dropping from the thermosphere onto the familiar ceremonial grounds of Tentaeve Spaceport. Londo was pushing it down from above.

The sleek family hypership hit the pavement. Police trotted onto the greens in an armed mob that coalesced into attentive battle lines to meet it. Within the group were various army personnel, identifiable by their uniforms.

Zipping in from every direction but especially that of Drape-Tessay, atmospheric flitters swarmed the restricted perimeter around the airfield to land. From them burst reporter after reporter, cameras hanging in the air around them like bubbles that couldn't break free. Camera drones filled in the air spaces they'd left open behind them.

More soldiers trotted from the hangars in two squads. They knocked the reporters out of their way.

"You are *not* going there." Kanti's hand gripped Lina's upper arm. Another hand gripped her from the other side: Jae.

"First person who shoots, gets taken to the Shit Flats!" Londo landed in their midst. He reached to the door of the flitter and opened it by pulling it as if it were a pop-top can of fruit. The metal let out an ear-splitting screech, and weapons fire came from within. Only to be absorbed by Lon's shield, of course.

"Welcome back to Aldierra, Patriarch," Londo bellowed so all recording equipment could catch it. "You won't be leaving, at least before Deadline."

Beside Lina and Kanti, Jae watched the feed. With a hand he signaled someone. "I've already set up a cell for him in the Flats," Jae said, and Lina leaned to her right to alert that facility to await his message.

The crowd around the flitter were shouting, "Coward! Coward!" Some added, "Traitor!"

Lon walked into the flitter and unceremoniously pulled out Lupoff. With the tips of his fingers he pushed him toward the waiting police. "Truss him up," Lon instructed, and then turned to the other passengers inside.

From behind him came the sudden short whine of an energy weapon. Even as Londo whirled, Lupoff crumpled in the arms of one of the officers.

For a moment everyone froze in shock. Then the whine sparked again. Londo looked up. Lina scanned the crowd of officers and army personnel, only to see one slump.

"Red Army," she reported. She could hear the echo of her words from someone's speaker in the crowd, loud enough to be picked up by the news. "An assassin in Red!"

The one who fell certainly wore a red uniform. One of the old crowd, supposedly loyal to Lupoff.

Jae gestured to the computer. "Not so loyal," Jae said even as his image appeared over the field. Next to him in holographic form, stood Major Dule in full uniform. They must have planned something like this to do it so smoothly, so quickly after the fact. It probably happened earlier than scheduled, though.

****Assassination was never in play,**** Jae assured her.

Lon knelt next to the fallen red-uniformed man. "Karf Lupoff," he said as he checked identification. "His nephew, I believe, though there were rumors he was a biological son."

"At least we won't need to hold a trial," Dule announced to the gathered audience.

"Not over this," Jae agreed. "However, we have the remains of the last of a series of insurrections to bring to justice. I command all who have been working with us to act now, so the perpetrators can't slip away. Those who know, know what to do."

Dule nodded as any networks that hadn't begun broadcasting the events, broadcast them now. "For about a month the real Major General Kettite has been in custody for high crimes. We've had a double assuming his place as we rooted out his traitorous plans.

"I hereby take command of his brigades. We will work with Field Marshal Bracken, who has been loyal to Aldierra all along, as well as Ganiva of the Aldierra Corps and Kar-Kolder of the planetary planning board. We will take charge of political units that have previously been overseen by the armies. We will work with the civilian authorities. We all stand ready to lend our full strength to whatever the Three Worlds ask of us. When Deadline comes and goes, I will direct the armies to reorganize fully to peaceful purposes. For the betterment and protection of the people and the planet."

CHAPTER

36

Both Lon and Jae escorted Mimik to Lina's office. "One hero to beam out," Lon announced proudly of his teammate.

Mimik, in her normal form, held her duffel and a small box of possessions she had collected during the mission, but Lon handled her equipment box, setting it down beside her as Lina rose to join them.

"I'm not sure exactly what you did, but I do know it was a lot and it was extremely dangerous," Lina said. "Thank you for everything. Now: are we through with the sneaky stuff?" Lina asked Mimik, though she glanced at both Jae and Londo as well.

"Sneaky stuff is my profession," Mimik told her. "But I believe I am through on Aldierra. For the moment. I don't think I will stick around for your Deadline." Her mouth moved in a comical, wavy way. "This world of yours may miss her aim here and there."

"We are both putting commendations on your record," Jae told her. "Though of course they'll be classified Unlimited until such time as… Well, you know the procedure."

"Of course."

"Which isn't to say that someday history books won't have chapters devoted to your work here," Londo said. "Take as much time off as you need, Mimik, and then return to the Legion to command my team. It might be yours someday."

Lina blinked. Was Londo was considering his future role as Protector over that of being Legionnaire Valiant? Then she shrugged to herself. Whichever path he took it would always be intertwined with that of the Legion. He had free will.

Plus choices made one moment could always be altered later as circumstances changed.

JAE PACED THEIR QUARTERS. The cats gave him room, skittering to the corners.

Thirty minutes.

He could feel Lina at a housing complex, touching everyone she could and reassuring them that whichever way The Decision went, it would be all right. They'd done a marvelous job so far, and would continue to do so in the future. Galactic sectors far and wide were being inspired by their work.

And if the Doom went against them, well, spiritual life was bliss; it was going home to paradise.

They were not that soothed, but it was all Lina could do and some seemed mollified by it, he felt through their link.

Lon? Of course Lon was attending to details: straightening equipment poised to build the next project on his list. He was talking to Bracken, to his chiefs, to a few of the larger platoons around the planet, pretty much telling them the same thing Lina was conveying to the civilians. It was what the three of them had broadcast yesterday.

"If the decision does go against us," Lina had told the cameras, "I think it will be quick. Painless."

But don't hold her to that promise, Jae knew.

Taking a long breath, then another just to clear his energy as best he could, Jae exited his home and took off into the sky to Plegerit. Fanning out from a park on a bluff overlooking the lesser city, tens of thousands gathered in relative quiet, with even more out in the streets.

It was a terrible quiet, one filled with aching uncertainty and fear.

Someone called out defiantly, 'Houses together! Houses together!"

Many in the crowd took up the cry for a few rounds, then returned to their uneasy silence.

Wiley was there, waiting. Stoan's image along with Andri, Riz, and Mimik's, stood near Wiley and Chim, who were next to Nesh and Yusuf. Nesh was trying her best to look cool and businesslike – professional, Jae decided. She was building a new reputation both for her position and herself. She was obviously proud of the work she'd done and waiting for a grade. Confident in her results.

Jae wished he was.

Thankfully Yusuf was sweating.

"You won't be hurt," Jae murmured to him as he landed.

Yusuf drew back to give him room. "Just tell that to the villagers on Santara," he said. "Tell it to my staff."

Where were their own staff? Jae checked. The higher-ups were in the largest conference room back at HQ. Kanti and Walker looked at him on their monitor to give him a nod. They'd set up wall-sized screens that had them practically members of the mob here.

In Communications, a pale Wicker stood ready to broadcast. He had two scripts ready. One of his non-Aldierran aides stood by in case they would be needed to deliver the second one.

As Lon flew down to join his spouses and friends, Jae gave him a shaky nod and then hug before checking out the hundreds of press personnel. Some were part of the Three Worlds' staff, but so many more had come in from the sector and beyond to document this.

The Rands checked in via monitor. Lon had asked them to stay away, in case things… didn't turn out. They stood hugging each other.

Lina checked the small scientific observation station she'd had set up for Wiley and posterity, making sure everything was ready for… whatever would happen. The researchers there, despite their skin color showing their non-Aldierran ethnicity, did not look particularly excited to be on-site during this occasion.

Wiley of course was coordinating the research from the ground and making sure everything had been calibrated exactly.

Lina finally ported to be next to Jae and Lon. They took each other's hands and held tight.

"I am going to faint," she announced.

"Any word from Aldierra?" Lon asked before Jae could.

Lina shook her head. "If she's giving a thumbs-down she doesn't want us to know ahead of time. If she's giving thumbs-up…"

"She's playing with us," Jae surmised, and Lina nodded.

"How often does a planet get to do this?" Lina asked, her mind not on the question as she scanned the crowd and its increasingly frantic murmurs. "How often does one planet get to be the center of attention in its sector?"

"But Aldierra doesn't have much ego," Jae countered. "Ego is a low vibration."

"Yes. There is that. Still…"

"She gets a kick out of it," Lon finished for her.

At the sky's zenith a countdown clock ticked off the moments to Doom. Thousands of these had been set up over every concentrated population center on the planet.

"Are we sure she's going by the exact moment?" Wiley asked quietly.

"Nope."

In hushed tones some in the crowd began to count down with the clock. At the fifteen-second mark, half the crowd did. For the final ten, everyone joined in, many shouting. In defiance? In relief that either way, it was over?

"Seriously," Lina said at the five second mark. "Faint."

Jae put his left hand on her shoulder and squeezed, then did the same for Lon with his right shoulder.

– – –

FOUR. THREE. Did Aldierra even pay attention to how humans measured planetary tilts and orbits? Two. One.

Tears streaming from his eyes, Jae had joined the crowd in chanting down. Now he held his–

A sound. Very high, a non-mechanical *screeeeeee*.

And then something happened to the sky. Today was partially cloudy, but the sky darkened.

The crowd gasped in their distress: this was Doom beginning.

But then a fiery, spinning corkscrew of a magenta spark zipped across the sky, north to south. It was quickly joined by others, green, gold, red, blue, purple, white… A dazzling net of activity.

The sparks began to dance around each other. The background color of the sky became a sheet of rainbow, with clouds pulsing below in neon violets.

And joy–! Jae felt laughter well within himself. It wasn't him; it was coming from without, from all around. He joined it.

It held energy that no stim could ever reproduce. Every cell in his body woke up to join in. Jae laughed, and then wondered at the love that lay beneath that joy. It was a part of it. Joy and love, forever entwined.

He danced to it, hearing music in his head made from instruments no human hand had ever touched. This was far beyond that, a pureness of frequency and melody he'd never experienced.

So he danced. He wanted to hug someone. Lina was nearest. And Lon. He hugged them both, and they danced with him, giggling like children.

Then came Wiley, who hopped about with more formal dance steps. He threw back his head to give belly laughs, only to be echoed by Chim. She launched herself at him and they skidded off in a dance that had no rules.

Everyone was hugging everyone else. Everyone was joining in on the dance. Those who couldn't were simply jumping and waving their arms in the air as they shouted with glee. Jae could feel the connection, the conscious combining of auras and spirits as the people of Aldierra became one community, twenty billion-plus points of loving joy.

From somewhere he could hear Stoan laughing as well, and people from off-world joining in the community. Hal's booming laughter joined the melee.

Unity. Individual souls, all of them, but knowing they were part of a larger entity.

How long did it last? Some people sat on the ground when their legs couldn't hold them up any more. They sat enthralled by it all. Their faces reflected their inner joy, and they moved their arms as part of the dance.

Some just lay on the ground and laughed until their laughter became chuckles, then quiet delight.

Then all the light in the sky ceased. A moment later came a flash of lavender light, brighter than the brightest firework display had ever been.

Jae stood with the rest, taking in the fading embers of the show.

"I believe we have passed the test," he said to no one in particular.

But then he put his face in his palms and began to weep.

He sobbed. Then he wailed with an earnestness that sucked at all the darkness he had carried with him since he was ten.

It was an ocean. Guilt. Fear. Self-loathing.

Loss.

Arms enfolded him. Lon and Lina were also weeping, though not nearly as dreadfully as he. They were all weeping out their worries and stress, but Jae wept from years of emotions that not only included Feith but also Aldierra and all the work he had done on its behalf. All the darkness and despair this mission had forced him to work with. He hadn't been able to save Feith but by the Orb, he'd saved Aldierra. Source be praised!

CHAPTER

37

No one in the Three Worlds organization took a vacation afterward. The call center on Earth reported that everyone there, even the kitchen providers and janitors, had fully felt the joy the moment it had happened on Aldierra.

Other-world heroes, consultants and equipment suppliers had also been included, to their surprise and awe.

Lina and her husbands took time to check what others told them was the best of the reporting, or the most intriguing, as other worlds tried to make sense of twenty billion-plus people suddenly experiencing such phenomena. Tishana leaders assured everyone that they had monitored it, had gotten a first-person report from Chim, and that just one person or even all three of the Starharts together could not remotely have caused this event.

They were dealing with a sentient planet.

It had set a deadline doom, billions of people had worked hard to improve both themselves and their planet, and doom had been averted.

But they couldn't stop now.

There were still the occasional riot, bits of disbanded armies making an appearance here and there. Domestic violence, natural disasters, political shenanigans.

"The usual," unimpressed Lon commented over his breakfast.

Cities still needed to be reorganized, demolished, and/or rebuilt. Wildlife corridors had to be expanded and conserved. The poles had a long way to go before they were cool enough to sustain a healthy atmospheric system. And now there was added the problem of uncontrolled weather.

But they'd come so far.

Wicker and his staff delighted in inundating both Aldierran and offworld networks with "before" and "after" videos, as well as ones targeting the next areas needing help. Aldierra as a populace had only begun their new purpose.

Work schedules were adjusted to a more leisurely pace, though. Medics were instructed to keep watch on how much rest the three principals and their higher staffs got. Alternating vacations were scheduled for all staff and expected to be used. Department heads met to discuss how the organization would need to restructure for its new phase. Some set out to Sarastor and Earth to oversee the establishment of new headquarters there.

Three Worlds was about to expand onto two more planets. Before that happened, a long-anticipated honeymoon would commence in three weeks.

"We'll set up things here," Lon summarized. "Make sure everyone knows what they're to do while we're gone. Lord knows we've given them enough practice of working without us."

"We make sure they know that we are incommunicado," Jae insisted.

"We need to check in on the cats now and then," Lina said.

"Yes, yes. Maybe they'll even join us a few times. But they won't want to be with us for most of it. It will be too exciting for them. Noisy. We shall leave a path of wanton destruction and delight in our wake. We'll see every sight worth seeing in four sectors. We'll taste unbelievable food – and rate it, one to ten, on Lina's lists. We'll test every position in Delwyn's *Guide for Thruples*. We'll sing new love songs. And we'll go through two dozen beds. At least. People will guess where we are, but only after we've gone."

"Incommunicado," Londo agreed.

You will relax. You will rediscover joy, Lina's guides ordered. They so rarely did that.

"Except for absolute, end of the world emergencies," Lina added. Then she realized that they'd just come through such. There couldn't be another to deal with for, oh, at least three months.

Finally there was time to take a deep, collective breath. She was going to enjoy every second of it.

ABOUT THE AUTHOR

When you think of strong women and strange worlds, think Carol A. Strickland.

Although born in a small town in Illinois noted for its Nineteenth Century demonic possession cases, Carol claims that all those voices inside her head are a result of having stories to tell and books to write. Even so, her strange devotion to and study of Wonder Woman would seem to indicate an abby-normal brain.

A one-time comics letterhack and outspoken member of various comics message boards, Carol has found herself the basis for two comic book villains (at times her opinions have not been taken well by the books' creators) (both villains were soundly thrashed) (and both, for some perverse reason, were male) and had one superhero wear her costume design. (Light Lass!)

Carol has also become an award-winning painter and certified tarot reader. Her primary talent, though, is procrastination. See what else she wastes time on at her website: www.CarolAStrickland.com or check out her other books at www.CarolAStricklandBooks.com . She's also on Instagram under @CarolA.Strickland.